I'm Not Home

Magnolia Moon Publishing, LLC

magnoliamoonpublishing@gmail.com
Charleston, South Carolina

Cover images by Casey Sekulovski

Cover design by Jovan Sekulovski

ISBN Paperback: 979-8-9930492-2-9
ISBN Ebook: 979-8-9930492-1-2

First Edition November 2025

I'm Not Home

Casey Sekulovski

To my husband, Petar. Thank you for the endless inspiration and for always encouraging me to finish this book for the world to see. May we find each other in every lifetime.

And to my children, Oliver and Lily.
I hope to make you proud, even though
I hope you aren't reading this book.

Ben

It's an eerie feeling, being in the passenger side of my mother's car, driving through my hometown, Yelton. The streets are covered in big white signs that say "Welcome home, Ben Phillips!" written in red and blue. Every time we pass one, my mother says, "Look, another!" I force a smile, but no part of me feels at *home*.

We live in a small town, the kind where everyone knows everyone; therefore, I can't say I am surprised that everyone knows about me coming home. As we pull into the center of the town, all the storefronts have paintings of the American flag and Welcome Home written on them, my name written on others. We get deeper into the center of town. People are standing outside with signs and cheering, cop cars and fire trucks with flags attached to them, and light posts that should have the annual holiday decorations on are replaced with flags and signs.

My mom turns to me with her soft brown eyes, her brown hair just lying on her shoulders, but there is a subtle touch of gray that I don't remember being there before. "It's a little much, I know. But you know how everyone celebrates a welcome back home. Especially after the Morris boy…"

Daniel Morris enrolled in the army a day after his 18th birthday and died a week before he was supposed to come home. It was an enormous loss for our town; he was always involved with the town and wanted to become a soldier as soon as he learned to walk. Everyone expected him to become at least a Lieutenant Colonel. It was a letdown for everyone when he never made it that far.

Being the first one back home makes it that much of a bigger deal.

"This is a little much, Mom." It's not the feeling of being anxious that is stopping me from being excited; it's just the overall inability to feel excited.

She pulls into a parking lot so we can get out and see everyone. Before she can put the car in park, I ask her, "Is Dad going to come?" My voice was almost a whisper, too scared to hear the answer.

"I don't know, honey. He said he is going to try."

"Just thought that his son coming home from war would be something to show up for." I slam the car door behind me when I get out and curve my lips into what a person would call a smile. The feeling of two arms wrapped around my waist stops me in my tracks. My kid brother Sean appears at my waist, looking up at me with a smile that has a few teeth missing. I pick him up and swing him around, his endless laughter making him unable to speak the words "stop". I ruffle his hair as I put him down in the same spot I picked him up from.

"How old are you now?" I ask him.

"I just turned nine! Don't you remember?"

"Of course!" I lie to him to make sure he doesn't know how his brother forgot about his birthday.

"My last birthday you came to was… my 5th!"

"Yeah buddy. You have grown a lot since then."

"So did you!" My stepfather, Paul, says with a giant smile on his face. He greets me with a hug, "Good to have you home, kid."

As soon as we turn the corner onto Main Street, people bombard me as if I were a crumb and they are the ants. The townspeople start filling my ear right away with, "thank you for what you have done", "you look so different", "it is so nice you are home", "your mother would always talk about you". I smile and shake hands while walking through. I am not sure where I am even walking until my mom comes up to me and tells me to walk to the stage up ahead in the center.

"The mayor just wants to greet you back home."

"Can we go home after this? I am exhausted." I feel like a little kid asking his mom to leave a family party full of grown-ups.

"Yes, of course," She smiles sweetly at me, and that smile I most definitely remember being there.

I get up on the stage and shake hands with the mayor. "Ben, it is an honor to have you part of this town and for you to be home. The town offers you anything you may need any time of the day." The mayor continues, and I look down at the crowd and see

Mrs. Morris standing there, slow, light teardrops on her face like morning dew. I smile at her, and she gives a forced half smile. I know she wishes it was her son standing here listening to the mayor's speech about how my presence is such an honor and how I have "brought a light back into this town today."

"Thank you, everyone, for this warm welcome back. I appreciate all the kind words and gestures. I would like to take a moment of silence for Private Daniel Morris and other fallen soldiers." The town is silent for a few seconds, then looks back up at me, waiting for my approval to speak again. "Thank you," I get off the stage, and Mrs. Morris greets me at the bottom step.

"Thank you. I really appreciate that," she kisses my cheek and scurries off.

"I need to stop somewhere," I tell my mother on the car ride back home. I give her a piece of paper with an address on it.

She looks at it skeptically, but then looks back at me, nodding. When we get to the location of the house, I get out and walk to the front door, knocking.

A man opens the door, "Charles? Cohens sent me," I say.

"Yes," he walks back into the house, "come in," he tells me, and I follow behind him. The house is in shambles, with beer bottles covering the floor, old blankets that are ripped covering the windows and letting holes of light in, and dirty ashtrays on every table.

"Want a beer?"

"No, I am good, thank you. I can't stay long."

He goes into the kitchen and comes back out with four pill bottles and hands them to me. "Xanax, Adderall, Ambien, and Seroquel, that is all the order said."

"Yeah, that is all of it," I take the bottles from him and look at the amount of pills in each, and they are all full to the brim.

"What is going to happen when I run out? You can refill it?"

"If you take the dosage like you're supposed to, then yeah, I can refill. Don't overuse. I can only get it when it needs to be refilled." He pauses and looks around, "I am not a drug dealer, just so you know."

"I understand." We both look around his house, and his face turns red when he makes eye contact with me. He looks me up and down, taking notice of my uniform.

"Listen, my brother couldn't get the help he needed because he wasn't allowed to be mentally ill while serving, and ended up killing himself. So if I can help others and help prevent that from happening again, then I am going to try."

"Trust me, I appreciate it and understand."

I get back into the car with my mother's eyes just staring at me.

"What was that about?" She looks past me at the house, wondering why I would ever come to a house with broken shutters, peeling paint, and a stripped-down car parked to the side.

"Just visiting a friend."

She starts driving home and asks me, "Glad to be home?"

"Guess so," my voice trails off, and I just remain looking out the window. The truth is that I don't know if I am glad because everything is so foreign.

"Your grandparents are going to come over for dinner, just so you know."

"Good. Any word from Dad?"

"No, sweetie. Not yet," she sounds disappointed in me.

"Figures." It would be nice to see my father, as I haven't seen him in four years, and I just got back from where I now refer to it as "plaga mortis" or "death zone," especially because he is now halfway across the country with his new family.

We pull up to the house, driving up the long driveway where I would always ride my bike up and down, and it is exactly how I remember. Just now, with more soon-to-be-dead flowers planted in the front yard. The house looks like it could be on a magazine cover. The lawn is perfectly green and the grass freshly cut, the water glistening behind it, the cicadas buzzing loud enough I can hear it from inside the car.

Sean is sitting on the front steps while Paul is sitting in the swing on the deck. Our house was always the one where the 4th of July parties would be held. I would be lying if I didn't say we had the nicer house out of the friend group my parents had created. My mother is a college professor at the local university, and Paul is a real estate agent in the big beach areas. My father owns his engineering firm and gives my mother child support even though I am over 18, so he can still call himself "dad". So with all their income, we can live *nicely.*

"Did you move my room?" I ask, walking up to the second floor with everyone following behind me, the stairs feeling even more endless than usual.

"No, it is the same!" My mother says proudly. I almost forgot how big the house was. The staircase has been redone and now has white railings instead of the dark brown. When I get to the top of the stairs, I look at the room right there as soon as I walk in and see how it is now redone with dinosaurs and Hot Wheels all over the floor, which is Sean's room.

I turn right and walk down a couple of feet and look into my room, which is the same. The dark blue walls put a strain on your eyes from the cream-colored walls in the rest of the house. The bathroom in my room looks the same, just a lot cleaner than when I left it, attached to it being just a room that was used as a spare room and office. I always locked the other door so nobody could come in from the other side.

Then my mom and Paul's room is at the end of the hallway, which I imagine probably looks the same. My favorite part of my mom's room was her window seat that looks out over the water. Even though my room has a big window that has a similar view, I always loved sitting by her window.

I put my bag down and sit on my bed while everyone is standing in the doorway, waiting for some type of confirmation that

I am fine. "I am just going to get settled," I say, breaking the silence in hopes they will walk away.

"Yeah, of course," Paul pulls my mom's arm that way she gets the hint to give me space.

"Is there enough hot water for me to take a shower?" I ask my mom before she closes my door. For the past four years, I have had tepid water that only lasts about a minute until it gets cold or someone stops pouring the water over my head so I can wash myself.

"What?" she asks, confused, and I remind myself that, of course, there is hot water, everyone here could take a hot shower, and there would still be some left.

"Nothing," I say, my voice trailing off.

A yellow Labrador puppy greets me in my bedroom after I come out of the shower. The puppy was just sitting on my bed with his tongue hanging out, just waiting for attention, and I couldn't help but bend down on my knees and pet him. "Hey, little guy," I say in a higher-pitched voice.

"His name is Sam. We got him three years ago for Christmas," Sean says to me while standing in my doorway. I jump up at the sound of his voice, grabbing my towel around my waist before it slips down.

"My dad convinced Mom to let me get him, she said it would keep us company." I think back to Christmas three years ago, which was the beginning of the time that I would stop calling my mom.

"Yeah, that was a good idea of his. Mom never let me get a dog. Glad Paul- your dad convinced her," I pat Sam's head.

"Come on, Sam! Time to go outside! Mom said I could only get him if I was the one to take care of him," he laughs and runs downstairs with Sam.

I look through my dresser drawers and pull out a pair of underwear that fails to fit around my legs, ripping the seams as I try to pull it up. My build was a lot different before I left; now I am wider and full of muscles. I end up just opening my baggage and pulling out a pair of cargo pants and a white shirt that I know will fit just fine. Although my abs do obnoxiously show through the shirt. I can see Sean and Sam playing catch outside by the lake as Paul stands outside watching them, drinking a cup of coffee, with a sailboat on the water. I lay on my bed, wondering how I ever thought such a soft bed was comfortable.

I must have dozed off because I woke up hearing a man's voice downstairs that isn't Paul's. "I got here as soon as I could," he says.

"You could have at least said you were coming," my mother says sternly back.

"You could have told me sooner when he was coming home. I got the first flight I could back."

"I have been telling you for months when he was coming home."

I walk downstairs and see my dad standing in the entryway. He has more wrinkles on his face, but his freshly shaved face keeps him looking younger. My dad was blessed with genes that help keep him looking young.

He smiles widely at me with bright eyes and hugs me. "I got the first flight out of Seattle when I knew you were home. That's why I haven't been answering my phone," he looks at my mother, making sure she heard the last comment.

"I am glad you made it."

He pulls away and grabs my upper arms, "Got some muscles on you now, kid."

"Not much else to do when you're sitting in the middle of a desert for days than to do a push-up contest. How long are you staying for, by the way?"

"The weekend. Have to go find a hotel room somewhere…"

My mother sighs, knowing what he is hinting at, "You can stay in the guest room, Mike."

My mom always tried to be civil with my father for my sake and even for her mental health. They have been divorced for about eleven years, and both have separate families now, so it is easier for each party not to be bitter. But I remember when it first happened, and there were constant arguments in the house. If I ever talked about my dad to my mom, she would always snap at me and get frustrated. Or when my father and his mistress flew in one time and I had dinner with them afterwards, my mom asked how it went and I said it was good and dad's new girlfriend was pretty, my mom burst into tears and that was the last time we ever mentioned her.

"I will bring your bags upstairs," I tell my dad.

"No, you don't have to," he insists.

"I have to grab my phone upstairs anyway." I grab his bag and go upstairs, grabbing my cell phone from my room on the way back down. When I get to the bottom of the stairs, I hear my parents and Paul in the kitchen talking quietly, and I stop in my tracks to listen.

"He just seems so... different," my mother says.

"He was just away at war for four years, Sarah. What else do you expect?" My dad answers.

"He has rarely smiled. I just feel like he has no emotions," she says again.

"It will just take time," Paul comforts her. "Once he gets settled, sees family and friends. Just have to get back in the groove."

"He asked me to stop at this house today. It looked like a drug house or a serial killer's house. I know all of his friends and where they live; that wasn't one of them."

"Could be someone he met while he was away," my dad answers.

"I don't know, Mike. It seemed very strange."

"Did you ask him about it?" Paul asks.

"Yes, he said it was a friend," her voice is skeptical.

"Then it was a friend!" Paul says, making it sound like it was a straight answer.

"Paul, why don't you ask Leon to check up on the house? See what it is." Leon is a cop friend of Paul's.

"You're being paranoid, Sarah. Leave the kid alone," my dad butts in, putting an end to my mother's worried mind.

I walk into the kitchen and smile at my mom. "Good to see you smiling!" My dad says, and looks over at my mom, and she rolls her eyes.

"I might stop at Chris's house tonight after dinner. It might be good for me to see friends. Friends that you know…" I pour a glass of water with my back turned to my mother, I smile to myself, and my dad lets out a burst of laughter. I turn to see my mother's face, which is as red as a tomato because she knows she got caught. I kiss her on the cheek, "I am fine." I smile at her and walk outside to the back, where Sam is lying on the grass. I pick up the ball and throw it, and he jumps up like a rabbit and runs for it.

I look in the mirror on my dresser and pull my dog tag out of my shirt, looking at the indents on it, rubbing it in between my fingers then touching the silver coin behind it tracing the Statue of Liberty's crown, placing them both back down on my chest.

"Did you kill all of the bad guys?" Sean says, standing at my doorway.

His presence and his question startle me. How do you explain to a nine-year-old that there will always be bad guys? I turn around and look at him, "You don't ever have to worry about any bad guys."

12

"There is a boy in my class named Aameen, and everyone always says his family is going to hurt the Americans."

I get slight anxiety by the way this conversation is turning, and that nine-year-olds are already being exposed to racism, "Is his last name Sala?" Since we live in a small town and there is only one Muslim family in the town, I know exactly who he is talking about.

"Yes," he says.

"I went to school with his older brother, Syed. I have been to his house before; I have met his family before. There is nothing for you to worry about."

"Did you kill a lot of people?" He asks.

"Hey buddy, this isn't a conversation we should be having, okay? How about you go to your room with Sam, and I will see you tomorrow."

A heavy weight sits in my chest as a gnawing pit eats through my stomach like a vicious animal. The deep breaths Cohens told me to practice don't get very far, but I know the Xanax sitting in my drawer will.

Chris is standing around a high-top table with his brother and a few other friends from high school that we talked to back in the day. There is more alcohol on the table than there is behind the bar. I get greeted with hugs, handshakes, and a shot of tequila.

Chris is short and stocky; before I went away, we would go to the gym every day, but it looks like he hasn't gone since then. "You have no idea how much I missed you," He says to me.

"Yeah, I know. Me too," I tighten my hug around him. He stumbles back to the table, knocking some bottles over when he finally gets there. "Looks like I am a little behind," I say, grabbing a beer that someone just got me.

Jason, a cocky, arrogant guy that we are friends with for some reason, comes up to me with his phone, taking a video of us together on TikTok Live, 'I am out here with my man, Benny Boy! Dude just got back from fighting for his life in the war. If any of you ladies love a good soldier, this is the one. Now let's get him drunk!"

Before I know it, I am drunk and a drink away from the room spinning, and now on TikTok Live. A couple of girls are around our table now; Jason is a fireman and uses it as his way to get girls to find him interesting and attractive, which is probably how he has so many followers on his social media. "Wouldn't even be able to tell that he has a girlfriend," Chris says, looking over at Jason kissing some drunk girl. I roll my eyes, looking at him.

My head feels like it is full of bricks when I open my eyes in the morning. I can't remember the last time I had a bad hangover this bad. My mom's footsteps creep up to my bedroom door and stop. I know she is waiting for a sign to see if I am awake or not. When I look over at my door, I notice all my pill bottles are out on my nightstand. The sound of her opening the door jolts me into action, and I shove the pills into my drawer. "Good morning!" She says brightly and cheerfully.

"I have the worst hangover right now," I say to her as I pull the covers over my face.

"You might have Advil in your drawer. Let me check," she goes to open my nightstand drawer, I pull the comforters off, and jump up, holding it closed.

"I don't. Already checked."

"Okay..." she hesitates, wondering why I would act so quickly.

"Mom, I have my gun in this drawer right now, and I would rather you just not open it."

Her timed wrinkles on her face settle down to a relaxed position.

I go back to sleep to try and sleep off the hangover, and I am greeted with a horrific dream, well, more so a flashback than a dream.

"Phillip's gets Youngs. He is on the west side, in the pit."

I walk over and look down into the pit. Youngs is trapped under dirt and rocks. "Pull me out! Pull me out!" he keeps yelling to me.

I grab his arm and start to pull, when he comes out of the dirt, everything from the waist down is cut off. I let go of his arm in shock. He looks down and sees he has no legs and starts screaming till his lungs' capacity. "What happened to them? What happened?"

"Ben. Ben. Ben," the sound of Sean's voice wakes me up. He stands at the edge of my bed just looking down at me.

"What?" I answer in a daze, looking around the room to confirm where I am.

"Your dad is looking for you."

I walk downstairs in the kitchen and see my dad sitting at the island. "I want to take a ride with you," he says.

"Dad, I feel terrible..." hoping I can get out of going.

"Take a shower, grab a cup of coffee, and let's go. Your mother said we could use her car."

I do as he says and jump into the shower, putting on another pair of cargo shorts and a white t-shirt from my luggage. "Guess I am going out with dad," I tell my mother as I pass her in the hallway.

She turns around and looks at me, "I think it will be good for you both. Especially because he leaves later tonight." She then looks me up and down, "We need to buy you some new clothes. I don't like those."

I look at my outfit, "Why, what is wrong with it?"

"Doesn't... doesn't look like you. I will give you some money, and you can go into town this week and get some," she then turns back and goes downstairs. The lack of Vineyard Vines clothing I'm wearing must seem off-putting to her.

We drive around aimlessly on the outskirts of town so we don't have to deal with the people in town gawking at me.

"So how are you feeling?" my dad asks while driving.

"I have a headache right now."

"No, I don't mean the hangover. I mean, in general."

"Fine."

"Okay, let me ask again and give me a genuine answer. How are you?"

"I don't know, to be honest. I feel strange. Doesn't *really* feel like home."

"Well, you haven't been here in four years. Thanksgiving is next week, and maybe seeing your family will help."

"Yeah, hopefully."

"I need to ask you something. I know it happened a while ago, but are you mad at me for what I did to you and your mother?" He asks.

"I was mad at you, yes. And I don't idolize you, but I am not mad about it anymore. I guess I am more mad that you picked up and moved, but I guess I kind of did the same thing, didn't I?"

"I didn't mean to hurt you or your mother."

"Dad, I have been through so much shit lately. The last thing that can bother me right now is something that happened years ago between you and Mom. If you feel like less of a man for walking out on your family, then that is your problem. If I hated you, I wouldn't be sitting in the passenger seat right now."

He doesn't say anything back to me for a few seconds, then breaks the silence by saying, "You have grown up to be a great man."

"Thanks, Dad."

A few minutes of silence pass by. "How was last night?" He asks, trying to find a new conversation.

"It was fun. Good to see all the guys. Jason is still a douchebag, though."

"Yeah, he was always a little strange."

We drive around for another 20 minutes, and for some reason, I bring up his other family that I have no interest in knowing about. "How is your other family?"

He rolls his eyes and sighs, "Is this an actual question, or are you just busting with me?"

"Genuine."

"Sophia is good, our son Marco just started playing baseball, so we're excited about that, and Bella just started preschool!"

"Who is Bella?" I ask.

"Oh… our daughter."

"I didn't know you had a daughter."

"Yeah… she is 4 now."

"Congratulations," I put my hand on his shoulder so he knows it wasn't sarcasm.

"Thank you. She is definitely a handful."

"Didn't even know I had a sister," my voice trails off.

"Yeah… yeah, you do. I want you to meet her. I want you to know my side of the family as well."

"Is it strange to say that I feel like Sean isn't my brother?" I ask him. There has always been something about my dad, despite everything, that I always felt like I could be vulnerable with him.

"I think you just need time to adjust back to life here. It will take time."

After I drop Sean off at school, I get a text from Chris.

I am getting a tattoo right now. Come meet me at the place in town.

I go to meet him and walk into the parlor, and he is sitting there with a dumb look on his face, grinning at me. "I can only imagine what you're getting," I say to him.

"The American flag." He says.

"Yeah, yeah."

"No, I am serious. It is for you."

"Jesus, Chris. You don't need to get a tattoo for me."

"I want to. Get a tattoo with me."

"I don't even know what I would get."

"Think about it for a few then," Chris says, then jumps up on the seat, pulling his sleeve up. "Ready!" he says to Martin, the only tattoo artist in town.

After half an hour, Chris is done with his and shows it to me. "It came out good," I hug him after, appreciating the fact that he got it in my honor.

"So what are you getting?" Chris asks me.

"Going to get a saying on my back. I want it to say, 'I will always place the mission first. I will never accept defeat. I will never quit. I will never leave a fallen comrade.' But can you tattoo over a scar?"

"Yeah, might come out a little strange though and rigid looking. Especially since it is writing."

"That's fine."

"Right on, dude," Martin says. I take off my shirt and sit down on the chair. Chris, who is behind me, stumbles back and knocks into a table that is full of equipment, knocking half of the tools to the ground. "Jesus," Martin says.

"I'm sorry…" I hear Chris say, all flustered.

I know his reaction was towards the countless scars that are all over my back. "Can we just get on with it?" I say in annoyance.

"Yeah, man."

"You still can do it, right?"

"Yeah, I will take care of it," Martin says, comforting me, understanding that these are battle wounds.

Just as he finishes, I get a call from my mom, "Hello?" I answer.

"I need you to get Sean from school ASAP. He got into a fight, and I am stuck at work. Go pick him up and talk to his principal."

"Yeah, I will take care of it," I hang up. "I have to get Sean; he got into a fight at school."

"Here, take a look at it first," Martin says, handing me a mirror.

I look at it, and it looks better than I thought it would. "It looks amazing, dude."

"Good, it was a pleasure. Just make sure you put some ointment on it."

"How much do I owe you?"

"Don't worry about it," he shakes his head.

"Come on. I have to give you something."

"No, seriously. It is fine. My treat."

I hand him $100. "I appreciate it," I leave before he can give me back the money. Chris comes running out after me.

"Listen, I am sorry about what happened before. I just… wasn't expecting that," I look at him, confused. "The whole thing with your back."

"It is fine. I know it looks like I got mauled by a bear," I laugh. "I am free tonight if you want to go out. Call me later," I say and get into the car.

I get to Sean's school, and he is sitting in the main office with his head down. I take a deep breath and walk up to the secretary. "Hi, I am Ben Phillips, Sean's big brother. My mother called me and told me something had happened."

"Oh, yes," she says sternly, almost offended. "Mr. Ryan is in his office with Sean's teacher, Ms. Dale. You can go in," her eyes narrow in on me, which confirms my suspicion that she was offended.

I walk in and feel as if I am the one about to get into trouble. They both stand up and shake my hand, "Thank you for coming in," Mr. Ryan says. He is a middle-aged man with slicked-back hair, fit, and he straightens his tie as he sits back down. "Please have a seat." I sit down next to Sean's extremely attractive teacher. She looks like this is her first year teaching, long brown hair that is pulled into a ponytail, a skirt that has a little slit in it that reveals a little extra thigh, but has tights on to make it less visible, and a red button-up shirt that is all the way buttoned so it is not revealing any cleavage. My dick starts to harden until I remember I am sitting in a principal's office of an elementary school because my little brother is in trouble, and I remember I am also the adult in the room.

"Today in class, Sean had an incident," Mr. Ryan says. "Ms. Dale, can you explain what happened?"

"We were doing partner work and Sean and a classmate named Aameen Sala were working together." I prepared myself for what I could imagine she was about to tell me. After Sean's conversation the other day, I don't want to know where this is about to turn. "They started arguing, so I went over to talk to them, and I heard Sean say, 'I will have my brother kill the rest of your family before you kill us.'"

My eyes widen in complete shock, I put my head down into my hands and mumble, "fuck." After a few seconds, I raise my head back up, "Sorry for my language," I say.

"It is very shocking, especially because they usually work so well together during partner work," she then says.

"I don't want your brother getting the wrong idea about you either," Mr. Ryan says.

"I just had a conversation about this the other night as well," I say back. "So, now what?"

"We need to excuse him from school for a few days. This is a threat, a racist threat nonetheless," Mr. Ryan says.

"Suspended?" I ask, shocked.

"Yes, Mr. Phillips," he replies. He looks at his calendar, "let's see, today is Monday, and their vacation for Thanksgiving starts Wednesday…" he writes on his calendar and mumbles more, "he can return next Wednesday."

I close my eyes and sigh for a second. I stand up, "I will talk to him." I walk out of the office, and Sean looks up at me. I can smell the fear coming from him. "Get up, NOW!" I yell at him and walk out of the office, with him following behind me.

We walk to the car, him just trailing behind me. "Are you mad?" he whimpers before we get to the car.

I turn around and look at him, standing over him, so he can feel the authority figure. "You made a racist threat to your classmate! Yes, I am mad at you. And you put me in that? Do you know how that looks? For both of us?" My voice is getting angrier with each rhetorical question. Sean doesn't make any type of noise, but all of a sudden, he starts to pee his pants. I pull back and am slightly confused. "You don't get to say something like that to someone and get to piss your pants after that either."

We get to the car, and as he is about to get in, I say, "Take a floor mat and put it on the seat. You're not sitting on the seat with that." I start to drive and try to find something to say, scrambling for words. "I don't know what to do, Sean. I am not your parent, so I cannot punish you… I do know how to be in charge of people, though…" I keep trying to find something to say, and nothing seems right.

"Are you going to shoot me?" he whimpers out.

I stop the car and pull over, turning around to look at him, "I don't understand what you think it is that I do. Why would I shoot you?"

He raises his hand and points to my waist, where I have my gun. "You have your gun on you."

"I always have it."

"Why?"

"I just do. Can you tell me why you said that to Aameen?"

"He was being mean to me, and it just came out."

"Curse words just come out, not an entire threat. Do you understand how this looks? This makes it seem like I am telling you that I kill people like Aameen. Better yet, do you know what this does to Aameen? Saying things like that hurt him. You shouldn't say that about anyone, no matter what their religion is or their ethnicity. During this break from school, you are going to write an apology letter to Aameen and go to his house and read it out loud to him and his family. Do you understand?"

"Yes," he answers quietly. "Are you going to tell Mom and my dad?"

"Absolutely," I start driving again.

After I tell my mom and Paul what happened, I listen to them yell at each other, at Sean, and my mom cries, all of the emotions. "I think he is just confused," I butt in and say to them in between fights.

"That is no excuse," Paul says, slamming his fist down on the kitchen counter.

"I will take the blame for it. I should have told him better what I do," I reply.

"I don't need you taking the blame or sticking up for him, Ben," his voice was getting angrier with me.

"I told him he has to write an apology letter and read it out loud to the Sala family."

"Well, it isn't your job to tell him what to do. It is my son, and I will tell him what to do," he snaps at me and turns to walk out of the kitchen. Before he is too far away, I hear him mumble, "Maybe your father should have raised you right."

"I'm not the one going around threatening people, that is YOUR son who is," I yell back.

"No, you're just the one going around killing them." He walks out the front door, slamming it behind him, and my mother runs after him.

I know he said it out of anger and didn't actually mean it, so I just roll my eyes and go upstairs to get ready to go out with Chris.

I turn around from my dresser, and there is a man shot on my floor, he is wearing an American uniform, he is one of my own. I bend down and look at him to see if he is still alive, and he grabs my wrist. "Help... me," he says while blood spills out of his mouth. I look around for a first aid kit, pulling things out of my drawer, but nothing. I run to the bathroom and pull everything out of the medicine cabinet, just some rubbing alcohol. I grab it and run back into my room. His body disappeared, vanished.

I realize I am holding a bottle of rubbing alcohol and go put it back in the bathroom, and notice everything that was in the medicine cabinet is now all over the counter. "What the hell?" I say to myself, confused as to how this mess got here. I walk into my room and notice that everything that was also in my bedside drawer is now all over the floor, including my pills and gun. I pick up the pill bottles, reading the label "Seroquel." Realizing that I must have just had an episode. I don't take a pill even though I should, since the hallucinations are coming back.

I get to the bar in Randall, which is a town that is a little bit bigger than Yelton, where most people from our town go out. I spot Chris and give him the one-second hand while I stop at the bar first, "Beer, please," I ask the bartender.

"Ben?" an angry man's voice says behind me. I turn around and see Syed Sala.

"Hey, Syed," I answer, friendly, trying to keep it light.

"You have some nerve," he steps closer to me.

"Listen, I am sure your family is upset. My family is punishing Sean, and he is going to apologize."

"I don't want your apology. Is this what you tell your little brother that you do? He must have gotten this idea from somewhere."

"Actually, he had the idea from other kids at school. But I am also not going to fight with you about my nine-year-old brother in a bar. We can talk another time," I start to walk away, and he pulls my arm, my beer dropping and shattering at our feet.

"You good?" Chris comes up and says. Syed's friend then pushes Chris back. "Not your fight," he tells him.

"There is no fight," I say in response and start to walk away again.

"I don't know, Ben. I am thinking your shit little brother must have gotten these racial slurs from your white picket fence family," Syed calls out to me, trying to push me into starting a fight.

"So you're going to name-call a nine-year-old? Get a grip, Syed," I turn my back on him.

"No wonder your dad left you."

There isn't much time between his last comment and me punching him in the face, which then escalates into a bigger fight. And that results in us on the floor, which is covered in the beer I just dropped and all the other spilled drinks. I don't fight my best, allowing him to get more hits in. The punches almost feel good, a reminder that I am alive and giving me an adrenaline rush. There is no reason for me to prove my strength, knowing I could have knocked him out with the first punch I threw.

The next thing I know, Jason is pulling Syed off of me and pulling me up. "You good?" He asks.

"Yeah," I wipe the dirt off my clothes. "Why did you pull me off? We were just getting started!" I yell, and Syed gives me a side eye and spits in my direction.

"Here," Jason uses the sleeve of his shirt to wipe my split lip.

"Your mom is going to be so pissed when you come home with that!" Chris says, laughing.

"She will probably beat my ass harder than Syed can," I say back, laughing as well.

"Feels kind of good, doesn't it?" Jason says in my ear, "Don't worry, I know you could have destroyed him." It is a reminder that Jason isn't a bad friend, just isn't a great person. He and I both knew that if he needed to step in, he would have been it was my fight that I could easily fight myself. "Now we have to get you laid!" He says with a giant smirk.

"I wouldn't mind getting laid!" Chris yells to us while we start walking to a high-top table.

Jason comes to our table with two girls in his arms, "This is Lily and Mel," he says. I don't find either of them attractive, so I excuse myself to the bathroom so Jason and Chris can move in on them.

I walk into the bathroom and go into a stall since all the urinals are taken. I walk in and see the same man who was on my bedroom floor sitting on the toilet, holding his stomach where he was shot. I bend down to meet his eye level; his eyes glaze over, but still blinking. I run out of the stall and get paper towels. I go back to the stall, but someone goes in there and locks the stall. "Don't do anything, I can help him," I yell in the stall and bang on the door. Then a gunshot goes off. A man then walks out of the stall, and I grab him, "What did you do? Did you kill him?" I yell while shaking him. He pushes me off of him, and I stumble back into the counter, turning around and looking in the mirror.

"Someone had too many drugs," a guy says, who is walking out of the bathroom.

"I will take two of what he is having," someone else says.

I look around the bathroom, then realize that I am standing there with an entire roll of paper towels in my hand. Two hallucinations already, not good. I go up to Chris and Jason and tell them I will see them later.

Ben

The feeling of dread and even embarrassment starts to set in that night, realizing that the hallucinations are beginning. How can I face the world when I can't even trust my own eyes?

Around late noon, my mom comes in, "Are you going to get up? I was thinking we could go out to get you an outfit for Thanksgiving," she says and sits on my bed next to me. I don't turn away from the wall, so we can't make eye contact.

"No," I answer.

"No, as in you don't want to go shopping today?"

"No, as in I am not getting up."

"Do you want something to eat at least?" She asks, trying to get me to do anything.

"Not now. Can you shut the door on your way out?" I ask, hinting towards the fact that I want her out of my room. I open my drawer and take out the Ambien, cutting it into a quarter and taking it.

The Ambien must have kicked in because I wake up to my mom knocking on my door, and I see that the sun is now setting. She walks into my room and has a plate of food, "I made you some dinner. It is chicken and noodles." I don't say anything, and she puts it on the nightstand. "Are you okay?" She asks.

"Fine. You can close the door."

She walks out, and I hear her talking to Paul down the hall a bit, "he hasn't moved all day." She is concerned.

"Might just be having a lazy day," Paul tries to reassure her. I roll my eyes at the whole situation.

It is Wednesday now, day two of not leaving bed. The sun is extra bright this morning, and I grab the sheet from my bed and hang it over the windows. My door must not have been closed all the way because Sam pushes it open and lies at the bottom of my bed. A few minutes later, Sean comes into my room, "There you are!" He says in a high-pitched voice and goes up to Sam.

Then my mom walks in a second later, "Oh, you're awake!" She exclaims. Even though she can barely see my eyes open, she is guessing since everyone is in here. "Do you want something to eat?"

"No," I answer. "Can you close the door?" Sean is still playing with Sam at the end of my bed, and she is still standing in my doorway.

"Are you staying in bed all day again?" Her voice was now annoyed.

"Probably."

"Are you sick?" She comes over to me and puts her hand on my head. "You feel fine. Sean, sweetie, can you take Sam outside?" trying to get them out of the room to try and talk to me about something. "What is going on?"

"Nothing," I answer and turn my head away to face the wall.

"I can't help you if you don't tell me what is wrong."

"Didn't ask."

"Benjamin, you can't just lie in bed all day. Thanksgiving is tomorrow, you know."

"Okay."

She lets out a sigh before she leaves. I take another quarter of the Ambien. Maybe I can sleep through Thanksgiving tomorrow.

I wake up and hear my mom on the phone, "I don't know what is wrong with him, Mike. He won't leave his bed…. Yes, I know that is what Paul said too, but it has been two days now… No, I am going to take him to the doctors… Because this is not right… He doesn't even talk in sentences or even eat… Okay, I will let you know later… Whatever, Mike, have a good Thanksgiving."

A few seconds later, I hear her at my doorway, "Okay, I am taking you to the hospital," she says as soon as she walks in and turns the lights on.

"Why?" I say very blasé.

"What do you mean, why! Look at yourself!" I don't move. "Ben, get up!"

"I have been away for four fucking years, can't I just spend a couple of days lying in my bed without you thinking I need to go to the hospital. Damn."

"Are you on drugs?"

"NO. I am just lying in my bed."

"Just eat something, please."

"I'm saving my appetite for Thanksgiving. Can you close the door and turn the lights off?"

"No, I am going to make you something now, and you are going to eat it. Clearly, you haven't had anything." I know she is referring to the three plates that are now stacked on my nightstand that she left today.

She comes back a little while later and sets a new plate down in place of the other three. "I was going to go out with your brother and Paul to get outfits for tomorrow for all of you, but I'm not sure if you should be home alone…"

"Okay."

"Paul will stay here. If you need anything, just yell for him."

"Okay."

The sound of Sean's voice causes me to open my eyes: "Mom will yell at you if you don't get out of bed today."

"Probably."

"Especially because it is your first Thanksgiving home again."

"Okay," I close my eyes and turn back over.

Sean walks out of the room, and my mom must have seen him in here and asks him if I am awake. "You need to get up and shower soon, and also cut this attitude," she says like a strict parent enforcing their rules about curfew. The sound of my grandparents fills the rest of the house. My grandma is yelling at my grandpa for turning the volume on the television too loud while he tells her that the parade is a monumental moment of the year.

"You should come help soon," Paul says to me from my doorway.

"Yeah," I say back in hopes he doesn't come in here to talk to me.

"Listen," I should have hoped harder. "For the past four years, your mom cried at every holiday just wishing you were home. Even just wishing you could call her or Skype her, like most stories she read, but you couldn't because you were too busy and couldn't get that privilege. I am just asking if you could just give her a nice Thanksgiving…"

"Yeah," I know he is trying to guilt me, and I am not in the mood for it, nor do I feel guilty. He sighs and walks out of the room. Seems like everyone sighs when they are leaving my room, and I am just curious as to why they keep coming back then.

I must have fallen back to sleep because I wake up and see a small child standing in front of me. "Who are you?" I say when I wake up, not even sure if this is a hallucination, a dream, or reality.

"Clay," he answers, he seems so young, I am surprised he even knows his name. "Who are you?" He asks back.

"Ben. I don't know you."

"I don't know you." Touché.

"There you are!" A woman says at my doorway and comes in and grabs the kid. I don't know her either. "I am so sorry about him, he loves to wander!" She picks him up and walks out.

My mom then, of course, comes into my room right after, "Oh, you met Clay and Lori!"

"Who are they?"

"Your cousin Nick's wife and child."

"Didn't know he was married or had a child…"

"Everyone is starting to get here, do you want to get up now?" She asks, but we both know it wasn't a question but rather a command. She pulls down the sheet that was hanging over my window. "You aren't a vampire," I close my eyes at the sudden burst of light.

"I will get up," I tell her.

"Be down in 15, your new outfit is hanging on the door in your bathroom."

When she leaves the room, I then open the Adderall bottle and take half to wake me up a bit more for today. I look at the Seroquel bottle, holding it in my hand, wondering if I should start taking it. I drop it back in the drawer and shut it.

My mother greets me at the bottom of the stairs with a smile on her face that falls to a frown as I get closer to her and she grabs my chin, "Wait a second, what is on your face? You have a split lip."

I forgot it was even there. "It is nothing. Got into a fight with Syed Sala the other night."

"What is it with this family and theirs right now? We will talk about that later." We walk into the kitchen together, "Look who is here!" She yells out to everyone, introducing me. Her voice was excited as if she wasn't just arguing with me for days about my depressive episode.

I smile and wave at everyone. When I look around the house full of people, there are faces I don't recognize. "Who did you invite here?" I turn and whisper to my mom.

"What do you mean? It is just family."

"I don't know these people," I say, worried.

"Sure you do." She starts pointing out people and naming them, half of whom look different from when I saw them, some I haven't even met. "Here, take the corn and bring it to the table." She hands me a bowl, and I am not sure if it's the steam from the corn or the anxiety that starts blurring my vision. Everything starts moving in slow motion, the voices surrounding me are loud, yet I have no idea what words are even coming out of their mouths. Kids running past me laughing, a baby crying, voices that don't sound like my family fill my head.

"Ben? Ben?" My mom's voice next to me is the only one I can understand.

I grab her hand and squeeze it, "I don't know these people." I say to her, turning around and going upstairs.

"Are you okay?" Her voice is shaky, like she is about to cry.

"Yeah, just need a minute," I walk into my room and close the door behind me. I sit on my bed with my head in my hands, my lungs struggling to fill with air, feeling like I am breathing through a straw.

Fuck. This.

Willow

"Do you still love River?" Lily asks me while she sips her lemon tea on my couch, covered in her silk flower-patterned shawl, which is her go-to comfort outfit. She has always been so effortlessly beautiful.

"No. What we had was special, it was. But it didn't work, and I don't think I should focus on that part. I want to remember him when we were good," I respond, pulling my white blanket that my mom made for me up closer, the scent of jasmine forever stitched into it.

She grabs my hand and looks at my palm, "Yeah, like I always say, your love line is super long and deep." Lily loves to palm read and has started card reading. One time, she even tried to tell me about how I was going to get hurt emotionally, and the next day, my dog died. After that, we like to believe she has a psychic ability.

"Are you coming to the fundraiser tomorrow at my store?" I ask her.

"I wish I could, my parents are having their sweat ceremony tomorrow and I can't miss it or else they will probably release some bad mojo on me!"

A sweat ceremony is where they all sit in a hot room with essential oils and sweat out their bad feelings and share their feelings. Lily's family is more intense with their "hippy traditions" than my family is. Her family celebrates the body and their culture, whereas my family is just kind of free-spirited and has the logic of "do what feels right in that moment". This allows a lot of actions without thinking of long-term consequences, which I fall victim to very often.

"I have to make a few calls to the store to see how it is going and everything," I tell Lily, so she understands it is time for her to leave.

"Okay, I have to go get everything ready for tomorrow anyway. I have to get flowers. My mom wants to throw rose petals or some shit at people," she gets up off the couch, which is a slight struggle since my couch is so deep, and wraps her shawl around herself tighter.

When she leaves I open my computer and check on book orders for my store and look over the bills, I call Nikki who is at the store now, "Hey, did the new orders come in?"

"Yeah, I am just finishing stocking them now. Someone called and asked if we could put one of the new books on the side for them, and they will be in tomorrow. Is that cool?"

"Yeah, you can do that, it's fine. But if they aren't there by the end of the day tomorrow, then just put it back on the shelves. You are going to be there for the fundraiser tomorrow, right?"

"Of course!" Nikki was one of my first employees when I opened the bookstore. She loved the idea of selling big books along with classics, but loved the idea of letting people bring their own books in to sell. Being the only bookstore in Randall, Yelton, and even Branchville, we get plenty of business. I published a book, *A Double Standard*, that became more popular than I ever imagined. My favorite part of the book tour was going to little bookshops, and it just made me want to open my own. Within six months, I was starting to make a profit, very little profit, but it was better than none.

Three knocks bang on my door, "Okay, Nikki. I will see you tomorrow," I go to open it, and it is River standing there with a giant smile on his face and his man bun nicely tied up. He walks in and tries to kiss me.

"River, please don't. You know this is over, let's not pretend it's not."

"Okay, Willow. But you look so beautiful today."

"Are you still coming tomorrow, at least?" I ask him.

"To what?"

"The fundraiser at my store."

"Fundraiser for what?"

I sigh because I know I have told him about it multiple times, "People are coming to donate children's books to the local schools or donate money for the schools. There is going to be an open mic too for people to come and read their stories or poetry as well."

"Oh, no, I'm not coming."

"Why?"

"I don't want to," he tells me bluntly.

"Wow…" I say, shocked.

"I am sure you will have plenty of people, though. Lily, your parents."

"Lily isn't going; she has a sweat ceremony with everyone."

"Right. I might go to that since you'll be busy," I roll my eyes at him.

"I would like it if you didn't hang out with my friends anymore." I put my jacket on.

"Where are you going?" He asks, ignoring my last statement.

"I am going to run up to my parents. They have some books they want me to bring to the store."

"I will come with you to help," River says.

"No, don't. Get the rest of your stuff out of the house. You can leave the key on the table."

Living in my parents' backyard guest house allows me to keep my space from them while maintaining a closeness as well, and staying with the farm animals is also a significant perk. The sounds of the chickens greet me as soon as I go outside, as they scatter around my feet while I walk over to my parents' house. The living room is full of boxes when I walk in. I look in them and see books, pictures, statues, art pieces, and other random artifacts they have collected from traveling or markets they have been to.

"Mom, what are you doing with all of this stuff?" I yell out to her, not knowing where she is in the house.

She pops her head up from behind a bookshelf in the living room, she smiles sweetly at me, and then comes running into the living room. Her gray hair is in a bun like River's, but my mom makes it look a lot better, her long yellow dress following her.

"I'm not sure yet, but I haven't seen some of these pieces in ages!"

"Joy, I found these pictures in the attic!" My dad says enthusiastically. He hands my mom a couple of 8x10 pictures.

"Oh my goodness! I forgot we ever took these! Willie, come look!" My mom says to me. I go over to see the pictures, and it is pictures of her nude in a grass field. "We need to hang these up, Jerry. I will look later to see if we have some extra frames."

"Are you staying for dinner?" My dad asks me and kisses me on the head.

"No, I am going to the store. By the way, are Coy and Rain coming to Thanksgiving?" It has been almost a year since Coy has been home after traveling all over the West Coast. He used to stop back every few months, but the time got longer and longer between visits. Meanwhile, Rain still manages to come once or twice a month despite living a few hours away. Being the youngest sibling can feel very lonely at times when the older siblings have fled the nest.

"Rain wants to be called Rachel now, remember?" My mom says.

"Oh, right. Well, to me, she is still Rain, so she can deal with it."

"She changed it legally now."

"That is unreal," I roll my eyes. She should take pride in her name.

"If that is what she wants, then so be it. Not everyone has to like their birth name. If that is what she feels like should be her name, then that is her name." At times, I admire my mom's positivity and the ability to not get annoyed or upset by situations, but then there are times I wish she would agree with me and complain about things.

"Well, are they coming?" I remind her that she still hasn't answered my question.

"Rachel is, yes. You know how Coy is."

"Hopefully, he does. I won't be able to deal with RAIN without him. I will call him tomorrow. He likes me more anyway," I give a sly smile and text Coy, telling him to call me when he sees this.

"Hello?" I answer.

"Willie!" Coy's voice on the other line warms my ears immediately. I can tell he isn't sober, but this isn't anything I didn't expect anyway.

"Are you coming for Thanksgiving? I can buy you a plane ticket."

"Sure, yeah!"

"Really?" I say excited and shocked.

"Yeah!"

"Okay! I will buy it right now and send you all the information!" I open my computer and start looking for flights.

"Sounds good! Can't wait to see you and see what you did with your house and see your store! Mom said it looks amazing. But I have to go right now. Love you!"

"Love you too! I will send you the info!" I say right before he hangs up. I then decide to call Rain.

"Hello?" She answers, her voice already sounding annoyed.

"Hey!"

"Why are you calling this late?"

I look at the time, "It is only 10:30."

"Well, when you have a full-time job and a baby that is asleep, that is late."

"Okay, whatever. You are coming to Thanksgiving, right?"

"Obviously."

"I am buying Coy a plane ticket now for him."

She gives a sarcastic laugh, "That's funny."

"Why?" Now I have an annoyed tone.

"He isn't going to come. He never does. I don't know why you even try. You're like a little kid still waiting for Santa Claus."

"Except Coy is real."

"Barely. Anyway, I will see you on Thursday. Tell Mom I am bringing the pies."

I hung up the phone in frustration with her. Once she turned 18 and could move out, she did. She looked at our family as an embarrassment and did everything against us. I used to think it was because she was the middle child, but I think she has more issues than just that. She always acts like her childhood was terrible and our parents were the worst, yet all they ever did was love us and make sure we were always happy.

The guests start arriving at the store around 5 pm, and the line forming outside the door makes me feel so proud of the work I have accomplished and the fact that I have created a safe space for people to share their emotions in their work. Our first open mic was from a regular named Dave, who always writes powerful poetry and sometimes talks with so much energy that he loses his words halfway through, but continues because he knows it gives it more meaning.

"Your parents just got here," Nikki comes and tells me as I stand near the stage where Dave is reading. My parents wave at me when we make eye contact. Once Dave is done with his poetry, I get up on stage to welcome everyone.

"Thank you, Dave. I am always in complete awe of your poetry. Thank you for sharing with us. I want to say thank you and welcome everyone here tonight. I appreciate it from the bottom of my heart. As some of you know, I put my all into this store and love it more than anything. But most importantly, this store wouldn't be what it is without all of you. So thank you, and I hope you all have a great time tonight!" Everyone claps for me after I put the microphone down.

"You are so good at speaking publicly," My mom comes up to me and says, putting her hand on my back. "Your sister wanted to come tonight, but the baby is sick, so she couldn't make it."

"No problem. By the way, I got Coy a plane ticket for tomorrow, so he will be here on Wednesday."

She smiles at me and walks away, most likely thinking the same thing Rain did, but doesn't want to say it. I check my phone and see a text from Lily saying how I hope a good night, and she wants to grab a drink when I am done because the sweat ceremony is going to drive her crazy.

Around 9 pm, it starts to slow down with only a couple of people still performing their work. I go up to Nikki and ask, "I think I am going to go across the street to the bar later to meet up with a friend of mine for a drink, if you want to come?"

"Yeah, I will join. You go now, though, I can stay here."

"I can't let you do that!"

"It's fine! I don't mind. Plus, you'll only be right across the street!"

"You sure?"

"Yes!" she gives me a reassuring smile.

"Don't worry about cleaning up, I will come early in the morning and do it. I have to do a few things anyway before we close on Thursday. Plus, since Chelsea decided not to come tonight to help out and is working tomorrow morning, she can help clean!" We both give each other a smirk at the unlucky Chelsea. "Join me when you're done!"

I walk across the street and go into the bar. As soon as I walk up to the bar to grab a drink, I hear two men arguing a bit a couple of feet away from me.

"I hope this turns into something!" A man sitting at the bar says to me about the argument that is happening behind us.

"Honestly, I am just trying to get a drink," I reply. I stand there waiting while the bartender is down at the other side, waving to get his attention.

The bartender makes his way back down to me and smiles at me, "What can I get you?" He asks, his voice growing louder with each word to block out the fight sounds happening a few feet from us.

"Vodka tonic with two limes, please," I reply with a smile, our eye contact lingering for a few extra seconds before he goes and makes my drink.

The fight ends shortly after I get my drink, and I maintain my spot while I wait for Lily to come. There is no way of missing her when she comes in because it is easy to spot her in any crowd. She makes her way over to me and sits down, ordering herself a drink too.

"How did it go tonight?" She asks and twirls my hair around her finger.

"Awesome!" I say and take a sip of my drink. "What about you?"

"It was fine. I smoked some weed before, though, so that helped it a little bit. River was there and was so high, pretty sure he was hitting on my mom, but who knows."

My eyes roll at the thought of River because none of it surprises me, "Aren't you supposed to be sober doing it?" I ask.

"Yeah, but I won't be able to deal with that if I'm not on anything! Mel is meeting us here by the way." Once Mel arrives, they both find some guys to hang with. I decline the invitation this time because I can feel the exhaustion of the night creeping up on me.

I pace around my house, waiting for Coy to respond to my text about whether he landed yet. According to the flight information, he has already landed. I light up a joint to take the edge off a bit. I assume he is getting high in the airport bathroom, but it's on my 16th call that he finally answers.

"Hello?" He says, like I just woke him up.

"Yeah, where are you? Did you land?"

"Oh man. I forgot about that! I thought it was next Thursday for some reason." I hold back my tears and just respond by saying Okay. "I will be there for Christmas, I promise."

"Sure you will," I hang up the phone and let out the tears, like a dam breaking loose. I don't know what I am dreading more, him not being here or Rain telling me that she told me so. My mom then knocks on my front door, almost knowing that I was upset and needed her. I answer the door, and she sees my tears and hugs me right away. "He isn't coming. Just like Rain said."

"Sweetie, I am so sorry. I know you wanted him to be here."

"Please just tell Rain not to say anything to me about it."

"I can't control what someone says, Willie."

"Please, just tell her I don't want to hear it," I plead with her, and she kisses my head.

"Well, I came here to tell you that she will be here in 10 minutes. I will say something to her for you."

"Okay, well, I have to run to the store real quick to close up for tomorrow and everything."

The car ride to the store is silent, allowing myself the space to think. Twirling my fingers around the loose pieces of braid as I drive and look out the window, admiring the scenery of my drive, never gets old. When I get to the store, a few people are starting to pay, and I tell Nikki she can leave when they are done.

"Are you still open?" A woman walks in and asks us. Her voice is almost a whisper, but she seems more timid of herself than us. Nikki looks at me to give an answer, and I tell her yes, matching her tone of voice to comfort her.

She goes up and down the aisles, and it is obvious she is looking for something that she can't find. "Can I help you with anything?" I ask her softly.

She jumps at my voice, 'Oh shit! Oh, sorry," she continues to look around the books around her in the aisle, "I saw online that you have this book?" She showed me a piece of paper from a book titled *Lost Connections: How to Regain Them.*

"Yeah, so that will be over here in this section," I reach out my hand for her to take, and she gives me a forced half smile, but takes it, and lets out a deep breath.

"Thank you," she says as I hand her the book.

"Do you need anything else?" I ask her, and she shakes her head no and walks to the front of the store to pay.

I don't go over to my parents till later, after I know my mom said something to Rain about Coy. When I walk into the house, my nephew Aiden, who is 3 now, greets me with a hug. "Aunt Will!" he says in his chipmunk-like voice. Rain then walks into the main entryway with the baby and hugs me. I look down at my new niece.

"Hi, Brittany!" I say to her in a baby voice to grab her undivided attention. She looks up at me with spit flowing out of her mouth. "She looks exactly like you!" I say to Rain. "Where is Hank?" I ask.

Her husband Hank is the most boring person ever, and I am convinced she only married him because he is so unlike our family.

"He should be here any second. He had to finish up some work at the office." Within seconds, his car shows up, and she opens the door, excited to see him, which I don't understand how he can bring any excitement to anyone. He walks in, and my parents must have sensed it because they both come in from the kitchen. My mom walks up to Hank first.

"So glad you made it!" she says and is about to do her traditional welcome kiss hello. Rain puts her arm in front of my mom, stopping her in her tracks.

"Hug only," Rain commands. My mom then hugs him hello, and then my dad starts to go up, and Rain says, "You too." Making sure my dad knows hugs only as well. Right as my dad is about to go in for the hug, he kisses him, and I burst out into laughter, which causes my parents to do the same. Rain now takes this as a chance to make a snarky remark, "Oh, where is Coy, Willow?"

I ignore her because I know it is best to just let it slide rather than argue with her. We all join in the living room, and my phone starts ringing, and River's name shows up.

"Hello?" I answer.

"Can we talk?" He asks.

"No, I am with my family."

"Alright," he hangs up.

"No phones, please. It is after 8 pm, and we start our radiation detox at this time," my mom says to me, I then shut it off and put it on the table. The rest of the night is spent playing board games and card games. Although it was fun playing the games and laughing with everyone, once we played Pictionary, I got gloomy because it was always Coy's favorite.

I spent the night on the couch, letting Rain stay in my house since she has the kids. The smell of Thanksgiving meals being cooked already fills the air early in the morning, and I take a deep breath, allowing it to fully sink into my lungs. I lay there for a minute and enjoy the sound of my parents' laughter and the clanking of spoons. Once I hear Aiden come into the house, I put the Thanksgiving Parade on for him. As a child, it was always my favorite, and I want him to feel that excitement as well.

Ben

"Mom!" I call out from my bedroom, about ten seconds later, she comes running in as if I had yelled that there was danger.

"What?" She asks, slightly out of breath since she just ran up the stairs.

"Can you put this ointment on my back?" I ask my anticlimactic question.

She grabs the ointment from my hand, "Why do you need this on?"

"I got a tattoo the other day. I forgot to put this on."

"What? You got a tattoo?" She asks, shocked. I forgot that I still have yet to show it to her.

"Yeah, with Chris," I pull my shirt up, and as soon as I do, she lets out a giant gasp. I also forgot that she has yet to see my back.

She touches my back and I hear her crying behind me, "What did they do to you? What happened to you?"

"Nothing, can you just put the stuff on?"

"Ben, what happened to you?"

"Nothing, I don't want to talk about it."

"You have to talk about it. What if I take you to see someone? Would that help?"

"What are you talking about, seeing someone?" I turn around and look at her.

"Like a therapist."

"Why would I need to see a therapist?"

"Because you're depressed."

"I am? This is news to me."

"That is why you didn't get out of bed for three days the other day."

"I am not depressed. Please, don't go around saying that I am or that something is wrong with me. Don't even say anything to Paul or Dad about it."

"They need to know what is wrong with you."

"No, I am serious. Don't say anything; don't even talk about the whole thing about me not getting out of bed. If anyone asks, I am fine, I am great, and I am just like how I was."

"Just tell me what happened to your back," she says softly.

"No, I have to live through it daily in my head. I don't need to talk about it," I turn back around and go into my dresser to find a shirt, and my mom puts her hand on my back.

"I am so sorry," she says, her voice shaky, and I know she is holding back more tears. I turn around and wrap my arms around her.

"I am okay," I kiss the top of her head, and she hugs me tighter.

She then lets go of me and pushes my body around so my back faces her and puts the ointment on me. I hear her let out a deep breath and sniffle to try to get rid of the tears she was trying to avoid shedding. Her hands move across my back as she lightly puts on the ointment. It feels soothing at first until I start to feel panicky about being touched. Before I get too into my head, she breaks the silence, "My friend Jen Donald's daughter was asking about you. I told her I would see if you wanted to go on a date with her. She is a cute girl, her name is Olivia."

"I guess," I respond by trying to pull myself back to the present. This feels more like it's for my mother than for me. A confirmation that I am fine. "Are we done now?" I ask her in a rush so I can get to Jason's house.

"Yes, yes. Have fun," she closes the door behind her.

As I get to Jason's house, I see Jason's girlfriend and immediately feel uncomfortable, seeing as how the other week he was just making out with some random girl at the bar.

"I have a date tomorrow night," I say, grabbing another slice of pizza from the coffee table.

"With who?" Chris asks excitedly, the couch squeaks as he moves in excitement for me.

"Her name is Olivia."

"Oh shit, Olivia Donald?" Chris got even more excited.

"Yeah."

"She is hot. Where are you going to go?"

"I don't know, grab a drink somewhere."

"Hopefully, she has a fake I.D then," Jason says.

"Why?" My mouth full of food, I grab a napkin and wipe it to not be too disgusting.

"She isn't 21 yet, man," Jason says and laughs a bit.

"Shit." I say. "How old is she?"

"Do you really want to know?" Jason asks.

"Yeah."

"I am pretty sure she is 19."

"Tell me you are kidding. No way my mom would set me up with her if she were 19."

Jason starts laughing hysterically, "Your mom set you up with her?" He can barely say the words from laughing so hard.

I throw a pillow at him from the couch, "Shut up."

"Maybe she didn't know," Jason's girlfriend says. The only sentence she said the entire time.

"I can't be with someone who is 19!"

"It's legal. No harm done," Jason says and shrugs his shoulders. He then pulls a cigarette out of the drawer next to him and lights it.

"Still smoking, huh?" I say to him.

"Yeah, my lungs are already shot, so who cares?" I know he is referring to when he was 15 and got stuck in a house fire and was put on a ventilator for months. He hands his girlfriend one and asks Chris if he wants one, and he takes one as well. "You want?" He asks me.

"No, I am good." For the last three years, I was a habitual smoker. After days of sitting in a desert with a few guys and only being able to move around a couple of feet, there is nothing much else to do than to burn packs of cigarettes and eat protein bars that coat your throat in grains. But eventually, it turned into a coping mechanism more than just a way to pass the time.

As Chris and I are about to leave, instead he asks me, "I am going to this bookstore in Randall, want to come for a ride?" I think about my other options, which are just sitting at home, so I agree.

"There is a bookstore in Randall now?"

"Yeah, it opened a little while ago. I have to get this one book for my mom. She is in some book club."

We walk into The Listening Post, a quaint bookstore that smells like essential oils and the classic smell of books as soon as you walk in. Chris goes up to the cash register to ask for the book, and I walk around looking at the store. The inside is bigger than you would imagine from seeing it outside. I go down one aisle and start looking around. "Can I help you with anything?" A girl's voice says to me.

"No, I am good. Just looking," I say, then look at her. My eyes don't come off her, though. Her smile forms a slight dimple on the right side. Her shirt is tied together in the front, and I try not to pay too much attention to the fact that I can see her belly button through it.

"Don't start a fight in here," she says, pushing one side of her long, dark blonde hair to the other side. She looks at me with wide hazel eyes, but I look at her, confused by her comment. "You got into a fight the other night at the bar," she leans on the bookshelf next to me, propping her elbow on one of the shelves and resting her chin in her hand.

"Yeah, I did. How do you know?"

"I was there. You were right behind me. You got your ass kicked!"

"Yeah, I let him win."

"HA! I am sure you did," she smiles and then turns around and walks away. I do an awkward leap up to her and get in front of her.

"I am Ben," I say, and put my hand out to shake hers.

"I am Willow," her voice is almost raspy, but doesn't sound rough; there is a soothing sound to it. She shakes my hand back, and it is warm and soft. I need to remind myself to let go of it. I see Chris standing at the end of the aisle, and when he notices that I am talking to someone, he just turns around and walks away.

"So, you were at the bar, huh? Are you Yelton?" I ask as she stops at a cart full of books and starts putting them on the shelves. I follow her each time she moves a couple of feet away.

"I live right on the outskirts of Randall on a farm. Do you cause fights at bars often?" She laughs and walks over to the next aisle.

"Not usually, only if action calls."

She stands on her tiptoes to reach a shelf, her lips slightly parted, and she tries to concentrate to reach higher. I grab the book from her hand and put it on the shelf for her.

"Your friend is waiting for you outside," she says, walking another couple of feet, pushing the cart to finish her organizing. I selfishly take a longer second to catch up to her so I can look at her from the back. I never thought an hourglass shape existed on a girl until now.

"Can I get your number before I leave?"

She stops in her tracks and takes a second before turning around. She smiles, and that dimple is more prominent now. "I have an idea. Let's play a game of fate. I am going to put my number in a book tonight when I close the store. You have to find it, and then you can call me."

"Alright, I will play this game. But can I have a hint at least? There are a lot of books here…"

"Can I ask you something?"

"Sure."

"How do men act on a sinking ship? Do they hold each other? Do they pass around the whisky? Do they cry?" She asks.

"I have no idea," she then turns and walks away. "What is the hint?" I yell out to her, but she keeps walking away. I go to find her and see her at the cash register, now helping someone.

Chris and I get in the car. "Who was that girl?" He asks me right away.

"Her name is Willow, she was beautiful, wasn't she?"

"Extremely!"

When I get home, I start thinking about the conversation I had with Willow and remember that she asked me a peculiar question, which, now thinking about it, might be a hint to the book she is putting her number in. Unfortunately, I was too distracted by her giving me a hint that I didn't realize it was a hint. All I remember is something about a man and a sinking ship, the Titanic being the first and only thing that comes to mind, although that seems too easy and generic, and this girl seems like anything but that.

A text message from an unknown number pops up on my phone, I read it, and it says, *Hey, it's Olivia! Just figured I would reach out to confirm dinner tomorrow night!* I don't answer and instead just take an Ambien. After doing so, I realize that I am hungry and find myself tiptoeing downstairs and reheating leftover pasta that my mom made for dinner. Paul is sitting on the couch watching TV, and I sit down and join him, sitting there without speaking.

"Your mom said you have a date tomorrow," he says all of a sudden during a generic ibuprofen commercial.

"Yeah, we will see how that goes. By any chance, do you know what book this quote is from? It's something like What do men do on a sinking ship? They drink and cry," I ask Paul.

"It sounds familiar. Let me think for a second," He sits there with a concentrated face, even rubbing his chin as if that will help. "Why not just look it up?" He grabs his phone and looks it up, "Ah! The Perfect Storm, that's it!"

"Perfect! Thank you!" I go upstairs and Google *The Perfect Storm* on my laptop, then remember I should text Olivia back.

Yeah, sounds good. I can pick you up around 6:00.

I wake up and look at my phone, and see that I have a text from Olivia saying *Sounds good. I am excited to see you!* I look through my texts and see that I was texting her last night, but I have no recollection of it. I also see my laptop open next to me and see that I was Googling *The Perfect Storm* for some reason; I shake my head at myself and close it out.

Arriving at Olivia's house made me feel uncomfortable in a way. Wondering if I have to go meet her parents and sit down and have a conversation with them, if they are going to tell me to bring her home at a certain time, just all the cliché first date conversations in old high school films. I decide that I don't even care enough and just text her and say I am outside her house. She comes outside and looks prettier than I thought she would. She is casually dressed in black jeans and a flannel, her hair is light brown and short, and she has red lipstick on. She gets in the car, and then all of a sudden, I remember coming here one time with my mom when I was younger and seeing her playing with her dolls. "Hey!" I try to sound as excited as I can be.

"Hey!" She says back. I then awkwardly hug her while she is sitting in the passenger seat.

"So where do you want to go?"

"There is a place in the center of town that just opened up."

"Yeah, we can do that," I start driving and then turn the radio on at a low volume so there is no awkward silence if we can't find conversation, but not too loud so we can have a conversation. I keep telling myself to at least try tonight.

"So how long were you in the army for?" She asks.

"Four years."

"Are you going to go back?" I pause for a second when she asks because I haven't thought about it yet.

"Not sure yet. What do you do?" Trying to avoid talking about myself.

"Right now I am going to school. Your mom is one of my teachers!"

"Oh, I didn't know that. What are you going to school for?"

"International communications, I want to work with foreign policy."

"That is really great. Let me know if you need help with anything. Do you like it so far?"

"Thank you! Yeah, I do actually! The only class that I am struggling with is my language class."

"What language are you taking?"

"Arabic." Something about it when she says it gets to me. The thought of how beautiful the language can be, but also how scared I was when I first heard it and didn't know what anyone was saying, how once you know some words that are being said, you find out that they are horrific, and there is nothing beautiful about it.

"Alkalb," I tell her to see if she knows what it means.

"Dog, right?" she says, excited at the fact that I actually knew a word and she knew it as well.

"Yeah."

"Do you know a lot of words?"

"I know a few."

"What other words do you know?" She asks. I try to think of a word that I know that isn't terrible, and nothing comes to mind.

"Is this the restaurant?" I change the subject and point to a place.

"Yeah, this is it!"

We sit down, and I can see how alluring she is now since it is better lighting. Chris wasn't lying when he said she is hot. Even though her looks are enticing, she seems smart and put together, for some reason, I can't get that girl Willow out of my mind. She is stuck in my mind like plastic wrap sticking to itself. Then all of a sudden, I remembered why I was looking up *The Perfect Storm*. It is from the hint Willow gave me. It was a complete epiphany, an eureka moment. A part of me wants to get up and run to the bookstore real quick, but I know I shouldn't. I try to pull myself back to reality and focus on what Olivia is saying to me. We both try to make small talk about what has changed around the town, and how she is liking school. It is all normal surface-level conversation for a first date.

After dinner, I ask her if she cares if we stop at the bookstore, and she says no. There is a sense of guilt about going to get the book with her there, but now I also need to know for my satisfaction if I am right or not. When we get there, I say, "I just have to run inside and pick up a book if you want to wait in the car."

"I will come in with you," she says.

We walk into the store, and I look over at the girl at the register. It is the same girl who was here the other night when I came in. She raises her eyebrow at me and smirks, "Need something?" she asks.

"*Perfect Storm?*"

"You got it," she winks, confirming that I have the correct book, and starts walking toward an aisle, and I follow behind her. Olivia stays in the front and skims through the local author's book section.

I open the book, and there it is, her number. "Does your date know what you're looking for?"

"She knows I am looking for a book, yeah." When I look back up, I see two Arabic men standing at the end of the aisle looking at me, then all of a sudden one pulls out a gun and shoots towards me, but misses me. I get startled and jump, falling into the shelves a bit.

The girl who helped me looks back at me, "You okay?" She asks, concerned.

"What?" I say, straightening myself since I am leaning into the shelves, "Yeah, yeah, I am fine," I realize what must have just happened and just go up to the front of the store to pay for the book. I walk outside, and Olivia follows. I take a deep breath to try to calm myself a bit. "I'm not feeling good right now, do you mind if I bring you home?" I say to her.

"Yeah, that is fine. You okay?" She puts her hand on my back to try and comfort me.

"Just a sudden headache."

When I get to her house, I get out of the car to hug her goodbye and tell her I had a nice time, which I did. As soon as I get back home, my mom bombards me with questions about how the date went, and I tell her it was good. My head starts throbbing so badly that I don't even bother trying to call Willow tonight. The pain in my head prevents me from falling asleep, so I go for my crutch of an Ambien. Something catches my attention when I open my drawer; someone is standing a couple of feet away from me. I turn on my lamp that is on the nightstand. It is Abba Akil, "Where is he?" I ask him. I pull out my gun and point it at him.

"I do not have him," he says to me.

"That is a lie. I saw you take him. Where is he?" I shake my gun at him in frustration.

"If you saw, why didn't you do anything? Jaban."

I look down at my hand and see that I am pointing my gun at my door, and I get terrified at the fact that if someone walked into my room, I don't know what I would have done. I put my gun back in my drawer and look at the Seroquel bottle that is sitting there, unopened, wondering if it is now time I should start taking it. I close the drawer and turn my light off, going to sleep.

I wake up in a mood again in the morning, where I don't want to leave my bed, and I know I should do something about it before it gets worse again. I decide to call Willow and hope that gives me something to do.

"Hello?" She answers.

"Found it. The Perfect Storm."

"How did you figure it out?"

"I have no idea, I figured it out one night when I was on sleeping medication and remembered it later on."

"Were you on like NyQuil or something?" She mocks me a bit.

"Ambien."

"Oh, so you actually like have an issue." She says bluntly.

"What are you doing right now?" I ask her, changing the subject.

"Lying on my couch. What are you doing?" Something about talking to her feels natural and casual, like we're just two friends talking on the phone.

"Lying in bed, do you want to do something?" I ask her.

"In an hour we can."

"Alright, where do you want to meet?" I catch myself smiling to myself as I talk to her. I let it sit on my face instead of trying to brush it off.

"Meet at the bookstore."

"Okay, see you then," I say, as I am about to hang up.

"Why are you hanging up?" She asks, confused.

"Am I not supposed to?" I prop myself up in bed so get more comfortable.

"Thought we were talking."

"I will have nothing to talk about when I see you then."

"I am sure you will find something," she says as if it were a given. "What are you wearing?" She laughs.

"Right now? Shorts. What are you wearing?" I laugh back at how ridiculous this is.

"Pajama shorts and a tank top. I turned up the heat in my house last night because I wanted to wear these pajamas."

"Seems logical to me." The smile on my face has grown wider and I welcome it with each sentence she says.

"I think so. What are you going to wear later?"

"Why are you so curious about my outfit choices?"

"You can tell a lot by what a person wears!"

"I am going to wear jeans and a t-shirt. What does that say about me?"

"Says you're boring and keep it simple."

"I mean, I guess I keep it simple," I feel slightly embarrassed for some reason.

"I am just kidding. I was making it up. I was only asking about your outfit choices because I have nothing else to talk about."

"I am sure you can find something," I say, mocking her.

"You are very right, Ben."

My mom then walks into my room, "Oh, you're awake!" she says and then realizes I am on the phone, "Is that Olivia?" She asks.

"No," I say sternly, and she backs up and leaves the room.

"Ooo, who is Olivia?" Willow says.

"Nobody."

"Is that the girl you were with when you found my number?" She lets out a small giggle, "Well, you can tell me later. I am going to get ready, see you in an hour," she then hangs up abruptly. I sit there smirking for a few seconds, then call Chris.

"Hey!" He answers.

"I am going on a second date right now," I jump out of bed and start getting ready.

"So it went well with Olivia?" he asks.

"No, not with Olivia. The girl from the bookstore."

"Damn, look at you!"

I go into my bathroom and go to start the shower, I pull the curtain back and Abba Akil is standing there, "Shit I say, startled.

"What happened?" Chris says on the phone.

"What?" I ask him, confused.

"You just yelled shit."

"Nothing, just saw a giant spider." I make something up quickly. "I am going to go get ready. I will let you know how it goes," I hang up and think to myself how these hallucinations just need to stop for today. I also think about how it might be helpful if I could even remember what I am hallucinating. Am I making situations up, or am I reliving moments that I have already suffered through?

I show up at the bookstore and walk in, and see Willow behind the cash register. She looks up at me and smiles. "At least it isn't a t-shirt," she jokes in reference to how I am wearing a flannel instead. Although I did roll up my sleeves a bit so she could see my arms in hopes she'd be impressed by a muscular forearm.

"Didn't want to be boring."

She smiles at me and then looks back down at the notebook she was writing in. Her hair is down this time and is covering most of her face. When she looks down, she keeps pushing it back behind her ears, but it keeps slipping. "I am leaving now, Natalie!" she yells out. A girl then comes down one of the book aisles and looks at me, and then looks at Willow and goes behind the counter. "Ready?" Willow asks me, and we walk outside.

"I haven't had coffee yet. Want to grab some?" I ask her.

"You're the one who asked me to hang out! Everything is up to you!"

"Where is there good coffee around here?"

"Beans is good, it's just down the street," she says.

We start walking. Slowly, we drift closer until we're walking side by side. She's no taller than 5'4", and with the foot of height I have on her, and my broader shoulders, she feels even more delicate next to me. It's as if there is a magnet pulling us closer together with each step.

"How long have you been working at the bookstore?" I ask, looking down at her as she keeps pushing her hair behind her ear like she did at the bookstore.

"I own it!" She exclaims, looking back up at me with wide eyes of excitement.

"Really? I didn't know that."

"Yeah. I wrote a book, and it became popular so I was able to open up this bookstore."

"What is your book called?"

"It is called *A Double Standard.*"

"And what is it about?" I ask even though the title seems pretty obvious about what it would be about.

"It is literally about double standards in America. I interviewed a whole bunch of groups of people and asked them questions and talked about the unfairness in America," I let out a dry laugh. "Is that funny?" She asks seriously.

"You just sound like every other feminist."

"No, I sound like every other American who knows what is going on. Are you saying that America is fair?"

"Never said that. But I do love my country, that is why I fight for it."

She bursts into a laugh, "Wow! You're one of those people."

"One of those people?"

"Those people who think their country is the greatest!" She then stops in her tracks and looks at me, "Oh… oh, I'm sorry. That was rude." I look at her quizzically. "You… you are *the* army boy."

"Yes, I am." I start walking then.

"You don't need to agree with my book for whatever reasons you need to not agree with it, but just don't sit here and talk down upon it. I worked really hard on it and put a lot of dedication into it, and it gave me my store, which is my life."

There is something about what she says and how she says it that makes me feel like she understands that there is almost a reason I can't agree with what she is saying in her book. "And you don't trash-talk what I do," I say, adding to this deal we just made.

She puts her hand out to shake on it, "Deal," I shake her hand and we start walking again.

Willow

Ben and I sit across from each other at Beans. I glance at his clean-shaven face and his grown-out crew cut hair. He is so different from most of the guys around here, and especially from the ones I've dated. I let my eyes linger, taking in the rugged features. There's an intensity in the way he holds himself, something unmistakably different. I should've known he was the Army guy the moment I saw him. A faint scar runs just along his hairline on the right. I notice scars and calluses cover his hands as he fidgets with them on the table.

"The coffee is good, isn't it?" I ask.

He takes another sip, "You were right!"

"So who was Olivia, by the way?" I tease him.

He blushes a little, "This girl I went out on a date with last night."

"Look at you! Two dates in two days with two different girls! How did it go?"

"Fine. Nice girl, pretty. Just not sure if there was something."

"I can understand that. I was just with someone for about two years, and our connection just… got lost."

"That is a while for a connection to just disappear."

"It is complicated."

"Ahh, nothing like the cliché saying of it being complicated."

"I know, I just hate talking about it. And everyone keeps trying to bring it up."

"Okay, we don't need to ever talk about it then. Anyway, this might sound strange, but I have to go to the hardware store. Want to come with me after this coffee?" He asks me and scratches his head.

"Yeah, I don't mind!" We sit there drinking our coffees, I look up at him and he is staring wide-eyed at the door, I look behind me to see what he is looking at and see nothing. While I keep looking at the door, trying to figure it out, I hear a loud crash and turn back around and see that he dropped his coffee mug on the floor.

"Shit," he says and stands up. An employee comes over and starts to clean it up. "I am so sorry," he tells the adolescent boy with the broom.

"No problem, man," he reassures Ben.

The vibe of humiliation radiates from Ben, and my natural reaction is to drop my mug as well. They both look at me, "I drank so much coffee today that I am literally shaking!" I blurt out to try and make an excuse. "I am so sorry, Neil!" I come here enough that

I know the employees. Neil is also about 15 and tried hitting on me the other day so I don't feel bad.

Ben and I walk out of the coffee shop and start walking to the hardware store, which is around the block. "Olivia Donald?" I ask suddenly.

"What?"

"Did you go on a date with Olivia Donald?"

"Yeah, how do you know?"

"That is my co-workers little cousin!" I giggle a little. "So, you like the younger girls, huh?" I tease.

He does a face-palm, "I was set up! I didn't know her age till later."

"Probably why there was no connection. She is mature for her age, but there is something about a big age gap. It is like older wine, it's just different when it is older." We then get into the store, "What are you looking for anyways?"

"A safe," he answers while looking up and down aisles. Then all of a sudden we turn an aisle and it is no other than River right in front of Ben.

"Excuse me," Ben says to River and walks around him. He makes River look so much shorter and smaller in comparison to his build. I never thought much about a guy's build but after seeing Ben, I can see the appeal.

"What are you doing here?" River asks me and Ben then turns around to see that I am stopped.

"I am with my friend Ben. What are you doing here?" I ask, knowing that it must be for something absurd.

"Getting some wood and rope to make a statue. I didn't know you had a friend Ben."

"We just became friends."

"Is this why you haven't been calling me back?"

"No, I haven't called you back because I don't want to. There isn't anything left to talk about."

"I suppose you're right. I just can't pretend that a world where we exist is no longer a world."

"River, please stop making this harder than it needs to be. Just... go on with your life and your art."

"I see and I understand. Just keep in mind you will always be a muse for me."

"Thanks, River."

"Have a good rest of your day, Willow and Ben. Namaste." River then walks past me, and I take a few steps up to Ben.

"I can see how it must be complicated." He says. My face turns red. "Like I said, we don't need to talk about it."

He then finally finds a safe and says "ta-da!" when he does so. "What do you need it for?" I ask, being nosey.

"My gun."

"That one?" I ask, pointing at his hip.

"Yes, this one," he grins at me and touches it, almost reassuring himself that it is there.

We walk out of the store, and I ask, "Do you want to go to this place down the block a bit?"

"What is it?" He asks curiously.

"Just this place I like to go sometimes…" I leave it mysterious for him.

"Sure, let me just put this safe in my car."

I bring him to a little park area where it is just a land of grass and a big tree in the center, an old tire swing swaying from the branches in the light breeze.

"My parents call this the tree of life. I come here sometimes to read. Not many people come to this side of town since it is a dead end."

"Why do they call it the tree of life?"

"My mom's water broke when she was pregnant with me when she and my dad were sitting here." We sit down under the tree with our backs resting against it.

"What are your parents like?" He asks and puts his one ankle over the other, his black boots crushing leaves and sticks beneath him as he settles in.

"They are amazing. To say their parenting style is indulgent would be an understatement. They believe that we should do whatever we want if it makes us happy."

"If only it was that easy." When he says it he sounds so disappointed that life is difficult, whereas I believe it isn't that hard. You really should do what makes you happy in that moment after all; you're only living to die one day so why not focus on your happiness in that moment. Then I feel sad for him, sad that he can't do what makes him happy and that his life isn't set up like that. It is tragic in a way. "Are you an only child?" He then asks.

"I have an older brother and an older sister. What about you?"

"I have a younger brother." He stops for a second and then continues to talk, "I also have another younger brother and just found out a little sister. I never met them though and I forget I even have them. They're all half siblings though."

We sit there without talking for a little while; the only noise is the leaves rustling from the wind, cars from the main street every so often, a dog barking in the distance, birds talking back and forth with each other. I start imagining that the birds are on a first date as well. They're asking each other about their family and where they like to go eat and if they come to this tree often.

"I get it now!" He exclaims while looking up at the tree.

"Get what?" I ask.

He points at the tree, "Willow," he looks at me and points at "Willow."

I start laughing, "Ah, yes! Forgot to mention that's where I get my name from!"

"I want to read your book, by the way," he says to me, My heart flutters in excitement that he wants to read it.

"But you don't like the concept of it," I remind him.

"So? It is something you put yourself into and are proud of. Just because I don't agree with some of it doesn't mean I don't want to read it. People don't agree with the newspapers but continue to read them every day."

"There is something I like about hanging out with you," I tell him.

"Maybe it is because of my insanely good looks," he smiles and shrugs his arm around mine.

"Probably," I smile at him; "It is also because there is something real about you."

"Do you usually hang out with imaginary people?" He jokes.

"Maybe it is because River was nonexistent."

"Was he that bad?"

"No, he was the sweetest. He wouldn't hurt a fly. He just was kind of always floating on a cloud, it seemed like. There was nothing concrete about him," I pause; I usually open up easily to people and never had a problem expressing my feelings or ever feeling scared to say anything on my mind, but with Ben, there is more of a sense of realness with it. It isn't just opening up, but feels more like confiding.

We walk back to his car. "Hey, do you want to come over tomorrow night for dinner?" I ask him.

"Wow, already asking to hang out for a second time," he smirks, "sounds good though. Let me ask you something, is it too early for you to have a friendship with a guy after your break-up?"

"No. And I know it has been weird with me talking about him and then him showing up. But he won't be a problem."

"Okay, if you say so," he then hugs me goodbye before he gets into his car, which lingers. My head settles right under his heart, his dark green and black flannel feeling soft on my cheek, and he smells like spearmint and cedar. We both pull away at the same time and smile at each other goodbye.

Ben

I spend about an hour trying to figure out what to wear to dinner at Willow's, feeling ridiculous that it is taking me this long to figure out. My mom walks into my room as I stand, looking into my dresser, and five different button-up shirts are lying on my bed.

"Where are you going tonight?" she asks me with a slight smile on my face.

"I am going to this girl's house for dinner," I say while I try on a different shirt.

"Put the dark blue one on, it is nice but casual, along with some khaki shorts."

I do as she says, and it does look good. "Do you think Paul will care if I use some of his cologne? I just ran out," I ask.

"Go ahead, it is in our room."

I walk down the hallway into their room, and I look in the dresser to find cologne, but instead find a small safe inside one of the drawers. The need to open fills my desire for some reason, but fail to get the correct combination of numbers. My mom makes her way down the hallway so I abort the mission and get to the bathroom before she sees what I was doing.

Willow's street is a long gravel road, and at the dead end is this colorful yellow house. The entrance door is blue, and the windows on the house are stained glass and vary in color, there is a porch wrapping around the house, and sunflowers that welcome you in. I remember that she texted me multiple times, though, saying go to the back house. I see a house towards the back left and drive on the lawn where the grass is dead, which leads to Willow's car, which is a light blue Beetle convertible. I laugh out loud in my car at how cliché it is that she has one.

Her house is the same yellow as the other house, and her door is red instead, with a little porch outside. I get out of the car and look around the yard. In the distance, there are woods, and then behind the main house is a mini farm. I see a chicken coop and hear a pig snorting around. It is difficult to get the main idea of what it looks like since the moon only lights so much of the yard. The only thing I can clearly tell is that it is the only house on the dead end, and there is also a lot of green land around.

I knock on her front door, and she opens it with a wide smile. She is wearing a longer white dress that has a flower pattern throughout. Her lipstick is a dark cherry red, much like her front door. "Welcome!" She says and spreads her arms open to welcome me in. I walk into the house, and it is small inside. You walk right into the living room, which is painted a yellowish-tan, and plants are all over the living room.

"Nice little place you have," I say, and she closes the door behind me.

"Yeah, it's small, but I don't need anything bigger!"

"So what are we ordering for dinner?" I ask.

"Nothing!" she exclaims and starts walking to the kitchen. "I am making dinner. I am making pesto pasta with chicken," she says while she is at the stove.

"You're not cooking one of those chickens that is outside, right?"

She laughs loudly, "No! Those are our pets. My parents' house is the other house. They're vegan, so no animals outside get eaten! Make yourself comfortable by the way."

I walk around her living room a bit, looking at all the pictures she has hanging on the walls. Most of them are just scenery pictures, views from the top of mountains or deep in the woods, then there is a picture of her and one man who is much taller than her, even though that isn't hard to accomplish, and skinny. "Who is this?" I ask, being slightly invasive.

She walks over with two glasses of red wine in her hand and hands me one. "That is my big brother, Coy," she takes a sip of her wine and keeps looking at the picture with me.

I look around at the other pictures and notice that there are no other pictures of anyone else. "Is he the only one who makes the cut?" I ask.

"I was always a lot closer to my brother," she walks back into the kitchen. She seems bothered about this subject, which is my cue to drop it. I take a sip of the wine, which is more bitter than normal red wine, but still enjoyable. All of a sudden, the smell of garlic and pesto fills the air and my nostrils all at once. "I hope you like the wine, I made it myself!" She yells out.

I take another sip, "I do actually. It's bitter, but I like it."

After dinner, we sit on the couch talking while we still drink wine, "The blue button-up and khakis are definitely not a boring outfit!" she says, laughing.

"You can blame my mom for it; she picked it out!"

She starts laughing louder, and I start as well, "Your mom picked it out?"

"She did help, yes!"

"That is so funny!" We both keep laughing, "No, no, it is a nice outfit!" She puts her hand on my knee and we both look at each other. About five long seconds after looking at each other, she jumps up off the couch, "I am going to make brownies!" She runs into the kitchen.

I wonder why she is so suddenly flustered, and I get up and walk to the kitchen. I didn't realize how much I drank until I stood up and felt unbalanced. "This wine is a lot stronger than I thought it would be!"

"My wine usually is strong. I should have warned you!" she starts pulling pots and pans out of the blue-colored cabinets. She finishes mixing everything and puts it in the oven.

I take notice of the fact that she has a record player and plays whatever vinyl she has on it. "Gregory Alan Isakov," she says, walking into the living room. I take her hand and start dancing with her around the living room.

"I must say, young lady, you are a fine dancer!" I say in a British accent.

"Oh, well, thank you! My mother took me to dance classes when I was crawling!" She says in a British accent as well. We both start laughing and then she rests her head on my chest. We dance slowly and quietly, just letting the music fill the air. The lyrics sit deep in my chest as I listen.

"I could share it with you, if you gave me the time. I'm all bloody knuckles, longing for home. If it weren't for second chances, we'd all be alone."

Every few seconds, one of us pulls the other one a little bit closer and harder, and her head relaxes even more and more on my chest with each sway. My head rests down on the top of her head and I close my eyes, enjoying the sweet citrus smell of her hair. I wonder if she can feel how fast my heart is beating.

With the next loop around from our swaying, I open my eyes and see that the kitchen is filled with smoke and I run to it, taking hockey puck brownies out of the oven.

"Guess we aren't having brownies," she says, laughing behind me.

"No, I guess we aren't! But you need to get the smoke alarm looked at."

Around 2 am, I notice the time as we sit on the couch talking again, "I am going to call my friend Chris to come get me. I didn't realize how drunk I was until it was too late, and I can't drive now," I say standing up.

"You can sleep here if you want. You can stay on the couch," she offers. I stand there and think for a few seconds.

I rub my face, "Yeah. If you don't mind."

"I mean, can't say I have plenty of room, but yes, you can stay! Let me go get you some blankets," she walks into her bedroom, which I still have not seen.

The couch isn't long enough, and I have nowhere to put my legs; no part of me can sleep. I toss and turn back and forth, then all of a sudden, Willow comes walking out of her room in silk pajama shorts that are white with black polka dots and a black long-sleeve shirt. She tiptoes into the kitchen and pours water, not knowing that I am awake. I see her standing in the kitchen and just stare at her long, toned legs, looking at them like a kid in a candy store. I close my eyes and pretend I am asleep when she turns around and walks back to her room, leaving the door cracked open a little bit.

I must have fallen asleep because I come to my senses of reality when I smell the aroma of freshly brewed coffee in the air. I sit up on the couch and look around for a few seconds to become aware of my surroundings. "Good morning," I say to Willow and get up.

She jumps a little, startled at me suddenly talking, "I hope I didn't wake you."

"No, you're fine. Thanks for letting me stay over," I say.

"Do you want coffee?"

"No, I am good, thank you. Do you know what time it is?" I asked, confused.

"It is… 6:45," she says perky. She comes into the living room and has a floral, multicolored robe on and her glasses now. "I had fun last night," She says and sits down on the couch next to me, pulls her legs up so she is in a fetal position, almost, and snuggles up with her coffee in her hands.

"I did too," I stand up and grab my jacket, and she jumps up, running to the door so she can open it. "In that much of a rush to get me out?" I say jokingly.

"No, just didn't want to be rude and not walk you out. Yet people say chivalry is dead," we look at each other like we have been as if one person is trying to tell the other person to go in for a kiss, but neither of us wants to do it first.

Willow

Spending two weeks' worth of time with Ben isn't something worth complaining about because his company isn't just there to give me something to do, but rather just time well spent. Today we would be together, but he said he wanted to go running and start working out again, so he doesn't get out of shape. It is strange to me that only after spending two weeks together, there is a sense of empty quiet when I am alone.

I start walking over to my parents' house and see my mom in the backyard doing yoga. "Come join!" She says when she sees me walking by. I join her, and about ten minutes in, she asks me, "Who is that guy that has been coming around?"

"Just a friend," I ask, changing from a child's pose to downward dog.

"That wasn't my question. I asked who he was."

I almost feel nervous telling her because I don't know how she will react to the fact that he was away at war. Actually, I know exactly how she will react, and that's the problem. Even though she doesn't get upset about situations and gives everyone a chance, war is one situation she does not agree with. She even said they chose to live in Randall instead of Yelton because Yelton was once a war ground and every mayor of that town was once in the war. They are only 15 minutes apart from each other, so I don't think there is that much of a difference, especially since most people from Yelton come here because we have a bigger town and stores. She said it's the principle of it.

"If you don't tell me, I will just introduce myself to him." She says, since I haven't answered yet. "Bring him by the house for dinner tomorrow night, Will."

"Okay," I change into a tree pose and look out to the woods for my eye of concentration. Ben and I have never talked about him being deployed, and his vibe screams that it is not a topic to bring up.

All of a sudden, I hear Lily's voice from a small distance yell my name. I lose sight of the woods and put my leg down so I have full balance and turn my head to see her standing at my front door, waving to me. "I'll see you later," I tell my mom and kiss her cheek while she is still fully balanced in her tree pose.

"Hey, stranger, where have you been?" Lily asks me while we walk into my house.

I can't help but start grinning as soon as she asks, or maybe it was as soon as I thought about Ben or the fact that I can talk about Ben. I walk into the kitchen and pour us a cup of coffee, put a spoon of sugar and milk, making it a nice caramel color. I sit on the couch next to her, which is our go-to spot at my house.

"So what has been going on? I haven't heard from you or seen you in a while."

"I started seeing someone…" I say and look away, all embarrassed.

She does a little squeal like a little girl who got a new toy, "I knew it by that freakin smirk on your face! Who?"

"His name is Ben, he is from Yelton."

"Tell me everything about him! So you and River finally called it quits, huh?"

"Yeah, River and I are done. I just couldn't do it anymore. But anyways, do you want like general details or specific ones?" I raise my eyebrows to make it sound like I am telling her something scandalous.

"I want to know everything about this guy and why he has been taking over your life, that I haven't even heard from you!"

"Well, he is over 6 feet tall, pretty built, like has these insane muscles, which I never thought would be something I am into, but I like looking at them when he wears short sleeves. He is clean-shaven, just clean-cut, all in general. Has short buzz-cut hair that is dark chocolate brown, and these beautiful hazel eyes that, when he wears a certain color shirt, look different. The other day, he wore a blue shirt and his eyes looked brighter than usual. Then, if he is laughing hard, he has dimples, which I noticed when I was drunk, so that means they stand out! He is also hilarious. I don't think I have ever laughed that hard with a guy before. My cheeks hurt by the end of the night."

"You're joking, right?" She says seriously.

"No, why?" Confused as to what made this seem like a joke.

"He sounds really wonderful, but every guy you have ever been with looks like you pulled them out of the woods in your backyard. But also I have never heard you talk about someone like this! You actually like this dude."

I start laughing hysterically at her analogy especially since it is pretty accurate. "Maybe that is why it never worked out. They were all the same!"

She turns her head, her wavy hair almost dipping into the coffee that she is holding, "What is his last name?" There it is. She figured it out. I start smirking and cover my mouth with my hands. "Oh… my… god. Your parents are going to actually die when they hear about this one! Are you mad at them or something and trying to rebel?"

"Hey! My parents are understanding and accepting," I add in quickly.

"They are going to take one look at him and just imagine him holding a gun. Oh wow, please let me be there when they meet," she starts laughing, "oh, and let me be there for the conversation that follows after he leaves."

"He is going to come over tomorrow for dinner. Well, I still have to ask, but my mom told me to ask him," I cover my eyes with both my hands, knowing that it isn't going to be fun.

"Hopefully the sex is worth it."

"Honestly, we haven't even kissed."

"What? You're this infatuated with a dude you have never even kissed? Does he not have lips or something?" She then pulls out a joint from her small yellow round purse that is still attached across her body and lights it up.

"Oh no, he most definitely has some lips. I know it's weird, and it's like we both want to but don't go for it."

"Maybe he forgot how," she says before she starts coughing from the smoke. I wait to see if she was making a joke when she said that, but she just sits there looking at me, waiting for a response. I don't know what to say, so I sit there quietly hoping she says something next, which she does, "How long was he gone for?"

"Four years. We don't talk about it, I just know that's how long."

"Imagine going through all that for four years," she says and takes another hit from her joint. Something about her saying that bothers me, not for myself, but imagining him worrying about his life for four years. It causes my mind to have so many questions that I wish I could just ask him, but I know the right to privacy. I saw the reaction people get when you ask them about war when I was writing my book, and I didn't want to ask him, but the curiosity in me was going mad, and the questions swirl in my head every night.

"Then again, if he can deal with war, I am sure he can deal with your family," she says, snapping me back to reality as my mind starts to race with thoughts.

My phone starts to ring, which is on the table closer to Lily. She goes to pick it up and hands it to me, "Speak of the devil!" She says with a giant smirk on her face and rattles the phone around, teasing me with it. I snatch it out of her hand and answer.

"Hey!" I say.

"Hey, what are you up to?" Ben says back.

"I am spending time with my friend Lily. How was your day full of workouts?"

"It was good, my body is going to ache tomorrow since I haven't been very active since I have been home. But it was good. Would it be weird if you came out tonight with my friends? You can bring Lily if you want."

"Why would it be weird?"

He didn't say anything for a few seconds as if the question was obvious, "I don't know," he rushes to say.

"Just text me and let me know what time and where."

"Okay, sounds good."

"Wait! Real quick," I say before he hangs up, "my parents are making dinner tomorrow night, care to come?"

"Yeah, that sounds good," he says without hesitation. We then hang up.

I look over at Lily, "Want to go out tonight?" I ask with a raised eyebrow and a grin. She gives me a giant grin, taking that as a yes.

We get to the bar and I see Ben standing outside with two other people. Lily then grabs my arm before we cross the street and stops me. "Oh my God, I made out with that one guy," she says, pointing at one of the men standing with Ben.

"Great, then you will have someone else you know tonight," I say and walk across the street, Lily trailing behind me.

"Hey," Ben says happily when he sees me. We exchange smiles, "This is Jason and Chris, guys, this is Willow," I give them both a hug hello.

"This is Lily," I introduce her to everyone, and her face turns bright red when she and Jason make eye contact.

"Well, let's get this started!" Chris says, and we walk inside.

Ben

We all dance together on the dance floor with drinks in our hands, vodka spilling on the floor from everyone moving so much. "I am going to get a drink!" Willow yells up to me over the music. She then walks away, and I go and follow her; the only dancing I want to be doing is with her. We stand at the bar, and both bartenders are already occupied with other customers.

My eyes look Willow up and down while we wait, which is not a bad way to wait. Her dress is held together by tied strings around her neck, leaving her back exposed. I try to pull my eyes away from her legs, but it feels impossible to. She keeps dancing while we stand there, just swaying her body back and forth, and her hair follows each move.

Before I stare too long at her, I tell her to wait, and I will go searching down at the other end for the bartender. I stand at the other end waiting to get the bartender's attention, and I look back over at Willow and see she is talking to some guy with an angry expression on her face. She then pushes him a little.

I start to push sweaty, drunk people out of my way to get to her, and I see her trying to walk away from him, but he grabs her arm and pulls her closer.

"Let me see," he says and pulls the string around her neck. Before it can fall off her, I grab it in my hands.

"Do we have a problem here?" I say, pushing Willow behind me. I don't let go of the strings of her dress until her hands are on them securely, and as soon as I do, I push the guy.

"No problem. But I saw her giving me eyes before, and I know she wants it. Don't be a fucking tease," he says and tries to push past me again. He must be drunk if he thinks he can size me up.

"You know you want it," the voice now sounding like a voice I know. His face turns into a face that haunts me. He turns into Sargent Reynolds, and he keeps saying "You know you want it" over and over again. Without hesitation, I punch him right in the face. He tries to stand up, and I just keep punching him, falling onto the ground, and I am now straddling him and nonstop punching him. "She doesn't want it," I keep saying.

"Ben! Ben! Stop!" Willow is saying behind me. I get up off the ground, and the guy is lying on the ground, covered in blood. Security men come over, "That guy wouldn't stop touching me!" Willow yells to them, pointing to the guy on the floor. They pull him off the ground and drag him somewhere else.

I remember the guy touching Willow, what he was saying to her, going over there knowing I was going to punch him, but the entire time I was punching him, I don't remember. But unlike all the other hallucinations that I don't know what triggers them, this one I *do* know.

I look at Willow who looks startled and look over at Chris, Jason, and Lily who are now standing there and I just turn around and walk away, going outside. I stand outside with my back against the brick wall and my knees bent, elbows resting on them. I look down at my knuckles, which are blood-coated now. Willow comes walking out and comes up to me. "Remind me to never go to a bar with you again, any time I was at one with you, you got into a fight," she says lightly.

"Sorry," I say without looking at her.

"While I don't condone violence, that was terrifying. He probably would have assaulted me if you didn't come."

"Please don't say that. Makes me sick to think about." I say and stand up, straightening myself. "I can't go back in there."

"Okay, we can go. I will text Lily and let her know," she says. We start walking down the street and everything that has transpired in the past ten minutes keeps playing over and over again in my head.

I stop walking, "I need a second," I say, and then suddenly it feels as if I am breathing through a straw. Trying to catch my breath and not being able to. I stumble to the building next to me and lean my back against it.

"I think you're having a panic attack," she says and stands in front of me. "Just focus on breathing in and out. In through your nose and out through your mouth, close your eyes, and just breathe."

I do as she says, but I just keep having flashbacks in my head. Not hallucinations, but actual flashbacks, which might be worse because it is just reliving it. *I hear the woman screaming in the other room, the room that I am guarding, so nobody comes in. "Help!" She keeps saying. "Nobody is going to help you," Reynolds says to her every time she yells it.*

"Ben, you're going to make yourself pass out if you don't calm down."

"Help me, please. Help."

"Okay, I am bringing you to the hospital," I hear Willow say.

I grab her wrist, "I can't go. I can't go there. Bring me home." My breathing starts to become more regular, still feeling anxiety in my chest, but at least now I can breathe. "You drive, I will tell you where to go."

We get to my house, and before I get out of the car, I turn to Willow and say, "You are more than welcome to come inside, but you will probably have to play 20 questions with my mom."

"The same thing is going to happen to you tomorrow, so I will share your pain," she says and turns off the car, getting out. We walk into the house, and I look behind me at Willow, looking around the entryway of the house. "Your house is huge," she says while looking up at the chandelier that is hanging above her.

"You're back home soon," my mom yells from the kitchen. I walk in there with Willow following behind me.

"Yeah, it wasn't the place for us," I say to her, making sure I keep my knuckles under the counter so she can't see them. "This is Willow, by the way."

"Oh, nice to finally meet you," my mom says and comes around the counter to shake her hand.

Willow smiles big and bright at her, ignoring her hand and hugs her, "Hi, nice to meet you!"

"I am just going to run upstairs real quick. I will give you a quick tour of the house if you want," I tell Willow.

"Yeah, sure!" We start walking up the stairs. "Your mom is beautiful," she says to me.

"Thanks," I say sincerely. We get to the top of the stairs, "That is my brother's room. He is at basketball practice right now with my step-dad, so you won't be seeing them tonight." We then walk down the hallway into my room, and I go to my drawer and open it, grabbing a Xanax. She walks in and looks around the room. There isn't much to see in the room except a few family pictures my mom put on my dresser for me. She picks one up and looks at it. It is a picture from when I was 17 and skinny, and my skin was seven shades lighter than it is now.

"Can I ask you something, it feels strange asking," she starts to say, I look at her with encouraging eyes to continue, "Why haven't you kissed me?" It wasn't the question I was expecting as she set the picture back down.

"Honestly? I haven't felt the right time for it."

"Fair enough," she says and then continues to look around my room.

"I should probably go wash my hands," I say while looking down at my knuckles. I go into the bathroom and pour rubbing alcohol on them.

"You have a nice view," Willow says from my room. I walk back into the bedroom and see her standing there looking outside my window.

"We can go outside," I say and go to my closet, giving her a black pullover sweater that has my last name and the army logo on the side of the sleeve. She looks at it and makes an upside-down smile as she runs her fingers across the lettering.

We stand outside in the backyard, the cold grass under our shoes, the brisk air giving us goosebumps, the lake still with the stars and moon lighting it up. We both just look out to the other side of the lake, which is just trees and I grab her hand and put it in my sweater pocket so I can keep it warm while also holding it. I turn my body to face hers and she turns as well, I put my hand on the lower back of her head, cradling it, and lean in to kiss her. Her lips felt soft and tasted like a mix of cherry and coconut.

Her tongue enters between my lips, and I part my mouth, allowing her in. Our tongues circle around each other, and the taste of her is even better than I imagined, and I *definitely* did imagine this moment. I pull her head closer, not allowing any space between us, my other arm now reaching behind her and resting on her back where it's open. Her skin is soft and smooth, and the feeling of her makes me intensify my kiss. I bite her lower lip softly, and she lets out the smallest gasp of air. I pull on her hair tightly and then pull away from her before anything else happens.

"I think that was the right time," she says with a smile on her face. Her big eyes look directly into mine, and I can't help but kiss her again.

"That was definitely worth the wait," I say as my lips leave hers.

I wake up in the morning with a high from last night's kiss with Willow. The smell of coffee takes over the kitchen when I go downstairs. I sit down at the kitchen counter as my mom makes her breakfast. "Want some eggs?" She asks me and hands me a cup of coffee.

"Sure," I say.

"So, Willow is very pretty," she says with a hint of wanting to know more. Before I can answer, my phone rings and I pick it up.

"Hello?" I answer.

"Phillips? It's Nick Bell," Nick and I were in the same squad for the majority of the time while we were in the army. We both went home at the same time. As much as I would be excited to hear from him right now, the tone of his voice doesn't sound very exciting.

"Hey, brother. What is going on?" I say, trying to get him to get straight to the point.

"They found Nelson's body. I don't know many details, but they said that he wasn't killed right away and was tortured for a while. He was found in some shit hole."

My head goes spinning, and I try to keep it together so I can finish the conversation, "Who found him?"

"Hawk Eyes found him," Hawk Eyes is a squad that I was once a leader of before I got transferred to a secret mission. I rub my face.

"Shit. Alright, I will give you a call back later," I hang up.

"Everything okay?" My mom asks me with a worried look on her face. I push back from the counter and go upstairs, each step heavier than the last. The high I had shatters instantly, now, all that's left is the crushing weight of its memory. I get into my room and shut the door behind me, feeling as if today is now going to be impossible to get through. I lie in my bed and close my eyes.

Nelson and I walk in the empty field, trying to find our camp since we both got lost and disoriented after the explosion went off in the middle of a shooting field. "Split up so we cover more ground in case anyone is lying around out here," I command him. The moon is low tonight. We have very little light to be looking at. All of a sudden a car comes driving through the sandy crop field and we both duck down and it stops a few feet away from Nelson. A couple of men get out and start yelling at each other and the only word I can understand is American. Then a voice speaks and I know exactly who it is, Abba Akil. The one man that we have been looking for.

My heart starts beating fast at the fact that a terrorist is standing in the same crop field as me and I can't even kill him because I have no authority nor backup. All of a sudden I hear a gunshot go off, Nelson. For some reason, he thought it was a good idea to try and kill Abba Akil in the middle of a sandy crop field with just us two in the middle of the night. Within seconds, he is being dragged to the car and thrown in. I just sit there in shock not being able to do anything.

A week later at camp, out of the three tents we have set up in the desert, a man comes up to my tent as I am walking out. I look down at his uniform and read, "Nelson" and look at his face and realize that it is not Nelson. Just as he starts to raise his gun, I beat him to it. Everyone comes running out of their tents with their guns up. "It wasn't him," I keep saying it over and over again.

Nobody knows how he got Nelson's uniform; where Nelson was, who took him, and they don't know that I was there.

It feels almost like a relief knowing that Nelson was dead, that he couldn't tell anyone what happened, and that I didn't say anything about it. But at the same time, the guilt I already had eating at me has grown hungrier.

I lie in bed, and my mom doesn't come in at all and bothers me, knowing that the phone call I got wasn't good. I hear my phone vibrate with a text and don't have any energy to turn it over to see who it's from. Then I get a call when I check it I see that it is Willow.

"Hello?" I answer, monotone.

"Hey… you okay?" She asks, hearing the emotionless voice.

"Bad day," I answer shortly.

"Oh, well, I was calling to see if you were still coming over for dinner tonight with my parents."

I completely forgot about it, and I take a second to think if I can pull it together today enough to see them. I can't. "Can we do it tomorrow? I am just not having a good day."

"Yeah, that is fine. Do you need company?" Her voice understanding.

"No," I say, then hang up and let the phone roll out of my hand and onto the floor.

The feeling of having my body and brain completely shut down is exhausting. It also feels uncontrollable, which makes it feel even worse. I am not upset about them finding Nelson's body, but my own body just shuts down to the point where it feels nearly impossible to even get out of bed. It feels as if my body and brain just go completely paralyzed. I lie there the entire day just looking up at the ceiling or occasionally turning and looking at the door, seeing the crack of light underneath it, poking through as people walk by every so often. I even see my mom's feet by the door for a few seconds, her listening at my door to see if she can hear anything. When she doesn't for a few seconds, she walks away.

The next morning, I wake up and call Willow, "Hello?" She answers.

"Hope you don't think I am an ass for canceling yesterday," I say apologetically.

"No, you aren't. I understand. But also, if meeting my parents is too much for you, just tell me."

"It isn't, and it wasn't. I just got some bad news yesterday, and it kind of took a toll on me."

"Want to talk about it?" Her voice is soft and sincere, making it sound inviting to actually talk about it.

"No, I am fine," I say anyway. "I will see you tonight."

I pull myself together and decide to go running around the block. When I am about to walk out the front door, sneakers tied, headphones in, I see Sam sitting by the front door with a look in his eye, almost asking me to take him with me. I pet his head, grab his black leash that is hanging by the front door, and hook it onto him. We both run around the block as fast as we can, almost competing with each other to see who can go faster. It also reminds me how much I miss running with my brothers back at base, makes me wish I was back there. I know Cohens gets back in a couple of months, and I can't wait to get in touch with him again.

Cohens was my greatest friend there and helped me with every problem I encountered, kept every secret I ever told him, one of them being when I told him I thought I was going to need medication when I got back home. Cohens told me that the first time he went back home, he struggled with it, and I should have the medication just in case. Anxiety and insomnia, on the other hand, are something I knew I would have a problem with.

I get back home and start doing pull-ups on the bar I installed in my bathroom doorway, then do push-ups, sit-ups, and all over again, turning it into a circuit. Before I knew it, it was time to start getting ready for dinner with Willow.

Willow greets me at her front door with a wide smile and a kiss, exactly what I needed.

"How are you feeling today?" She asks me, cocking her head to the side.

"Better," I smile at her, "Do I look okay?" I ask and look down at my outfit, a simple blue button-up and khaki pants.

"You look very handsome," she smiles back at me with a softness in her eyes. We start to walk to the main house, stepping over a chicken on our way there. She stops in her tracks, "My parents may come across as strange to you, just so you know."

"I'm not too worried about it," we walk up to the house and walk in. It looks almost exactly like Willow's house, just bigger. The color scheme is the same, and there are more plants around the house. Not one thing in the house matches or goes together, and it's full of every color possible.

Her parents then come into the entryway from the kitchen. Her mom has long, full gray hair and is wearing a long, loose tie-dye dress that hangs off the shoulders; her dad has matching gray hair that is only slightly shorter and a deep V-neck shirt and rings on almost every finger. All I can think is that my parents would never.

"Mom, Dad, this is Ben. Ben, this is Joy and Jerry," Willow says.

"So nice to finally meet you," Joy says excitedly, I go to put my hand out to shake hers, but she walks right past my hand and grabs my face, pulling it down to her and kissing me. Jerry then walks over to me and does the same thing. I look over at Willow, and she is just staring at me, waiting for a reaction from me. Her eyes are big and she is doing her upside-down smile.

"It's nice to meet you as well. It smells good in here." It smells like oranges and rosemary, and the two of them complement each other nicely.

"Come into the kitchen," Joy says and starts to walk away with Jerry.

"Sorry for their weird greeting," Willow whispers to me as we walk a couple of feet behind them.

"I have seen so many cultures, I get that each one has different greetings," I say to her.

We walk into the kitchen, and Joy and Jerry continue cooking, "Want anything to drink?" Jerry asks me.

"Anything is fine, just not Willow's wine," I say jokingly.

"I don't blame you," He says.

We sit at the dining room make-shift table, on the table is a salad in a wooden bowl, which has a mixture of spinach and other greens in it, cranberries, almonds, and a light vignette dressing, side dishes of asparagus tossed in garlic, cauliflower and a main meal of lemon chicken and grilled tofu for Joy and Jerry.

"So, what do you do, Ben?" Jerry asks me while I lean over to put the mixtures of foods on my blue, hand-painted plate.

I look over at Willow and see her looking at me, clearly looking nervous about her parents' reaction. She has never actually told me that her parents don't approve of war, but I can already tell that it won't go well. It is obvious they come from a free-spirited belief, and war is the complete opposite of that belief. "I was actually away in the Middle East for a couple of years," I say.

"Oh, really, what for? We were there a couple of years ago in Egypt for vacation; it was so beautiful there. The pyramids were so beautiful! Where in the Middle East did you visit?" Joy asks me, sounding excited to hear about some groundbreaking vacation that I took.

"I don't think he was there for vacation," Jerry sternly says, snapping Joy back to reality while staring directly at me.
I have never felt embarrassed or like I needed to hide that I was in the army; there is no reason to, but for some reason, the way he looked at me made me feel like I had something to be ashamed of. Joy looks at Jerry, slightly confused, then at me.

"Yeah, I was there at war."

"OH!" Joy says, shocked.

"I had a feeling as soon as I looked at you," Jerry says, not breaking eye contact with me.

"Well, just because we don't agree with what you do doesn't mean we have to dislike you for it," Joy says, keeping a monotone voice, and then continues to eat.

"I just don't think he will be very good for Willow," Jerry says out loud, just speaking out loud instead of directly toward me.

"Dad, you don't even know him," Willow comes in to my defense.

"You are right, I just don't see how your lifestyles will coincide," he says.

"I am sure we will figure it out," I say, and then start to eat my food as well. In the corner of my eye, I see Willow smirk a little.

Willow

I call Lily after dinner and tell her to come over. I didn't say much to my parents after Ben left. I don't feel angry with them. I knew they weren't going to like the idea of him being in the army, but I can't help but be disappointed in the fact that they always taught me to never judge a person, and yet here they are doing exactly that.

Lily gets here shortly, bursting into my house with excitement since she knew tonight was the dinner night. "How did it go?" she says enthusiastically, wearing her shawl that she usually wears, and walks into the kitchen, immediately making coffee and lighting a joint.

"Not good," I say, sitting on the couch.

"Tell me all of it," she hands me the coffee in one hand and puts the joint in my mouth. I take a hit before I take a sip.

"They asked him what he does, and he was like, oh, I was in the Middle East for a couple of years, and my mom was asking him where, and then my dad said, you weren't there for vacation.

Implying that he knew what it was for. Then my dad said that he doesn't think Ben and I will be good for each other. It was just awkward. I mean, after that, it was just normal conversation, nothing crazy, and we had a few good laughs and conversations. But it just goes against everything my parents ever told me. Just a little hypocritical."

"I am sure they will eventually get over it, though."

"Yeah, " I say, my voice full of doubt.

"I have an idea," she says, taking the joint from my mouth, "Have him come to the sweat ceremony. We are having another one next month. That way, your parents can see that he can be part of your whole world."

"That's if he would even want to go."

"Well, being in a relationship is just doing a lot of activities that you don't even want to do," she shrugs.

Before I go to bed, I drink my last sip of my lemon tea and text Ben, trying to make light of the situation and say I hope he isn't scared off. He replied quickly and said he isn't. But then Lily's comment returns to my mind, where she said we are in a relationship, are we?

I toss and turn all night, and around Devil's hour, and I hear a knock at my door. I open the door, assuming it is my parents or even Lily who is coming over drunk. I let out an excited scream when I open the door.

"Coy!" I yell out and jump into my brother's arms, squeezing him tightly, making sure that I am not imagining him.

His jet black hair pulled back into a thick bun, he is wearing a deep V-neck purple t-shirt and a loose black and white tribal print cardigan, and torn up jeans and Converse. He looks the same as he always does, effortlessly beautiful and oozing charm from just a smile. Everyone he ever met loved him because he was just genuine and pure; he was never mean to people. I remember one time that I had a crush on one of his friends, and one day I walked into Coy's room and saw them making out. I was so upset because I thought it was unfair that Coy got that hot guy, and I didn't. It wasn't till I grew up a little and learned about sexuality realized that I was nowhere near his type.

He was always into smoking weed, which my parents were okay with since it was natural. But then, eventually, he started getting more into things such as LSD, opium, shrooms, and I remember a couple of times he was using cocaine. My parents didn't care much about this either because it was the same drugs they were using back in their time, and they figured he was just exploring and experiencing life in his own way.

Coy eventually started traveling to California and Colorado because life there was more laid back and casual. He came back home for Christmas two years ago and was obviously drugged out, and Rain was so mortified by it that she was begging him to go to rehab and tried convincing my parents to send him. It didn't end up working out in her favor. That was the last time we saw him. Until right now, where he is standing on my front porch.

"Surprise, baby sister!" He says excitedly, his voice still calm and mellow.

"This is the greatest surprise!"

He comes into the house and goes to the kitchen, "Hope you don't mind," he says as he starts raiding my fridge.

"Go ahead," I tell him. "Does anyone know you're here?"

"No, I didn't tell anyone. I will surprise Mom and Dad in the morning," he starts eating the turkey and avocado sandwich he just made and sits at my little table. I sit across from him, resting my chin on my hand. "Is it okay if I sleep in here tonight?"

"Yeah, you can share my bed."

The smell of fresh coffee being made wakes me up but I look over next to me to notice Coy wasn't there. When I come into the living room I see Coy sitting on the couch smoking a joint, drinking coffee. I grab a cup of coffee and sit next to him.

"How is everything?" I ask.

"It is fine. Well…" his voice trails off and he looks around the room, "My boyfriend and I broke up and he kicked me out." As soon as he says it, I realize that is why he is here; he has nowhere else to live.

"Sorry to hear," my voice has an attitude to it. He can hear it, and he then puts his head on my lap and looks at me with wide eyes and a big smile.

"How is my little sister?" His voice was sweet and innocent. I take his hair out of his bun and start playing with it, running my fingers through it. He plays with the ends of my hair, braiding that few inches that he can reach.

I can't help but smile when I think about Ben, "Well, I met a guy," I look down at him as my smile grows.

"Tell me," he says excitedly.

"His name is Ben, and he is so different from any guy I have dated. He can hold a conversation and is just so interesting. I don't know, I just feel awakened."

"That is beautiful, Will."

"Mom and Dad met him," my voice trails off.

"Oh, and? It didn't go well?"

"Yeah… it didn't go well."

"Why? What happened? Stop gatekeeping and spill it already."

"I forgot to mention… Ben is in the military."

"Wow, okay. Yeah, you didn't mention that when you were gushing about him," he picks his head up off my lap and stands up. "Just confused as to how that would appeal to you," he sounds almost offended.

"Because…. I don't know. It doesn't seem like that big of a deal."

"Okay, Willow. I mean, I know our parents are pretty open, but war? Violence? Death? Guess you are more like Rain than I thought," he says and then walks out the front door. His comment was offensive, especially because we always mock Rain for being so closed-minded. I stood there for a second with my arms crossed against my chest like a child who isn't getting what they want, and realized just how uncool he is being. I throw my arms to my side and run out the door after Coy.

"So you're allowed to leave for months and go explore yourself and your body, but once I do something you don't agree with, then you freak out?" I yell to him as his back is towards me and halfway to my parents. "Don't leave and then come back and pretend to be a big brother."

He turns around and looks at me, "You're right," he says, and then turns back around and walks away from me.

I didn't see Coy for the rest of the day; as a matter of fact, I didn't see anyone for the rest of the day because I stayed in my house all day. That was until Ben came knocking on my door. I answer it, and his broad shoulders kind of just hover over me; it was like I forgot how tall he was.

"Hope you don't mind the surprise," he says with a welcoming smile on his face. He kisses the top of my head and hands me flowers that were behind his back.

"Not at all," I say, grabbing the flowers.

We sit on the couch, facing each other, backs on the armrest, both our legs on each other's laps. He tells me a funny story about when he was younger, and he would always run around his yard naked. He said he figured I would like this story because of the free-spirit part of me.

"I need to see a picture of you when you were little so I can get the full image," I tell him.

"My parents hated it. They were always so worried the neighbors would see, even though our house is completely enclosed. Them freaking out about it made me love it even more."

"So you were a rebellious little thing, huh?"

"If there were a way to annoy my parents, I would do it. Looking back at it, though, I think I only got into trouble most of the time because it was the only time all of us would talk. I think my dad was having an affair long before we ever actually knew about it," he says it so casually, and the thought of a broken marriage and broken family makes me sad. The word divorce was never in our vocabulary.

"How come they got a divorce? " I ask him. I run my hand up and down his leg, applying light pressure to release the tension that I can feel he's holding from running.

"They got officially divorced about eleven years ago, but it was a long process because they couldn't agree on anything. Since my father also moved away, it was harder because he had to always travel back and forth any time they needed to meet with an attorney. But at that time, my mom got together with my stepdad. He was a guest speaker at the college my mother teaches at, and they ran into each other and started talking, and then just hit it off."

"So he was having an affair?" I ask curiously.

"Yeah, he met an intern. He says that was the first time he ever cheated on my mom, but I don't know about that. Their marriage always seemed rocky. I mean, they were great parents, but they weren't good together. But I was a rebellious child before everything started happening, and then once they got worse, I did too."

"How so?" I move in closer, getting more intrigued with the story.

"I got into fights at school, skipped classes, and failed. Just caused an issue anywhere I went. I had no chance of getting into college unless it was a community college. My mom was so mortified. Here she is a professor, and her child can't even pass high school English. I didn't know what I wanted to do in school anyway. Then one day my parents were fighting about me and I heard my dad say 'just send him to a boot camp or some shit' and then I got the idea to join the army and it stuck in my head like a leech."

"Were they okay with it?" My hand moving to the other leg to rub it.

"No. Absolutely not. My dad only said that idea because my mom was crying about how she didn't know what to do with me, and my behavior was so bad."

"So then, of course, them saying no to you made you want to do it more?" I ask, understanding all the motives more.

"Exactly. Then once I got into the army, my parents realized how respected it is to be in the army, and they loved being able to say that their son is enlisted. I think it was more of a way for my mom to justify the fact that I wasn't in school."

"Then it turned into four years of being there. Could have gotten a degree in that time," I say with a laugh.

"I could have," he answers back with a laugh. "I could have come home sooner. But once I was there, I realized that it was what I was meant to do. That rebellious teenage part of me had that aggressive behavior to be there, but then they trained me how to put that to good use. I just felt *right* there."

"It was your calling. I understand that. So, putting that aggressive behavior in bars is a good way to use it?" I raise my eyebrow and smirk.

"All of those situations were deemed necessary for aggression. Especially that last one. By the way, I don't want you to think I was talking down about my parents by the way. They were great and still are. I don't forgive my father for what he did, but I have learned to deal with it. I don't hate him, and we don't have a terrible relationship," he says. While he says this, I wonder which one of us he is trying to convince that his parents aren't bad. He tried to make it a point multiple times, and I am wondering who the point is for.

My front door then swings open, and Coy is standing there. We make eye contact, and I say, "What the hell, man?"

Ben instantly jumps up and, within seconds, is standing in front of me, guarding me. "Who is this?" His voice instantly changing tone from vulnerability to sternness.

"Oh, right, I forgot to tell you, too, that Coy is here."

"So this is Ben?" Coy says, scratching his head, and by the looks of it, I can tell he is withdrawing from something.

Ben's eyes narrow in at him, and I can tell he can also tell that Coy is withdrawing, "And this is Coy."

"Yeah, I am not digging the vibes here, so let's end it now," I say, standing up between them.

"Peace and love, man! Peace for all, love for all, lots and lots of freakin peace," Coy holds up the peace sign and walks away into my bedroom, closing the door behind him.

My eyes go straight back to Ben, "Peace and love," he says to me, and we both let out a giggle.

Ben

I have learned how to control my hallucinations in a way. Maybe not control, but lately it is easier for me to understand when it is a hallucination. It is when I stay focused and aware that I am able to realize it isn't real. This also means I need to take my Adderall so I can stay focused. But then that leads to either sleepless nights or taking more Ambien.

Every time I open my drawer and see the pill bottles, I am hopeless. I keep reminding myself that as long as I don't need the Seroquel, then I am fine. There is nothing wrong with me. Everyone takes Adderall or Ambien or Xanax, high school kids even sell them, that is how common it is. Just as long as it isn't the Seroquel.

I sit on my bed and start reading Willow's book, then Sean comes in, "Want to come to the park with me and my dad? We're going to play catch," he asks.

I pause and think for a second, "Sure," I say and get up, and put my sneakers on.

We get to the park, and I sit on the hard metal bleachers with Sam lying down next to me while Sean and Paul play catch. I wanted to read a chapter from the book before I saw Willow tonight, so I can talk about it with her.

The first chapter talks about women getting paid less in the job field. She interviewed men and women from two companies too but they aren't named because neither employee wanted to speak out about the company. Willow mentions how sad this is that these women who are getting paid less don't even want to actually speak out about it because they are afraid of the consequences. Willow even collects pay stubs, tax returns, and transcripts from their schools so she can compare the women's and men's credentials.

I was going to play catch after the first chapter, but I actually couldn't put the book down. The next chapter was a bit darker.

In the next chapter, she explains how men feel as if they cannot come forward about being a sexual assault victim. She interviews two men who were sexually assaulted: one man came forward to their family and police but was ignored and ridiculed, and the second man did not come forward because he was afraid of being mocked.

For the first man, she went over police documents and records, and hospital records to see that he actually reported it. During this, she discovered that the case was closed, but it was never solved, and nobody was charged, even though the hospital record clearly stated he was assaulted.

I was so impressed while reading this; she went into full detail about everything and did actual research to prove her facts and ideas. I also noticed that she does a good job of showing *each* gender's inequality.

"Alright, let me show you two how to play catch," I say as I put the book down and jog up to Sean and Paul.

"Let's see what you got," Paul says.

After throwing the ball for a bit, Paul and I sit on the bleachers with tired arms while Sean plays catch with Sam. "So your mom says you have been seeing a girl lately," Paul says.

"Yeah, her name is Willow."

He looks down at the book next to me, "Wait, this Willow?" He asks, picking up the book.

"That is the one. She wrote the book, and it is interesting, actually. Just about inequality and everything."

"Your mom said she was a pretty girl," Paul says. I can understand that he is trying to pull more information out of me and trying to start a larger conversation.

"Yeah, she's gorgeous. Smart, too. Not just book smart, but intellectually. Her family is this hippie family, though. It's strange to me."

"Wow, talk about two opposites."

"Her family isn't too big on the whole army thing."

"Well, what you do is courageous. I could never do that, not many people can."

"I know. Just their beliefs, everyone is entitled to their opinion."

"Why don't you invite her over for dinner this weekend?"

I think about it for a second, it can't be much worse than dinner with her family, "Yeah, I will ask her."

I don't even know what to pack in my overnight bag for Willow's. Then a thought hit me: do I need to pack condoms? This thought then led to my next to one, which ultimately led to me getting an erection. I can barely remember the last time I had sex. The last person I slept with was Madison, and it was a week before I left.

"Where are you going?" My mom says in my doorway, breaking me out of my thoughts. It takes me by surprise, and it reminds me that I have something to hide from her.

"What? Uh…" I get fidgety and just shove my clothes in the bag, keeping my back towards my mom until my hard-on softens. "Sleeping at Willow's."

"Okay, I feel like I haven't seen you in a while," she says and then sits down on my bed.

I turn my body so my back is still facing her a bit, and the more I try to ignore it, the worse it gets. "Yeah, just been busy."

"Okay," she gets up and starts walking out of my room. "I hope you aren't rushing anything," she says before she fully walks out.

"I don't even know what you're referring to," I scoff.

"The relationship, you have been spending a lot of time together, and I hope you just aren't rushing into anything."

"Can you be more specific?" I ask, my erection and patience are now fully dissolved.

"Just get back into the groove of being back home before you get involved with a serious relationship. A couple of weeks ago, you were refusing to get out of bed and got mad at me for bringing up the fact that something might be wrong. If this ends badly, I don't need you getting worse," she says it in an aggravated voice to make sure I understand her point.

"Okay," I say to brush her off.

"Benjamin Phillips, I am serious," she snaps at me.

"I am fine."

"Until in a few weeks you are refusing to leave your bed," she doesn't wait for a response and just walks out and downstairs, slamming her feet on each step she takes.

I rub my temples in annoyance and just zip up my bag and leave. I get in my car, and Sargent Reynolds is sitting in the passenger seat. "How is the girlfriend treating you?" He asks me.

"No, I am not doing this tonight. Not in the mood for this," I respond. I know he isn't there, but it is difficult not to respond or react.

"Bet I can get you in the mood," he says slyly. I ignore him and just start driving. "If you sleep with her, she will see your back," I still ignore him. "She will see how ugly you are."

"Why are you even here?" I ask finally.

"Ask yourself that. Why would I be?" After he says that, he is gone.

Willow's soft lips, big eyes, and contagious laugh make everything better when I get to her house; her homemade pizza is also an added bonus.

"Can I ask you something?" She asks in between bites of her pizza.

"Sure," I say.

"So there is going to be this sweat ceremony, and I was wondering if you would come. It is when you just sit in a hot tent and sweat, but you share your feelings and thoughts. It is getting rid of the bad energy."

The idea to me sounds ridiculous, but I can see that she seems serious about it.

"Sure," I say hesitantly.

She smiles and then takes a bite of her pizza. "Good," she squirms a little in her chair as if she was getting comfortable and pleased to hear my answer.

"I read a couple of chapters in your book," I tell her.

She throws her pizza down on the plate, "Really?" She says excitedly and surprised.

"Yeah, it was good. You put a lot of effort into it, and I appreciate that."

"I did, I really did," she says, still excited that she is being acknowledged.

"I do have a question though. I only read the first two chapters, but do you write anything about…" my voice traveling, I break eye contact with her and look down at my half-eaten pizza, "Inequality in the army."

Her smile fades quickly. "Are you asking because you know there is an inequality?"

"Just answer the question, please," I say, slightly frustrated.

"Yes. I talk about the 'Don't Ask, Don't Tell' policy."

"That's it?" I ask.

"It was the only topic that didn't fall through. I tried to talk about the homeless men who served, but they didn't have anything concrete. I tried to talk about mental health, but nobody had any documents to prove anything. Plus, a lot of people I talked to didn't even want to talk to me about it."

"Okay," I say, still not looking at her. A part of me feels angry for some reason. "Where is your brother tonight?" I ask to change the topic.

"He went out with his friends. He is staying out tonight," there is agitation in her voice.

I reach around the table and pull her arm, trying to get her to come up and come to me. She lets out a little smirk, then gets off the chair, standing next to me. I move my seat back, it screeches beneath me, and pull her onto my lap. Her smirk gets bigger, and I start to kiss her, starting with her neck and making my way up to her dark pink lips. She wraps her arms around my neck and pulls herself closer to me. She then pulls away and moves her legs so they are straddling me instead of sitting sideways. I cross my arms around her lower back, pulling her closer.

All of a sudden, she pulls her silk tank top over her head, and to my surprise, she isn't wearing a bra. My first reaction was to grab her breast; it fits perfectly in my hand. I start to kiss her collarbone down to her breast, putting her erect nipple in my mouth, slowly tugging at it with my teeth. She moans and puts her hand down my pants, and as soon as her hand touches my hard dick, there is a sudden release of pressure. My pants are then suddenly wet and sticky, and she pulls her hand out of my pants, her hands being just as wet.

"Oh," she says, looking down at her hand, calmly, though.

"I uh…" I stutter. "I am going to the bathroom," I get up, her struggling to her feet quickly from nearly being pushed off me. I grab my overnight bag on my way to the bathroom. I jump in her shower quickly to thoroughly wash myself off.

When I get out of the shower, Reynolds is standing there. I grab the towel quickly, covering myself as a natural reaction. He starts laughing, "Wow, what a disappointment," he says through his laugh. I don't answer. "You can't even properly give it to a girl! At least one of us can."

I put my clothes on and walk out of the bathroom, leaving Reynolds in there.

When I get out of the bathroom, I see her cleaning up dinner. "I am," I start saying and sit on the couch.

"If you are about to apologize, I will punch you. I think I have learned a thing or two from you," she stops cleaning and leans against the dining room table to look at me.

"I haven't been with anyone since I got back. I wasn't with anyone for the past four years."

"I understand, don't worry. But can I ask you something?" She says, her eyes narrow in at me and turn soft.

Still mortified, I don't even want to know the question. "Yeah," I say, I try to avoid her eye contact but her eyes keep bringing me back in.

"Are you ready for that next step? We never really talked about it," she pushes against the table to come a little closer to me.

"Shouldn't I be asking you that question?" I say, my eyebrows furrowed.

"Is this a gender role question?" She cocks her head and raises an eyebrow.

"Yeah, I suppose it was," I answer.

"Well, are you going to answer?" She asks me again.

I wait a few seconds before I reply, "Yes. I thought it was pretty obvious," I say.

"Then why am I here?" Reynolds says, standing next to her.

"I don't know why you are," I respond to Reynolds.

"You don't know why I am what?" Willow asks.

I try to cover it up, "I don't know why you are asking."

"Just making sure," she says, and then cleans up more.

"Are you?" I ask her.

"My instincts tell me that I want to have sex with you, so yes. I have never shied away from sex but there feels something very fucking different about you," she sits next to me on the couch, "I want to know more about you. I find you so intriguing."

"Okay, ask me a question and I will answer. Find out more," we look into each other's eyes for a moment, really look into them. She bites her lip, and for the first time in a long time, I feel peace and comfort.

"Longest relationship," she then says and sits back more into the couch.

"About three years, but we were on and off, it was in high school. We broke up officially because I was leaving; she was also the last person I had a physical relationship with. You?"

"River, for two years. If you could live anywhere, where would it be?"

"Japan, I enjoyed it there."

"I would live somewhere tropical, Earthy."

I laugh, "That doesn't surprise me one bit!"

"Do you want to go back?"

"To Japan? Yeah, definitely."

"No, I mean, do you want to reenlist?" Her voice almost sounds sad at the end of the sentence.

I pause and scratch my face where there would be a beard, "I strongly believe so, yes."

"What are we?" She says. It takes me by surprise.

"Humans?" I say slightly joking, even though I knew what she meant.

She rolls her eyes, "Seriously."

"Well, I don't know. Do you want to be my official girlfriend?" I say with a giant grin on my face and sit up, and start moving closer to her.

"I don't think I would mind it," she says with a smile. Our lips then meet, and she pulls away an inch, "Hope you have an extra pair of pants if you plan on kissing me," she says teasingly.

"Oh, you think you're funny, huh?" I say and then start tickling her, and she starts squirming around and fills the room with joyous laughter.

All of a sudden, her phone starts ringing, and she sighs in disgust when she hears it. "Hello?" She answers. "Are you serious? Okay, send me the address," she then hangs up.

"What's up?" I ask.

"Coy needs a ride home," she tosses her phone on the floor.

"Okay, I will drive," I say and get up.

"I am sorry," she says apologetic regarding our fun being paused.

"Don't be. Plus, you're right. I don't have that many extra pants. And you just became my girlfriend, can't see me naked yet." I lean over, my body on top of hers, and my arms holding me up. She wraps her hands around my arms, and I lean down to get closer to her, our lips almost touching. Her breathing gets slightly heavier,

"I really fucking like this," I say and stand up. I hear her catch her breath behind me.

We pick Coy up near the college my mom teaches at, except he is in an old apartment building that looks like it hasn't been used in years and is about to fall. We wait outside for Coy, and out comes walking Charles, holding a backpack, which I assume is some type of illegally prescribed medication. I put my hand on the side of my face so he can't see me. Right after he walks out, Coy walks out. He gets in the car and smells like pot and alcohol. I sigh.

"Thanks again," he says while trying to find the handle to close the door. I start driving, and Coy appears between Willow and me, between our seats. He shoves a little bag in Willow's face. "Want some?" He asks, slurring his words.

She pushes it out of her face, "No."

He then returns to the back seat and then all of a sudden he yells, "Oh shit!" Willow turns to look back, and then he says, "Oh, never mind. We're good."

I then look in my review mirror and see cop lights going off behind me, "Cover your shit," I demand Coy, knowing that he must have drugs out in the open.

I pull over and look back at Coy before the cop comes to the window and sees a bigger bag of cocaine sitting in the back seat as if it were a new passenger I picked up. I grab it and shove it under my seat. "Hey!" Coy exclaims.

"Shush," I demand again.

The cop comes to the window and I roll it down, "Oh wow," the cop exclaims, "Phillips, is that you?"

"Ken, hey man," I say. Ken was a guy from high school who would come hang out with us every so often.

"Hey, you went through a red light back there. Just so you know," he says. He then looks over at Willow, then looks in the backseat at Coy. "What are you doing with this one?" He asks, his voice now changing into a stern tone.

"It is my girlfriend's brother," I say, pointing to Willow.

"Yeah, but why are you with these people?" His question shocks me a bit, but before I could answer, Coy opens his mouth.

"What do you mean, these people?" He says.

"Coy, I would shut your mouth. I guarantee I could find some drugs on you right now and take you in. But I don't feel like dealing with the paperwork."

"Okay, we good here?" I say, trying to end an argument that I could see happening.

"Yeah, we are. Be careful," Ken says and walks away, tapping on the trunk of the car as he passes it.

"Girlfriend, huh?" Coy mumbles in the back. I roll my eyes. Now, this I fucking don't like.

Willow's bedroom is low-lit and full of pillows on the bed, a bookshelf full of books and a small desk covered in papers, a wall full of Polaroid pictures and concert tickets, and other souvenirs from things she has done. Her room is full of life and warmth. I look over at her, her back to me as she changes her clothes. First, her shirt, leaving it bare, and then her pants, which, to my surprise, she does not have underwear on. She puts on an oversized t-shirt that only comes to the very bottom of her ass cheek, and I take note that she never puts anything else on. I take off my jeans and throw them on the desk chair.

We both get into bed, and she turns on her side to look at me, her head resting on her hand as she props herself up with her elbow. I turn and do the same so we can look at each other.

"When is that ceremony?" I ask her.

"It is in two weeks," she says excitedly, remembering that I am going.

"I don't need to get high or anything for it, do I?"

She lets out a laugh, "No! It is encouraged to NOT get high so that your experience and feelings are pure. The only thing we inhale is some essential oils."

"What can I expect from it?"

"To sweat a lot," she laughs again, "you just sit around and share your feelings."

"Am I obligated to?" The thought of telling strangers my thoughts makes me uncomfortable.

"A little bit, yeah," she then sits up and climbs up on my lap in a straddling position again. "Listen, I know it is probably going to be weird at first, but everyone talks about how they feel. You don't need to reach deep inside you and tell a story, but share something."

I put my hands on her thighs, "Can I explain how you sitting on me like this turns me on?"

"No, I want to hear that all by myself," she says, and then leans down and starts kissing me again. I open her mouth with my tongue, trying to get as deep as I can by pulling her head closer to mine.

She then gets up off me and walks over to her dresser, opening a drawer. She turns around and shows me that she is holding a condom. Guess I didn't need to bring one. "Want to try?" She says, her voice like velvet.

I get off the bed and go up to her, pulling her into me. My hand reaches beneath her shirt to grab her ass. I drag my finger from the top of the slit between her cheeks all the way to the bottom, my finger landing right at the entrance of her ass hole. I pull my hand away and put it on her lower back.

"I guess that is a yes," she says in my ear, deep breathing. She pulls her shirt off and throws the condom on my chest.

She looks down at my boxers and sees nothing is happening, and gets on top of me and starts kissing me again. She moves her soft hands down my pants and starts rubbing me. Still, nothing happens. This continues for a few minutes, which feels like painful hours. I try to put the condom on myself and fail because it just doesn't stay on.

"We don't have to if you don't want to," she then eventually says.

"NO, no, I do. I don't know what is going on," I say aggravated. "I am turned on by you, I don't know why it isn't… showing."

"Okay, just calm down. Is there something you want me to do specifically?" She asks, trying to solve the problem.

"No," I respond in a harsh voice from frustration.

"Okay, we don't need to do anything," she kisses my cheek and then gets off my lap.

"I am going to clean this shit off of me," I say while looking down at the lubricant on my hands from the condom. I put on my boxers and go to the bathroom.

Of course, when I walk into the bathroom, Reynolds is standing there with a grin on his face. "At least one of us can get it up."

"Don't start," I snap back while washing my hands.

"Are you just mad because your manhood isn't working?"

"I am mad cause you are here. Why are you here?"

"I told you, ask yourself that."

"I don't know. I don't know why you are," I exclaim.

"Since your dick can't show up, at least I can." His grin still on his face, just standing there behind me while I wash my hands. "Do you want me to show her how it feels to have a man?"

All of a sudden, I swing my body back with a full fist and aim to punch him, but since he isn't there, I end up just punching right through him and into the wall, where he then disappears as soon as my fist goes through.

I look at my fist on the wall and pull it back to me, looking at my red knuckles, my half-healed cuts broken open. Within a few seconds, Willow walks into the bathroom and looks at me, then at the wall.

"Are… are you okay?" She asks, confused.

I look at the wall, then back at her, "Yeah. I…" I don't even know what to say.

"Is this because we couldn't have sex?" Her eyebrows cave into the middle of her face.

"What? No," I respond as if that were an obscene question, which it was. Yes, I am annoyed that I couldn't perform, but I am not that angry.

"Then… then why did you just punch a hole in my bathroom wall?" She points at the hole as if I needed to be reminded.

"I will fix it," I say.

"I don't care about you fixing it; I care about *why* you did it."

"I can't explain it," my voice sounding like a plea for her to stop questioning me.

"Try," she demands.

I grab her shoulders, "I am sorry about the wall. But the reason why I did it, I can't explain right now. Just… just understand and trust me on this."

She looks up at me with my eyes and says, "Okay," in an understanding tone.

Willow

I stand in the bathroom and just look at the fresh new design Ben created on my wall. I heard him talking in the bathroom prior to hitting the wall, but I didn't even get to clearly hear what he was saying. But whatever it was, it led to this. I trace over the hole with my fingers. There has never been a hole in a wall in our house; nobody ever got that angry, where it ever led to it. I don't want it to be fixed or covered up. This was art to me; this shows an emotion of some sort, and this is what Ben did in a moment where he felt out of control in some way.

"Girly pop!" Lily says as she comes into the house. I walk out of the bathroom and close the door behind me. Lighting the joint I had in my pocket, taking a long drag, coughing as I let it out. "You good?" She asks when she notices my drag is longer than typical. "So, how is it having Coy back?" she asks me while she looks at my vinyl collection in the living room, even though she knows what everything is.

"Uh, interesting," I lean on the wall next to her. "Coy and Ben don't seem to really… hit it off."

"Not surprising. Just give it time," she grabs the joint from my mouth and takes a hit even longer than mine, not coughing because she can handle it.

"Ben slept here last night for the first time."

"Oh yeah? How did that go?"

"Fine," as open as I usually am, telling Lily what happened isn't invading my privacy but rather Ben's.

"Okay… worst information ever," she says with an eye roll.

"Anyways, he said he is going to come to the sweat ceremony."

"That should be interesting," she says with an undertone of skepticism.

"You told me to ask!"

"Yeah, and I think it will be interesting."

"Yeah," I say quietly under my breath.

After work that night, I head over to Ben's for dinner with his parents. Ben opens the door with a wide smile, his perfect white teeth glowing out of his pale pink lips, his face freshly shaven, so that when I touch his face before kissing him, I can feel the dampness on his skin. "Hey, babe," he says to me. I don't think I have ever been called "babe" seriously, and my heart flutters at the sound of it.

"Hey, cutie," I say back.

We walk into the kitchen, where his mother is, just like last time when I saw her. His stepfather then emerges from the other room, his blonde hair slicked back and a button-up shirt tucked into his pants. They are both the epitome of a picture-perfect family from this rich neighborhood, poised and seemingly flawless.

He stands up and walks over to me, "Hello, I am Paul," he says and puts out his hand to shake. I forget how tall and broad Ben is until he is standing next to someone else, since he is nearly towering over him.

"Hello, I am Willow," I move past his hands and go straight in for a hug.

"Nice to see you again, sweetie," his mom says to me with a warm smile. She has beautiful blue eyes that stand out against her shoulder-length dark brown hair that is curled. She is wearing a loose white silk button-up with the sleeves rolled up and black slacks. "Do you want wine?" She asks.

"Yeah, sure," I say. She then pours me a glass and hands me it.

"Willow makes her own wine," Ben says.

"Oh yeah?" She says, surprised. "You will have to bring some next time."

"Oh, actually here. These are for you. I picked them from our garden," I hand her the small bouquet I had saved for her. "Do you need help with anything?" I then ask.

"Aren't you just so sweet! Thank you," she grabs the flowers from me and starts to put them in a vase that she has under the sink. "No, I am fine. If you just want to bring these plates to the table," she hands me plates that were on the counter. They are just pure white glass plates, the complete opposite of what I use at home.

I put them down at the table and turn to Ben and ask who the other plate is for.

"My brother Sean," he says, and then a few seconds later, his mom is yelling for Sean to come down to the table. We sit down at the table, and then Sean comes running down with a childlike smile on his face. He reminds me of a little Ben, and I can't help but smile when I see him.

"Sean, this is Willow," Ben says.

"Hey," Sean says, his voice sounding almost like a cartoon character.

"Hey there," I say back, and he sits down across from me.

We start eating, and in between bites, I would be asked questions, "Ben says you wrote a book," Paul says to me as he dips his buttered white bread into the spaghetti sauce.

I finish chewing and then answer, "Yes, I did actually. I now own a bookstore." Ben's mom then looks up at me with a fork full of spaghetti in her hand, and that is when it dawned on me, I have seen her before, she was the woman who came into my store a while ago looking for a book called *Lost Connections*. I then look over at Ben, who is just sitting there eating with one hand on my leg and the other hand twirling spaghetti with a fork. But then, when I look back over at his mom, I see her looking at Ben, then at me, and I remember the hole in the wall. The book was for her because of him.

"Your father called today," his mother says. I assume it is because she does not want to bring up the fact that I have seen her in the store before.

"Oh, yeah?" Ben answers.

"He is flying in next month and wants to get dinner with you. He is bringing," she pauses for a second, "his wife and children."

"I will call him later."

The rest of the dinner was awkward in the sense that it was mostly silent. Every so often, Sean would share an anecdote from school, or someone would ask me a question about my family. The silence after I said I didn't go to college was even more uncomfortable because I could feel Ben's mom just unimpressed and unpleased about it.

Once we finish dinner, I help Ben's mom clean up the dishes. She notices we are alone and grabs my arm lightly, whispering, "I know we have encountered each other previously, but if you could just not mention it, I would appreciate it," she was intimidating, not because she is my new boyfriend's mother, but because her voice is stern and everything she says sounds more like a command.

"Yeah, of course," I don't move away right away because I wonder if I should bring up the fact that he punched a hole in my wall.

"I want to talk to you in private in a little bit, if that is okay," she says. It doesn't sound much like a question but rather a demand.

"Okay, sounds good," I say with a smile on my face and walk away.

I walk up to Ben and whisper in his ear, "Your mom is so serious."

He laughs a bit and looks at her in the kitchen, then at me, "Just straightforward," he says.

My family is straightforward as well, but we don't come across as intimidating- at least I don't think so. I think about my family and how everyone is usually wearing some type of bright color and talks slowly and upbeat, we are not intimidating.

Ben's mom and I walk in the backyard, we both look out over the lake and I can't help but think of me and Ben's first kiss. We then sit down on the white wooden lounge chairs that are in the middle of the backyard, the light from inside the house illuminating us.

She takes a sip of wine and then begins to talk, "I talked to Ben about this the other day, but I doubt he listened or cared what I had to say. Ben was just away for many years, and I want him to be able to come home and adjust properly before he starts to adjust to… other things."

The other things being me. "I understand," I say, but after I say it, I realize that I don't understand. "Wait, so are you asking me to stay away from him or keep an eye on him?"

"I suppose both," she says sternly. I understand why Ben was rebellious when he was young. There is something about her that makes you want to do the opposite of what she says.

"I don't understand how that is possible."

"Ben is stubborn, so he won't listen to anyone, but he also likes to make sure everyone is taken care of. You need to make sure there is a balance. Don't pressure him into doing things or going places or telling you things. But make sure he is taken care of. Does that make sense?"

"Yeah," I get a flashback of him standing in my bathroom with red knuckles and a hole in the wall a few feet from him. I want to tell her in case it pertains to something else, but it was like I was too scared to tell her. "He is a great guy," I say instead.

"Yes, he is," she says as if it were a fact, making sure there was no confusion on that.

Ben and I lay in his bed, my head on his chest, and his arms wrapped around me.

"Your mom thinks the world of you," I say to him.

"Oh yeah? What did she say?" he asks, his voice sounding slightly defensive, as if he knew that she voiced a concern to me.

"She was just telling me that you smell pretty weird and I should remind you to shower," I say playfully, and he smiles at me.

"Yeah, yeah!" he grabs me and pulls me on top of him and nuzzles in my neck.

"Did I tell you how beautiful you look tonight?" He says.

"No, I don't think you did! Why not tell me again?"

"You look very beautiful tonight," he then grabs my face and looks in my eyes right before he kisses me. He then takes his hand off my face and slides it up my dress. Goosebumps start forming on my skin from the excitement. But then I remember the last time we tried doing anything like this, and it never ended well. He then flips me over so he is on top of me, he then reaches over to his drawer and grabs something, which I assume is a condom.

"You sure?" I ask him.

"Yes," he says, then flashes a smile at me. We go back to kissing for a few minutes, "Will you shut up?" He says suddenly in an angry tone.

I put my hands on his chest and push him back, "What?" I say offended.

He looks at me, confused, "What?" he says back to me.

"You just told me to shut up," I respond.

"No, that wasn't to you," he then starts kissing me again, and I push him off of me and sit up in the bed.

"What do you mean that wasn't to me?"

He sits up and closes his eyes, pinching the bridge of his nose. "Can you pretend that didn't happen?"

"You can't think I will let that go, do you?" I ask him, surprised that he would even ask that. He doesn't respond to me, and I grab his hand. "Who is it?" I ask, breaking the silence.

"What do you mean?" He looks at me with confused eyes.

"I have seen Coy on drugs before, and there have been times he has seen people or things and responds to them. It seems as if… as if that is what is going on here," I say, almost watching what I say so he doesn't take it the wrong way.

"I am not on drugs," he snaps at me, his voice sounding so defensive.

"I am not implying that. I am saying I know when someone is hallucinating."

He looks away from me, "Please," even though his voice was in a whisper, I could hear the strong plea in it.

"I just want to help you."

"I don't want your help, I don't need it. So please, just don't ask," he still doesn't look at me, his voice still in a whisper.

"Is it the same person as last time?"

"I thought I just said to stop asking about it," his voice growing more agitated, he gets off the bed and paces around his room a little bit. It scared me a bit since I had never seen him this angry. I didn't know what would happen next, then a knock on his bedroom door. "Come in," he said, calmer than before.

His mom opens the door slowly, peeking her head around the door, and looks around the room. Ben lets out a quiet sigh and raises his eyebrows, waiting for his mom to move faster. "Your phone keeps buzzing with text messages. I looked at it, and it said something about a funeral. Someone named Nelson?"

He lets out another sigh, "Oh, right. Okay," his mom then leaves the room, leaving the door open. Ben goes over to the door, closing it loudly, almost a slam. I just sit on the edge of the bed with my legs swinging off, looking at him. He is pacing the room again. He scratches his head and then looks at me, "Want to come to a funeral with me?" He then asks.

I let go of the last five minutes, "Yeah… yeah, I can do that. When is it?"

"We would have to leave in two days. It is a 15-hour drive to Georgia."

"Okay, I will have someone watch the store while I am gone." I have never been to a funeral before, and the thought of it makes my skin crawl. "Who is it for, by the way?"

"One of my partners died."

"I am so sorry. How did it happen?"

"Uh, I don't know," his voice sounding slightly flustered, and from previous conversations, I know that if he doesn't want to talk about something, it is best not to talk about it.

Ben

I wait outside of Willow's house, just thinking about how dreadful this funeral is going to be. I check my bags about seven times to make sure I have all my pills in there. When I go to check again, I see Willow coming out of her house in the corner of my eye. I check the bag one last time quickly before she gets in the car. She opens the doors and greets me with a kiss and a smile.

"Got everything?" I ask her.

"I believe so!" she says, closing the door behind her. "Do you?"

I grab her hand and kiss it, "I do now."

After listening to music for a while, Willow dances her little fingers to the volume knob down, "So were you good friends?" She then asks.

I was surprised by her question, "I mean, we were friends."

"I know you're going to say no to this question, but can you tell me a war story? I just want to know more about that part of your life."

"I don't want to expose you to that."

"Just tell me," she grabs my hand and rubs my fingers.

My hand white knuckling the steering wheel, she has never asked me about what it was like being away or what I have done, which I appreciate. And I do understand why she is asking, and now would be the time to share stories. It is just that I don't want to tell her. I think for a few seconds about something that has happened that won't pain me to talk about.

"There was this one time when we had to blow up a building, it was me and about six other guys. We separated into twos and placed the bombs throughout the building. When it was time to ignite it, this kid Pierce, who was a walking dead man. He was convinced he was about to die any second. It was irritating to be with him. Always so fearful, which added stress. Anyways, he turned to me and said he must have dropped his picture of his wife in the building. He said he wouldn't die without her by his side. As soon as he went into the building, one of the guys hit the button."

"Wow. I mean, don't they communicate to make sure everyone is out?" She asks.

"Yeah, he should've. We had a time limit and should have been out by then, but he still should have made sure. They were all a bunch of idiots. I wasn't with that team for long."

"What did you do while you were there? Like, what was your specific role?"

"I mostly did combat missions. I would go into cities and patrol them, spend a lot of days driving around checking for IEDs. I also worked with transportation, so I was able to spend some time traveling and networking. I did a few hostage missions, too. I did anything that kept me busy and moving. My captain wanted me to get behind enemy lines and do more of the intelligence work or special forces."

"How come you didn't do that?" She asks.

"Honestly? Because at the time, I didn't want to put in the work or training. I wanted to do the easy work with adrenaline. Although I think I am still trying to come down from that adrenaline. But now that I've got that all out of my system, I would do special forces. I'd be fucking good at it."

She clenches onto my hand tighter, "The thought of someone shooting at you pains me to think about."

I let go of the wheel and roll up my right sleeve, showing a scar on my shoulder of where I was once shot, "It's happened."

She traces over it with her finger, then kisses it. She sighs heavily and then says, "I hope that is the only one."

I pull up my shirt a little and show her the one on my left side, "Nope, afraid not."

"I don't want to see any more."

"Then you wouldn't want to see my back." When I said it, I said it in a joking voice, but right after, it reminded me of how my back does look.

"Why?" she asks and then tries to pull up my shirt.

I pull it back down and move her hand away, "Not today." I hear her laugh a little, the type of laugh where it sounds more like a sigh. "What?" I ask her.

"You have seen me pretty much naked, and I have never seen you without a shirt on," I look over at her, and she has an eyebrow raised.

"If it makes you feel any better, you have touched my genitals before I have touched yours," I say, making a joke out of it.

"I barely even touched it," she says in a whisper and a smirk on her face.

"Oh, you think you're funny, huh?" She starts laughing back at me, and I join her.

We get to the motel where everyone is staying for the next two nights. Everyone is sitting outside by the pool, drinking beer. Nick is the first person I say hello to since he is the one who told me about the funeral. He introduces me and Willow to his girlfriend, Idia, a beautiful, tall brunette with blue eyes, with a thick Australian accent. Nick is an average-looking man, and I question how he managed to get this girl. Willow greets both of them with a hug. I find it comical watching Idia bend down to hug Willow, making Willow seem so much smaller. While I think of how lucky Nick is to have such a beautiful girlfriend, I look over at my own girlfriend, who is so imperfectly perfect. Willow doesn't have these long legs or curled hair that looks like it was done for her. Willow is just so herself, and in this moment, I realize how much luckier I am.

I grab her hand and kiss it, then put my hand around her waist, dragging her along to meet other people. People that I have been on a squad with, just know from being around, and other people whom I have never met.

"I couldn't have done this without you," I whisper into Willow's ear. She looks up at me and smiles.

We say hello to everyone, and make our way into our room to put our things down and clean up before we join everyone outside for beers and food. "I am going to jump in the shower," I tell Willow and grab my clothes from my bag to bring to the bathroom with me.

After a few minutes of being in the shower, she knocks on the door. "Do you have a phone charger?" She asks.

"Yeah, it is in my bag," I yell back out to her. After I get out and get changed, I walk back into the room, and she is just standing by the bed with her arms crossed.

"What?" I ask.

She puts her hand in my bag and pulls out the pill bottles and drops them on the bed. "Why didn't you tell me?"

I went over to them and put them back in my bag, "Didn't know I needed to."

"I mean, it isn't that big of a deal. It just would've been nice to know. I know you already don't tell me things, and that's fine. This is new and all. But it just," she stops talking, and I look up at her. "I just feel like sometimes I don't know you."

"Takes time to get to know someone. Can you just do me a favor and not mention this to anyone?"

"Is it because it is illegally prescribed?" She says with confidence in her voice. "I know the name on the bottles; he is friends with Coy."

"That and just because nobody can know I am taking anything. Okay?"

"I am going to get changed," she says, changing the topic. She pulls out a long blue skirt from her bag and takes off her tight, dark blue jeans. This girl needs to start wearing underwear before I lose it.

"Do you have to do that here?" I ask her with a smile on my face. Before she puts the skirt on, she walks over to me, like a flower in the wind. She is so dainty that it makes her even more irresistible to me.

"Does it bother you seeing me with no pants on?" Her body is only inches away from me. I pick her up and she wraps her legs around me, my hands grasping her ass. She starts kissing my neck, and when I look past her shoulder.

Reynolds is standing by the door, leaning on it. "Oh yes! I have such a good view of her ass over here," he makes a fist and bites his knuckles. "Are you finally going to have sex with her today? If you don't, I might have to. She is definitely asking for it, no panties." He then walks over to her jeans and picks them up, and smells them. "Still smells like her ass."

"You're seriously sick," I say and put Willow back on the ground, and when I look back up, he is gone.

"That wasn't to me, right?" She asks fearfully.

I scratch my forehead, "No, sweetie," I say and kiss her head. She turns around and puts her skirt on.

"I won't try anymore," she says with her back turned to me.

"It isn't you," trying to reassure her.

"I know it isn't. You're just extremely complicated," she still doesn't face me and just heads towards the door, "Ready?"

"Yeah," I reply sheepishly.

Willow grabs us both a beer immediately once we get outside to join everyone.

"I am going to sit by Nick and Idia," she says, and I follow behind her. Joining them on a hard plastic white pool chair. Idia is lying down on the chair, and Nick is sitting on the side of the chair holding her hand. When I sit down next to Willow, she puts her head on my shoulder, raising her hand and touching where she knows my scar is underneath my shirt.

"How long have you two been dating?" Nick asks.

"About a month or so?" Willow pondered, looking at me for some type of clarification.

"Yeah, about that," I agreed.

"So what do you do, Idia?" Willow curiously asks.

"I own a magazine company." It is hard to tell if Idia is sincere or if she comes across as snobby due to her accent, a monotone voice, and a lack of facial expression.

"Willow wrote a book and owns a bookstore," I input, almost bragging.

"That's cool," Idia responds, still monotone.

"I was thinking about writing a book," Nick stated. "Maybe like an autobiography or something. I figured I have enough to say that it could be in a book. Ben, you probably could write a book with all the shit you've been through!"

"Yeah," I snuffle.

"Ben was the kind of guy that you heard stories about, where you had to ask him once you saw him if the story you heard was true or not. This guy has seen some shit."

Nick takes his last gulp of beer and opens another right after. "Cohens comes home soon," he adds.

My ears perk up, "Yeah, he does," I say with a little excitement in my voice.

"You two are the dream team. I would have you two on my squad any day," he sits up closer, his elbows resting on his knees, "Can I tell you something?" He whispers.

"What?" I respond and look around to make sure there are no eavesdroppers.

"Idia, want to grab a drink with me?" Willow asks, getting the hint that this conversation is only made for two.

"Okay," Idia says and stands up, and walks to the grill. Willow smiles down at me when she stands up.

"I am not surprised Nelson is dead," he then says in a low hush.

I wince, "Why?"

"He ran his mouth too much," he adds.

"What?" I say, shocked, this news is new to me.

"Yeah, he just always had something to say and it pissed a lot of guys off."

I remember Nick telling me that he doesn't know how Nelson was killed, "You think one of us did it?" I ask.

"Wouldn't surprise me," he takes a sip of his beer, as do I, simultaneously. He pulls out a cigarette and hands one to me.

"Huh, and no thanks, I'm not smoking these days," I try to play into his conspiracy theory, pretending I was giving it a thought. I guess it isn't that crazy of a conspiracy theory; one of us *did* get him killed.

The rest of the night is spent with everyone drinking, laughing, and dancing to the music blasting. Everyone is completely drunk, Willow and I included. It is amusing looking at Willow this drunk. Her face is rose colored, every movement is like a dance, she just moves freely like wind in the air. Looking at her is more intoxicating than the alcohol itself.

I somehow manage to get talked into jumping into the pool with a few other guys. I strip off my jeans and hand them to Willow and stand at the edge of the pool in a lineup. The people who aren't jumping stand across from us on the other side of the pool, counting down when we should jump. 3…2…1

"Jump in!" I yell out to Willow while in the pool.

"No!" She yells back with a giant smile on her face. I pull myself up on the ledge of the pool and run up to her and grab her.

She starts playfully screaming, and I jump into the pool with her in my arms.

"Ben!" She shrieks out humorously.

We lay in bed together, the room close to spinning from being so drunk. "This might sound messed up... but I am happy being here with you," she says softly.

"I am glad you're here," I roll over and kiss her head, then pull her close to me. My arms wrap around her, and she holds on to my forearm, slowly dragging her fingers up and down. My hand caresses her cheek as I rub my thumb slowly on it. I pull myself closer to her so I am suffocating in her hair. I can tell she is starting to fall asleep by how her fingers decrease in speed. I allow myself a few more minutes of this before I attempt to fall asleep as well.

Despite falling asleep in peace, as soon as I wake up, I am already anxiety-driven. The thought of seeing Nelson's body- and not knowing what it looks like- sends me into complete stress. "Wow! You look handsome," Willow says to me when she comes out of the bathroom and sees me in my Army Service Uniform. I look at her in her high-neck, long black dress, hair pulled back.

"Thanks," I say briefly.

"First time I have seen you in your uniform," her voice traveling at the end, as if there was some underlying point. "Makes it feel a lot more real."

"Feels strange being in it."

She walks over to me and places her hand on my chest where my last name rests in stitching. She traces over it, and I see her look down at the medals and ribbons that fill my chest. Her finger then leaps to the purple ribbon sitting right in the center. She taps it with her finger and sighs. I grab her hand off my chest and kiss it. We head to the car without saying anything else.

When we get to the church, there are people everywhere- complete chaos. Men and women in uniform, dressed in suits and dresses, people of different ages and races. Looking at people walking into the church with tears on their faces, tissues in hand. My heart starts beating faster than I can catch up to it.

"There is a spot over there," Willow says, snapping me back to the now. I pull into the spot and take a deep breath. She grabs my hand and squeezes it, and we get out of the car.

Right when I am about to close my door, "See you inside," Reynolds says from the backseat.

I catch the door before it shuts and look at him, "What? What did you say? You're coming to this?"

"Why wouldn't I be? I knew him, and thanks to you, I am back in the States now."

The thought of Reynolds being here didn't cross my mind until now. I look at the entrance of the church to see if I can see him, as if in that exact moment, he would be walking in. Better yet, how would I even be able to tell if it is him or not? I get back in the car, and I see Willow turn around and look at me in the car, and come back in.

"What is going on?" She asks, shutting the door behind her.

"I… I… I can't. I can't go in there," my breathing becomes heavy and hard to catch, I reach for my bag behind me and stumble around it looking inside.

"What are you looking for?" She asks. I just dump the bag over and pull everything out of it, pushing clothes out of the way. "Ben! What? I can help you," she yells at me. I grab the Xanax and put two in my hand, swallowing them immediately.

"I can't go in," I say to her.

"Why? What happened?"

"I'm just not," I say sternly. "I am sorry for bringing you here, but I am not going."

"Tell me why, and I will drop it and we can leave." She pushes me for an answer.

"I said I'm not fucking going in," I snap at her when I didn't intend for that to happen. She pulls her body back and looks out the windshield.

"Let me drive. You're too wound up," I don't argue with her since it is the least I could do at this point, and I just get out of the car to switch seats.

We start driving, and I end up falling asleep, which is most likely more of a Xanax induced sleep. I wake up feeling more at ease, as if the thought of seeing Reynolds didn't send me into panic mode. "Want to switch?" I suddenly say to Willow. She looks over at me, assessing me to make sure I am fully awake and alert.

"You sure you're good with driving?" she asks while taking glances at me.

"Yeah, I'm fine," she pulls over on the side of the highway, which only has about three cars driving on. We get out of the car to switch seats, once again. When I get to the driver seat, I push the seat back. If I sat as close as Willow did to the wheel, my knees would be in my eyes.

The seat doesn't move back, and I keep pushing it, "Damn thing." I say under my breath. Then all of a sudden, as it slides back, a giant pop. It sounds as if a balloon came in contact with a needle. I look down and see white powder covering the floor.

"What the hell is this?" I ask out loud.

Willow looks over at it, then up at me, making eye contact. "Babe, that's coke."

My eyes widen as I remember that I put Coy's coke under my seat a few weeks ago. I take a second and take a deep sigh, closing my eyes. "This isn't happening," I say, opening my eyes. "I am going to start by saying that I am not mad at you right now."

"Okay," she says apprehensively.

I slam the door shut and yell, "FUCK!" I go to the side of the highway where there is just a field of grass and sit down with my head in my hands.

"Remember last time we were in a field together?" A voice says, but it startles me because it isn't Reynolds' voice, it's Nelson's.

I look at him, confused, "Why are you bringing that up?"

"Just look out there and tell me what you see," he says.

I turn around and look out into the field, and four men are walking towards me. I jump up immediately, and they start to pick up their pace and are now running to me. I instinctively grab my gun from my side.

"Stop right there," I yell out.

They yell out to me, and I can't make out what they're saying, but they don't slow their pace.

"I said fucking stop!" I then shoot one of the men in the head. "Now will you stop?" I say. Two of them stop in their tracks, but one keeps walking toward me.

He finally gets up to me, and I say, "What did you do to Nelson?"

"Not me. You," I then point my gun right at his head.

"I didn't do anything."

All of the men start yelling, and the man standing in front of me points his gun over my shoulder. I turn around and see a young woman behind me wearing a Niqab.

"What are you doing?" She asks me.

"Is she with you?" I turn around, looking at the man, and ask him.

"This is not my abeed. She must be yours. I know what you people do to them."

"Ben? Ben?" Willow says to me.

I look at her with confusion, not remembering her coming up to me, "What?" I respond.

"Are you okay?" she asks with sadness and confusion on her face, eyebrows furrowed.

"What do you mean?"

"I mean, you were just standing out here talking to yourself with your hand pointed out like a gun, and when I came up to you, it was like you didn't recognize me."

"Oh," I look away from her and try walking past her, but she slams her hand on the middle of my chest. "It was a hallucination."

"Yeah, I know you get them, but you usually aren't so out of it when you do."

I sigh in realization that I can't just drop this one. She has given me a free pass so much already. "Okay... so I guess I get two different types of hallucinations. I get the kind where I know it's not real. I mean, granted, just because I know it isn't real doesn't stop me from responding to it. Those are the kind I have been getting lately. But then there are ones I get where I don't know it is fake, and when I wake up from it, it just feels more like a dream you can't remember. I have a sense that it happened, but I don't know for sure or what it even was."

"So you don't know what you just saw?"

"No. I don't think I would have even realized that it happened if you didn't point it out. I mean, since you did, I can kind of remember not being present for a bit, but I don't remember what it was."

"Seems a lot scarier," she says with a deep sadness in her eyes.

"Yeah, but at the same time, I would rather have that than feel like my head is going to explode every time I hear Reynolds make a comment."

"Reynolds? Is that who you see? Is that who you have been talking to?"

I suddenly feel flustered, not even realizing that I said his name. "Oh, come on, you better not tell her. You know she won't be able to keep her mouth shut if she knows," Reynolds says, standing behind her.

"Drop that one," I tell her, and try to start walking back to the car again.

"You know they have medication for it," she yells at me.

I turn around and walk back up to her, "Seroquel, yeah, I know. I have it sitting in my nightstand at home. But once I take it," I look down and kick a little rock, watching it hop over a few pebbles and bounce into the grass where it gets lost. "Once I take it, then it means that there is something wrong with me. And if there is something wrong with me, then I can't serve."

"Right, I should've known. I should've realized it. And if you talk about it, then it means it's real and you can't take it back." I look up at her, and it was as if she knew exactly what I was thinking.

"I should report you for being crazy. That seems like fair payback." Reynolds drops in again.

"You can't because you aren't even real," I respond with an eye roll. I turn around and go back to the car. Before I open the car door, I stop for a moment, "There is coke all over my car," I say to Willow.

"Right," she opens the backseat door and grabs something, then pushes past me and opens the door. I look over her shoulder and see that she is scooping the coke with her hands and putting it into her overnight bag.

"What are you doing?" I ask.

"Where else would I put it?" I raise my eyebrows, realizing that she has a valid point, and I don't answer. "I will vacuum the rest of it when we get home," she closes her bag and starts walking back to the passenger side. As soon as she walks by me, I turn around, grab her arm, and spin her back around. I take her face in my hands and kiss her with full force.

I pull away and look at her, "I'm sure your brother will want that back anyway," I smirk, and she laughs out loud.

"Unfortunately, that would be the first thing he would ask for if I told him what happened."

Willow

The car ride home is silent, while we both ponder what the hell has happened in the last 24 hours. I spend the entire time looking out the window that is slightly cracked enough just for a breeze to come in to make it feel like there is some type of movement and life in the car. My mind is full of questions, more than usual.

"It is an object," Ben suddenly says.

"What?" I say, breaking out of my trance of thought.

"I am thinking of an object. Guess what it is," he says with this smirk on his face. I can't help but smile back at his interest in playing a silly car game to lighten the stifling air in the car.

"Is it in the car?" I ask, looking around.

He lets out a big laugh, "Yeah."

"What color is it?" I ask while looking around.

"No, you're only allowed to ask yes or no questions!"

I sigh and squint my eyes in fake annoyance, "Is it large?"

"No."

I look down at the cup holders and see a cup of coffee and water, "Is it something you can drink?"

He lets out another big laugh, "No, but close."

"Can you eat it?"

"Yes," he says through his unfaded smirk.

"Why do you keep laughing? What could it be?" I look around the car more and see a pack of gum and pick it up, "This?" I say, nearly shoving it in his face.

"No!"

"Okay, just tell me!" I command.

"You're giving up that easily?" His smirk grew into a sly smile. A smile where you can see his white teeth and the front tooth that is cracked a little, which I still have yet to ask why. His light pink lips curved upwards, resulting in his right dimple showing. I couldn't help but smile looking at him.

"Just tell me!" I roll my eyes at him.

"It's the coke in your bag," he laughs so loudly as if he had said the cleverest joke. But that is when I felt *it*. I felt my heart flutter, skip a beat, stomach turn into knots, and feel as if I was going to let it come out of my mouth. It is realizing that even after an insane trip of one thing going wrong after another, he still releases the tension in the air. It's the realization that he has put himself in front of me at any moment he senses there is danger. The realization that his kisses and touch are full of not only want but need, and I fucking feel it every single time he lays a finger on me. It's the realization that, despite whatever is going on with him, I have the need to protect and help him. It's the realization that this was something so much more from the moment he walked into my store.

"I have strong feelings for you," I say suddenly. It pours outo of my mouth before I have a chance to fully think about it myself. He looks at me, his smile depleted, and my mind races thinking he is about to tell me he doesn't feel the same way or something. Anxiety doesn't exist in my world. I have felt nervous before, such as when I opened my store or broke Coy's favorite pipe, but never *anxious*. I've lived by the phrase of whatever will be, will be. My face starts to burn as it turns to red with embarrassment and regret for saying something.

"Don't do this now," he says and grabs my hand, almost reassuring me that it isn't a full rejection.

He drops me off at home and kisses me goodbye before I get out of the car. I can't get the sense of embarrassment away from me, though, and I force a smile when I leave. I get into my house and see Coy sitting on my couch, eating cereal. I throw my bag at the back of his head, and he spills drops of coconut milk onto the floor.

"Hello to you, too," he says, turning around, looking at me. He puts the bowl on the table and comes up to me and hugs me, "You look radiant. You really do. This dress looks so beautiful on you," he is being sincere, and I appreciate it. He pushes a strand of my hair behind my ear. "Why do you look so beautiful but look so miserable?"

"That bag is full of your coke, Coy," I say, pointing at the bag that is on the couch.

"Well, thank you for the gift," he says. He grabs my chin and looks at me.

"It spilled all over Ben's car. From when he took it from you," I push his hand away from me.

"Okay, that is his fault for taking it and leaving it there," he turns around and sits back on the couch, opening the bag.

"No, it is your fault for having it in the first place," I walk over to the couch and stand in front of him.

"You changed. When did you start giving a shit about what other people do?"

"When it affects someone I love," I finally said it out loud, the big L word.

His eyes widen, "Wow, you did not just say love," he says it judgmental.

"I did, Coy."

"I don't know how you can love someone who is just so violent," he says in disbelief.

"Is this in reference to the whole army thing?" I say, rolling my eyes wondering this will stop being such a controversial topic about Ben.

He stands up from the couch and raises his voice, "No, it is about the fucking hole in your bathroom wall, Will," pointing to the bathroom. "I am assuming that is from him because last time I checked, you don't punch things. Was he mad at you? Was it directed to you?"

"No, it wasn't like that," I say defensively. Then I understood why he punched the wall. It was a hallucination, and I didn't put the pieces together until now.

"Already making excuses for him," Coy rolls his eyes and starts to walk out.

"When did we start arguing so much?" I ask him before he opens the door.

"I just don't agree with what you're doing."

"And you think I agreed with all the things you did? No. But I didn't hate you for it and argue with you about it. You give me no choice but to be defensive."

He sighs and turns around to look at me, "I just don't want to see you get wrapped up in something you don't believe in or getting hurt."

"That is for me to decide and let it happen. I didn't want to see you wrapped up in God knows what it is that you do. By doing this, you're putting a wedge between us, Coy. I'm not going to end things with him just because you don't like it."

He lets out a big breath; "You were always the stubborn one," he smiles at me and hugs me. His warm body reminding me of the comfort I have in him. "So, love, huh?" I don't need to look at him to know he is smiling sarcastically.

"Yeah," he then lets go of me, and we sit on the couch together. Then I hear a knock on my door and open it to find Lily standing there, as if she knew a story was about to happen without her.

"You're home," she says, surprised.

"Uhh… yes?" Confused as to why she would be here if I wasn't home.

"I came here to hang out with Coy, but this is even better!" she says.

"You're in time for story time!" Coy says to her, patting the couch for her to sit. "Will just told me she is in love!" He holds his hands and brings them to his face, batting his eyelashes.

"I never said IN love. Just that I love him."

"Did you tell him?" Lily says excitedly, nearly falling off the couch. I walk into the kitchen and pour all of us a cup of coffee.

"I mean," I take a sip of coffee while Coy pulls out his bong from under the table. "We were in the car, and I told him I had strong feelings for him, and he just told me not to do this right now."

"What does that even mean?" Coy says as he packs a bowl.

"Maybe he wants to be the one to say it," Lily comes to Ben's defense. "Coy, I want some!"

"Yeah, I mean, we waited a while to even kiss."

"Well, when you two kiss and have sex, do you feel that passion of love, or does it just feel lustful?" Coy asks and then takes a hit. The bubbles fill the silence in the room before I answer.

"When we kiss, it definitely feels strong," I try to ignore the other part of the question, but I know it won't work.

"Is he still coming to the sweat ceremony this weekend?" Coy asks.

"I forgot about that, yeah, I assume he is," I grab the bong from Coy as soon as he finishes and take a hit, one that doesn't make me cough. After the rollercoaster of emotions on the last day, weed doesn't even make a dent in my thoughts.

Just a bit past midnight, Lily leaves, and Coy and I stay on the couch, curled up in a blanket, watching television, when I get a call from Ben. "Hello?" I answer.

"Hey, I can't sleep, and I was wondering if I could come over," he asks.

"Yeah, sure. I am awake anyway."

"Okay," he takes a pause; "I am actually coming up your driveway now." I laugh and say okay and open my front door.

"What would you have done if I said no?" I say, standing in the doorway when he gets out of his car.

"Turned around," he comes up to me and grabs my face and kisses me. I always feel so giddy after he kisses me like that. He walks in, and Coy turns around and looks at him. "Hey, Coy."

"Hey, man," Coy responds and turns back around to the TV.

"We're going to go to my room," I tell Coy.

We walk into my room and I suggest for him to take a hot shower and use lavender essential oil because it can help him fall asleep, while I make tea. I go into the kitchen and put water on the stove to heat up, and grab Chamomile tea. I hear him get out of the shower, and I walk into my bedroom with both cups of tea in my hand. When I walk in, I see a towel wrapped around his waist, and

I look up at his back and see countless scars all over his back. Small scars, long scars, wide scars, some on an angle, there wasn't a spot on his back that didn't have a scar. His tattoo on his back covers the top half, but they are still visible through the ink.

The mugs slip right from my hands, smashing on the floor. He turns around and looks at me, stunned. I hear Coy walking quickly to my bedroom door, asking what happened, and Ben just reaches behind me and shuts it before Coy can come in. I didn't even know I was crying until Ben wiped away the tears on my cheeks.

"I am… I am so sorry," I mumble. He picks me up and carries me to the bed.

"I don't want you to cut your feet on the glass," he says and then gets dressed quickly.

"I didn't mean to react that way," I quickly say.

"It isn't anything new," he starts picking up the bigger pieces of glass. "Are you okay? Did you hurt your feet?"

I look down at my feet, and they are cherry red from the scorching hot tea spilling on them. I ignore it and just walk up to him, hugging him from behind while he is bent down. "Who? How?"

"Willow, please," he says the words softly, but they feel intense. He grabs my hand and kisses it before he gets up and walks out of the room with the glass in his hand.

"Let me see it again," I demand when he walks back into the room.

"I don't feel like cleaning up any more glass," he says with a slight joking tone to his voice.

"Ben, I haven't asked anything of you," I remind him, and he doesn't say anything but just lies on the bed on his stomach, his face buried in the pillow. I look at and put my fingers on one of the many scars and wince as soon as I touch it, pulling back, but then putting my finger on it again. "Were you tortured?" I ask.

"No," he says briefly.

"I can't imagine someone hurting you like this. I don't want to imagine you getting hurt."

"I am fine now."

My heart is pounding as fast as thoughts are racing in my head, "Do you know who did it?"

"Yes."

"Did you do anything about it?"

"Please stop asking questions," he demands.

"Did they get in trouble?"

"Willow, please," his demand frustrates me, the fact that whenever I ask a question he just ignores it.

"Why did they do it?"

"I said stop," his voice cracks at the end.

"Just answer me," he doesn't say anything, "Literally answer any of those questions." He still doesn't say anything. "Ben, this is a big-" Before I finish my sentence I notice he is gripping onto the pillow, his knuckles white. Then I hear him hyperventilating.

"I… I can't…" he says, turning over. I jump off the bed and lunge for the bag that he brought with him and pull everything out looking for his Xanax, I put a pill in my hand and bring it over to him. "When I say to stop asking I mean stop," he throws the pill to the back of his throat and looks up at me.

"I just want you to be able to talk to me," I say sadly.

"I can, I just don't want to talk about this shit, Willow. I don't know why you can't get that," he sits up from the bed and puts his shirt on.

"Where are you going?" I ask.

"I am going home."

"Why?"

"Because I don't feel like being with you right now, honestly."

"Ben, I am sorry for pushing you," he goes to open the bedroom door, and I jump up, "I lo-"

"Don't."

"Why? Is it because you don't feel the same?" I have never been one to sound desperate but right now, I am not much of myself.

He turns around, "Because you aren't just going to say that right now, like this, just so I don't leave or so I can become less pissed or whatever the reason is for you doing it right now."

"Then why did you stop me when I was in the car?"

"Because it didn't seem like the best time."

"Why do you get to decide when it is the best time for everything? When do I get a fucking say, Ben?"

"When you start thinking about something other than your own curiosity. When you grasp the fact that I said I am not talking about it. When you stop being so damn selfish. Start fucking thinking, Willow."

"You are being so cruel right now," I say and feel a tear drip down my cheek.

"No, Willow. I'm not. You are," he sighs, "maybe I'm not ready for this," he walks out of the bedroom. And for the first time, I cried over a boy. I have felt a heartbreak. This isn't whatever will be, will be.

When I close the store at 8 pm, I go straight home and start a hot bubble bath. I check my phone for the 10th time in the last two minutes to see if Ben has reached out. I start undressing and see the hole in the wall behind me in the mirror. Overwhelming anger fills my veins, an anger that I have never felt before. I turn around and try to create another hole in the wall with my fist, but it just results in my fist being red. Before the water fills the tub, I grab weed that I know Lily has left in my bedroom and decide to smoke it while I am in the tub.

I thought it would help me relax, but it just makes my thoughts feel more out of control. I imagine Ben being helpless while someone stabs him in the back, and I try everything to get the thought out of my head and fail.

Did he kill them after? If it were one of his enemies, why wouldn't they just stab him in the chest, where it would kill him? There clearly wasn't much of a fight since he is left with so many scars. Did he let them do it? That would explain why he didn't fight back. Or did he think he deserved it, so he just let them continue? I take another hit from the joint.

More questions float around my head as I think about our road trip together. Why did he suddenly not want to go to the funeral? And who is Reynolds, and why does he keep showing up in his hallucinations? All of a sudden, the bathroom door swings open, and Coy walks in.

I jump, splashing water on the ground, "Do you knock?"

"I have been," He says and sits down on the toilet, grabbing the joint from my hand and relighting it and smoking it. "You smoking?"

"No, I am holding it for fun," I sarcastically say. "Get in with me."

He stumbles as he pulls off his clothes, already high, and gets in the bathtub, sitting across from me. We pass the joint back and forth.

"So would this gloomy ass bath have anything to do with last night?" He says with a slight hesitation in his voice.

"Possibly," I take a hit.

"And that he broke up with you?"

"What are you talking about?"

"Before he left, he said maybe he isn't ready for a relationship."

"Okay, that doesn't mean we broke up," I look down at the bath water and draw circles in it with my fingers.

"Have you talked to him since then?"

"No."

"And you don't think that is odd?" He splashes me with water to try and lighten the mood. "Turn around, let me wash your hair."

I turn around, and he pours lavender shampoo in my hair and starts rubbing it in. Taking baths together is always a common theme when we're going through a rough patch, taking turns washing each other's hair. When we were kids, we always bathed together, Rain included, but then she grew out of it. But then, when Coy went through a tough breakup as well as a withdrawal, we realized that these baths together were essential for us mentally.

I went to bed, and due to my restless sleep, I was up before the sun. I go outside and do yoga until the sun comes up and warms my face. While I am in warrior two pose, I remembered that today is the sweat ceremony. My hands fall to my side, and I grunt in annoyance.

While in downward dog, I open my eyes and see a coffee cup right under my head. I drop my knees down and look to my right and see Ben standing there in a squatting position.

"What are you doing here?" I ask, shocked.

"To see you?"

I move the coffee off my yoga mat onto the grass and sit in child's pose. Energy starts moving next to me, and I look over and see Ben attempting the child's pose; I don't say anything but rather just watch him. He then suddenly jumps up, feet kicking dirt underneath him. I turn my head down on my mat, pretending I didn't see anything that happened.

I sit up with my butt resting on my heels, "Thought you couldn't deal with having a relationship?"

"I am sorry for what I said and how I acted. I am just trying to figure out how to deal with all the emotions and crazy shit that is going on in my head. So, trying to figure that out and how to incorporate a relationship with it all... I would be lying if I said it wasn't a challenge," he takes a breath and looks around the yard. "I would also be lying if I said it isn't going to be difficult, but if you want to keep trying, then I want to as well."

"I just want to help you and know what is going on," I plead.

"There are just some things I can't tell you. Then there are things that I don't know how to tell you. It was wrong of me to call you selfish. I know you are trying to help. But there are a multitude of reasons why I won't tell you. So trust me on that."

"I don't have a choice, do I?"

"Baby, even if you knew everything, you wouldn't be able to help. It's better if all that wasn't in your head," he taps my head. "Listen, you know about the hallucinations, that's already more than what anyone else knows. So if you know about them, then you can help manage that. And that is how you can help," he kisses the top of my head and puts his hand under my chin so I meet his gaze. I let out a forced smile, but when he returns it with a genuine smile, I can't help but match it. "When is the sweat ceremony?" He asks.

"Uh, like 8 tonight," I say, now lost in gaze and trying to take in everything he has said.

"I will see you then," he kisses the top of my head again and walks away. "Enjoy your coffee," he says before getting into his car, reminding me that it was even there.

Willow

I finish setting up the tents with Coy and my parents for the ceremony, six tents that will be filled with groups of eight and a guide, Lily's parents, my parents, and two of their mutual friends being the guides of a tent. Lily is going in with her mother and six other people who are learning how to become a guide in a sweat ceremony. I decided it would be best to be in a tent with Lily's father. That way, it is someone I am most comfortable around without it being with my parents.

Ben arrives at 7:00 and greets me with a kiss, and I can automatically feel the vibe of uneasiness radiating off of him. He plays it very cool, though, not even showing it. "Do you need help setting up anything?" He asks, while fidgeting with his hands.

"Actually, yeah, do you mind helping my dad bring the stones into the tents?" I ask.

"Sure," he says and walks away.

Coy then walks up next to me while I stand there watching Ben help my dad; "I am going to sit in your tent tonight. I can tell this might get entertaining."

"No. You will make it worse!"

"He just looks so out of place," I know Coy is referring to the fact that Ben is wearing tan cargo shorts and a black t-shirt while everyone else is wearing loose, colorful clothing. "I am glad he came, though," he then adds.

"Me too," he says genuinely and squeezes my hand. "If you need help with anything, let me know," he says and walks away.

Around 8:30 pm, after everyone has arrived and mingled a bit, everyone goes into their tent. Ben and I walk to our tent, and I grab his hand, filling my hand with sweat. We get into the tent, and the heat fills your body as soon as you walk in.

"Ahh, perfect," Lily's dad says. Everyone takes a seat in a circle around the pit of hot stones on their pillows. In our tent, it is Ben and I, the other guide's daughter and son, and their friends.

"Thank you all for coming. My name is Tet, and I will be your guide in this journey. This experience is to let go of the negativity and let in the light. We will go around the circle and share a little information about ourselves so that we create a relationship with each other. I will then light some incense, and we will sit here for a little bit, and then you will tell everyone what you want to let go of. Fairly easy. This tent is a safety area; there is no judgment, no reason to be scared or nervous. Everyone here has a purpose, and I want to help you through it. Whatever emotion arises in this ceremony, it is encouraged for you to act upon it."

"Aspen, do you want to start?" Tet looks over to Aspen, who is sitting to his left. Her long black hair is pulled into a braid, and she is wearing a white skirt with a black tank top. "Hello, my name is Aspen. I am currently growing cannabis in my backyard and selling it to people who need it medically but are unable to get it legally. I love helping people."

"Hey, everyone, I am Ivy," I look over at Ivy, and she has this dirty blonde shoulder-length hair that is curled nicely. She is wearing a dark green dress that hangs off her shoulder, her voice sounding almost childlike. She waves to everyone, "I am currently attending school to get a degree in nursing. This is my second time coming to one of these, and the last time it was uplifting and empowering. So I am happy to be here again," she then turns to Ben, "I have never met you!" And hugs him, and he wraps his arms around her, hugging her back.

And for some reason, I felt *jealous*. Ivy is beautiful, but she seems traditional. Like the type of girl that his mother would love, and that is what made me jealous.

Ben cracks his knuckles as it was his turn to introduce himself, "Hello, I am Ben. I uhh, I have never been to one of these. The past four years I was serving in the army," he says, then looks down.

I start talking right away so he doesn't feel awkward, "I am Willow, I am not new to this! I have been feeling a wave of new emotions, and I am trying to understand them. I am hoping this will allow me to grasp them a bit better."

Tet lights the incense once everyone finishes their introduction. He shakes it around the room so the scent is everywhere, then he rests it near the stones so they continue to burn and starts to play a singing bowl.

I look over and see Ben put his face down into his hands. I then start to feel slightly lightheaded; it has been a while since I have done this, and I forgot how. If you haven't done it in a while, it is easier to feel out of it and can hallucinate. I see flowers growing on the tent walls, and it makes me feel jovial. Then, in the slightest whisper, I hear Ben say, "Why are you here?" His head is still in his hands.

"No, you need to leave," his voice was slightly louder. "No, that's not what it is. That isn't what I am doing." I put my hand on his back, and he jumps up and looks at me. "Tell them that's not what I am doing," he says to me.

"Who?" I ask.

He looks around the tent and comes closer to me, whispering in my ear, "All the men think I am converting."

"Who is Reynolds?" I ask. Part of me asks because I am out of it and not thinking straight, but another part of me knows he is not fully aware of what is going on, and I can use it to find out answers. It is selfish and stupid, but the part of me that is not coherent can't make me stop.

He jumps back a little and shakes his head, "No, he isn't here. No…"

Aspen must have overheard us talking and said, "He is right outside the tent."

"Willow, tell me he isn't here. Tell me," his voice is frantic, and before I can answer, he says an answer that I have been searching for: "He is going to stab me again."

My tongue is nearly swollen, and I can't respond right away. Ivy puts her hands on Ben's face and twists his head so he is facing her.

"Nobody is here, Ben," then kisses him. My stomach drops. He doesn't do anything, doesn't get intimate, but also doesn't pull back. Her hands still on his face, she sits up on her knees, and her dress falls off her shoulders even more. She then lets go of his face, "Nobody is here," she says again.

Ivy stands up and starts dancing, and I look over at the two other guys in the tent, and they are making out. Aspen is looking at the incense closely, watching it burn. Ben is sitting there looking down at the ground.

"What are you thinking?" I ask Ben.

He looks up at me, "I killed Nelson."

"Ben, what are you talking about?" I ask, scared.

"I saw them take him, and I didn't do anything about it. I killed him. I have killed so many people. They're all dead because of me."

"That's not true," I didn't know what to say because it is true. They are dead because of him.

"They won't leave me alone. Nobody will," he turns his head and looks at Ivy. "She kissed me," he then smirks a little.

"I saw," my voice slightly annoyed at his reminder. He then grabs the back of my neck and kisses me. His warm tongue pressing against mine, getting me aroused, I climb on top of his lap and get more aggressive in my kissing.

"I need to know what it is like to have you naked on me," he whispers in my ear.

"Trust me, I want to be," I suddenly feel hands grab my face and twist my head, and when I open my eyes, I notice it is Ivy, and she starts to kiss me. I suppose sweat ceremonies bring out an erotic emotion in her. She then lets go of me and turns to Ben and starts kissing him. I stay sitting on his lap, watching them kiss.

"I forgot to mention I am also a therapist to help people learn better ways to have sex," she whispers to Ben.

"I'm already pretty good at sex," he then pulls away from Ivy and pulls me back in to kiss me. I selfishly think about how I wish I knew if he was any good at sex.

Ivy grabs the back of my neck again and puts her hand on my left breast, grasping it firmly. Ben gets hard while I sit on his lap and he watches. She moves her hand onto my thigh, slowly moving it up, and then she starts to rub me through my underwear. I pull my face away from hers and go to kiss Ben. Suddenly, I then hear Coy's voice behind me saying, "Is this an orgy tent?" Ben then pushes me off of him and jumps up.

He looks over at Ivy, "You fucking lied."

"What?" She looks at him with scared eyes.

Ben turns and looks at me, "Why is he here? Why is he here?"

"Who?" I ask.

"Reynolds. Why is he here?" I look over at Coy and believe that Ben thinks it is Reynolds. Coy starts walking over to me, and as soon as he is standing in front of me, Ben pushes me behind him. "Don't come near her."

"It's just Coy," I try to bring him back to reality.

He puts his hands over his ears and looks down, "That's not true. That's not true, I didn't," I stand in front of him and pull his hands down from his ears.

"You're okay," I grab his face to kiss him, and he pulls away.

"I can't."

"Ben…"

"Willow, please let me go. I can't be in here," he walks out, and I start to follow, and Coy stops me.

"Let me go," Coy then walks out of the tent, leaving me standing there with sweat covering my body.

Ben

I wake up in Willow's bed and turn around to say good morning to her and realize Coy is the one lying next to me. "What are you doing here?" I ask, rubbing my eyes.

"You were pretty out of it last night. I didn't want to leave you alone. Plus, I am more trained with fucked up people than Willow."

"Should I even ask what happened?"

"I got there at the end. You yelled at me to get away from Willow. I think you thought I was some guy named Robbins… Regan… Reynolds!"

"Shit."

"You know Willow is going to question you up and down."

I get up and walk out of the bedroom, and see Willow sleeping on the couch. "You're going to tell her? I swear to god, kid, if someone finds out… If someone comes knocking on my door asking questions, I will slit your throat. You ruined enough of my life." Reynolds' voice threatens from behind the couch.

His words mean nothing to me anymore, "I don't care."

"While you're dead, I will take care of your girl."

"You're not even actually here. It doesn't matter what you say."

"No, but you know I am real and I can show up anywhere, anytime, you dumb shit."

"He isn't there," Coy says behind me.

"I am going home. Can you just, I don't know, tell Willow," I stammer to Coy.

"Yeah, I will take care of it."

My mom is on a ladder on the stairs trying to hang a picture when I get back home. "Hi, sweetie," she says to me when I close the front door.

"Need help?" I ask and walk to the ladder. She comes down from the ladder and hands me the picture of her, Paul, and Sean. It is replacing the spot where a picture of her, my dad, and me once hung.

I think back to the time that the picture of all of us came crashing down. I lay in my bed while my parents were out for dinner. My mom already knew about the affair, but they wanted to try to work it out. I knew better than to have any hope that their marriage could be salvaged, and this dinner wouldn't help it. Their fights were constant and daily, and tonight was no different when I heard the door slam behind them when they came home. My mom went running up the stairs into their bedroom,

"Get out, just get out already!" She yelled. "I can't believe you would do this to me, to your son!"

I came out of my room to look at what was going on and saw my mom standing over the banister, throwing clothes down at my dad, who was standing below. "What is going on now?" I asked.

"Why don't you tell your son what is going on?" Her voice fills the house.

I looked down and saw my dad standing there with tears rolling down his face, something I had never seen before. "I didn't want to tell you like this," he sniffled.

"What did you fuck up now?" I questioned.

"Tell him. Tell him what you are doing to us," my mom demanded with tears pouring down her face.

"I am moving to Seattle," he said nervously. "Sophia is pregnant…"

My mother grabbed the picture of all of us from the wall and threw it over the banister, smashing it only inches away from my dad.

"We're not a family anymore," she wept before going to her room.

I look down at my mom, Paul, and Sean smiling in this picture, and almost feel angry or sad. As if it is a replacement of my dad and me, and even though nothing sat on the wall, why did she find the need to put something up now? "Just because dad isn't your husband anymore doesn't mean I'm not your son," I say, and climb up the ladder, hanging the picture on the nail that was still jammed into the wall.

"Ben, we took that picture a year ago. I'm not replacing you." I start to head up the stairs to my room, "What else am I supposed to do, Ben?"

I turn around and look at her, "What do you mean?"

"I am not the one who left. I fought so hard for your father. He was the love of my life, and it still pains me not to be with him some days. I love Paul, and he has done so much for this family, more than you know. But there are still times that I wish your father would walk through that door and tell me he loves me. He has moved on, and I needed to as well."

It breaks my heart hearing that, the sorrow in her voice. "I'm sorry," I say and go to my room. I close my bedroom door behind me and think about whether I should be mad at my father for what he did, but it's as if I can't get angry. And as petty as it feels, I am mad I am not in that picture with them. I am mad I'm not in a picture with my dad and his new family. I am mad that I'm not *in* a family.

I call my dad, "Hello?" He asks.

"Hey, Dad," I say back. "I was just wondering if you were coming here any time soon."

"Yeah, I can fly in soon."

"Can you bring everyone?" I know he will appreciate me asking about them.

"Yes!" he says enthusiastically.

"Daddy, who is that?" I hear a little voice on the other line.

"It's your brother Ben, Bella," he responds to the voice.

"Hi Ben!" She yells into the phone.

A giant smile fills my face, "Hi Bella!" I reply.

"Sweetie, go play in the other room while I talk to your brother."

He says, then a few seconds later, he asks, "Are you okay?"

"I don't know," I clarified truthfully.

"What is going on?" He inquires, his voice soft and comforting.

"I guess just a hard time adjusting. It's not like I thought everyone's life would just stop while I was gone. But I didn't think it would move on so quickly."

"When I flew in every time from Seattle and saw you and your mother, I felt the same way. Especially with you, I didn't want your life to stop because I left. But every time I saw you, it was like seeing a new person."

"I just feel as if I don't have a place."

"Ben, you will always have a place. But you're a new person now, your attitude has changed, you have grown up. You're not the kid who would ride his bike up and down the driveway or throw parties when we went out of town. Nobody knows you, just like you don't know anybody."

"I guess I just need my dad right now."

"I will look at flights, and we will come in as soon as we can. Okay?"

"Okay," I say, then hang up quickly.

"Mommy and daddy don't love you anymore?" Reynolds says, leaning on my door.

I throw my phone at him, "Leave me the fuck alone!"

"Just take the Seroquel. I'll go away then."

"Shut up."

"Oh, you don't want to be remembered as a crazy person? I am going to destroy you, right back."

"How is my family? Did you see them?" I look up and see Nelson standing right next to Reynolds. "Do you even know what they did to me when they took me?"

"Damn, you ruined my life and Nelson's!" Reynolds says. "Nelson, enlighten us on what happened to you."

"I don't want to hear it!" I say to them.

"They didn't feed me for weeks, then when they did, they gave me actual goat shit. They ripped out all my fingernails. They made me sit outside all day long and would pour boiling water on my sunburn."

"So, what you're saying is that you died very painfully?" Reynolds says.

"I can't imagine anything more painful," he answers.

"Think about all the other people you didn't save, all the women crying out to you, begging you to help them and save them."

A woman then stands at the doorway of my bathroom, crying and shouting, "Help." Then another one appears next to her, and another, and then a younger girl stands right in front of me.

"Why didn't you help us? I spoke English, you knew what I was saying," the young girl says to me.

"Look at all these people, you ruined all of their lives," Reynolds says. "There is more too, do you want me to bring them in?"

"STOP! Please just stop. Stop," I put my head in my hands and close my eyes.

"Why didn't you protect us?" The girl says to me again.

I drop down to my knees in front of her, "What was I supposed to do? What do you all want me to do? Why are you here?"

"You let me die. You let me die in the worst way possible. Why didn't you say anything?" The girl keeps saying.

"I am sorry! What do you want? Just tell me."

"I didn't die peacefully, you don't get to live peacefully," she answers.

I just sit there with my head down, then arms wrap around me. I don't even need to open my eyes to know it is Willow sitting in front of me. She pulls me up and brings me over to my bed, and lies next to me in bed and scratches my head, her head lying on my chest. Her fingers reach up to my dog tag, and she rubs it, looking at my name embedded in it. She then grabs my coin that rests behind it and stares at it.

"What's this?" Her voice is low.

"Uh, it's a souvenir. I found it somewhere," I take it from her hand and hold it until I fall asleep.

"Not again, Ben," the sound of my mother's voice wakes me up. The mental breakdown was enough exhaustion, but not enough to help me stay asleep all night; the Ambien had to do that. I don't even turn over to look at her. But I can tell that Willow is no longer in bed with me, and it isn't long until I hear her next to my mom.

"Babe, why don't we go outside? It's nice out, and it would be good to get fresh air right now," Willow attempts to encourage me.

"Can someone just close the door?" I grumble.

"Benjamin Phillips, you're not doing this shit again," my mother shouts at me.

"Just go take care of your other son," I attack back.

"Is he on something?" She questions Willow.

"No," she lies without hesitation, and I can't help but smirk.

My mother stomps her feet across the room and lands next to me. I assume she is going to check on me, but I hear her open the nightstand drawer with full force. There is no energy left in me to try and stop her. She gasps, "What is this?" The pill bottles shake as she takes them out.

"Please just get out," I sigh.

"I'm taking these," she tells me.

"Do you just pick and choose when you want me to be your son?"

"What is this whole kick you're on today about you not being my son? Am I a bad mother? Do I not take care of you?" I don't answer her, and I hear her throw the pill bottles across the room. "I don't know what you want, Benjamin."

"Thought you said you were taking them?" I provoke her.

"What is going on?" I hear Phil say from the hallway.

"Just know he gets in these depressive states sometimes, Willow."

My mom warns Willow.

I then hear the door close and the lights shut off. Willow comes crawling onto the bed and lies back down next to me. "You hungry?" She asks. I don't answer and just close my eyes again.

I lose track of the days, but I am guessing it has been about two, and Willow hasn't left my side the entire time, unless it is to go downstairs and eat. She doesn't ask questions or try making me talk to her, which is nice because I don't want to talk.

With my back to my door, I hear it open and assume it is Willow coming in after she finished her breakfast, but then I hear an unexpected voice say, "Hey, son," I don't turn around and look at my dad right away, wishing that he had just waited a few more days to come here, so he doesn't see me like this.

He then sits at the end of my bed, "Sophia and the kids are coming in two days. I called your mom, telling her I was coming in, and she told me you weren't being yourself, so I came alone," I don't answer him. "She said that this has happened before. She also said she found some pills."

"She makes it sound like I am on drugs," I finally respond.

"She didn't tell me what they were, I don't think she even knows."

Anything I should be concerned with?" He asks.

"Just for sleeping and anxiety and shit. But no."

"I am staying in the guest room until Sophia gets here. If you need me, I will be here," he says and then gets up. "I met your girlfriend by the way. She really cares about you," he tells me. As he gets up, I grab his arm, and he looks over at me.

"Thanks for coming," I warmly tell him.

"You could have called sooner," I let go of his arm, and he pats me on the chest.

Willow

The sound of light whispering wakes me up, and when I roll over to check on Ben, I notice he isn't in bed anymore. It takes me a second for my eyes to adjust to the darkness, but the moon is nearly full and lights up the room just enough for me to see him standing by his bathroom door. When I go to sit up in the bed, there is a wetness on the sheets, and the sense of wrongness fills my body when I realize that he must have wet the bed in his sleep. I take a deep breath before I get out of bed, not knowing what I am about to walk into.

"Babe," I say to him while walking up to him. In a low whisper, I hear him just saying I am sorry, I don't know what you want. "Ben," I say.

He turns around and grabs me by the shoulders, "You should leave," his face looks blank, even though he is looking at me; it's as if he's looking right through me. I realize very quickly he is hallucinating and doesn't know it. Even though we have been through this before, I can't help but feel scared. Coherent Ben would protect me from everything possible, but I don't feel so safe around this version of Ben. Research on this didn't get me too far on the topic either. All I can do is use my best judgment.

"Hey, I know this feels pretty real, but it's just me, Willow," I calmly and slowly tell him.

With no hope, he says to me, "I will take care of him, just hide over there," he points to the bed and walks into his bathroom. I follow behind him and see him standing over his sink, looking into the mirror.

"Just leave her alone," he says. His voice then getting louder, "I said leave her alone." A coil of dread tightens in my gut, and I take a few steps back as his voice grows louder, "Don't fucking touch her." The mirror then shatters everywhere, and his knuckles are covered in blood.

My natural reaction is to run up to him and grab his hand to look at it. The glass is stuck between his knuckles, and blood starts pooling in droplets in the bathroom sink. I push the rock in my stomach down and pull out a piece of glass from his hand and throw it in the sink. He hasn't reacted, and I have no clue where his mind is right now.

"Let's get in the shower so I can clean you off," I turn him around, shutting and locking his bathroom door behind me. My hands guide him over to the shower, stepping over the few pieces of glass that scatter around on the floor. We both get into the shower, and I throw the water on whatever setting it lands on, in hopes it helps him come back to reality.

His arms reach up instinctively while I pull his shirt up off of him, his legs stepping out of his shorts when I tug them down. It turns out that he feels even larger when he is naked. I look down at myself and see my shirt has blood splatter on it, and I undress myself, throwing both of our clothes on the bathroom floor.

This is the first time we have been this close together while naked, and I can't help but take a second to admire him while I wash him with the bar of soap. His muscles created valleys in his torso, scars etched in him to create a story of his pain, his tan body showing in even the dim light.

The sound of a knock on the bathroom door brings me back to the fact that this isn't a romantic moment where I can take time to take him all in.

"What is going on?" I hear his mom ask, panic filling her voice.

"Nothing," I yell out. But then she keeps knocking.

I then hear his dad say from outside the door, "What is going on?"

"What the fuck are you doing, dude?" Ben starts asking me as he pushes my hand away from him.

"Ben, it's me. It's your GIRLFRIEND."

"Willow, open the door," his mom demands outside the door.

"Ben, I need you to snap out of it like right now," I plead knowing that his parents are going to end up seeing him like this.

"NOW, Willow," his mom demands again.

Then I say the first thing I could think of, "We're having sex," I wince at my comment.

"Then why isn't he saying anything, Mike? I know I heard glass break," I hear his mom whisper to his dad. Then a second later, I hear the door slam open. "I told you there is glass," his mom exasperates as she bulldozes into the bathroom.

"What are you doing?" Ben pokes his head around the shower curtain to look at his mom. I can tell by his voice he is coherent. His voice is less defensive and softer, just irritated.

"What is going on?" She asks. My eyes shutting as I am completely cringing inside.

"What do you think is going on?" He says rhetorically.

"I told you," his dad says, and then the door closes.

Ben pulls his head back in the shower and looks at me, "Do I want to ask?"

"You peed in your sleep and punched a mirror, that is the short version."

He looks down at his knuckles, "Yeah, I noticed that part," Tthen looks back up at me. His hands grip my shoulders and he pushes me back and looks me up and down, "Did I hurt you?" He asks me.

I shake my head no.

"Are you mad at me for some reason?" Concern filling his voice. I shake my head no again. "Perfect, because even though I have no idea what the hell just happened, I am very aware that you are naked in front of me and I would be a fucking fool to ignore that."

In a swift move, he pushes me against the shower wall, and my heart thumps hard enough for him to feel it against his chest. His finger drags from the inside of my thigh until he reaches my swollen vagina lips that are also pulsing.

"Our timing is so fucked up on this, isn't it?" He says quietly in my ear.

"Slightly," I breathe heavily while his other finger joins in, lightly touching my vagina and I clench in anticipation.

"Something about seeing your face in the toughest times just really makes me want to touch you. And you'd be lying if you said you didn't feel the same. Because it's not just the shower that is making you this wet, is it?" He finally inserts his fingers inside of me, and I moan at the release of anticipation, but I tighten around his fingers in need of more. His thumb slightly grazes over my clit in a circular motion. I wrap my arm around his neck to hold myself steady, his other arm reaching behind my back to help stabilize me as his fingers move faster inside of me.

I use my other hand to push him back ever so slightly so I can see his abs because no man who has felt like he's made of marble has touched me like this. My hands trace the lines of his body, slowly making their way down to his shaft. I hear him let out a slight moan when my hands touch him, unable to fully grasp his hard dick with one hand. He starts kissing my neck, starting from my ear and moving his mouth down to my collarbone, his fingers never slowing in motion.

"Let go of me," he says in between kisses. My hand drops off from his dick, and he grabs it instantly, pinning it behind me. Suddenly, his fingers come out of me, and he puts them in his mouth. "Exactly what I have imagined. Tell me, Willow, what is that you want?"

I look at him wide-eyed, "Right now? I think it's pretty obvious," I say in between breaths that I am trying to catch.

"I want to hear it," his other hand grabs my other arm, and he pins it behind me, pushing his chest closer to me while keeping his still hard dick away from touching me.

"You in every way," I say to him.

"I can't give you that, but I can give you a great fucking orgasm," he lets go of my arm and puts his fingers back in me. His fingers curl inside me as they hit the perfect spot, and I start tightening myself around him, needing more of it. He was right, it isn't the shower that is making me this wet. His thumb continues to strum my clit, each finger doing its job perfectly. He takes my nipple into my mouth as I am on the rise of my climax. The warmth of his mouth around me sends all the nerves in my body into action.

"Ben," I moan out louder than I should.

"Go ahead, baby, let it out," he says, then puts my nipple back into his mouth, tugging on it with his teeth. And that sends me into full release. I grab the back of his neck again to try to keep myself up, "That's right," he holds me up with his free arm while his fingers slow down to let me come down from my release.

When my orgasm slows down and I can let out a breath I yell, "fuck!"

"That's a moan that sounds way better than I could have imagined," he kisses me, slipping his tongue into my mouth and I accept it fully.

He was right again, that was a great orgasm.

Ben

My father and I sit by the water on overly priced lawn chairs, the cicadas buzzing in the near distance and frogs croaking to one another. The rest of the family went to Paul's sister's house for dinner, which I think my mother purposely did just to see if my dad could get answers from me.

"So what is going on, kid?" He says after a few minutes of silence.

"Which part?" I cross-question.

"Any part."

I don't answer right away, trying to figure out where I should even start. The fact that he is even here right now makes me feel comforted, "Well, I guess to start, mom still isn't over you. Not sure if that has anything to do with anything, but it has been lingering in my head," my dad's presence, despite everything, brings an ease to me.

He sighs, "How do you feel about that?" He asks.

"That mom still isn't over you? I don't know. I think I just feel bad for her right now in general because I know I am pissing her off."

"I don't think you're pissing her off. I think she is just confused. Are you angry with me for your mother?" I look over at him and see him looking at me, scared to know my answer.

"No. I mean, you went about the marriage and divorce the wrong way, but I don't hate you for not wanting to be with mom."

I think back to when I found out my dad was having an affair. I sat at his computer and went to email my teacher a paper, and when I went into the emails, I saw an email from Sophia. The email talked about hotel arrangements in Hilton Head and ended with an "I love you" and a "can't wait to spend the weekend alone with you."

I went up to my dad and said, "How is Sophia?"

He didn't even turn and look at me, but said, "She is good," apprehensive to answer.

I then replied and said, "I bet she is good at fucking." He was so shocked, he didn't even answer. I found later that my mom already knew about it, so I didn't have to break the bad news.

"Anything else you want to talk about?" My dad then asks.

"Is this about last night?" I crack open a cold beer and start to drink it.

"Sure, if that is what you want to talk about."

I debate on telling him about my hallucinations, but the unknown of how that conversation will go puts that thought aside. "No. Not really."

"I probably would have ended things with Sophia if she didn't get pregnant," he then says while looking out to the water.

I look over at him, "You should probably use a condom if you're going to have an affair," I say lightly to not offend him.

He sighs, "Yeah, guess so." We sit there quietly for a little bit and then he continues to say, "Did your mom ever tell you about the time she cheated on Paul?"

I look at him, shocked and confused, "No, With who?"

He raises his hand, "Me. It was a couple of months before the divorce was final and I came back one time and Paul was out of state for a conference, you were at some party and I stopped by. We got a little drunk and one thing led to another. I think she just loved the idea that I was cheating on Sophia with her. That is what drove her to do it. It had nothing to do with Paul or me, it was revenge on Sophia. She wanted to go to bed that night knowing that she slept with me behind her back."

"Jesus," I say surprised.

"Don't mess things up with Willow like I did with your mom," he looks over at me and we both take a long sip of our beer. He reaches into his pocket and pulls out two cigars, handing me one.

"I don't plan on it. But it wouldn't surprise me if she didn't feel like dealing with my shit. I put her through enough," we light our cigars and take a slow draw from it, letting the smoke fill the air between our thoughts.

"If she cares about you like I think she does, she will deal with it. I talked to her a bit when I got here, and she is something else. A breath of fresh air, I would say."

"Trust me, I know."

"I know you didn't want to talk about last night, and you're a grown man, but we don't need to have a conversation about protection, right? Since I lacked in that department," he asks with an uncomfortable chuckle.

"That would involve us having sex. So no, I don't need the talk," I stand up and pick up a rock, skipping it on the water.

"Wait, but I thought you were? At least, according to last night, that is what it seemed like."

"Nope. I had a nightmare, pissed the bed, and she was helping me in the shower," I don't look back at him to see his facial expression.

"Makes more sense as to why you didn't say anything. You weren't kidding about putting her through some shit, huh."

"Speaking of me being a grown man, my birthday is in a week. I think Mom said she is going to have people over Saturday for a birthday gathering party thing. If you are still here."

"Yeah, we were going to leave on Friday, but we can stay for an extra day."

We sit in silence as we smoke our cigars and drink our beer. He breaks the stillness in the air when he grabs my upper arm, and we both look at each other. "Care for some fatherly words?" He asks, raising his eyebrow. "I will give it regardless. If you love this girl, I want you to know something about her. She is terrible at lying, and from the conversation I had with her, which of course I asked her a bit about how you're doing, she is holding a lot of shit in. Don't put all that on her."

I nod my head because what in the actual fuck do I say to that?

Willow comes walking out of her house to the car, and I get out to greet her. Despite her pastel striped dress that comes down to her shins, she looks tempting. My mind can't help but wonder if she is wearing underwear under that dress because it is obvious she is not wearing a bra. Her hair is in a high ponytail tail leaving her neck exposed and waiting for my lips to caress it.

I bite my knuckles as she approaches, "Am I a lucky guy or what?" I say and pull her in for a kiss, my hand reaches behind her back to make sure she is close enough to me. She bites my lower lip lightly before she pulls away and gets in the car.

The restaurant is lowly lit, and the aroma of Italian food enters your nose the second you walk in. I can see my father and his family sitting at the table when we enter, and the kids are sitting still in their chairs, coloring, teasing each other by drawing on the other one's paper, but keeping the bickering to a low sound and playful.

"Your dad's girlfriend looks younger than me," Willow leans over to me as we approach the table.

"She probably is, Will," I respond.

Sophia stands up and comes to hug us once we get to them. I understood the appeal of Sophia. She knew her strongest attributes were her legs and she always made sure to show them off.

"You don't even look the same!" She grabs my forearms and does a look over at me. The last time I saw her was before they moved to Seattle. It was a brief meet and greet and she wasn't showing her pregnancy yet. And with the way she looks right now, it looks as if those kids were never in her.

"You look exactly the same. This is Willow," I introduce.

"It is nice to meet you," Willow says, hugging her.

"This is Marco and Bella," My dad says, introducing my brother and sister. They both wave to us shyly from across the table.

Our glasses are full of red wine before our asses meet the chair.

"If you don't mind me asking," Willow starts to say, "How old are you, Sophia? You look so young to have children," Willow turns her head to the side when she asks, her voice soft.

"I am turning 30 in two months," Sophia responds while helping Bella draw a picture.

"Wow, so you were only 19 when you had Marco?" Willow asks.

"About that," she answers awkwardly and nervously. My eyes narrow toward my dad as he looks down while fiddling with his napkin. I never did the math about her age, but I am sure my mother did.

"That is so young. Well, you seem like a great mother. How long did you and Mike know each other before you had Marco?" She asks, taking a sip of her wine.

"Hey, Will. We don't need to talk about how long my dad had an affair before he accidentally got his mistress pregnant. Okay?" I whisper in her ear.

"My dad says you were in the army," Marco breaks the silence that I created.

"I was, yes," I place my hand on Willow's thigh to keep myself grounded.

"I want to be in the army one day," he says. "Did you shoot your gun a lot?" And there it was, the question that every little boy asks, and I don't want to answer.

My dad must have felt my uneasiness as well as his own, "Marco, you don't ask those types of questions," he commands him.

"Did you ever get shot?" He then asks. My dad turns and looks at me, wanting to know the answer but not wanting to hear it.

"Yeah," I answer quickly.

"Did it hurt?" He asks almost excitedly, like it was an action movie.

"Yeah, it hurts a lot."

"Where?" He starts looking around at my arms.

"Marco, enough," my dad snarls at him.

"My shoulder and arm," I answer.

"That's so cool. You are like a real-life superhero. Did you ever throw a grenade?" His voice was still excited.

My dad didn't think it was very cool, though, he slams his fist down on the table, "God dammit, Marco. I said enough."

Sophia puts her hand on my dad's shoulder, "Mike," her voice defensive.

"No, I don't need to imagine my son getting shot at, and he doesn't need to relive it. When I say enough, I mean it," the anger and pain in my dad's voice get the point across to everyone at the table.

Lost in my hardships, I forget that everyone else has to face them alongside me. The thought of telling them what has happened to me is harder than actually living through it all.

Sophia gets up from the table to bring Bella and Marco to the bathroom, Willow following along. I lean closer to the table to whisper to my dad, "Do I even want to know how old she was when you started the affair?"

"Nope," he replies and drinks his wine.

Willow comes walking back to the table with Bella in her arms and sits down next to me with Bella in her lap. "I made a friend," Willow says to me with a smile on her face.

"I can see that," I say gleefully.

"I also learned a secret," she says to me.

"What is it?"

"I can't tell, you'll find out soon."

My dad then says, "Okay, well, Sophia just told Willow so I might as well say it now." I look at Willow, then my dad, and I can feel where this is going. "Sophia is pregnant."

A wave of emotions hit me, and the first thing I say is, "Was this one a mistake too?"

"Ben," Willow says.

"I'm sorry but why didn't you tell me this last night?" I ask my dad.

"Sophia wanted to be here when I told you," his voice coated in guilt.

"And I didn't want Sophia to ruin our family, but here we are."

"Ben, uncalled for," Willow warns me, trying to make sure I don't take it any farther.

"No, I feel betrayed right now. Yesterday would have been a fine time to tell me. Yesterday, when I was telling you how my girlfriend had to help in the shower. Or when you were telling me-"

My father cuts me off before I can reveal any secrets that he told me, "Ben," he says sternly as a warning.

"Yesterday, when we were having a personal conversation, would have been a fine time to tell me," I get up from the table, shoving my seat away from me, leaving the echoes of screeches as I leave, "I just need a second."

I walk outside and walk down the street a little bit until I hear footsteps running after me, "Hey!" I look behind me and see Willow ignoring her call-out.

She runs in front of me and stops, "What?" I ask her, raising my eyebrows.

"Is it cause he is having another baby?"

"It's because he didn't tell me. I sat there in front of him and we told each other personal shit, and he couldn't tell me that? It's because he is having children left and right, and I'm having my issues with our sex life because I can't touch you without a voice telling me I am assaulting you. It's because I don't even know how to hold a baby. I never held a baby that's aliv…"

"You'll learn how to hold one," she tries to comfort me, cutting me off before I can say words we both don't want to hear. "Did you tell him about the hallucinations?"

"No, I told him I had a bad dream and pissed the bed, and you were helping," I answer with irritation.

"You aren't assaulting me…" she then says.

"Will, please," I grab the bridge of my nose and close my eyes.

"Well, you aren't."

"Yes, I know. But when you have a voice in your head saying you are and then making comments about you, I can't do it."

"Who is the voice?" She asks, not caring about the repercussions of the question.

"Willow, just stop," I warn her again.

"Is it that Reynolds guy you always briefly mention and are terrified of? The one that stabbed you?"

I look at her, surprised, "What?" I never told her about that.

"You said it in the tent. You told me he stabbed you. That's why you're all cut on your back." I don't answer her, "Did… did he sexually assault you?"

"Jesus Christ, Willow," I start walking away from her.

"What am I supposed to think, Ben? The only information I ever get from you is when you're hallucinating."

"No, Willow. It wasn't like that. He-" and before I can say it, there he is.

"You have got to be kidding. You made it this far. I knew it, I knew you would tell. This bitch won't keep her mouth shut. But I know what will," he unbuttons his pants.

"I'm not going to," I respond.

"He isn't here, Ben. Stop giving him the power," Willow grabs me by the shoulders and looks at me. Reynolds stands behind her. Glaring down at her, scratching his grown-out beard.

"You know I take power no matter what," he spits on the ground and chills run down my spine at the noise.

"Everyone, please stop talking," I plead.

"It is only me talking."

"If you want, I can stop her," he walks up closer behind her.

"Willow, please. Please just stop."

"Please stop, oh please!" Reynolds mimics in a high-pitched voice. "If I had a penny for every time I heard that," he looks over her shoulder while making eye contact with me.

"My head is going to explode," I say.

"I bet Nelson's head exploded."

"Will you just shut up?" I yell out.

Willow grabs my face and looks me in the eyes, "It is only me here. Me and you."

"I want to go home," I say.

When I get back home, I tell Willow just to go home so I can talk to my mother. I walk in, closing the heavy wooden door behind me, echoing louder than usual. The sound of the teapot whistling steam comes from the kitchen. My mom stands there by the stove with her black rope tightly tied, "Want some?" She asks when she sees me enter.

I sit down at the kitchen counter, "Sure."

She pulls out another blue and white floral mug from the counter and pours the boiling water in, handing it to me. I don't make eye contact with her and run my finger over the wide mouth of the mug. "How was dinner?" She finally asks.

"Did he tell you?" I ask her.

"Tell me what?" Her face is curious as she is bent over on the kitchen counter, mug in between her hands.

"He is having another kid," I say, slowly looking up at her.

Her body jolts up into a standing position, "Oh. No, he didn't." She doesn't say anything for about a few seconds and then says, "How old is she again? Isn't it dangerous to have a child at this age?"

My stomach turns as I am about to tell her that she is almost 20 years younger than she is. "She is almost 30."

"Oh, right, I forgot your father should be on a sex offender registry," her voice snaps. "Good for them," she says before taking her tea and going upstairs.

Willow

I look in the reflection of my car window, retying my bandana again for added security. My chest feels heavy knowing that I am about to spend the evening with Ben's family and friends tonight. I knock on the front door, and a brown box with a loosely tied blue ribbon sits in my tight grip.

Ben opens the door with a bright smile, wearing a white collared shirt and tan cargo shorts, and black sneakers. I put my hand out that has the little box. "For me?" He asks modestly.

"Well, this is your birthday party, isn't it?"

"And Memorial Day. Don't make it all about me."

I roll my eyes, "Well, doesn't that kind of involve you as well?"

"Nope. Memorial Day is for people who have died." He brings the box up to his ear and shakes it, "Hmm…"

"You will just have to open it later," I say, walking past him to come inside.

"Are you excited to see everyone?" Ben asks, coming up behind me, putting his hand around my lower waist, and leading me to the backyard.

He introduces me to his family, his arm never coming off of me unless it was for me to hug someone hello and even then his fingertips still grazed me.

"Babe, come get another drink with me," Ben says to me after we finish up a conversation with a cousin of his. I follow him to the coolers where the beer is. At this point I have lost count of how many drinks we have and my fuzzy head will not allow me to even attempt to try, granted the weed I smoked beforehand probably doesn't help much.

"Want to do something mischievous?" He then asks, opening another beer.

I shrug, "Sure."

He takes my hand, lacing our fingers together. His feet moving faster than mine can keep up as he leads me to his mother's room, shutting the door behind us.

"I saw this in here one day and I want to know what is in it," he says as he starts to fiddle around with a safe that was in a dresser drawer. A loud beep and a red light kept flashing every time he tried a different set of codes. "It is a different number than she would usually use," his brows furrow as he keeps trying.

"Maybe she doesn't want you in it then," I tell him.

"What would she be hiding?" He says, still putting combinations of numbers in.

"Maybe it's sex toys," I say laughing.

Then, suddenly, a green light appears and a POP sound of the clasps coming undone. "Got it!" He says and opens it.

I look down in the safe and just see papers, "Doesn't seem like anything exciting. It's probably just important documents, in case there's like a fire."

He pulls out a document and holds it up, "Her divorce papers from a decade ago are important documents?" He starts flipping through the document, and I see a birth certificate on the safe.

I pick it up and hold it up to him, "See, just birth certificates." I then look down at the certificate and see Sean's name written on it.

"Why is Paul's name written so much in their divorce agreements?" He asks himself out loud. I look over at him and see his eyes just running through the lines on the page. He then looks down at the other papers in the safe and sees a title on the document that says, "**ADOPTION FORM.**"

"What the fuck is this?" He says, "why is Sean's name on this? Is Sean adopted?"

"Ben," I hand him the birth certificate, and he reads, "Your dad's name is signed on the certificate," I grab the adoption papers from his hand and read them. "Paul adopted Sean."

He rips the paper from my hand and starts walking out of the room. I run after him. "Ben, listen. You don't want to do this now. Just wait. This is a family issue, don't make a scene here," he keeps moving through the house, and I can't catch up to him fast enough. Right before he steps outside the door, I say to him, "This isn't how you want Sean to find out." He stops in his tracks and thinks about it for about five seconds, and then walks out the door.

His mom and Paul are standing together talking to someone, and I look to my left side and see his dad and Sophia saying hello to someone else, since they must've just arrived. It was nearly perfect timing for this conversation to happen; all of them just standing a few feet away from each other.

Ben walks up to his mother, grabs her upper arm, and pulls her a couple of feet from the other guests. I stand closely behind Ben so I can hear what he says, shoving the papers in her chest, "What is this?" He asks angrily. She pulls the papers out of his hands and looks at them.

Her face red with shock and embarrassment, "Where did you find these?"

"It doesn't matter, what are they?"

Paul then comes up next to his confused wife and drunk, hostile step-son. "Everything okay?" He asks, unsure what he is walking into.

"What is it?" Ben's voice is growing louder and deeper.

His dad then walks over to them, leaving Sophia with guests who must be mutual friends of theirs. "What is going on over here?" His voice is stern and yet smoothing, it was such a *dad* tone of voice. I see so much of Ben in his father.

Ben grabs the papers from his mom's hand and gives it to his dad, "This."

He looks down at it and quickly realizes what it is, "Damnit Sarah, I thought you hid these."

"I did," she answers defensively.

"It doesn't matter. Can you just explain it?" Ben asks, getting impatient with their banter.

"We will talk about it tomorrow," Sarah says.

"No. We will talk about it now," Ben not budging from his stance.

Sarah sighs, ready to cave into Ben's demands, "A couple years ago your father and I got together…"

"Is this what you told me about the other day?" Ben asks, turning to his father. His father just slightly nods. "I should've put the time frame together," Ben adds quietly.

"You told him about that?" Sarah asks.

"Just keep going," Ben urges her.

"Well, I felt guilty about it and told Paul, which he understood and asked me to go to therapy to work through issues I encountered during the divorce. Once we found out I was pregnant, Paul also learned a month before that he can't have children. I didn't want your father to be a part of this child's life and we all agreed that he would sign his rights over to Paul."

Ben rubs his face, "This… this is insane." He looks over at his dad, "Anything else you want to tell me? Or am I going to find out in a week?" Ben turns around and quickly glances at me and then looks away. His shoulders are stiff as he walks away. I look over at his dad, who has slumped shoulders and sighs multiple times, cursing under his breath.

Quickly, I run up to Ben as he gets another beer from the cooler, "Ben…" I say carefully behind him, not knowing what emotion of his to expect.

"How many kids does this guy need?" He opens the beer and takes a sip. His eyes meet mine, and his eyes are just blank and hollow with emotion. "I need a minute," he says before he tries to walk into the house.

I grab his arm and pull him back to me, "Just tell me you're okay."

His eyes looking down at the ground, "Yeah," trying to pull away.

The thought of him being alone at a time like this makes my heart race. I clutch on to his arm tighter to a point where I will leave nail marks. He looks at me and flashes a smile, then kisses my head before he runs off inside.

Ben's dad grabs my arm as I start to join back with Chris and Jason. "Is he mad?" He asks me, looking past me to see if he can see Ben in the distance.

"I don't understand your relationship with each other, but I know that man is falling and he is trying to grab on to his father. But your hands are too preoccupied to grab him," the anger in my voice surprises me, I bite my tongue before I apologize to him for the aggressive behavior on my end, and I walk away.

The group of friends is drunk when I get back to them, laughing hysterically. I put on my facade, "What did I miss?" I ask with a smile.

Chris's face turns a little red when he looks at me, "Just an embarrassing story about Ben."

"Tell me!" I say excited.

"It's probably not one that you'd want to hear," Chris says, looking down.

"Why not?" I ask, looking around at the rest of the group.

"Because it's a sex story," Jason butts in and says.

"Impossible. He said I was his first," I say, and they all look at each other blankly and then at me, "I am kidding!"

They then start laughing at my small joke, "You really want to hear it?" Jason says.

"Come on, dude. Don't tell it to her," Chris says, backhanding Jason in the chest.

"I wouldn't want to know it," Melissa then says.

My head snaps looking at her, "Well, if everyone knows now, I need to know." My voice is slightly irritated.

"Don't tell him we told you," Chris adds in before Jason tells the story.

"I don't give a shit if you tell him," Jason laughs.

"So one time we had a party while his parents were away and his mom came home early in the middle of the party. Well, Ben was upstairs hooking up with his girlfriend Madison, and his mom walked in on him in the midst of coming on her face. When he told us it was the funniest thing I ever heard," Jason says with a chuckle at the end of the story.

I laugh to mask any insecurities they think I would have, "Did he hook up with a lot of girls back in the day?"

Jason and Chris look at each other then at me, "I mean…" Chris says.

"Yes, when he and Madison were on and off. But those two couldn't stop touching each other when they were together," Jason answers bluntly.

And that was the exact answer I was expecting. The reason as to why not being able to do it now bothers him.

Ben

I lie in bed staring at the ceiling while I hear Willow breathe softly in her sleep. I wrap my arm around her, pulling her closer to me. She turns over and nestles her head into my chest.

"Why are you still awake?" She asks quietly.

"Restless," I answer.

"Do you need to talk about anything?" Her voice was still hushed.

I kiss the top of her head, and she falls back to sleep in my chest. All of a sudden, I hear voices in my mother's room, and I get up from the bed and go towards my door, cracking it so I can hear them.

"Because he is MY son, Sarah," I hear Paul say.

"Well, I don't mean to tell him right now, Paul. But when he gets older," she responds.

"No! This is my son," his voice was full of anger, and trying not to yell.

"What if he finds out, though, Paul. He will never forgive us."

"Then he won't find out. Mike was just a sperm donor; I am his father."

A pit of guilt sits in my stomach at the thought of me causing this problem. If I had just never opened that safe, this wouldn't have happened. I lie back down in bed next to Willow, and the idea of sleep is far-gone now.

The sun shining through the window tells me it's about 7 am when my mom comes into my room, "Good, you're awake. Time to get up," she says.

"For what?" I ask.

"For the Memorial Day parade," her voice already sounded irritated.

"What parade?"

"The one you are speaking at, the one I told you about last week." She sighs, "You forgot."

"I'm not doing that," I turn over so my back is facing her. Willow shuffles around and starts waking up.

"Ben, I am not dealing with this today. Get up and get ready."

"Mom, I am not going to a parade."

"After the shit you pulled yesterday, yes, you are," her voice was now fully irritated and shaky.

"Oh, you mean find out the truth?" Ready to argue back with her.

After a weak argument but a lot of resilience, I stand at a podium on the same makeshift stage that I stood on when I first arrived in the center of my town with eyes looking up at me to give a speech. Daniel Morris's mom is front and center, looking at me again when nausea sucker punches me right in the stomach. The start of my hangover is coming full force now. Right before I start saying hello to everyone here, a chunk of vomit comes right up to my mouth, I put my hand over my mouth and swallow it.

Daniel Morris stands next to his mom, I close my eyes tightly, knowing this isn't real, he's not here. But when I open my eyes he is still standing there. The town is silent and I just hear him say to me, "Why do you get to be up there and not me?"

I look down at my hands as they rest on the podium sides and see them shaking, I grip on to it to make the shaking subside a bit. "This day is heavy on many hearts," I begin to say.

"Do you wish you were celebrating my death today?" Reynolds says next to me. I jump a little at the surprise of his voice.

"It is a day we recognize the brave men and women who risked their lives. People who I considered my brother."

"Do you consider me as your brother?" He says.

"Thank you for coming," I quickly say and turn around getting off stage. Willow greets me as soon as I get off stage, "I feel like I am going to puke." And as soon as I finish the sentence, Willow's white dress is covered in yellow vomit. She walks me over to the bench behind us and sits me down.

I sit there with my face in my hands and elbows on my knees, and I hear Willow ask someone for water.

"Do you hear my mom up there? Talking about me, telling everyone how brave and loyal I was," Morris says, standing next to me.

"At least he isn't the one who let you die," Nelson then says. "I am a fallen soldier because of him."

"Babe, drink some water," Willow says to me, and I see her hand me a bottle of water under my face. I grab it and start drinking the water slowly, getting another glimpse of the vomit on her dress.

"You let me die and then can't even go to my funeral. You go up there and say we were brothers. You're no brother of mine."

I throw the bottle of water in the direction that Nelson is standing. Willow grabs at my arm to try to get me to stand up, "Come on. Let's get out of here."

While walking to the car, I see a convenience store owned by Frank Langdon. I run inside the store and walk up to the counter, "Uhh, get me a pack of…" I look behind the counter at the different brands of cigarettes that sit there in a row, "Marlboro is fine."

"Hey, kid," he says, "I didn't know you were a smoker." He goes and grabs a pack.

"How much?"

"Don't worry about it," he pushes the white and gold label pack across the counter to me. I tap the pack on the palm of my hand and unwrap it, flipping one of the cigarettes upside down to

227

mark down my last one. "Here," he then puts matches on the counter.

The cigarette is lit between my lips before I even get out of the store. Willow stands up the street, looking at me with her mouth and eyes wide open. We both start walking towards each other and meet in the middle.

She grabs the cigarette out of my mouth, "What is this?"

"I just needed one right now," I grab it back from her.

"Just knew you never smoked," she sounds disappointed.

"I did while I was away."

She starts walking up the street to her car, "I'm ready whenever you are."

"Miller, go check the bodies and collect their shit."
Lieutenant Colby orders. There are only 10 dead men around us.

"Miller, I said, go check the bodies." He demands again.

"Sir, I would really like to not do that." He says.

"Private, I would really like to not be standing in the blistering sun right now. Now go check the god damn bodies."

"Sir, I do not feel comfortable just ransacking the bodies,"

I stand up and shove the gun that I was cleaning into Miller, "Do you feel comfortable cleaning a gun at least?"

I start checking the bodies, taking out any notes they had in their jackets, collecting dog tags, and taking anything that would be valuable to us. I pull out a pack of cigarettes from some guy and wipe the blood off the pack onto my pants. There are only two left but one is his upside down one. I take the other one and put it in my mouth and search around his pockets to find a match.

"I don't know how you can do that," Miller says while standing above me. I stand up so we can make eye contact.

"Do what?"

"Just take things from them," his eyes gazing down at the body at our feet.

"They're dead. They are our brothers, they would want us to take what they have instead of letting it go to waste."

"I just don't see it that way."

"Well, start Miller. If you think that taking some granola bars and cigarettes off of a body is disturbing then you have another thing coming."

Lieutenant Colby walks over, "Miller, you're on shit duty tonight. You're in charge of the burn pile. Maybe that'll teach ya to do what you're fucking told. Now everyone starts loading the bodies in the truck."

Miller and I start picking up some of the bodies and bring them to the back of the truck. As soon as we begin to grab one Colby warns us that there was a bombing in this area and to be careful with the bodies. Seconds later, the body we were picking up splits right in half.

Miller lets go and jumps back, falling on his ass and now hyperventilating. At this point, I am numb to it, and this isn't the *worst thing I have seen. I remember what it's like to be new, where dead bodies aren't an everyday sighting, especially ones that are cut in half while you're carrying them. I have had my fair share of mental breakdowns, and it helps when you have someone there for you.*

I walk up to him and get down to my knees, "I know it's hard, but you gotta push through. It'll get easier to digest it all."

After a Xanax-induced nap, I wake up feeling better than I did at the ceremony. Willow is lying next to me, reading a new book that she has brought over. I woke up just in time because my mother yells that dinner is ready and for us to come downstairs.

"My parents would love to have dinner with you guys one of these days," Willow says during dinner.

"That would be wonderful," my mother says, but I can tell by the tone of her voice that it's something she is not particularly interested in.

"What is your family like?" Paul asks her.

"They're very open and free-spirited. My parents were nudists for most of my childhood."

I look at her, shocked, and whisper, "I didn't know that."

My mom pauses before she puts her fork full of pasta in her mouth, "Nudists?"

"Yes, they believed that covering their body in front of their kids would over sexualize the human body."

"Well, I never allowed my boys to see me naked when they were growing up. I don't think that would be appropriate," my mother says, and then puts her fork in her mouth.

"That is why sex was such a big deal for Ben while he was growing up," I look over at Willow in disbelief that she is talking about my teenage sex life with my mother. Sean just looks up at Willow, but then looks back down at his food. And then she makes her next comment, "How come you circumcised him?"

"Oh my God," I say quietly and pinch the bridge of my nose. I hear my mom put her fork down.

"Uh… I uhm," She tries to gather her words.

"Willow," I turn and say.

"What? It's just a body part. It's like asking about someone's arm. I have just never seen one before."

"Am I circumcised?" Sean then suddenly asks.

"Okay, we're done with this," I interrupt.

Willow and I decide to sleep at her place tonight since I don't even want to look at my mom after the dinner conversation.

"I really wish…" I watch Willow as she goes through her drawers picking out what clothes to get rid of as I sit on her bed.

"What?"

"I don't know, a lot of things."

"What about this shirt?" She holds up a pink and blue flower patterned t-shirt that ties together on the stomach.

"Get rid of."

"You wish what?"

"I wish you didn't invite my mom and Paul for dinner or that you didn't say half the shit you said at dinner."

"Our parents should meet and say what shit at dinner?"

"All of it, actually."

"Ben, everyone has genitals, get over it. I'm sorry your mom decided to cut half of yours off while you were a baby."

"Why do you do that?" I say defensively.

"Do what?" She holds up a denim skirt waiting for me to answer if she should keep it.

"Keep. And say whatever you want."

"Why shouldn't I?"

"Because you need to be sensitive to people's feelings."

"Am I hurting your feelings?" She puts down a red sweater in the toss pile and looks at me with concern.

"No... but..."

"I don't think I say anything that would particularly hurt someone's feelings." Her eyes narrow in at me, waiting for me to challenge her.

"You make me uncomfortable at times, though." I start folding her keep pile back up.

"That is because of your own closed mind, that's not my fault." She shrugs her shoulders and continues looking through her clothes.

"My mom and your parents are going to hate each other." I sigh and learn back on the bed.

"My parents don't hate anyone, other than you," she smirks at me, except we both know it isn't much of a joke.

"Should I show them my gun collection?"

"What collection?" She says, rolling her eyes.

"Right here," I make a muscle with my arms, and she starts laughing hysterically.

"Better be careful, might hurt yourself," she ties a garbage bag full of clothes. "Can you bring this to my parents' house? My mom is going to donate them tomorrow."

I sigh and pick up the bag. When I go outside, I light up my second cigarette of the day. Easing my way back into this shitty habit.

"Bet my sister hates that," I hear Coy say from the chicken coop.

"I'm sure your sister hates plenty of things I do."

He walks up to me and takes the cigarette out of my mouth, and puts it in his. "Never understood the point, doesn't do anything."

"Debatable."

He grabs the bag from my hands, "I can take this up to my parents' house." He puts the cigarette back in my mouth, "Enjoy your night, lover boy."

I sigh and roll my eyes as he walks away. I finish the cigarette on the porch, the cicadas buzzing around to fill the silence.

Willow

"Am I allowed to be present for this?" Coy asks while I help set up the merging of two families' dinner.

"Of course," I kiss his cheek and straighten out the flowers that are in the center of the table.

"Willow, love, can you bring this plate out to the table?" My mom requests from the kitchen. I go grab it and see a beautiful plate full of colorful vegetables with homemade hummus sitting in the center waiting to be dipped in.

As soon as I place the plate on the table, the doorbell rings and I see my mom and dad emerge from the kitchen to open the door. She opens the door and I see Ben standing in front of his parents wearing dark jeans and a white and blue flannel, his growing hair pushed back.

"Hello, Ben," my mom says, hugging him and as she pulls away her forearm grazes his gun that is holstered. "Are we being robbed?" She says playfully.

"Good thing the military is here in case the veggies get out of hand," my dad then says and hugs him as well.

Sarah and Paul then walk in behind Ben and Sarah looks elegant like usual. She is wearing jeans that are cuffed and boots that have a slight heel. She is covered in a cream-colored turtle neck sweater with her hair pulled back into a low bun.

"Hello, I am Sarah, and this is Paul," she says to my parents.

"Wonderful! I am Joy, and this is Jerry," my parents do their usual greeting and kiss both of them, and Sarah and Paul just stand there for a few seconds afterwards in near shock. "Please, please, come in," my mom says backing up so they can walk in more.

I walk up to Ben and whisper in his ear, "Scale of one to ten, how excited are you?"

He looks at me with his hazel eyes, just piercing at me, and my stomach does a flip, "It's a negative."

"Here, come sit in the living room while the dinner finishes. Can I get you something to drink?"

"Do you have red wine?" Sarah asks.

"Yes, of course."

My mom disappears to grab the wine, and I see Sarah looking around the room. When my mom comes back, handing her the wine, she says, "Very colorful home you have here."

"Very vibrant!" Paul says.

"So these are the people who made Ben," Coy says, walking into the living room.

"Ahh, that one I can't take credit for," Paul remarked.

"Oh, right on. I'm Coy by the way," he hugs Paul and Sarah and then sits down on a chair next to Sarah.

"Is Ben your only child, Sarah?" My dad inquires.

"No, Paul and I have a son together. He is with Paul's sister tonight."

"How young is he?" My dad asks.

"Sean is nine," Paul answers, his voice stern.

"So Ben barely knows him." It is difficult to tell if my mother is asking a question or making a statement.

"Of course, I know him; he is my brother," Ben answers defensively.

"Sarah, if you don't mind me asking, how come your son went to the army?"

I see in the corner of my eye Ben glaring at me as if I could make my mother stop saying things that he would categorize as too invasive.

Before I could say anything, Sarah starts to answer. "Because he was an adult and he is allowed to do what he wants. If only we were able to control our kids, right?" Sarah lets out a sort of uncomfortable laugh.

"Well, see that's the thing, we can't control them, nor should we think we should. They are humans and people; they shouldn't be controlled. It is our job as parents to make sure we influence them to make the right choices. If children feel too controlled then they sneak around, it is better to know what your child is doing rather than them thinking they need to hide it."

Sarah's face turns red and she grabs her glass and starts to drink.

"I have always known what my children are doing and for that we have a mutual respect. Have you had that with Ben?"

"I actually don't need to sit here and listen to you tell me how I should raise my child. Ben is a wonderful child."

"I actually wrote parenting books, I studied psychology and child development and did many studies on parenting and coached many parents struggling with raising their children. I know what I am saying, I think you would be able to learn a lot, Sarah. For your other son's sake."

"Thank you, I appreciate your concern but my boys are perfect the way they are. Thank you for dinner but we are going to leave now," Sarah's tone of voice stays the same and it is shocking especially because I can tell how she is offended. I look over at Ben sitting on the couch pinching the bridge of his nose with his eyes closed, which I have learned is his look for when he is aggravated. Sarah stands up from the couch and Paul follows.

"Do you know that he is suffering through depression and anxiety? That he has punched a hole in my daughter's house? Do you know that he is now smoking?"

"You're right mom, you don't need to listen to this," Ben then stands up behind Paul and pushes him to get him moving.

"Because you want to continue to hide and lie to your mother? To yourself? This isn't helping anyone," my mom continues to add.

They get to the front door, and I grab Ben's arm, his eyes looking at me now with disappointment, "I... I'm sorry." I say.

"I don't care what your parents say to me. But to say that shit to my mom. Are you fucking kidding me? She doesn't deserve that, Will."

"I know, Ben. I know. She just knows a lot about parenting and-"

"That doesn't mean she can give unsolicited advice whenever."

"I know."

"Just answer one question and answer it honestly. Do you think what she did was wrong?"

"I think she went about it the wrong way."

"Is what she did wrong?" His voice growing deeper.

"I just answered," I answered cowardly.

"Yes or no?"

"She had good intentions, Ben."

"I knew it," and he did it, his nose in between his thumb and pointer, eyes shut. "Of course, you don't think it's wrong. Now I understand why you can never keep your mouth shut."

"You asked me to be honest."

"Yeah, but sometimes I wish you would just lie to me. Because the truth from you fucking sucks sometimes," he then walks out of the house following Sarah and Paul.

I take a deep breath and walk back into the living room. Coy and my parents suddenly stop talking as soon as they see me.

"What is it?" I ask.

"I just feel bad for the other son. I hope Sarah will talk to me and ask for advice on him."

"Not everyone wants help with their children," I tell her.

"I understand that. But Ben should have received more guidance."

"I'm done listening to this," I turn my back and start walking away.

"Should've just stayed with River," I hear my mom say. "That's what we were talking about. And you turning your back on us signifies a lot right now, Willow."

"I really hope you weren't part of that conversation, Coy," I look at him directly.

He looks down sheepishly, "He just would've been better for you."

"Fuck you, Coy. You have some nerves. He could've thrown your ass in jail when you sat there with coke in his car."

"I didn't say he was a bad guy. I said River just would've been better for you."

"I understand you're angry right now," my dad then joins the conversation.

"Well, I'm not leaving him," I say almost defeated, tired of this conversation.

"Nobody is asking you to, we are just having a conversation. You're the one who got angry," he then says.

"You are a lot like your sister right now, Will. Keep that in mind, love," my mom says before I walk out of the house.

I am greeted with a choking sense of humidity that is inescapable at this time of year and a chicken on the porch.

Ben

I reach over Paul as he sits in the passenger seat and grab cigarettes from the glove compartment. Pulling out a cigarette, placing it in between my lips, and lighting it before Paul or my mom can make a comment.

"When did this start?" My mom asks from the backseat as I roll down the window.

"While I was away."

I hear her sigh and a few seconds of silence until she asks, "Am I a bad mom?"

Then, my turn to sigh, "No. Don't listen to Willow's mom, her one daughter barely talks to her, Coy does drugs, and Willow is well… Willow."

"Did I fuck up?" I always find it strange when I hear my mom curse.

"Sarah, stop," Paul says.

"Ben, did I fuck up? Did I do something wrong?"

"No, mom. Not you directly," I take a longer inhale.

"What does that mean?"

"Just, the divorce," I look over at Paul to see his reaction, but he doesn't look phased.

"You know it wasn't my choice," her voice gets quieter, remembering that Paul is still sitting there. "Is that why you left?"

"Ben, you need to go to college," my mom said it for the third time today and the twelfth time this month. She puts down brochures for numerous colleges on the counter in front of me.

I roll my eyes, for the third time today and the twelfth time this month, "I told you I'm not going."

"At least community. It's a start, and you'll get accepted despite your grades from high school."

"Mom, enough."

"You're 18 years old, you need to do something."

I drop a 9" x 12" white envelope in front of her, and I see her face light up with excitement, knowing it is some type of acceptance letter.

"What school? What school did you get into?" Her fingers fumbling over each other, trying to open it. She pulls out a piece of paper that says on the top left corner in bold letters, "U.S Army." She throws the paper at me and says, "What is this, Benjamin James?"

There it was, the middle name was said. "You told me to go somewhere, I am."

"This is not what I meant, Benjamin. You damn well know that."

"Well, this is what I pick to do."

"Have you..." her voice lowers and softens, "talked to your dad about this?"

"No, fuck what he thinks."

"Benjamin... he is still your father."

"Maybe if I get blown up in the Middle East then he will give a fuck about me," I grab the packet and walk away.

"I didn't want to go to college," I say under my breath.

"So, it's because of me? Because I pushed you to go to school?" She squirms in her seat in the back.

"I'm a better person because of it. I believe that and I hope you do too. You remember what a shmuck I was prior."

"I don't want to mess up Sean."

"Sean will be fine," Paul jumps in.

"Are you depressed?" She then asks, another statement that Willow's mom had to announce.

"I'm fine," another long pull.

"You don't smoke around Sean, right?"

"No, mom," she rolls down the window, "I'm not a fan of this habit just so you know."

I lie in my bed looking at my phone debating on if I should call Willow or not, hoping that she will just call me so I don't have to make the choice.

"Ben?" I hear my mom's voice at my door.

"Come in."

She slowly closes the door behind her and sits on my bed, "Can we talk?"

"Yeah, go ahead," I sit up a little straighter as she sits down.

"I didn't want to talk about this with Paul, but do you think Sean should know the truth one day?"

"Do you think Paul is a good dad?" I grab her hand.

"Yes."

"Then let Sean keep thinking he is his dad. You can't destroy his life or Paul's like that because you made a mistake."

"Would you want to know?" She squeezes my hand, her eyebrows furrowed.

"It isn't about me," a pause, she is still waiting for an answer. "Would I want to know if my mom cheated on someone who I thought was my dad with a guy who left her because he had an affair? No, I wouldn't want to know," I lie.

"Okay, thank you."

"Burn the evidence."

"No. If your dad ever tries to come and take him from me..."

"Dad has enough kids. I also don't think he would ever sink that low. He cares for you too much to ever do that."

She wraps her arms around me before she gets up, "I do think you're a good kid." She whispers in my ear and looks in my eyes.

My phone then starts to vibrate, and I look down to see Willow's name. "I'm going to take this," I say to my mom.

"I do like her, Ben. Despite her family and her absurd comments, I do like her," she then gets up and walks out of the room. I answer the phone when I hear the door click shut.

"Hello," I answer.

"Hello, Mr. Phillips," she says properly. "How is your mom?"

"She is fine," I reply in annoyance.

"And how are you?" Her voice doesn't waver from sincerity.

"I am fine. I don't want to argue, I don't even feel like talking about it," I sigh in defeat.

"Okay. I have an idea," her voice is enthusiastic.

I sigh, "What is it?"

"Are you alone?"

Even though I know no one is around, I still look around the room, "Yes."

"Take off your pants."

"What?"

"Just do it."

I slide my gym shorts down and take them off; I lie there wearing just my black t-shirt and black boxers that are squeezing my thighs, "Okay, I did."

"I have one of your t-shirts on right now, nothing else," her voice sounds like velvet now. And that's when I understood what she was trying to do now, what her idea was.

"Nothing else on? I told you, you love bad timing with this type of stuff. You thrive off chaos, Ms. Willow."

"Yeah, yeah. I like you when you're vulnerable. And no, nothing else. Put your hands down your boxers. I have my hand in between my legs. I'm getting so wet. Are you getting hard?"

I close my eyes and try to imagine her; I pull down my boxers a bit and start jerking off.

She starts moaning softly, "Tell me how turned on you are." I look down at my still flaccid dick, "Ben?"

"Yeah yeah, working on it. Send me a picture."

"Oh, okay," she says surprised.

Within a few seconds my phone vibrates and I look at a picture of her breasts. Her nipples are hard and just wishing to be touched again by me. I envision my hands cupped around them and the taste of her skin, it tastes like lavender from the reminisce of her body oil.

"Does that help?" Her voice is soft and seductive again.

I look down and see that I am getting somewhere, "Yeah."

"I wish I could feel you inside me right now. Would you like that baby?"

"Yes," I grunt.

"Great, I am at the front door. Care to let me in?" She says.

I get flustered at the fact that she is here, "Oh! Yeah, let me unlock it from my phone, and you can come up." Within seconds, she's in my bedroom. She walks in like a dream, gentle and slow. She shuts the door behind her and walks up to me, our eyes not breaking contact. My mouth hangs open as I watch her, her nipples still visibly hard through her dress, and I can assume she is not wearing anything else under the dress, like usual.

She gets to the edge of my bed, and I run my hands up her thigh, and to no surprise, I was right. My fingers run along the outside of her vagina and lightly brush across her clit. Her head falls back, and I see her chest grow heavier with her breath. I stand up without letting my hand move away from her and move her strap down her arm from her dress to reveal her breast. As I put as much of her soft breast in my mouth, I quickly put my fingers inside of her.

Willow lets out a gasp and grabs a fistful of my hair as she nestles her mouth into my neck. "I'm here for you, not me," she whispers.

"This is for me, though," I slip off the rest of her dress and let it fall to the floor. I lay down on the bed and grab her arm to pull her on top of me. "Please, Willow. Let me taste you. Suffocate me with that pussy of yours."

She does just that and sits on my face. I can tell she is holding on to the headboard to hold herself up. I put my hands on her hips and pull her down onto me even more. My tongue finds each fold of hers, and I slowly lick it. Even her vagina tastes like lavender, I can taste her wetness grow with each flick of my tongue. My hands grab her ass as I pull her even closer into me. The tip of my tongue reaches her opening, and I can fully taste her.

I want to taste every inch of this girl, inside and out. My tongue goes deeper inside of her, and I hear her moan louder, encouraging me to keep going. "Ben," she moans. I move my fingers between her ass cheeks and separate them so I can insert my fingers into her. She gasps for air when I do. The full weight of her body on my face, and I can feel myself rock hard for her, begging for release, and as much as I want to, I can't let her go yet.

Her tight ass clenches around my fingers, her wetness and my saliva dripping down as lubricant. I use my free hand to rub her clit since I refuse to take my tongue out of her. She grabs the headboard so she doesn't fall forward and lets out a moan that I am sure can be heard through the house as she climaxes in my mouth. "Fuck, yes, yes, yes!" She yells out.

I take my fingers slowly out of her ass but continue to use my tongue to clean her up, not letting any of her wetness get past my taste buds. At this point, my cock is throbbing for her, and as much as I want to let her come down from her orgasm at a slow speed, I can't help myself. I flip her on her back and she looks at me with her big eyes widening even more. She smirks at me and it sends chills down my spine, making my dick pulse for her even more.

I want to stare at her for a little longer, to look at her rounded tip nose, the freckle on the left side of her neck. But all I can envision is my dick inside of her mouth, her full pink lips around me. I take another look at her and then put my thumb on her chin, reaching it up to her lower lip and pulling it down to open her mouth. She does as so and I put my cock inside of her.

The warmth of her mouth sends me spiraling immediately. She gags as she takes me in but continues to suck me. I take a fistful of her hair and pull at it, I can feel her moans on me as I pump myself in her mouth. We make eye contact the entire time and within seconds I fill her mouth with my come. She tries to swallow it, but some of it seeps from the side of her mouth.

I pull out of her mouth and wipe the corners of her mouth. "So am I forgiven for tonight?" She asks as we both sit up.

"Baby, I don't even remember what the fight was about at this point."

"You do know, you didn't ask her? If you could shove your hands in her asshole, you didn't ask her if you could put your dick in her mouth. She couldn't even talk because you held her down." The voice behind me says. My stomach drops at the realization of it. In the grand scheme of it all, I didn't ask only presumed.

My chest gets heavy, my breathing becomes shallow. My instinct is to numb it all, I grab the Xanax from my nightstand and throw one in my mouth instantly.

"What the fuck are you doing?"

"What?" I asked, confused.

"Taking all those pills. Are you trying to overdose? Right in front of me."

"No… I didn't mean… I didn't even realize I had that many," I look down and see three pills in the palm of my hand.

"So you're unaware of how many you're taking?" She grabs it from my hand and throws the pills back in the bottle. "I am at a loss, Ben. I think we're getting somewhere and then."

"Getting somewhere? What does that even mean?" I grab my boxers from the floor and put them on, handing her the dress she was wearing before all of this.

"Making progress," she mumbles as she slides her dress over her head.

"Progress of what?" I throw a t-shirt on. Something about this conversation feels as if clothes should be worn now.

"You! I don't know how to help," she throws her hands up in defeat.

"Did I ask you for help?" And while my voice screams sarcasm, I actually have no idea if I did ask her or not. " Better yet, why don't I ask your mother for help. She seems like she wants to give out advice on what to do."

"Oh, please. Suddenly, now that your dick isn't hard, you remember the fight? Just tell me what is going on."

I roll my eyes at her, "Nothing is going on."

"Tell me," she crawls to the edge of the bed and looks up at me.

"Nothing is fucking going on," I start to yell.

She takes a deep breath, "Just tell me." Her voice was still monotone. It almost makes me even angrier that she stays calm.

Her voice and words remind me of her mother right now, "Nothing, god damn it." My fist lands on the wall.

"Yeah, that looks like nothing," she pushes me aside and stands up. "I really enjoy it when you yell at me when it isn't even my fault. I didn't send you overseas, asshole. You put yourself there. You did this."

"I didn't do shit, Willow. There is nothing wrong."

She opens my nightstand and throws the pill bottles at me, "Yeah, this looks like nothing." She opens one of the pill bottles and takes one out. "Here, you want to take pills? You think that is what is going to help. Take the one that matters," she grabs my face and squeezes my cheeks, trying to put one of the pills in my mouth. My hand raises, and I push hers away, swatting the pill out of her hand.

"Damn it, Willow," I rub my face in exhaustion. My fingers still smell like her. "How do we go from screaming orgasms to this?" I plead.

Suddenly, Paul barges into the room with my mother following behind, "What is all the yelling about?" He asks.

My mom's eyes dart to the hole in the wall, "Maybe you should go, Willow."

"Do they know?" Willow is looking me in the eyes.

"Don't," I tell her.

"Know what?" My mom questions.

There is silence, and my mom asks the question again.

"Just that… he is actually having a hard time adjusting," Willow's voice is apprehensive. My dad was right, she will lie for me.

Willow

I look down at my feet, which are black from dirt. I don't feel any closer to the earth. In fact, I feel more distant. I feel like a fly caught in a web, getting ready to be eaten, looking around and seeing everything for the last time. The trees, the grass, and feeling the wind in my wings for the last time. The spider is creeping down in slow motion before it attacks, as it just forced me into this unfortunate circumstance.

What if I am the spider, though?

What if Ben is actually the fly?

I am the spider.

He is the fly.

The war was the spider.

The pills in his drawer are the spider.

The gun on his hip is the spider.

The world around him is the spider.

Ben is the fly.

Helpless, hopeless, every moment being the last.

There is a tap on my shoulder that causes me to wake up, and when I open my eyes, I see Coy standing in front of me.

"Why are you sleeping outside?" He asks.

I grab a fistful of grass and just let it sit in my hand, "I needed to feel the earth."

He sits down next to me and puts his hands on his knees, and starts to meditate. I grab another fistful of grass in my other hand, and I close my eyes to focus on the moment. "I need to go to the store."

I open my eyes and see Coy rolling a joint. "Want to feel the earth?" He asks as he finishes rolling it. I grab it from his hand and grab the lighter that is on the ground next to him. I take a couple of hits before I give it back to him.

As I am restocking the shelves, Lily walks in with two coffees in her hand. "Got you something," she says and hands me one.

"You're the best."

"I know. I figured I could find you here if you weren't at your second job."

"What second job?" I take a sip of the coffee, a caramel latte with a splash of white mocha.

"Ben."

I roll my eyes and take a sip of the coffee again, and place it on a shelf.

"I saw River the other day," she says as she slowly sips her coffee, waiting for my reaction.

"And?" I raise my eyebrow.

"He says he misses you, Will."

"Good for him," I continue to put the books on the shelf.

"Maybe you should try again with him," she leans her back on the shelf, crossing her legs at the ankles. I look over at her and give her a look, my eyes narrowing at her letting her know she's crossing a line.

The bell to the store rings and I look past Lily and see Ben standing there with two coffees in his hand. Lily turns around and sees him, "Speak of the devil."

"Hey," he says sheepishly.

"Lily beat you to the punch," I hold up the coffee to show him.

"I will head out," Lily hugs me and whispers, "think about what I said." And leaves.

"I feel like a dog with my tail between my legs," he says while walking up to me. "I am sorry for yelling at you last night."

"Another apology," I take a sip of the coffee Lily gave me.

"Come over tonight at 8. I have something for you."

"I will think about it," I say and turn my shoulder to him..

"Okay," he turns around to walk out and leaves the coffee on the front counter. I walk over to the coffee and see it is from the place we had our first date, written on the lid it says "Ben hearts Willow," and I can't help but smile at it. I trace the wording of his childlike handwriting with my finger.

I rummage through my closet looking for an outfit that says, "Willow hearts Ben, but I still don't forgive you." I stare at the closet blankly, skirts lying on my bed behind me, dresses hanging in my closet waiting to be worn. If this were a friend of mine, I would have given the same advice Lily gave me, and she doesn't even know most of it. But the gnawing ache I have in my chest when I'm not with him is something that can't be explained.

I settle on a cotton, shin-length dress that shows off my collarbones like a dream. I can give him a little something to look at.

When I get to his house, I see that the front door is open, and I walk in. The back door is open too, and I walk out there to find about a dozen candles lit to make a path leading to a blanket that Ben is sitting on. The sun has just set, and you can still see its orange haze on the still water.

"Thank god you came, or this would have been awkward," he says with a hopeful smirk.

"Yeah, probably," I walk towards him.

"You look beautiful," he says as I sit down on the blanket.

"Thanks. You look nice too," he is wearing a blue button-down with the sleeves rolled and khaki shorts. Blue looks so nice on him.

"I know I keep... I don't know. Messing up," his fingers fidget with each other as he speaks.

"You aren't messing up, Ben. I just don't want to see you struggling so hard," I grab his hands, and he interlocks our fingers.

"I know. I thought I could get through it, but I can't. I want to tell you, but it's so hard to form the words. To get all those images into words to tell you. I will tell you, but can we just enjoy tonight?"

I sigh, "Yes, babe." He lifts my hand and kisses the back of it.

"I love you, Willow," he says quietly.

I pull my hand away and look at him, "What?" I say with a slight smirk.

"I said that I love you. I know it has been rough to be with me, and I am shitty to you, and you deserve better. I know that with every fiber of my being. But I do love you, and I love that you have stayed by my side. I'm sorry for it all. Despite it all, my love and feelings for you are something I haven't questioned since I laid eyes on you. As a matter of fact, it's the *only* thing I have been sure of."

"I love you, too, Ben," I respond.

I have known that I have loved him for a while now, but saying it out loud to him fully made it seem more real. It makes me realize that the feeling I have when I'm with him is love that you only feel once in a lifetime. The kind that everyone always talks about, where words can't explain it, you just have to feel it for yourself. I keep my eyes on him as he runs his fingers through his hair. It has grown so much since I first met him.

The sound of a wine bottle popping pulls me out of my thoughts, and I look at Ben as he pours a glass of red wine into two wine glasses that are encrusted with a golden rim.

"Can I tell you?" he whispers apprehensively to me as he takes a sip.

"Tell me what?"

"All of it… well most of it," I look at him quizzical, "what I am so fucking terrified of."

It is the moment I have been waiting for but I know my curiosity shouldn't push him to do something he shouldn't feel right doing. "Only if you want," I give him a way out.

He grabs my hand, "I can't tell if it will make things worse or better between us but I know by hiding all this shit it isn't helping us."

I put my other hand on top of his, "Like I said, only if you want."

He lights a cigarette and lets out a sigh.

Ben

The sergeant didn't call it a demotion, but it sure as hell felt like one. He called it an "opportunity," which felt more like a nice way of saying "figuring new shit out for you". I had my own team, one that I oversaw. But he also told me I am a good person to have in the cities and would help broaden my knowledge of how to interact with people. And if you're smart, you never turn down an "opportunity".

When I got to the camp base, I was introduced to Reynolds and his team. They automatically had that "brother" bond that you can see from miles away. And I was an intruder coming into it. For the first few days, we walked on the streets in the city. Our job was to look around and see if we saw anything or anyone suspicious. This would include walking around the streets, going inside stores, meeting the community so they felt a sense of comfort around you and would tell you things, knocking on doors, and checking houses. On my first day with them, we saw a bomb on the street, homemade, but it was done nearly perfectly. The person who made it has done it before. So, the next part of our mission was to find out who did it.

The next day, I first met Nimaah, a girl who was fascinated by American culture. She had a silver dollar coin that she made into a necklace and would wear it. It was about 105 degrees that day, and the sun was at its highest. A few of the men had to stop because they were about to pass out. Our day was spent mostly looking for some shade to sit under. I took off my helmet, and after a few minutes, Nimaah came up to me with a cup of water and a piece of bread.

"Hot out," she said. "Take," she shook the cup a little to encourage me to take it.

I did and said thank you.

It happened the next day, the next, and the next. In between these water breaks, she would tell me these jokes that I wouldn't understand. They usually involved an animal of some sort, but she always laughed hard after telling them to me, and I would join in on it. I think she thought it was funnier that I had no idea what was going on, though. One day, we didn't go that route, and I didn't see her, and the next day she was mad at me. She said she made bread that day, and I didn't get to try it.

But that is when Reynolds started to show who he really was. He said that we needed to start checking more houses due to a bomb being found in the neighboring city. He said we should do morning ones because that is when the men will be out working and the women will be home, so it will be easier. The next morning, we went into a home, Reynolds knocked once and then opened the door, and two women sat on their couch, stunned and terrified that

American soldiers were suddenly in their house. He kept asking if
their husbands were home. They cried and said no and had their
hands over their heads. It wasn't his first time coming into the
house. And it wasn't their first time dealing with it either.

He told me to do a quick search of the house, and I did,
along with Jimmy, who came with me. We looked around the small
two-bedroom house and cleared it. When we came out of the
bedrooms back into the living room, I saw Reynolds ripping off one
of the woman's hijab. I assumed he found something and is trying
to get something out of her. But then he pulls down his pants to his
thighs and pulls her dress up, and starts to assault her. She screams
out, and he puts his hand over her mouth. Mc'Neal holds the other
girl back and looks away from Reynolds. I go to push Reynolds off
of her, and he turns back and elbows me in the jaw.

"What the fuck are you doing?" I ask.

"Don't worry about it, rookie," and then he continued. I
went to push him off again, and Jimmy stopped me.

"Don't," he says, warning me.

I figured this would just be a one-time thing. But it
happened again the next morning. And the next. My time spent with
Nimaah felt more meaningful because my heart ached. She was the
only innocent thing in this whole war. I started to ask her more
about herself. I asked her what her family was like, what she
enjoyed doing. It helped remind me that I am not completely
inhumane.

Then one morning, it was the same as it had been; we went in, Jimmy and I checked, and Reynolds started. Except this time, he didn't go for the wife; he went for the daughter. She was older than Nimaah, but she was still young. I pushed him off and punched him in the face. Without hesitation, he pulled out his gun and shot me in the thigh.

"Touch me one more time and I will shoot you in the ball-less dick you have," and as if nothing had happened, he just went on. I walked out of the house and sat outside. By this point in my career, I have become good at pulling bullets out of myself. Last year, I could pull a "rosebud" out of my arm without passing out, which was an accomplishment. A rosebud is a bullet that opens once it hits you; it isn't a clean extraction.

Jimmy came out while I was in the middle of taking out the bullet. "I told you not to. I know it's hard to watch, but Reynolds will fuck you up."

When I got back to base, I woke Cohens up and told him I had been shot and needed his help. He asked me what happened, and I just told him someone hit me from nowhere.

"You took it out by yourself?" He asked.

"Yeah."

He rolled his eyes because he knows I'm known for doing this despite him telling me repeatedly not to because it can cause an infection.

"What kind of bullet was it? It wasn't a rosebud, was it?"

"No, it was just one of ours," and then I closed my eyes, realizing I just told him it was from our gun.

"I have heard stories about him, Phillips. You'd better walk on eggshells around him."

"What have you heard?"

"Nothing specific. He just isn't easy to get along with. He is also trigger-happy."

For the next three mornings, we didn't go into houses. I continued my days by stopping by to visit Nimaah. At this point, we would also exchange some type of food. She tried chocolate pretzels for the first time and instantly loved them. The next day, I made sure to put in an order for them to be shipped so I could give her more.

Then one morning, Reynolds wanted to go into a house. We go in, same procedure, I don't even look at the women anymore when we walk in. They were in the kitchen, and I just walked straight past them. When I walk into the bedroom to check it, I see a bag of chocolate-covered pretzels on the bed. I run out into the kitchen, and I see Reynolds take off Nimaah's hijab. Her black hair covers part of her face.

"No, Reynolds. NO," I shout.

Nimaah looks behind and sees me. "Help me, Ben," she yells.

Her mom was being held back by Mc'Neal yelling "Help" over and over again.

"Shut her up, Mc'Neal," Reynolds demanded. He then put his hand over her mouth. He started with Nimaah. Her coin necklace dangling from her neck just swung back and forth while he forced himself on her. I'll take the bullet to the dick. I pushed him off and grabbed Nimaah.

"Oh, this is your little friend, isn't it?" He said, with a smirk on his face.

"Reynolds, enough," I told him.

Nimaah turned into my chest and cried, wrapping her arms around me. "Please, please help."

Reynolds took out his gun, "Go ahead and shoot me then. If that's what gets you off," I say.

"Did you suddenly grow a pair? You fucking pussy. Did you want her all to yourself?"

"Fuck you."

"Na, I have these bitches to fuck," he then turns the gun to Nimaah's head, "I think it is time we make a man out of you. Don't we agree, boys?"

Suddenly, the sound of a gunshot goes off. My ears are ringing, and I hear the faint sound of screaming. Blood soaks into my uniform instantly, head wounds are always the worst. I look up at Reynolds.

"What... what did you do?"

"She wasn't serving much use," he says and walks out.

I sit there with Nimaah still in my arms. I roll her over and look at her face. Her tears were still on her face, and now covered in blood. "I am so sorry," I whisper to her corpse. My ears still ringing, I grab her necklace off of her and put it into my pocket. I walk out of the house and go straight to the base.

I go into the sergeant's office, and he looks at me with wide eyes as I am covered in blood. "Sit, sit," he says to me, noting how distraught I look.

"Reynolds..." I start to tell him, grabbing at my ears. I then tell him everything. All of it. In every detail.

He looks shocked and at a loss.

"Fucking Reynolds. He broke so many laws I don't even know where to start to charge him with." He slammed his fist down on his desk. "Go get yourself cleaned up."

I left his office and headed to the showers. I sat under the faucet with my uniform still on. Nimaah's blood was just washing off me and spinning around in the drain.

The next night, I lay in bed, and as soon as I started to fall asleep, I felt hands around my wrists and ankles and then a body sitting on my back.

"You want to know how it feels to be stabbed in the fucking back?" Which I can tell was Reynolds' voice. Then suddenly I felt the tip of a knife blade go into my back, and then everywhere on my back. He picked up my head, shoving it into the pillow so I can't make a noise. The stabs are getting deeper and more aggressive each time. I screamed into my pillow and attempted to get him off or get his hands off me. This was it, this was where I died.

"You little tattle tell, pussy. I swear to god, if you tell anyone about this, I will find you and fucking kill you. Got it?" Then his last stab right at the bottom of my back, the worst one yet. He knew exactly where to place them to inflict pain without causing damage.

Three hands let go of me as Reynolds gets off of me, and then I hear Jimmy whisper in my ear, "I'm sorry, dude. He didn't give us a choice." Then he let go and walked out.

I heard them laughing outside, saying "snitches get stitches" like teenagers.

I don't move for a minute, and blood runs down my back, soaking into my sheets. I tried to sit up, but it felt impossible. I rolled off the bed but landed on my back.

"FUCK!" I screamed out. I dragged myself to the back door of the tent and pulled myself next door to Cohen's. I get to his bedside and pull on his arm, "Hey, hey," I whimper to him.

"What?" He said, waking up and turning on the light next to his bed. "Jesus!" he yelled, startled as he looked down at me.

He helped pick me up and walked me to the medical center. "Don't tell me it was Reynolds," he said as he helped me onto the bed.

"I really can't talk about it," I tell him as he cuts my shirt open.

"Some of these cuts need stitches, man."

"Just fix it, please."

"This isn't just a quick fix, Phillips. These are severe fucking stabs."

"It was him. But I can't talk about it. I can't."

He sighs, "I can give you a letter saying you hurt your back so you can stay at base for the next week."

"Thanks."

Willow

Ben pushes his oatmeal from side to side in his bowl, the brown mush just falling apart more with each shove of the spoon. He still has sweat dripping on his forehead from his morning run. The veins on his arm are more prominent after the countless push-ups he does post-run. He doesn't even hide the disgusted look on his face with each bite he takes, and eventually tosses the spoon, calling it quits and reaching for his coffee instead.

I take a sip of my coffee, "So, you're going to kill me when I say this…" I begin to say. He looks up at me with a raised eyebrow and a slight smirk on his face. "About 30 minutes away, in Bright Creek, there is a support group that gets together every week."

He put his coffee mug down; it only had the luxury of touching his lips once. He grabs both of my hands in his, "Thank you." He replies calmly, "For persistently trying to help me. I have never had someone put so much effort into trying to better me. I see it. I see your efforts, and I appreciate them." He kisses my hands and puts them back down, and brings his leftover mush to the sink. "I have thought about it. But talking about it won't help. I tried that last night. And I know I'm not alone in this shit. I don't need to compare stories with others."

I sigh and walk up behind him at the sink, wrapping my arms around him. "I just think if you talk about it, then you would be able to work through it all better," I squeeze him tighter.

He finishes washing his dishes and turns off the sink. He turns to me, making sure he has a steady grip on my arms so I don't let go, "Worry less about me. Isn't that what your whole thing is? To not care?" He smirks.

"I guess you broke me."

"Then maybe you need the fixing," he kisses the top of my head.

While Ben goes upstairs to shower, I go to sit outside by the water, and for some reason, I can't help myself but to search for Reynolds on the internet, just needing to see his face. It wasn't difficult to find his social media; he makes himself very visible. I come across his TikTok and start to watch some of his videos. The first few videos are of him working out in a garage or at a training base camp. He wears a hat and sunglasses, so I can't fully make out his face. I keep scrolling and reach a video of him when he was deployed, still, and I click on it.

The video is of him and another guy in the desert, "We are more likely to die by being bored to death," Reynolds says. The sound of his voice sends chills down my arm. He takes off his glasses in this video, and his eyes are stark blue. They are eyes you could see from miles away. He turns the camera to the other guy, and I read his last name on his uniform, and it reads, "Mc'Neal".

Within five minutes and $5.99 later, I have Reynolds' phone number. I don't call him until I am back home and alone. My thumb floats over the green button before I hit call. No plan of what I am going to say, and I am not entirely sure what I am even trying to get out of this phone call anyway. But I call anyway.

"Hello?" His voice is stern as he answers.

"Hi…" My mind starts racing through scenarios of how I can play this out, "This is Lola Dean, I am interviewing returning soldiers and I was wondering if I could speak to you. This is… Sargent Reynolds, correct?" I can feel my heart racing, I put the phone on speaker so I can wipe my sweaty palms.

"Yeah, this is Sargent Jacob Reynolds," he is quiet. "Okay, when?"

"Well, we could do a phone interview, but I would prefer to do a face-to-face one, depending on your location and availability."

"I am currently at Fort Moore," he clears his throat.

"That is about five hours from me," I look down at the time, "I can be there today around 2 pm if that works for you."

"Well, Lola, I am honored that you would drive here today just to interview me. But I can't help but to ask what this interview is exactly for."

"I am writing essays on soldier's home return. Just so civilians understand the sacrifice that you men have to go through.

I came across your TikTok videos, and you just really stood out to me," I try to feed into Reynolds' ego that I know he has.

"I can do it at 2 o'clock today. There is a coffee place on the corner of Broad Street, I can't remember the name of it. It's mocha something... java something... I don't know, Lola. Something coffee-related," he laughs.

I return the laugh, "I will see you there." I hang up the phone and ask myself aloud what the fuck I am doing.

Espresso Cup. Not Java or Mocha, but coffee-related. It is easy to spot him since he is in uniform. He holds a coffee mug between his hands, and his leg shakes as he waits for me, mannerisms that remind me of Ben. Which reminded me to text Ben back to tell him I am out this afternoon with Nikki, doing some things for the store.

"Jacob?" I say, walking up to him.

"Lola?" He stands up and pulls out the chair for me. It almost feels as if we are on a first date, except I already know his dirty secrets.

"Thank you."

"How was the drive?" We both take a seat in our chairs, and he looks at me with those piercing blue eyes. He isn't a terrible looking guy, unfortunately. I smile in my head, though, knowing my boyfriend has a bigger build, though, and that's why it took so many men to hold him down.

"Fine, not bad. So why are you in Fort Moore?"

271

"I am stationed here. I am helping some of the fresh blood get prepared."

"Oh, so you work at the base?" I take out a notepad and pen and start writing some things down to look official.

"Yeah," he takes a sip of his coffee.

I can't help but feel angered about him working here, after everything that has happened, and why he got sent home; they just sent him here to work? To train new men? To what, be like the fucked up hero that he is? I can't help but think about what Ben would say about it.

"Do you miss anything from being overseas?"

"My brothers," he smiles and moves closer, putting his elbows on the table.

"I could imagine that you develop some close relationships under those circumstances," I mirror him and also put my elbows on the table to get closer. I smile to try and hide the fact that my heart and stomach feel as if they're going to fall out of my body at any given moment.

"You do. But at the same time, you try not to get too close with them because at the end of the day, you don't know if you will be sleeping next to the same person again."

"Yeah, guess you have to appreciate what you have while you have it."

"Exactly. By the way did you want a coffee?"

"Oh yeah, thanks," he then gets up and goes inside. I check my phone and see a picture that Ben sent me of him with Sam, my heart automatically skipping a beat seeing him shirtless because it's a view that definitely never gets old.

Jacob comes back with a coffee and puts it down in front of me. "Is it hard being with all guys all day, every day? I know it can be difficult, especially when men try to," I begin to say.

"When men try to prove their dicks are bigger than each other's?" He laughs.

"Essentially. I have just interviewed other men who have spoken about how it is difficult to work with the same sex, especially in such a tough situation."

"I mean, yeah. You have some guys who think just because they can hit a target better than they are more manly. Everything is compared to one another. And you just got some people who aren't much of a team player." When I notice the table move slightly, I look down to see his leg shaking again.

"Can you give me an example?"

"I mean, it isn't anything particular. Just shit like one guy wants to go right and the other one wants to go left. So then it turns into a whole thing and everyone starts acting like they know better."

"In prior interviews, a lot of people have told me about the physical loneliness they deal with and the lack of privacy being an issue," my attempt at luring him into a story that I know he won't tell is desperate. I am flailing, and I hope he doesn't see it, but I am thinking the fact that my shirt is low-cut enough helps that.

273

"Of course, that is an issue. But you find ways," he laughs. "Some guys find a way, and some guys just struggle with being lonely."

"What guy were you?" I say almost flirtatious.

He laughs out loud, "Tell me something about yourself, Lola."

"This isn't an interview on me," I continue this flirty voice with a side smile.

"We can make it one."

"Is it hard to date when you got back?"

"Is this a personal question or a standard interview question?" He has a slight smirk. I look down at his hand on his mug, and I see a few cuts on his knuckles, dirt under his fingernails.

"Personal, off the record," I put my pen down and sit back.

"I go on dates, nothing happens out of it. I am trying to go back overseas soon anyway."

"How come you can't go back now?"

"Helping out here, plus I have a few things to clear up beforehand," he starts to shuffle in his seat.

"Such as?"

"I have a few charges against me. That's why I got sent home," he scratches his jawline.

"What were they? If you don't mind me asking."

"It's stupid and a misunderstanding. I was too friendly with civilians, and they said it looked unprofessional, so it's just something I have to clear up."

"Sounds like a shit situation," I say, pretending that I am in agreement with him.

"So how many of these interviews have you done?"

"A couple."

"Who else have you talked to? Maybe I know them."

I think for a second, thinking of names that Ben has mentioned to me before, but nothing comes to mind, so I make up a few names. I say generic first and last names, and Jacob thinks for a few seconds to see if he can recall the name. "Benjamin Phillips," I then say.

He thinks and shuts his left eye, raising his eyebrow. "I know him," he then says.

"Oh?" I say, acting surprised.

"Yeah," he chuckles.

"What is with the laugh?" I say, chuckling back.

"He is just a weird dude. How did that interview go? Let me guess, he was one of the guys who said he had trouble with loneliness?"

"It was a fine interview. And no, he was one of the ones who told me how hard it is to work with other guys for a long period of time."

"That's because he was a hard team player."

"So you knew him well?"

"I wouldn't say that, but we were on the same unit for a few weeks. With Phillips, it was his way and that was it and if you didn't agree he would raise hell about it."

"I see."

"Did he say anything else?" He bit his lip and started to tap his fingers one by one on the table. Pointer finger up. Down. Middle finger up. Down.

"Like what? I mean, yeah. It was an interview."

"Just about what it was like with other guys there. I just know he didn't have many friends."

"Just that he didn't get along with people. But nothing specific."

"Oh okay," he lets out a slight sigh. Yes, he told me that you assaulted women and stabbed him in the back if that is what you're asking. "If you want, you can come look at the base. We can finish the interview there."

"Yeah, that works," I take another sip of my coffee before standing up.

"I can drive us and you leave your car here."

"So, you're asking me to get in a car with a stranger?" I laugh.

"Yes. Granted, I can't reassure you that I'm not a killer," he laughs out loud, and I follow. But I can't help but feel bothered at the fact that he says it so lightly.

I follow behind his car as he leads me through the gates of the base. I should have smoked a joint with Coy when he asked me before I left. We pull into the driveway to a small red house, "I have to go inside real quick. Want to come in?" He asks as I am about to get out of the car.

"Yeah, sure. See where the magic happens," I say lightly.

"No magic here," he says.

We walk into the house, and there isn't much on the walls for decoration, just a three-seater brown couch, a coffee table that has a beer bottle with about two sips of beer left. I look at it, and he must have noticed because he asks if I want a beer. I tell him yes.

He grabs two from the fridge and opens them both, handing me one and taking a sip of the other. He sits down on the couch, and I sit next to him.

"I am going to make a judgment about you and correct me if I am wrong," I nod yes. "You don't have a boyfriend, do you?"

I lie and say no, "What makes you think that?"

"Because you're sitting on my couch drinking beer," I just respond with a smile. "Why don't you? You're a beautiful girl." My stomach starts to feel like it is in knots, and this beer is not going to sit in it for long.

"Busy with work," I circle my finger around the rim of the bottle.

"You can still have a relationship with work," his leg is shaking again as he sits there.

"Then I guess I could ask you the same question."

He leans back on the couch, "I don't think any girl wants to be with a guy who is going to leave the country soon. I don't know, you never come back home, and it's hard to be in a relationship when your head is shooting terrorists in Afghanistan. Personally, I think guys who come back home and date are selfish."

I can't help but disagree, thinking about Ben being selfish by being in a relationship. But damn, is he right about not being home.

"So, you're not looking for a relationship because of work?" He asks.

"No," I reply. "Why are you asking so many questions about my relationship status?"

He sits up and puts both of our beers on the table, and starts to come towards me. I freeze as he gets closer. He grabs my chin and starts to kiss me. Stop, I tell myself. Stop, I tell him in my head.

He then starts to put his hand up my shirt. "What are you doing?" Words finally come out of my mouth, and I am able to move.

"Having fun. Neither of us want anything serious and you're single."

"Okay, that doesn't mean I want this. I am at work."

"No you aren't," he starts to kiss me again.

I pull away and find my feet to stand up, "Interviewing you is my job. This is work."

"No it's not. Stop trying to play hard to get now."

"What?" I muster out.

"I know you aren't a fucking reporter. And I don't care, it's cool. But I can tell that this is why I kept up the act."

"What act?" I swallow hard.

"Willow Lady Storm from the town of Randall, daughter of Joy and Jerry Storm."

My heart stops, "What?" I asked confused.

"I ran your phone number when you called and then also your plates when you parked. Do you think I am dumb? Listen, it's fine. Sometimes people lie. But it's just funny because you are actually a writer, so I am confused as to why you didn't tell me your name. Want to share why?"

"I just…"

"It's cool. I get it, you're a bit of a military groupie," he stands up and pulls me to him and starts to kiss me again.

"I want to leave."

"We are just having fun. Is it that big of a deal?" His hand grazes my nipple under my shirt.

"Stop," I push him away as hard as I can.

"What is your fucking deal? I should be mad. You lied. You manipulated me!"

"You must seriously be suffering from delusions of grandeur. I'm surprised I am even your type, I thought you liked little girls," my face turns red with anger and shock after I say it. As I start to walk away, he grabs my arm, spinning my body around with the momentum.

"What the fuck did you say?" His eyes darken, and his voice gets deeper with anger.

"What, surprised, I know about you too? You got sent back because you were assaulting girls. And how you are still working here just hows how you fucking army men aren't heroes but rather boys who care about each other's dick."

"You little bitch. Who told you those fucking lies?"

"You think I am dumb?" He lets go of my arm, and I start walking to the door. As soon as I go to grab the handle, a beer bottle goes right past my head. I stop for a second and then open the door, but he's there in a second to shove it shut.

"It was that little pussy wasn't it?" He says with his arm over my shoulder, holding the door closed.

"What?" I say while looking at the door.

"Who told you?" I can feel the tension radiating off his body.

"Some guy who saw you do it," I scoff.

"Who?" He yells in my ear.

"Some guy," I should know what I am getting myself into, what this can lead to. I see Ben when he's angry, and what happens, and that is from a guy who loves me. I am playing a dangerous fucking game.

"Who the fuck was it, Willow?"

Him saying my name in that tone of voice sends chills down my spine. "Mc'Neal," I respond confidently, not letting my voice falter. Let him think his friend ratted him out for a minute.

"Mc'Neal? I call bullshit."

"Well, that's who it was," his arm starts to lower from the door, and he is trying to think of what to do next. I open the door once his arm is loosened off of it enough.

"How far is Yelton from Randall?" He says. I let go of the doorknob.

"I don't know."

"Yes, you do. Because I am sure you had your interview with Phillips there," he punches the door, and I can't help but jump. "I knew that area sounded familiar. You fucking cunt."

I turn around and look at him, "No. It was Mc'Neal."

He grabs my purse out of my hand and searches through it. "I'm sure you still have his number from when you interviewed him. Does he know you aren't Lola? How about we tell him about your lie, and he can tell you the truth about his lie about me. He is just a gay fuck who was jealous that I was able to get a girl, and no one wanted his little dick," his insecurity and guilt seeps from his words.

He takes out my phone from my purse and laughs out loud when he looks at it. "This is even better!" He turns the phone around and shows me the picture that Ben sent me earlier. He then starts scrolling through my texts with him, "Wait, you're dating this pussy?"

I try to grab the phone out of his hand. "Does he know? Does he know you're here? Because you told him you're with Nikki"

"Give me the phone," I try to grab it again from him.

"I have a better idea," he then grabs me by the back of the hair, pulling me close to his face and takes a picture of us. "He does now."

Ben

The sound of thunder rolling in comes from the distance as I lie in the grass smoking a cigar with Sam. The feeling of my phone vibrating from my pocket, my stomach drops instantly when I see a picture from Willow pop up of her and Reynolds.

What the fuck. What the fuck.

My hands start to sweat as I call her immediately.. It has to be a mistake. Maybe it's not him. Why would she even be with him?

"Phillips! So glad you called," he answers the phone. It's a voice I would never be able to forget.

"What are you doing?" I instantly demand.

"Your girl is here, she told me you have a little cock and she needs more. Her words, not mine. I apologize. But you know, all these girls just always beg for me to fuck them, and I can't help it."

I'm hallucinating. I must be.

"Ben," I hear Willow's voice in the background.

"I don't know what game you're playing right now," I try to sound stern, but I know my voice is on the verge of cracking.

"Well, we are going to play some drinking games, and we will see what goes from there."

"Don't fucking touch her," I say it from deep within my chest.

"What did I fucking say? I said you better not tell anyone your fucking lies. How is your back doing? Is it good?" He says, taunting me.

"What do you want?" I try not to sound desperate, but I know he hears it.

"I wanted you to listen. Now tell your girl that what you said was a lie."

"It was a lie," I huffed.

"Tell her you're a fucking liar and a coward," I know the tone of his voice; I have heard that frustration and anger before.

"I lied," I say again.

"Phillips, my hands are tied here. I don't know what to do."

"I won't say anything," I hear Willow plead.

"You both are liars, and I can't trust that," he sighs. "Alright, well Willow and I are going to go now. Good talk."

"I will burn you to the fucking ground if you touch her," I start to pace around the yard.

"Who are you on the phone with?" My mom comes out and asks, concerned.

"Well, too late for that, but Willow will just call you when she's done here."

"I swear to fucking God, I am going to kill you."

"You're a little bitch. No you won't."

"Who is that?" My mom asks again, now sounding more worried.

"Hey, ask your mom if she wants to join too."

"Where the fuck are you so I can come there and cut your fucking dick off?"

"She will be home soon," Reynolds then hangs up.

"FUCK!" I throw my phone across the yard. The anger in me overpowers the hyperventilating that is trying to come through.

"Who the hell was that, Benjamin James?" My mom asks again.

"I can't explain," I start circling the yard to look for my phone and when I finally find it I fumble to try and call Willow back. It rings for an eternity with no answer. After the second attempt, I decide to take a deep breath, closing my eyes and giving myself a second. Maybe this is a hallucination and she will see I called and call back to tell me that she and Nikki found some great books for the store.

I look back at my phone to see the time stamps of how long it has been, seven minutes. My mom stands on the patio talking to Paul and keeps looking at me with concern. "I am fine," I reassure her.

She's not there. She's not there. This isn't real.

"It is real. I am with her," Reynolds says from behind me. Shaking my head no, I start to go through my phone to see who would know where Reynolds actually is right now.

My first instinct is to text Cohens, but the text bounces right back to me with a red exclamation mark saying not delivered. Before I can look for someone else's number, Willow's face pops up on my phone as an incoming call. I stare at the picture of her blankly. She is sitting by the willow tree where we had our first date. She is wearing a short blue dress, and her hair is down with loose curls from the braid she just took out. She wore lip gloss that night. I remember the feeling of it on my lips because it was unusual for her. It's my favorite picture of her because I caught her in mid-laugh.

The phone vibrating brings me back to the moment to unfreeze, and I answer it quickly. I want to know she is safe, but the thought of not hearing just her voice on the other line makes my chest feel tight.

"Hello?" I answer apprehensively.

"I'm so sorry, Ben," she says, crying.

I sigh, "Are you alone?"

"Yes, yes. I am in my car by myself on the way home. Ben I..."

I scratch my head as I try to gather my thoughts, "Are you okay? That is my biggest concern. Well, that and trying to piece together if this is happening."

"Yes, I am fine. And it is real, Ben. I went to Fort Moore," she begins to tell me.

"Why the fuck did you go to Fort Moore?" Now that I know she is safe, the frustration and confusion start to make an appearance in my voice.

"It's a long story but, I just needed to see him. I needed to confront him for what he did to you," she scrambles for words.

"It isn't your issue to confront, Willow. You lied to me. You told me you were out with Nikki getting fucking books. Did he touch you?"

She is silent for a second, and I check my phone to see if we are still connected, "He kissed me." She starts to cry again, "He kissed me and went up my shirt."

Fuck, I mumble. "Are you okay to drive?"

"Yeah, yeah, I am fine," I can hear her trying to stop herself from crying.

"Come here so I can check you and we can talk. Just… put your fucking location on, on your phone so I can see where you are."

I take a Xanax to lessen the shakes in my hand, and so I don't lose my mind completely on Willow when I see her. When the Xanax doesn't quiet down the thoughts, I chain-smoke on the porch until she gets here.

My feet race to the ground when I see her pull into the driveway, and I am at her car door within seconds to pry it open. She jumps out of the car and wraps her arms around my neck as she stands on her tippy toes. I exhale with relief that she is home safely, but my bones feel like they're on fire.

"You lied to me, Willow," I say as I pull away from her and look at her. "And for what?"

"I don't know, I was just angry with what happened and I felt like I needed to do something. I needed to see what he looked like and how he acted. I wanted him to confess or something."

"There is a lot of I in that sentence, Will. I don't know what your intentions were. But you fucking lied to me. You are my constant. You are the one who I go to know the truth. You are the only thing I know that is real and what the fuck do I do with that now," I move back to the porch and sit down.

She follows behind me, and sits down, "I didn't," she murmurs and puts her head in her hands.

"Is his come coming out of you right now?" I stupidly ask.

She gasps and jerks her head up, "what is wrong with you?"

"I don't know what to think right now. Did he do something else to you, Willow?" I interrogate her.

"I told you, no," she says defensively.

"You also told me you were with Nikki, so what am I supposed to believe?" I look in her eyes and they well up again.

"It was wrong. I know, Just please believe me on this one. I am so sorry, Ben."

"I don't know if I can," I whisper. If there is anything I know for certain about Willow is that even though I don't know what her intentions were, I know she came from a place of goodness. Willow doesn't have a bad bone in her body. The fate of our being is in my hands right now as she looks at me with soft eyes that are bloodshot from crying. "You want honesty? You want me to be open?" I ask her.

"More than anything," she says.

"I can't just move past this... It is going to rot in my fucking brain like black mold. Simply because I know him, I have seen the shit he has done, and it's something I just ignore. The sound of his voice when he called me, I know that tone. But I love you, and it is what it is at this point. But I need you to know I am so damn disappointed in you, selfishly because I can't believe a thing now." I grab her hands and squeeze them, "In short, babe, I forgive you, but I can't fucking forget this."

Willow

"Has anyone ever told you that it's really difficult loving you?"
Ben asks me as we lie in his bed together. My head rests on his
chest, the wetness of my hair soaking through his shirt. Our hands
are clutched together on his belly, and he rubs my thumb. And even
though my body was resting, my guilty conscience wouldn't let my
mind settle.

"No, actually. Has anyone ever told you?"

"Yes, actually," I turn my body so I am on my stomach and
facing up at him. His hand moves to my back, and he glides his
fingers up my spine, then starts to twirl my hair around his finger.

I sit up on my elbows, "Your shirt is soaked."

"It's okay, I liked having you there," he sits up and pulls
off his shirt over his head. "Problem solved," he says as he lies
back down. My fingers circle his stomach; his perfectly sculpted
muscles make it hard to focus on anything else.

"It's easy to love you, by the way. It is also really easy to
want you when you look like that," I tell him and kiss his abs.

"Look who's talking," he replies and grabs my face in his
hands. I look up at him and crawl up to meet his face. We look into

each other's eyes before he pulls me in for a kiss, his hands never leaving my face. The force behind his kiss confirms everything I am feeling. It feels passionate but the anger and disappointment sits on his tongue.

"I'm sorry I didn't come drive to you when you were coming back home. I felt panicked and confused and it's not an excuse," he starts to say, his mouth inches away from mine still.

"I haven't thought twice about that. I was fine, it was better to have you here waiting for me," I go back in to kiss him, and I am just hoping he doesn't feel the guilt and hate I have for myself on my tongue.

He rolls me over onto my back, "You are the most undeniably beautiful girl I have laid my eyes on. I will do whatever it takes to keep you safe, my love. Just know you have my whole heart, Willow. And because of that, I want you to know that if someone touches you again without my permission, I will point blank shoot them without hesitation." And after tonight, I hate myself for finding so much comfort in that last part.

I pull the back of his neck to bring him in a kiss. My tongue finds his immediately and I pull the back of his hair. He bites the bottom of my lip harder than usual. The feeling of his lips cover my neck as he starts to lightly bite at it. He sits up on his knees and pulls off his boxers that I was wearing and pushes open my legs with the back of his hand. He's not slow when he puts his mouth on my vagina, as if he needs me now.

"You are my favorite thing to taste," he says as he puts his tongue inside me. He grabs my hips to pull me in closer to his mouth, holding me to him so there is no space. I help close the space by pulling the back of his head closer to me as he nibbles on my lips. His other hand reaches around and takes hold of my nipple, twisting it between his fingers. My hips sprout up at the feeling, but he pushes them back down with his other arm.

"I need you," I pant. His dog tag drags across my clit as his mouth moves up my body. My breast fills his mouth as he flicks my nipple with his tongue, sending waves of pleasure down my body. I pull his boxers down halfway, and he finishes taking them off fully. His massive dick rested on my vagina, just pulsing as he waits to get inside of me.

"I told you I need you. Please don't make me wait any longer. I have never needed someone so badly," I let the words fill the air so he knows I am giving him the okay. He kisses me on the head and puts himself in me, filling me instantly, hitting spots in me that I didn't even know existed. I gasp as he thrusts inside me.

"I am going to fuck you until your legs are shaking. But I also want to enjoy every second of your moans," he says to me and kisses my neck. I stretch open as he slowly pulses in me. "You're everything I imagined."

His hand slips between us as he starts rubbing my clit, and he takes me to a whole other level of euphoria. My legs tense around him as my orgasm starts to build, my walls squeezing his dick as I need him more. "Slow down, baby. I am in no rush," he says, continuing to stroke my clit.

"Easier said than done," I say between gasps. He builds me up and then stops rubbing my clit, slowing down his thrusts. "What..."

"Trust me, it'll be so much better the longer you wait," he moves his fingers from my clit to my ass and fingers me. I push his shoulders to try and turn his body to get on top. Without loss of connection, he flips us over. His tight grasp on my hips keeps me steady as I bounce up and down on him. I reach behind me and grab his full balls, sending him rolling his eyes back.

"Fuck," he groans. I start moving faster, seeing him enjoy it makes me that much wetter.

"Yes, come for me, baby," I moan as I bend down to kiss him, my hands around his neck as I keep my movement steady and fast.

He flips me over, "No, I told you *I* am fucking *you*." He twists his body to push my one leg open more to get even deeper inside me as he thrusts in and out of me with want and need. He hits my g-spot at the perfect angle, and he must know it because he has the biggest grin on his face, and he watches my eyes roll back.

"Go ahead, let it out. Be a good girl," he says. My orgasm builds all the way and releases. I let out a yell, his hand lightly covering my mouth as I moan even louder. "Just like that," he tells me in my ear. My nails dig into his back, and then he releases as well. His arms shake as he holds himself up and lets it out. My hands still on his back, I pull him down so he lies on top of me. He draws in a shaky breath as he starts to come down.

I scratch at his head as he lies there on my chest, "Give me a minute," he then says.

"You can stay here as long as you want," I tell him.

"No, I told you I am doing this until your legs are shaking. So, unless you say no to that, I am keeping true to my word."

I bend my head back and laugh, "You are more than welcome to stay true to it."

Sarah looks radiant as always, even at 7 in the morning. "Where is Ben?" She asks me as she pours her cup of coffee.

I sit at the kitchen island and take a sip of my coffee that is about five shades lighter than hers, "He went on a run."

"Great, I wanted to talk to you alone anyway," she leans on the counter with her elbows. "I don't want to embarrass Ben, so this stays between us. But next time you two are," she pauses. I raise my eyebrow as I take another sip. "Having sex, can you be mindful that there is a little boy only a few feet away from you?" She continues.

"Oh!" I say, rather shocked, "I mean sex is a beautiful…"

She interrupts me, "No, let's just leave it at that. Okay?" I shake my head yes. "And the other thing I wanted to talk about. I don't know what happened between the two of you yesterday, but from the phone call; it didn't sound great. But clearly, you two worked it out just fine last night. I want you to know Ben takes this relationship very seriously, and I hope you do too. I like you,

Willow. Despite whatever it was between us and your parents, I think you are good for Ben," she takes a step back and leans on the stove as she drinks her coffee.

"I do as well, and I love Ben. Yesterday was-"

She lifts her hand to stop me, "I don't need to know. But as a mother, I ask you to be mindful. I am sure at this point you know him better than I do and what is going on with him."

I hang my head sheepishly out of guilt that she is correct about that. Ben then comes running in from the back door filling the awkward silence in the room.

"We were just talking about you," Sarah mentions.

"I can only imagine," he sits down in the chair next to me while he catches his breath. "About what?"

"How hot you look when you come home from running," I kiss his sweaty forehead and hand him my coffee to finish. "I should also tell you how my sister texted me saying she is coming down for the weekend and wants to meet you."

"Oh, good, you know I love your family," he says and smirks at me. Sarah lets out a giant laugh as she walks to the backyard.

"Yeah, well, this one you might actually get along with."

No part of me is nervous about Ben and Rain meeting; of course, they will get along. He walks into my house wearing jeans and a flannel, his gun sticking out more than usual from his belt.

"What is with this?" I ask, pointing to it.

"Honestly? I am doing it to piss your parents off," he shrugs.

"You're being petty," he comes over and kisses me on the head.

"Your parents pretty much told my mom that she isn't a good mom. But yes, I am being petty."

"Whatever you want to do," I say, lighting a joint.

He grabs a beer from the fridge and stands in the kitchen speaking loudly to me, "So, anything I need to know about your sister?"

"She has no interest in our family, so I am surprised she is here. She has a baby daughter named Brittany, a three-year-old son, Aidan, and her husband is a drag."

"What is wrong with her husband?" He asks, walking into the room.

"Just a boring dude."

"Boring or normal?" He raises his eyebrow and sits next to me.

"No, actually boring," I lay back on the couch and put my feet on Ben's lap. "Even you would find him boring." I take another hit of my joint.

"What does that mean?" He stands up and pulls me up by the arm, "Come outside to smoke with me," we sit on the front patio, he lights his cigarette, and I continue to smoke. "Well?" He continues.

"Just that you're not boring. You're the most complex, not boring guy I have ever dated," I look over at him as he stares out to the empty field.

"This feels like a backhanded compliment," he looks over at me, narrowing his eyes.

"I think it is," I respond honestly. The smell of our smoke battles the air as we sit there quietly.

Ben

If I didn't know Rain and Willow were sisters, I would have never guessed. Willow is wearing one of her loose, long dresses that is yellow and covered in flowers, she has one piece of hair in a braid that is tucked behind her ear. Rain, on the other hand, is wearing dark jeans and a white button-down shirt that is tucked in. I look down at her hand and see a giant engagement ring that she wears, something that I would imagine Willow hating.

Her husband Hank is wearing nearly the same outfit but with a blue button-down tucked in, his hair combed back with gel in it. People who would be in my family, not Willow's.

"So you are the man I have heard all about?" Rain says, shaking my hand.

"And you are the sister I have heard about," I respond.

"Nice to meet you, this is my husband, Hank."

"Hey man, nice to meet you," he says, shaking my hand. "What you got there? A M17 or M18?" He asks about my gun.

"M18," I say, shocked.

"Hank is a cop," Willow announces to me.

I can't help but laugh out loud, knowing how much this must annoy Willow and her family. "They just love it," he whispers closer to me.

"Oh, I'm sure," there is no way I could find this guy boring, and at the very least, he is someone I can have a conversation with.

"Okay, well, you can both have a bromance later, I am hungry," Rain says. "Hank, can you get Brittany's bottle from the diaper bag and heat it?"

"You aren't breastfeeding?" Joy asks, mortified.

"No, I'm not," she rolls her eyes and continues into the house.

"Oh, Rain," Joy says disappointed.

"Don't start," she warns. I purse my lips and try to hold back my smile. I love hearing someone talk back to Willow's mom.

As we sit down for dinner, I look over at Rain and Hank as their hands are folded and they are praying. "Didn't know you were suddenly religious," Willow says as she starts to eat.

"What I believe in is personal to me and my husband," she says already defending herself.

"I am just saying," she sucks in a breath.

"Where is Coy?" Rain asks while cutting her food.

"He went out tonight," Jerry responds.

"What he does with his friends is personal to him and his friends," Willow says with a snarky tone.

"Yeah, getting high and having unsafe sex is a personal matter," Rain says. "So, you were in the army?"

"Oh, yeah," I answer off guard.

"And now you're dating someone in this family, interesting."

I look over at Joy and Jerry, "Can't say it isn't difficult."

Rain laughs out loud, "Amen to that."

"Is it?" Joy asks. "Are you having difficulty?"

"I don't know, last time I was here you told my mom that she was doing a shitty job at being a parent, so you tell me," I shrug.

"Ben," Willow says almost warning me to not go any further with this argument.

"It was just me voicing an opinion of what I have noticed. I am sure Willow is having difficulty trying to fit in your lifestyle too. Are you, Willow?" She looks straight at Willow who has a green bean about to enter her mouth.

Her face gets immediately red and she takes her bite of food to buy her time from answering. "This isn't therapy, mother. Let them deal with their relationship," Rain says, trying to diffuse the situation.

"I want to make sure my daughter's feelings are being accounted for," my eyes narrow at her.

"They are," I strongly answer. I get up from the table, "I will be right back." I whisper to Willow.

She grabs my arm, "Where are you going?"

"Outside."

"You okay?"

"Yeah," I kiss the top of her head and walk out. As I start to light a cigarette, Rain comes out.

"Can I have one?" She asks, standing next to me.

"HA!" I pull one out and give it to her, lighting it as it is in between her lips.

"What?" She takes a pull from it and exhales.

"You sure you are related to this family?"

"Unfortunately. I know my family can be a lot, which is why I can't help but ask why you're with Willow?" She turns her body to me.

"Hank is with you," I turn towards her.

"I am not them," she points back to the house. "Willow is."

"Being with her is good for me. I need someone understanding."

"What are you going to do when she realizes this isn't the life she wants?" I watch her as she takes another inhale.

"What do you mean?"

"She isn't going to deal with holes in her walls for the rest of her life. You can take that literally or metaphorically."

I don't respond and just continue to concentrate on my cigarette. "Are you trying to tell me to break up with her?" I finally say.

"I am telling you to watch your own back."

"Thanks for that."

I help Willow take off the pillows on the bed and notice she keeps looking at me, waiting for me to say something. "So, that is my sister," she says after taking the last pillow.

"Am I missing something?"

"What are you talking about?" Willow sits on the bed, her legs tucked under herself.

"Are we meant to be together?" I sit on the bed, scratching my jaw as I think out loud.

"Isn't that something you should be asking yourself? Did she say something?" Her eyes turn into worry.

"Yeah, but it's just everyone. Your mom, sister, my mom. I heard you talking to my mom this morning, but I won't comment about the other part of the conversation you guys had."

"Your mom said we are a good match. My mom just knows what is going on."

"Stop telling your mom my issues, okay?" I stand back up defensively.

"Sorry, I will talk to my mom about things happening in my life," she doesn't flinch from her position.

"She is using it against us, Willow. Can't you see that?" I turn my head and look at her. How can someone be so oblivious and naive?

"No, she just wants you to recognize it and work on it."

"Why do you all think my issues are for all of you to worry about and fix?" My voice gets louder.

"That is what it is like to have someone care about your mental and emotional health. Emotional health is just as important."

I roll my eyes, "The lack of an answer tonight at dinner is fucking concerning by the way."

"Are you dense? I mean, really think about it, Ben. Fuck, babe, you can't be that crazy, can you?" She lets out a huff and I look at her, confused, "Of course, I don't fit in your lifestyle. Guns? Violence? Your lack of communication? In what world do I fit into that? But can't you see I am doing everything to do it anyway because I love you? You're not trying to change me; you have accepted that this is how I am. And I love you for that. I love the look on your face when you wake up and look at me and smile, or at least when you pretend to wake up because we both know you are not sleeping. I love the way you still come to these horrible dinners because you know I want you there," she continues, her eyes getting full of tears as she talks.

I go around to her side of the bed and get on my knees so I can see her eye to eye. "Will."

"You say you would burn the world for me, but baby, I am walking through fire every day for you."

I pick her up from the bed as I stand up and place her down on her pillow. I lie next to her and brush her hair behind her ear. A pit in my stomach grows because, despite lying here with a girl who is out of my league, who loves me endlessly, it still doesn't feel like home.

Willow

The feeling of wetness on my clothes wakes me up. I assume it is Ben until I realize it was me who is sweating, remembering the dream of Jacob's hands on me. I turn to look at Ben and feel a sense of guilt, and light up the joint that sits next to my bedside, waiting for me to put my lips around it.

His hands up my shirt, his tongue in my mouth, the taste of beer from his saliva transferring into my mouth. I step outside into the night sky, stretching my body left to right, embracing nighttime yoga and the stars around me for support. Taking a moment of reflection.

I walk back into the bedroom as quietly as I can, but I can already feel the weed hitting me more than I thought it would, which causes me to close the bedroom door harder than planned. Ben suddenly jumps up, gun already in hand.

"Chill, it's me," I say, trying not to laugh.

"What are you doing?" He asks, aggravated.

"I was outside."

"Are you high?" He asks.

"Yeah," I giggle slightly. "I couldn't sleep."

"Me or you?" He asks.

"What? I said I couldn't sleep."

"The bed is soaked," he sits up and pats his own body, it wouldn't be the first time he also had night sweats either though.

"Me. I had a bad dream," I take off the shirt I was wearing and replace it with one of Ben's that sat on the chair. As soon as I put it over my head I can smell him on it. The smell of cedar and his natural body scent.

"Ms. Willow have a bad dream, I can't imagine," he takes off his shirt and throws it on the floor, it must also have been wet from the crossfire of my own.

"Yeah, yeah. Guess that's what happens when you are face to face with a psycho, get the consequences of a nightmare."

His head snaps to look at me as he winces, "What are you talking about?"

"Nothing, love you," I kiss his forehead and lay down.

"What are you talking about?" He says sternly.

"Nothing, I am really high right now," I rub my head as I lay on my pillow. Fuck, was that joint laced with something?

"What was your dream?" He is using his serious tone, where it is borderline about to yell.

"It was just a dumb dream about Jacob," I close my eyes.

"Who?" He is quiet, "Reynolds? Did you just refer to him by his first... What was the dream?"

"It was like a memory, I don't know, dude," I don't bother looking at him as I slowly start to fall back to sleep.

"How high are you right now? What was the memory?"

"Just of him like all over me," I mumble.

"What happened after he hung up the phone?" The tension in his body prevents me from falling asleep any longer. I sit up and look at him.

"I left," I say, looking into his eyes.

"That's bullshit, I can tell by the time difference of everything, it doesn't add up."

"I left," I repeat.

"How did you get in contact with him?"

"I called him. I found his number online. Babe, I am tired. Can we just stop with this shit already?"

"You're going to make me go crazy with this, you know that, Willow? You fucking know that?"

"Okay, go crazy in the morning." I lay back down and close my eyes.

"Glad you think this is amusing," he lies back down, and I look past his shoulder, out the window to count the stars. One, two, three, four, five, six, seven. "Nope, no. Give me your phone." Ben says as he shoots up from the bed.

"Why?" I ask, handing it over to him.

"Because I can't do this, what don't you get? Then you come in here and tell me this guy is giving you nightmares," his fist goes through my bedroom wall, and I jump at the noise. He doesn't take more than a second to start looking through my phone, and proceeds to make a phone call.

"What are you doing?" I ask.

"Nice to hear from you again," I hear Jacob on the other line.

"Fuck you. Tell me what happened," Ben says.

"Of course it's you. Happened with what?"

"Tell me what fucking happened," he starts to walk away, and I can't hear what the response was. I jump out of bed, trailing behind Ben into the living room. "Bullshit, what is the truth?"

"That is what happened, is she telling you differently?" Jacob says.

"Tell me the truth."

"That is."

Ben hangs up the phone and throws it across the living room, I assume leaving a dent on the wall it hit in its path. "What did he say?"

"The truth," he responds, walking past me to go back into the bedroom.

"Which is what?"

"What, you don't know what it is? How about you tell me what it is you think he said?"

"I left."

"Yeah, I can see that," he starts to put his pants on.

"Where are you going?" I ask, following him as he walks back out the door.

"I don't know, for a run," he slams the door behind him.

"FUCK YOU," I yell at the door as it shuts.

He swings the door open, hitting the wall as it opens, "What?" For the first time he has felt intimidating to me and I take a step back from him. His broad shoulders take up most of the door frame and he raises his eyebrow waiting for me to answer.

"Nothing," I whimper out.

"I am going for a run, I will be back. You don't need to yell at me behind my back like a coward. Try not to do anything ludicrous again while I am gone. I am going to shut the door now, anything you need to say before I do?"

"Yeah, I love you," I smile after I say it in hopes it eases the tension.

"Great," he doesn't return the smile and shuts the door closed again. What is it that Jacob said that he believes that he won't believe from me? What is Jacob's version of the truth, what is Ben's idea of truth?

I end up falling asleep on the couch before Ben gets back and the only way I know he is back is by waking up to him carrying me to the bedroom. He kisses me on my head and whispers, "I'm sorry" as he puts me down. I don't open my eyes to show him that I heard him. In my head, I whisper I'm sorry back.

We don't talk about what happened, but I can tell there is a shift in him; he has grown quieter. While I am at work, he only texts with one-word responses, and when I call him out on it he makes up an excuse about him working out or playing a game with Sean, but still acts cold when we see each other. I take advantage of his mom asking me if I want to go to the store with her and Sean one afternoon to see if she notices anything different about him.

In the car on the way back home, I ask her how he has been doing since I have been busy with work. "Usual Ben self. He spent yesterday in bed, but he was coughing a lot, so I think it's just from his cold."

"Yeah, he has just been acting weird," I look down at my fingers, twisting the ring on my finger around in endless circles.

"Isn't he always?" Sean says from the backseat. Sarah looks in the rearview mirror at him.

"Headphones," she commands. "Anything we should be worried about?" I appreciate the fact that she is including me in this situation; it makes me feel as if we are joining a rebellion. A rebellion against Ben. I just shrug. "Well, has anything happened?"

"Not that I can put my finger on." Other than the fact that he freaked out in the middle of the night, made a crazy, almost threatening phone call, then went on a run at 2 am, but then came home and said sorry.

"He reminds me of his father. The lack of communication. His dad just thought he could handle any issue by himself."

"Yeah, sounds a lot like Ben. He tries to carry the world on his shoulders."

"Willow…" Her voice sounds concerning, like a warning, "I looked into a facility. A facility that helps people return to civilian life. I know he's struggling. Just tell me if I am being paranoid or if I am on the right track."

"He won't go," I say.

"He needs to, doesn't he?"

"I have suggested he talk to someone."

"I don't want to ship him off again, but there is only so much we can do. I just want you to be prepared for when I talk to him about it. I am going to call his dad later to have him fly here and help me with this talk. I don't want it to feel like an intervention, but I know it isn't easy. I have read stories; I live with him. But is there something I am missing? You're the one who sees him differently."

"You aren't doing the wrong thing," I validate her thoughts.

"Please tell me. Tell me what he is going through."

"I just know he's struggling."

"Okay, I just know his father is going to call me crazy when I tell him."

"He hallucinates," I admit.

She releases a heavy sigh, "My poor baby. What does he hallucinate?"

"People. People being in his room or talking to him."

"Jesus Christ. How often?" I see that she keeps looking back in the mirror to make sure Sean isn't listening.

"Too many to count."

"Okay. I'm not trying to use this against him or you, but I need to tell his dad concrete evidence or else he won't agree. I know Ben still looks up to his dad."

"He does."

"Fuck," we both let out a deep breath. We both know she's going to fail at this attempt but we both know that she needs to make the attempt.

When we get back to the house Sean and I start bringing in groceries, while Sarah waters her purple pansies that lay perfectly grown at the front of the deck. Sean runs ahead of me and I can hear him laughing when he gets in the house, "are we playing cops and robbers?" He exclaims from the kitchen.

"Put your hands up," Ben responds from inside of the house. The hair on my arm raises instantly when I hear the inflection in Ben's voice.

"Oooo, I want a gun too!" Sean continues, I run into the house, sliding into the kitchen.

"I said put your hands up," Ben turns to me and says, he has a gun pointed at Sean and then turns it to me. "Who else is here?" He asks.

"Ben!" Sarah shouts when she walks into the kitchen, dropping the bags of groceries on the floor.

"Who else is in the fucking house?" He asks.

I try to think of what to do, but Sarah starts crying and moves towards Sean, "Don't move," Ben says, and she stops in her tracks.

"Ben, babe, you are home. It's me, Willow."

"How many times do I need to ask who is in the house? Who else is fucking here." A pot of water starts boiling over the top and lands on the stove, sizzling as it makes its way down. I inch slowly so I can stand in front of Sean while maintaining eye contact with Ben.

"Willow," Sarah says to me.

"No one else. It is just us," I respond, Ben and I don't drop eye contact, and he is blank inside. The hazel eyes that were looking into mine last night have vanished. He is looking right at me and has no clue who I am. He could shoot me right now, and I have no recollection of it.

And as if timing was set up to destroy our universe, Paul walks into the house from the back door. "Daddy!" Sean yells, terrified.

Ben moves his gun and points it at Paul, "You said no one else is here."

"What the fuck?" Paul exclaims as he looks up.

"Daddy!" Sean starts to run to Paul.

I start to move towards Ben, "Hey, it's me," I say as calmly as I can.

"Back the fuck up," He says, moving the gun to me.

"Willow," I hear Sarah say in tears behind me. She is looking at me for help that I don't even know if I can provide."

"Everyone, just let me handle it," I tell them. "Ben, it's me." I think hard about what to say next, and even though the books say not to go along with the hallucinations, the books also don't outline what to do when your PTSD boyfriend has a gun pointed at you, either. "It's me, Nimaah," I sigh, hating to do what I have to do.

He grabs me by the arm and pulls me behind him, so I shut off the stove instantly. He looks over at me, lowering his gun for a second, but Paul starts to move, and Ben notices, which causes him to point it back up at Paul. Paul shoves Sean out the back door as best as he can without moving.

"Ben, put down the gun," Paul says.

Sarah starts saying something to Paul, but I can't fully make it out with her tears, "What is she saying?" Ben says. Sarah cries more. "What the fuck is she saying?" He starts to wave his gun at Paul.

"Put down the fucking gun," Paul says.

"Ben, look at me," I say. He glances at me for a second.

"Ben!" Paul exclaims, and Ben looks back at him.

"Shut up, Paul," I demand. "Ben, it's me. Nimaah. I am okay. Just get me out of here. Let's go."

He looks at me confused, studying my face and then back at Paul, "is he hurting you again?"

"What?" I say confused.

"Did he fucking touch you again?"

Then it clicks, he sees Paul as Jacob. I feel my heart racing at the sudden realization. "No, no. I want to go."

"Nimaah is dead." He looks at Paul, "and it's your fault." His voice getting more stern, he lowers the gun but starts to walk towards Paul, "what did you do to Willow?"

"Ben, no. No, that's not him. Ben," I cry out as his fist clench while the other one turns white knuckled around the handle of the gun.

"What did you fucking do?" Ben is face to face with Paul, who starts to back up against the wall.

I run up to Ben as he starts to raise his gun to Paul. The gun reaches up to Paul's stomach as I stand in front of him. Paul holds his breath so the gun doesn't push into his stomach anymore. "Babe! Ben, please. It's me, Willow."

"Move, so I can kill him for what he did," Ben starts to push me away.

"He didn't do anything. That isn't him. That is Paul," he knows it's me now so I put myself in front of Paul.

"No, no. He…" He looks at me, "I know. Willow, I know. Please stop lying."

"Give me the gun, Ben," I reach behind me and push Paul back, and he steps a few steps away.

"I can't," he picks up the gun and puts it to his head. Sarah screams.

"Ben, please. Stay with me."

"I can't. I can't take the ringing in my ear anymore. I can't do this," He says again.

"Ben, I love you," I plead.

"I can't," he closes his eyes, and I pull his arm down right before his finger pulls the trigger completely. The weight of his gun feels like a life in my hands, and I shove it into Paul's stomach for him to grab as I yank Ben away. Ben opens his eyes and looks at me.

"I am taking him upstairs," I say as I pull him away, leading him up the stairs. I block out the sounds of Sarah crying and Paul calling Ben horrible names under his breath.

He plops on his bed and then just lies down. "Do you know where you are?" I ask.

"I am in my bed, right?" He says, his eyes staying closed.

"Yes. Do you know who is talking to you?"

"Willow."

"Do you know what just happened?"

"I... I," He turns around with his back facing me.

"Ben, I need to know if you know what you just did."

"I don't know, Willow. I was making pasta, and then I had a gun in my hand. I don't know. Yes. No."

I can hear Sarah crying hysterically downstairs still, and I know he can hear it too, "Do you know, or do I need to tell you what happened? Because I am warning you now, this is going to have a consequence."

Nothing.

"Ben, I need you to answer me."

Nothing.

"Don't shut down on me now, I am trying to help you."

"Yes, Willow."

"Yes, you know what happened?"

"Yes, Willow."

"Be a man and fucking look at me, Ben. You need to give me more than just that."

He sits up from the bed and rolls his neck, "I was here... I wasn't here... I was there. I know where I thought I was. I can fill in the gaps of the reality of it all."

"Ben... tell me what you think the reality of it was."

"There was a boy with his mom. His dad came home. And I thought the situation was unsafe. Reynolds was... he was there, and you were there. I can fill in the blanks, okay?"

"I don't... you..." I try to muster up a thought and come up blank. This will give his dad the concrete evidence that is needed.

"Will, can you just go home?" He sighs, he doesn't look at me.

"No, I am not leaving you here alone," I snap back to say.

"Will, what I am about to deal with, I don't want you here."

"Ben, you put a gun to your head. I am not leaving you. Do you remember that part?" I ask.

"I didn't pull the trigger," he whispers.

"That is a bunch of bullshit because both you and I know that you started to. Sure, you hesitated, or didn't pull the trigger hard enough whatever the case may be. You can spew that lie to your mom but I was standing right there. Your blood would have been on *me*."

"Do you hear my mom right now?" I bring my ears back to the sound of her still crying. "I have to, I don't know what I have to do. Tell her something."

"Well, I am staying here. So go deal with it," I sit firmly on his bed and watch him walk out of the room.

Ben

I walk out of my room quietly, sitting on the top of the stairs to hear what my mom is saying before I see her.

"I know, Paul. But he is my son," she says.

"So is he, Sarah. We can't live like this. You need to tell him." Paul responds.

I decide to just walk down the stairs and into the kitchen. "Is Sean okay?" I ask.

"He is at the neighbor's house," Paul answers.

"I don't know what to say," I say, my head hanging low.

"Tell him, Sarah," Paul says.

I look up at my mom, "Tell me what?"

"I found a facility for you," she says.

"What?" I huff.

"I have been looking into one, and I was going to talk about it at a later date, but," she starts to cry again, and I can tell she is about to get up from her chair, but Paul puts his hand on her leg to have her stay seated.

"Benjamin, we think it is best if you leave," he says, coldly.

"We think or you think?" I try not to sound angry, figuring now isn't a time to get mad.

"We. Especially after today's events," Paul fills in the answers that my mom won't say.

"I fucked up, I know, but-" I argue a fight that I know I can't win.

"You pointed a gun at me, my wife, and my son's head today. This isn't a fuck up, Ben."

"Mom," I say, hoping that at some point she sticks up for me.

"This is what is best," Paul adds.

"Fuck you. Let her speak."

"You need to leave," he demands, "none of us feels safe in the house with you here. You need to leave my house, Ben. You have given us no choice."

"This isn't your house. This is my father's house. He paid for this."

"I am not dealing with semantics right now, okay?" He gets up from his chair and looks at my mom, "I told you, Sarah, I will take my son and leave."

"You're making her choose between me and you?"

He looks back at me, "This isn't a safe place for my son."

"What son? How about you stop trying to raise my father's children?"

"Someone needs to," he walks to the fridge, pouring himself a glass of water as if this is a casual conversation.

"What is going on, Mom?" I ask her, but she doesn't look at me. "This is bullshit. I know what just happened wasn't... I will talk to someone, but you aren't sending me away."

"You can't stay here, Ben," Paul says. "I am not sure how to make it much clearer to you."

I go into the living room and grab my phone from my pocket to call my dad immediately. Before he can even fully say hello, I start stumbling my words to him, "Come get your kid," I say.

"What?" He asks, confused.

"Either one of us. Paul is trying to... Paul is trying to send me away."

"Hey, slow down first. What is going on? Send you where?"

"I don't know, to some fucking place. He thinks I'm crazy, Dad. But he is over here raising a kid that isn't his. He's crazy. Not me. Him. And he is telling Mom to pick between me or him. He's crazy. I'm not. Dad, I fucked up and now they're trying to ship me away."

"Ben, calm down. Let me talk to your mother."

"Dad, they're trying to send me away. And they're making me go to this place."

"What place?"

"They're out to get me."

"We're not out to get you, Ben. Jesus Christ," Paul says from the kitchen as he rolls his eyes, rubbing my mom's back to comfort her.

"Just calm down, let me talk to your mother so I can find out what is going on," I walk over to her and hand her the phone. She doesn't look at me.

"Hello?" My mom answers. "You aren't here, you don't understand," she is quiet. "I even talked to Willow about it, and she can confirm."

"What? What did you do?" I say.

"Yes, he has been hallucinating. You have no idea what just happened here. You need to come here and talk to him."

"No, no," I say and go out the back door, "Sean! Sean! We are going to see Dad." I start yelling in the backyard.

"What are you doing?" Paul yells coming out the door.

"I am taking him to see his dad."

"Ben, stop it," my mom says, "Get here, now." My mom says before she hangs up the phone.

"Get in the house or I am calling the cops," Paul demands.

I raise my hands as if I am surrendering, "Okay, okay. You all think I am crazy, but do you hear yourselves?"

"I don't think you're crazy, honey. You just need a little help clearing your mind. That's all," my mom is hunched over and looks defeated. I have never seen her look so awful.

"I just got home, and you're trying to send me away, Mom. I want to be home with you. I haven't seen you in years, and you already want me gone," my voice pleading, I can see her starting to cry again, and as she starts walking towards me with open arms, Paul grabs her and puts her behind him.

"Sarah, don't fall for this. He is manipulating you. He was about to kill himself; he doesn't care about spending time with you. He can't decipher what is real and what isn't, he is high most of the time."

"High? What are you talking about?" I ask in confusion.

He pulls out pill bottles from his pockets and throws them at my feet, "These pills aren't even labeled with a name, a doctor didn't give these to you. You can't handle this life without being on something. You need help."

I step closer to him and grab him by his shirt, "You have this pretty life because I risked mine. You have no idea what life I have lived and what I can handle."

"Ben, love, we just want you to be the best you that you can be right now," my mom says, sounding like an inspirational quote that she would write on her board at the beginning of a class.

"Fuck you. Fuck both of you."

Seattle

Willow

"Have you talked to Ben recently?" Lily asks, flipping through a new book that she pulled out of the shipment box sitting on my couch.

"Nope," I answer from the kitchen, looking for a lighter in the drawers.

"So you don't know how he's doing?"

"Nope," I repeat myself.

"Well, do you think he is better at his dad's?"

"I don't know," my voice grows more irritated with each response.

"Well, it has been what, like a couple of weeks now?"

"I said, I haven't talked to him, Lily," I snap at her. I walk back into the living room, lighting the joint that is being smothered between my lips.

"Sorry, dude," she says apologetically, looking down at the floor to avoid my look at her.

"It's probably better. He needs to focus on himself. Plus, I am sure his mom will tell me if he kills himself."

She gasps, "Damn, that's heavy. You think he would?"

"Depending on the day. I don't know. Can we not talk about Ben anymore?" She must notice the sorrowful look on my face because she changes the subject to herself and about a guy she hooked up with the previous night.

I find myself high, drunk, and lying naked next to River to help keep the loneliness that I fight at bay. "Your vibe is totally off," River says.

"Been dealing with some things," I defend myself.

"I'm going camping next weekend. If you want to come, it might help."

"Yeah, I will think about it. Are you good for round two?" I shift my focus elsewhere.

"Always," he rolls over and gets on top. I would be lying if I said I didn't enjoy it, the mindless sex that is just about feeling each other and having a quick orgasm. But I would be lying if I said I didn't wish it were Ben.

As River goes to the bathroom, I can't help but text Ben. I begin to type, "thinking of you," but decide it sounds too cliché.

Hey… too casual.

Hope all is well… too formal.

Miss you… too desperate.

Hope the Seattle rain isn't drowning you… too passive.

Hope you didn't die or go crazy… too aggressive.

I'm looking at the hole you punched through my bedroom wall. I wish I could be mad about it, but it reminds me that you were here. That you were in my bedroom. That you were in my life, and I can't be mad about that. Send.

I put my phone on my nightstand, assuming there wouldn't be any return message, but as soon as I put it down, it vibrates.

A cold response of, *I can have someone come fix it for you.*

I can't help but answer back, *that's not what I am asking for. I am just saying... I miss you.*

Well, you shouldn't have a broken wall.

I throw my phone across the room, which ironically leaves a small dent in the wall.

While River rolls a joint in the living room, I grab my phone and look at the text conversation again, looking to see if there is some hidden message there or some glimpse of emotion reflecting some type of yearning. My mind starts to flutter with thoughts about how he just left without much of a goodbye, hasn't bothered to contact me to even express if he is doing well or even if he's doing shitty.

Screw this. I unexpectedly hear the tone of a phone ringing and register the fact that I just called him.

"Hello?" His voice was soft, as if he was just lying down, but it sounds huskier than I remember. But then I remember the huskiness of that voice is always after he yelled, and his throat is raw, red, bleeding with vexation and repentance that will never be disclosed.

"Hi," shock fills my voice.

"Are you calling me to get a quote for that wall?" A dry laugh as he attempts to make a joke. But my heart can't help but plummet into my stomach, sinking at the thought of him not being here. About us not being *us*. He is him. I am me. We are no longer us.

"Ha... no. I just... how are you?" My voice is striving to sound sincere.

"Fine. Seattle is nice, there is a lot to do, and things to see. I venture out on my good days."

"Good days? Guess you still have bad days?"

"We all do, Willow," his voice like sharp daggers directed right at me. "How is it there?" A softening in his voice.

But I can't help but feel disappointed at the false hope I created in my mind that he would tell me I should come visit. "It's how it always is, nothing new."

"Are we just doing small talk, or is there something else to this conversation?" He clears his throat.

"I can't make small talk with my boyfriend?" The words falling out of my mouth like water.

"Willow," his voice trailing off, sadness following behind it.

"What? We never ended this, and I don't know where you have been lately, but I'm here."

"I need to figure things out. I'm not good for you right now."

"Babe, got the blunt ready for you. I can also go for round three when you're ready, my testosterone is at an all-time high today!" River exclaims into the bedroom as if it were almost a calculated moment.

"You don't seem to be too lonely," Ben says, his voice turning ice again.

"It's not like that," I plead before I know the inevitable argument begins, or even worse, before he hangs up and ends this poor attempt at me trying to remain as us.

"I am glad you're not lonely. But I should have remembered," his voice remaining calm as if he was talking to a stranger, but I know there is more attached to this comment.

"What?"

"You will never be lonely. You're Willow. You will always find someone."

"I don't want someone. I want you, Ben."

"I can tell," then there it was, the sound of silence. Gone.

I text Coy, saying, *Bring over something strong. I need to leave the world for a little.*

Always babygurl

Ben

Even after five weeks, the bed still feels foreign to me. Maybe foreign is what I need right now, though, at least that's what I keep reminding myself. Before the rain starts again, I go to sit outside on the stoop smoking a cigarette as my dad pulls up in his black Tesla, the rain from earlier leaving wet marks on the windows. He puts down his briefcase in front of me and grabs my pack of cigarettes, pulling one out and lighting it.

"Don't let Sophia know about this," he warns me and takes a seat next to me.

"Lips are sealed," I respond, moving over more so he can sit.

"How are you liking it here?"

"Living in my dad's basement? Loving it here," I sarcastically answer.

"Well, have you thought about what you are going to do long term?" He asks, finding a place of comfort in his spot.

"Long term, as in what? As in getting my shit together mentally?" Another inhale.

"No, job-wise. I mean, yeah, that too, though."

"I am going back."

"When? Did you tell your mom? What are you going to do long term in Yelton then?"

"Yelton?" My voice reflecting a surprised tone, "I am going to re-enlist."

He stands up and turns to face me, "Like hell you are, Ben. I am not letting you do that."

"Letting me? You can't let or not let me do anything," my voice equally raising with his.

"You can't go back, look what it has done to you."

"What? What has it done to me, exactly?" Pushing him to say something, to admit that there is something wrong with me.

"You know what I am talking about."

"What? Just like how you believe I am fucked up like everyone else thinks."

"Do we need to bring up the incident that happened that got you here?" His voice hushed, as if he were trying to remind me what happened without attaching any guilt to it.

"Was the whole point of this conversation just to point out mistakes I have made or just to make me feel bad about myself?" I stand up and flick my cigarette into the driveway, but before I can fully walk away, he grabs my arm tightly, pulling me back.

"I just want to talk to my son. I am not trying to start an argument. Just stay and talk," he pleads. I hesitate, but I come back closer, so he lets go of my arm, and I sit back down on the steps. "How is Willow doing?" he then asks.

"I haven't talked to her."

"Since you have been here?" He sounds stunned.

"Yeah." A memory flickers in my head of her smile, the sound of her laugh that comes in waves, each laugh growing in amusement, her hair drowning me any time we lay together, her sleeping breath on my neck warming me as I lay there staring blindly at the moon-lit ceiling.

"Well, how come?" He asks.

"I'm just not right for her, Dad," he must hear the guilt and desperation in my voice because he puts his hand on my shoulder.

"And you think I am right for Sophia? I mean, God, she is the beautiful girl who just flows through the house like she's dancing, and I knock down plates from the table because I have no spatial awareness. She plays with the kids like she is their best friend, and I don't even know what Bella is talking about half the time with her LOK dolls or some shit. I am not right for her, but we both have the same goal, and that is to love each other endlessly."

I sigh, "It's just more than that."

"Because you're making it more than that."

Sophia places a white dinner plate in front of me, which consists of burnt meatloaf, canned corn that has streaming water running into the boxed mashed potatoes acting as a dam for it. I wouldn't say it's her best meal, but it's also not her worst. She wobbles to each of us, putting a plate down at the table, her pregnant belly nearly knocking into me each time.

"Bella, tell daddy how good you did at dance today," she says as she sits down and we all pick up our forks.

Gunshots fill the streets outside. I look over at the children who sit at the table with us and shout at them to get down in the little Arabic I know. They stare at me blankly.

"Philips, turn the lights off," Colby yells before he heads upstairs. I turn off the lights in the dining room we're in and start to head upstairs behind Colby.

The man who is hosting us here starts following behind me, asking what I am doing repeatedly. I turn around while I am halfway up the stairs, "Just turn the lights off and hide somewhere, okay?" I turn back around and start to go back up.

He grabs my arm and pulls me to look at him, which causes me to lose my balance and fall a step, landing in the middle of my back. I gasp for air as the wind gets knocked out of me, struggling to inhale some oxygen.

Reynolds starts walking up the stairs, "Get the fuck up and let's go." He passes by me and grabs the back of my collar slightly to try to get me to start moving.

As I finally catch my breath, I push the man's chest slightly, "Just, go take care of your family." I finally get upstairs and go to the north-facing room to see the streets. As I look out the window, the streets are empty, but the gunshots are still firing in the neighboring streets.

"Your head," a voice says behind me. I look over to find the man standing at the doorway of the bedroom.

"For fucks sake, I said go take care of your family," I say and start to walk towards him to push him out of the room while Colby and Reynolds start setting up snipers.

"Your head," he says again. I reach the back of my head and feel a wetness. When I look at my hand, I see it's covered with dark red blood like crushed raspberries.

I look back up from my hand and see my dad looking at me with concerned eyes as I look around the room. I notice a crib, a giant stuffed teddy bear sitting in the corner, light green walls with gray elephant wallpaper on the left wall. "It looks good in here, you did a good job painting,"

I say, hoping that I am in here because he was showing it to me. Hoping that I just blanked out on him bringing me in here, and I can play it off that I know what is going on.

"You hit your head when you fell," he says.

I look down at my hand and see it engulfed in blood. "The carpet!" Sophia's voice shrieking as she comes into the room, "It has blood on it!"

I turn around and look down and see droplets of blood on the white fuzzy carpet, a bad dinner party with spilt red wine. "I told you to wait downstairs, Sophia." My dad's voice was harsh and deep.

"The carpet," She squeals.

"Downstairs," he says again. The command in his voice is unforgiving, and she turns around to leave. "Let me put a bandage on you," he says, turning around.

I follow him into the bathroom and sit down on the toilet as he rummages through the medicine cabinet, mumbling curse words under his breath as unused toothbrushes from the dentist and cold medicine fall out of the cabinet.

He pours rubbing alcohol on a cotton ball, and I turn my body so the back of my head is facing him, "Your mother told me…" I try to focus on the stinging of the alcohol on my head, a pain I'd rather endure than this conversation. "It's just different when you see it."

"It's not always… I don't know how bad this one was. I mean, sometimes I know it's not real. Then there are times when I am just in a different place."

"Do you remember any of it?" He asks, still dabbing at the cut.

"No. I don't even really know if it's a real memory or something that I am making up. I can't remember any of it. It is like a dream that you just can't remember, but you feel like it was a nightmare."

"So, you don't know what just happened or what happened at your mom's?" He throws away the cotton balls and starts to open a bandage.

"No. I mean, everyone told me what happened at Mom's. But I don't remember it."

He sighs and finishes putting the bandage on my head, "So you don't know when it's going to happen or how severe it will be?" I can already tell there is a hidden question to this.

"Correct," I turn around and look at him, but he avoids eye contact. "What?"

"I have to think about everyone's safety in the house," he said, still not looking at me.

"Are you implying I need to leave?"

He finally makes eye contact, "No, not at all!" But then he looks right back down. "I have to lock your door at night."

"Oh, okay," I look down sheepishly and feel the bandage on my head.

"I am sorry, Ben. But if something were to happen while we were asleep or…"

"I get it," I stand up and hug him because I do get it.

As I sit in my now dungeon of a basement bedroom, the sound of a man's voice talking to Willow replays in my head. The voice sounds faintly familiar, but I can't put my finger on it. Regardless of who it is, she is still having sex with someone else. I swallow the idea of being petty, but it can't help but get stuck in my throat, revenge burning in my esophagus.

The window in my room is just big enough for me to crawl through and make my escape. Seattle is a great place for bars, a tag chaser who I can revenge fuck. A bar called, "The 51" grabs my attention with the bright neon green "open" sign hanging in the window. As I walk in, there is a group of ten college-aged kids sitting at a table, a liter of cheap beer in the middle of the table, and half-eaten pepperoni pizza lingering on their plates.

"I'll take a Stella," I ask the bartender. I stand there, looking at the kids at the table, seeing all of them tell each other jokes and teasing each other about failing a midterm, and I can't help but feel homesick for a place that no one would consider my home except for my brothers.

The laughter of a group of girls catches my attention. I look over at a pool table and see four girls attempting to play pool. One girl specifically grabs my curiosity, her long black hair swaying as she laughs, her belly button ring slightly showing when she moves, since her shirt is cropped, her black jean skirt revealing her legs. I can see the effort she tried to make to look this good, nothing like Willow, who is naturally flawless. Willow doesn't need tight clothes or shirts that don't fully fit to show what she has underneath.

"Bet none of you bitches can get any of these balls in," she says to the other girls and takes her last sip of her beer, walking towards the bar.

"Bet you can't get any of the balls in the pocket," I say to her as she stands at the bar.

She looks me up and down and then smiles, "If I get one in, then you buy me a beer."

"And if you don't?"

"What do you want?" She puts her elbows up at the bar and leans forward, revealing more cleavage.

"What do you have to offer?" I smirk at her.

She bites her lip, "Well, you want something specific, and that's why you're flirting with me."

"I can't make a friendly bet with someone?".

"If I don't make the ball in, then I will make out with you. Right here."

"I can agree to that one," we shake hands, and she walks back to the pool table and yanks the stick from one of her friend's hands.

"Any certain one you want me to get in?" She yells out to me as I walk over to her.

"The red 13 into the left top pocket," I say. Within seconds, she makes it in.

"I will take a Corona Light, thanks," she puts the stick down and walks up to me.

"Okay, I stand corrected,"

She whispers in my ear, "and don't forget the lime." We walk over to the bar, and I get her drink. "So, what's your name?" She asks.

"I'm Ben."

"Zoe. Guess I can join you in the three-lettered name. You here by yourself, Ben?"

"Yeah, I just came back home. I was in Iraq for a couple years, was living with my mom for a while but shit went wrong so I am here now."

"Iraq, huh?" She moves a little closer, just like I predicted. "So, you decided to come to a bar by yourself… on a Wednesday night?"

"Honestly? My ex-girlfriend just called me and she was fucking someone else so I figured a beer would be ideal."

"That's rough," she grabs my arm. "You know what they say, payback's a bitch."

"They do indeed say that. So what is your advice?" I put my hand on her lower back.

"You pocket call her while you fuck someone else."

"Uh-huh, and how would I manage that one?"

She leans into my ear, "I know just the girl for the job," she pulls away. "But first a shot of Fireball."

A shot of Fireball turned into four shots of Fireball, a shot of tequila, resulting in me licking salt off her neck and taking lime out of her mouth, her friends encouraging the behavior from both of us. She grabs my hand, announcing to her friends, "We're going to go fuck in the bathroom to make his ex-girlfriend jealous." Only one of her friends looks shocked, but it quickly fades as another one yells that they're getting another round.

She leads me to the men's bathroom, "they usually have condoms in here. Plus, boys care less about someone having sex in the bathroom than the girls do."

"Do you do this often?" I hesitantly ask.

"No, not often. But at least enough to know this gold mine of information."

We walk into the bathroom, and a drunk guy at the urinal turns around to look at us and gives me a head nod to congratulate me on my victory. Zoe wasn't wrong, there were a couple of condoms lying on the counter. She goes up to grab one and looks me up and down, "Is it safe to assume that you need a magnum?" She smirks and raises her eyebrow at me.

I let out a laugh, "That's safe to say."

She walks into the second stall, and I follow behind, locking the door. I look at her as she stands there smirking, trying to talk myself into not getting into my head about the situation. I say to her, "You know, we don't have to have sex. You could just pretend on the phone." Letting her have the option to opt out of a bar bathroom-stall revenge sex.

"But what fun would that be?" She says, starting to unbutton my pants. I put my hand on the back of her head, pulling her hair as I kiss her, spinning her around, and pushing her against the door.

She puts her hand down my pants, "good thing I grabbed the bigger condom."

I grab the condom and put it on, pulling her underwear down and pushing her skirt up. She jumps up and wraps her legs around my waist, her moans filling the bathroom as I hear people come in and out, saying "nice" when they hear us.

"Harder, harder," she yells. I put her down and bend her over the toilet, holding on to her hips as I thrust. "WAIT!" She suddenly yells, and I stop, "Get your phone, call her."

The thought of whose voice was on the other line, doing exactly what I am doing to Zoe to Willow crosses my mind. The thought of Willow yelling "harder, harder" to someone else, her lying there naked with her round breasts bouncing as someone fucks her, her unshaved vagina wet with excitement. I pull out my phone and call her, throwing it on the toilet paper holder and continuing to have sex with Zoe. Either Willow answers and hears it or gets a long voicemail of the sounds of sex.

Willow

"Ben is calling you," Coy yells from the living room, "do you want me to answer?"

I walk in from the kitchen and sit down next to Coy, staring at the phone. Preparing myself for the lecture I am about to receive as I click "accept".

"Hello?" I say reluctantly. Nothing except muffled noises, "Ben?" I say again more frantically than reluctantly now. "Ben, are you okay?"

"What? What's wrong?" Coy asks nervously.

"I don't know, I think something is wrong," I reply while putting the phone on speaker for Coy to hear now.

"Is that moaning? Oh god, did he call you while jerking off?" Coy says and starts to laugh.

Then, suddenly, a distinct, clear sentence, "Harder Ben, harder, fuck me harder." My stomach drops, and I just stare at my phone, frozen as the noises suddenly become clearer now that I know what the noises are.

"Hang up!" Coy yells. Yet I can't unfreeze myself to do so. The moaning was getting louder, Ben's name being repeated over and over again.

"You feel so fucking good, Zoe. My cock has never felt this good," I hear Ben say.

Coy grabs the phone and hangs up, "Weird sex talk," he says, trying to break any tension. The vase sitting on the coffee table meets its demise as it is greeted to a halt against the wall. Coy looks at me with wide eyes. "Willow…"

"Coy," anger boiling in my chest.

"I mean, you have been having sex with River."

"Don't even start," I stand up and pace from the kitchen back to the living room and back again. "You don't get it, Coy. Before he left, this is the kind of shit he did with girls. Then he came home and was all messed up, and I was there and I tried to help and I was there to love him, fully, truly, whole-fucking-heartedly. And he couldn't just fuck me like that at first because he's a bipolar schizophrenic in denial. And guess what, I was fine with that. But this? Who is Zoe? Why is she someone that he can shove his dick into?"

Tears start to fill my eyes, "I miss him, Coy. I love him and I want him back home." The tears finally make their way out. "I need shrooms and a bath," I say as I take out weed and a rolling paper to make a joint.

"I can get both for you, if you mean that," Coy says.

Bubbles pop like floating clouds that have exploded, creating more bubble clouds. They're blue, POP, pink, POP, purple, POP, blue, POP, yellow, POP, orange. They cling together like atoms holding on for dear life, the ocean of water trying to pull them apart. An island of bubbles clinging together, forming their own life simultaneously.

The sound of voices channeling from the living room. Ben is shirtless on the couch, a naked girl bouncing on him, her long blonde ponytail swaying like a swing on a windy day. "Ben, Ben," she moans. I yell out his name, but the words pop like the bubbles before they come out. "Ben, Ben," she keeps moaning. I try again, failing. "Ben," she becomes louder every time I try.

He can't hear me over her, and I need him to look at me, my feet ice skating to the couch, but when I get there, they're gone. Scathing whimpers echoing in the bedroom, Reynolds penetrating Ben's back with a knife, blood dripping on the floor like the aftermath of a hurricane.

"Stop," the words fully forming from my mouth this time. My back is against Reynolds' front door, the hardwood pushing on my crooked spine, his hands pushing against the door on each side of my head. "Stop," I repeat.

"Miss me?" He questions, his lips forcing themselves on mine. A tongue slithering like a snake tasting its prey. "This was fun the first time," his words were icy in my ear.

My body is playing limbo under his arm, he catches his prey. Bends her over the couch, pulling off her skin. Now she is the one penetrated.

My eyes gazing up in front of me, Ben and Zoe mirroring us. Ben's eyes were down, his face hidden. I reach my hand out, and Zoe grabs mine, squeezing it tightly. I call for Ben, but she mimics me every time.

"Ben," I yelp. They're gone, and I am alone. Wet footprints lead to the bathroom, and I follow. Opening the door to find Reynolds at the edge of the bathtub, holding someone down as he flips the coin that Ben wears on his necklace. Rain sits on the other end of the bathtub, staring down into the tub. Red and white roses start to bloom in the tub, overflowing onto the floor.

The sound of laughter and clinking of utensils on fine china comes from the kitchen as I follow it. My mother's carcass lies on the table as Ben and his parents pick at it and eat it. "What are you doing?" I yell, but none of them stop or even acknowledge me.

I'm in my bed with my head feeling as if there are a ton of bricks replacing my brain, Coy lying next to me asleep. "Coy," I shake him, attempting to wake him up. He just groans and ignores me as I keep trying to wake him. "Coy, wake up."

He rubs his eyes and looks at me, "Be aware I have nothing on below the waist."

"You just left me last night," as I sit up, a wave of nausea rushes over my stomach.

"I didn't know you needed a guide through your trip. I took some ecstasy and had my own party," he rolls over and grabs cocaine from the nightstand that he left there. "So, I am guessing it wasn't good?"

"I can only remember pieces of it, and it doesn't make sense. Ben was there a whole lot. I think I need to go to Seattle to see him," I start packing a bag, stuffing the first shirt I find in it.

"I don't think that is a good idea," Coy warns.

"Why?" I snap at him as he grabs my hand before I can put another random tank top in the bag.

"Because he clearly moved on and doesn't want you there, Will," he lets go of my hand and wraps one of my kimonos from the floor around his waist. "How about you call him first and see how that goes? A real conversation."

I think about what he says and try to talk myself into the logical idea. My hands are shaking as I go to call him. The phone rings a few times, and before I give up, he answers.

I can hear the sound of cars and birds in the background, and I picture him outside, I picture him wearing jeans and a t-shirt with a zip-up sweater, "Hello?" He says, I can hear him inhale his cigarette.

"I got a call from you last night," I say right away.

"I didn't call you," he states.

"You did, but it seemed like you were busy with someone," I try not to show the sadness in my voice.

"I must have pocket called you, sorry," the apology sounding like an obligation.

I click the FaceTime button on the phone call, waiting to see if he will accept, thinking that if he has to look at me, then he will feel sorry.

His hood is on, and his beard has grown even more. "It's nice to see your face, Ben."

The corner of his lips going up slightly to form a smile, "I am embarrassed."

"About the pocket call?"

He smokes his cigarette a few times before answering, and I grab a joint to match the mood. "No, Willow. About what happened," he finally says and there is a sense of relief I feel within about his honesty, an actual confession.

"Come home, baby. Let's do this together," I say, taking a longer drag to hide my sobs.

"My mom won't let me back in the house. Nay, fucking Paul won't."

"Who says you have to move back in with them?" I say.

"Where would I go?" He takes off his hood, and I can see his face more clearly. His hair has grown too, and he has it styled back, one piece of hair with a slight curl dangling on his forehead, and he pushes it back.

"Are you not understanding that I want to be with you?"

"Will, I can't put that burden on you," he tosses the cigarette he was smoking and lights another.

"Regardless of where you would be living, I am staying with you."

"I want to be happy with you. If I come back, if we do this, I want to do it, right."

"Then you need to get help, Ben," I tell him.

There is a moment of silence. I see Sophia walk out of the house behind him and the kids following behind her, "I could have taken them to daycare today," he states.

"No, it's okay," I hear her respond, her voice sounding stern as if he was a stranger.

He sighs and looks back at the phone at me, "There was an incident. I think she is more pissed about the blood on the carpet than anything else."

"Should I bother asking what happened?"

He rolls his eyes, "No, not worth it. Willow, I don't know where home is right now. Nowhere feels *right*. But the one thing I do know is that the closest thing I have felt to a home is being with you."

"Is that a yes, Ben?" I try to hide my excitement, but I know he can see it.

"We have a few things to talk about beforehand. How about I fly back this weekend and we talk and go from there?"

Ben

I know Willow is watching me from the window as I chain smoke and pace around the front yard. "Well, shit," Coy says as he is walking out of his parents' house and sees me.

"Hey, Coy."

"Do you want the lecture now or later?" He says, taking a drink from a flask.

"Can never be an option?" I say back. He raises the flask, offering me a sip, which I quickly accept, taking more than a sip.

"Good luck," he says, slapping my back and walking away.

I start walking to Willow's front door, a mix of feelings brewing in me like a tornado. The feeling of embarrassment of all the times she has seen me lower than the lowest, guilt of having sex with another girl and making her listen, anger of her having sex with someone else, sadness that it wasn't me, rage of what happened between Reynolds and her, but overall love which has brought me to this front door.

I knock on the door, and she answers. She is wearing a dress I have never seen before. It is light blue and loose, proving my point that she doesn't need tight clothes to show what she has underneath. Her hair is different from the last time I saw her, longer, less sun-kissed blonde. She smiles at me, her red lipstick making her lips more pronounced.

I scratch at my beard to try and cover my giant smile as I look at her. We stare at each other for a few seconds until she comes up and hugs me. I grab her tighter, breathing in the smell of her floral perfume and the slight hint of weed.

She pulls away and looks up at me. I grab her face in my hands and kiss her. We stumble into the house, and I close the door behind me, pushing her against the wall adjacent to the door. She starts to unbutton my flannel, and I pull her dress off over her head. I take a step back for a second to just look at her.

I don't feel embarrassed or guilty. I don't feel angry or enraged. She pulls me back in and jumps on top of me, wrapping her legs around my waist. My hands wrap around her ass, embracing her fully. We stumble into her bedroom, our mouths never separating from each other.

"I missed you," we both muffle into each other's mouths in between kisses. We find our way to the bed, tripping over each other like a bad choreographed dance. My fingers slowly slide up her thigh until I reach her clit. I start to rub her clit slowly to warm her up, but it feels as if she is already there. Two fingers enter her, knowing exactly what spot drives her crazy. The feeling of her getting instantly wetter makes me solid, my dick pulsing in my pants.

She grabs the back of my hair in a fistful, but then catches herself before she lets herself release and pushes me back slightly. Her fingers fumble as she starts to unbutton my jeans. I finish the job for her and take them off. I push her thighs open wider with the back of my hand and insert myself in her.

We both gasp at the initial contact. The warmth of her encapsulates my entire body, and I need to keep reminding myself to hold a little bit longer. I thrust in her, her nails scratching my back as she opens her legs wider to let me in deeper. I pull out and flip her over so I can see her from behind. Her ass is bouncing back into me as she takes me in whole.

"Harder," she moans, and I do as she commands. I reach one arm around her waist to hold her up more as I slam into her. "Yes, right there!" She exclaims right before she releases. My hard cock is soaking from her, and I follow her pursuit and fill her. Her body collapses onto the bed, and I roll off her, lying next to her.

"So, hello," Willow says, panting, lying there naked in sweat. She smiles at me, and I grab her to hold her. Her head rests on my chest.

"Hi, Willow," I kiss the top of her head.

"I made you dinner!" She exclaims and jumps up, putting her dress back on.

I get up and get dressed, following her to the kitchen, stopping to look at a hole in the wall by her bedroom door. "Do you only want me to move in to get rid of these holes?" I ask her, my finger circling the hole I left.

"It would be a benefit," she says as she pours wine and hands it to me.

She plates spaghetti and sauce on a plate and puts it in front of me as I sit at the kitchen table. "So what did your dad say about you leaving?"

"They tried very hard to hide their sigh of relief and attempted to make it sound sincere, convincing me to stay," I twirl my pasta around my fork before taking a mouthful of it.

"And your mom?"

"That would have to involve me telling her," I take a sip of wine after my bite.

"Ben, you have to tell her you're here!"

"I am here for you right now, not her. If I stay, then I will."

"So, that brings me to my next question? Want to jump into that conversation you mentioned earlier?" She grabs the wine bottle from the kitchen and pours more wine into our glasses. "Maybe this will help too," she then grabs a bottle of vodka and two shot glasses, placing them on the table.

"I think so," I pour both of us a shot, and we cheer before taking the shot. And another one. "I will take the medication, the Seroquel that I have been holding on to. I know there is something wrong, but you need to understand I can't talk to someone about it. I can't have a trace of it. But I also need you to understand that I am going to go back one day, not now, but I am."

She takes another shot and sighs, "Is any part of that up for conversation?"

I follow her lead and take another shot and sigh, "No, Willow. I am homesick for a place I never wanted to call home." She takes a second to mull over that last part, taking a sip of wine to push down the feeling in her throat that wants to explode.

"Do I get terms and conditions?" She smirks, attempting to switch the mood, and I can already tell I am in trouble. I nod to show my acceptance in listening to these terms. "The hair and beard stay. It's a good look, and River didn't have a beard, and it felt like I was kissing a child."

Then it dawned on me, the person she was having sex with was River, and I don't know if I should be relieved it was someone she already knew or angry that it was him. I remind myself that I just did the same thing in return. I push it in the back of my head to help ensure this night isn't ruined by jealousy.

"I also want honesty from you, no bullshit. That means full disclosure on everything," I can tell she is waiting to say something else, but is pausing.

"What is the main question you're asking, Willow?"

"I just need to know in detail about the girl you were with the other night. I need to know what it is that you keep seeing and what is making you hallucinate."

"Why would you want to even know that? And I don't even know or remember half the time. It's everything," I take a sip of wine, reminding myself not to get frustrated, reminding myself that she is the type of person who is open and literally every god-damn thing… everything except. "Great, let's be honest then. Tell me the truth,"

She looks at me, confused, "What are you talking about? The truth about what?" Then she breaks eye contact with me and looks down, fiddling with her fingers. She and I both know the truth, we both know what happened when the phone hung up. I also know she went there to get answers because I don't give her any. Regardless of whether we both know the truth, I need to hear it from her.

"I told you, nothing. When we hung up, he was just being an asshole, and I left," she doesn't look back up at me.

"So that is all?" I raise an eyebrow at her, leaning an inch closer to her.

"Ben, if you want the truth, that is it. If you want to hear something else, then I would be lying, but that is the answer you *need* to accept," her eyes look back at me now, her eyes big and round, sincere and waiting for my approval of her answer.

I tap my fingers on the table and pour another shot, "So you like the beard?"

She smiles, probably happier that we are done with that topic of conversation, "Love it! So are we okay with these terms?"

I put my hand out to shake hers, implying I agree. She returns the handshake and blatantly says, "So tell me about the girl you had sex with."

"Oh, so we're back to that? If that's really what you want to know, but then tell me why you had sex with River," I respond.

I tell her the details, starting with the incident earlier that night with the hallucination, since that is now part of our terms. I tell her how I met the girl, my poor flirting skills, and the overall ease with the girl was. I tell her every detail, down to telling her what color the girl's underwear was. She asked me how it felt and didn't show a hint of anger when I told her that I enjoyed it. Then she finally asked if it reminded me of who I was before I went away, and even though I didn't think of it prior, it did. But that is why I left home, because everything was meaningless.

We make our way to the couch, where she tells me she had sex with River because she was lonely, and I can't blame that. I am the one who left her out of nowhere, and what is going to happen if I leave again? Is this an issue we will have to keep facing? Revenge and jealousy over and over again? I pretend it never crossed my mind and try to enjoy the moment with her while it is still here.

Willow

Once Ben moved in, it finally felt like I could breathe knowing he was here with me. I am not sure if that stemmed from wanting to just be with him or if it's because I can keep an eye on him. The mornings were filled with pancakes, coffee, and occasionally a shot of vodka if we were feeling a little disobedient against the norms that morning. While his hallucinations seemed to simmer a bit, his night sweats did the complete opposite. The sheets needed to be washed every night, and while I did have some contribution to that, I would never tell him.

He came into the bedroom with a coffee in one hand and a shot in the other as I pulled myself up from laying down, "So, I think we should tell my mom where I am this weekend. My dad gave me some time to get settled and hasn't said anything to her," he hands me the coffee and the shot. I take the shot, letting it burn my throat on its way down as it hits my empty stomach.

"And I was thinking we can tell her I live with my wife," he says and drops down to one knee, pulling out a box where a ring lies perfectly still waiting for me to take it or leave it. I stare at the ring before I respond, the sunlight about to cast upon the green gemstone that is cushioned by a rose gold band. I have never given much thought about marriage in general, the idea of it seeming so conventional.

I look up at Ben, his eyes waiting for a response. Before I can say anything, he starts talking, "Willow, I know I am not good at expressing myself, but I am going to try. I love you more than I thought it could be possible to love someone. And I appreciate everything you do for me and how you have been by my side, and I am sorry I haven't done more for you because you deserve it. But, I want to spend the rest of my life making sure you are taken care of the best way that I can," he stays on his knee for another second as we both sit there in silence.

Moments of the past year with Ben flicker through my head like a slideshow on a speed run. The heavy moments slip through my mind, overpowered by the greatness we have shared.

"Through the good and bad, I will stand by your side. I would love to marry you, Benjamin James Phillips," I jump up from the bed, and he glides up off his knee and onto two feet to catch me as I wrap my arms around him.

"Now let's go make you my wife," he says and pulls away from me, making eye contact. I look at him in confusion, which he must notice and respond, "Let's go to the courthouse and get married. We know we want to get married, so why wait?"

I stand across from Ben in a white lace dress, the back of it revealing my whole back and the sleeves wrapping around my wrists. Ben wears his formal army uniform, which unfortunately means he had to shave his luscious beard off, his blue pants with creases in all the right places loosely fitting him, and a jacket that is filled with pins and medals for which I have no idea the meaning of any of them. Chris and Lily stand at our respective sides as an officiant reads us our vows to say to each other.

"Do you promise to love, honor, cherish, and protect him, forsaking all others and holding only unto him?" The officiant looks at me to respond.

"I do," my cheeks aching from smiling so hard.

"I, Benjamin, take the Willow, to be my wife. To have and to hold, in sickness and in health, for richer or for poorer, and I promise my love to you. With this ring I thee wed," Ben starts to put the ring we just got from the jewelry store on my finger. Both our hands are shaking slightly with nerves as sweat leaks from our pores. We make eye contact as it gets to the web of my fingers and smile.

"I, Willow, take the Benjamin, to be my husband. To have and to hold, in sickness and in health, for richer or for poorer, and I promise my love to you. With this ring I thee wed," in return, I put his wedding ring on his finger. Maybe marriage isn't quite as conventional as I thought it was.

"I now pronounce Mr. and Mrs. Benjamin Phillips, you may kiss the bride!" The officiant announces.

Ben grabs me, my face settling in his hands as he kisses me. The cheers from Lily and Chris fill the room as he continues to kiss me. He pulls away and whispers in my ear just for me to hear, "thank you for marrying me."

The rest of the night was spent going from bar to bar with Lily and Chris while other of our friends joined us as we came across them. We drank until we couldn't feel our faces. At our fifth bar we stopped at a place called Loca. Somehow Coy ended up meeting us there, which is where the blurriness of the night truly began. Ben's friend Jason convinced me and Ben to do body shots and said that Ben had to do one off his new wife, which automatically got us pumped up. It then ended up turning into me and Lily doing one together as the boys stood there wide eyed as I took the lime out of Lily's mouth, exchanging a little tongue between us.

Coy then initiates for us to head to more of a club atmosphere and by judging how our behavior was escalating it seemed like we were about to overstay our welcome here. Our group then gathers and drunkenly stumbles into the club called Highlander, where we are greeted with shots of liquor that is very new to me. I cough as I swallow it and look over at Ben who takes it like a champ and winks at me.

Lily grabs my hand and brings me to the center of the dance floor and yells, "You are fucking MARRIED!"

"I am fucking MARRIED!" I yell back. Ben then comes up behind me and turns me around to start dancing with him. Lily isn't alone for long, Chris and Jason put her right in between them.

Coy comes up to us and shows me a vial that is in the shape of a cross. He unscrews the top of it and pulls out a little spoon that has cocaine at the tip. "You want a bump?" He shouts over the music.

I cover one nostril and snort it. He refills the spoon and looks at Ben, offering him some, and without a beat, in utter disbelief, Ben accepts it. "Fuck yeah!" Coy exclaims in his excitement at Ben's sudden rebellion. We continue dancing, which then starts to end up in more making out than dancing. He puts his hands down my skirt that I am now wearing and starts fingering me. His fingers hit my G-spot immediately. I wrap my hands around his neck to help hold me up as my knees start to shake.

"Don't stop," I moan in his ear. And within a minute, he has me orgasming in the middle of the dance floor. I must have moaned loud enough because I see Lily and Coy look at me and then look down to see Ben taking his hands out of the waistband of my skirt.

Between more drinks and another bump, Ben and I end up in a bathroom stall, sharing a cigarette in between making out. I take another pull and hand him the cigarette, I unbutton his jeans and drop down to my knees for his turn to have an orgasm. I put my mouth around his erect dick, gagging as it hit the back of my throat. He grabs the back of my hair in his fist as salvia drips down my mouth onto the bathroom floor. I look up at him as he looks down at me. He takes one last pull from his cigarette before flicking it into the toilet and pulling me up off my knees from the back of my head.

He pulls my skirt up to my waist and bends me over the toilet, "I want my come dripping down your legs." He grabs onto my hips and starts fucking me, grabbing my hair in his hand again as I moan. I put my hands in front of me and hold on to the wall to keep balance. His hand slides down my back, his fingers tracing my spine as he keeps his thrusts steady. I turn my head to look at him, and we make eye contact as he finishes inside me.

Once we got back to the dance floor, he was indeed correct, his come did drip down my leg, and as soon as I told him about it, he took his finger and wiped it off my thigh, and with the other hand, grabbed my jaw for me to open my mouth. He took his finger and put it in my mouth, "Tell me you like it," he says to me afterwards.

"I fucking love it," I respond.

Ben

I wake up in a shirt that isn't mine, in between a naked Coy and my wife. The last memory living in my head is Facetiming my dad as we left a club and telling him I am married. I check my phone and see a text from him saying, *Call me in the morning.*

I roll over Coy not caring if I wake him up, realizing that my shirt smells like a mix of vodka, tequila and beer, gagging as I get a whiff of it. Stepping into the living room to find a passed out Lily and some other girl on the couch and Jason and Chris on the floor beside them. I walk over a few beer bottles making my way to the front porch.

"You're alive," my dad says as he answers my Facetime.

"Barely," I pinch the bridge of my nose and look at him with squinting eyes.

"So married, huh?" He gives a smirk.

"That's what I came back for, isn't it?"

"I suppose it is, well congratulations. By the sound of it seemed like you had a good celebration last night," he laughs at my obvious hungover misery.

"From what I remember," I respond, trying to match his laugh but failing.

"Well, between the alcohol and drugs, it seems that," he says. I look at him, confused. "Well, you very… willingly… did drugs last night,"

"Huh?"

"You took a nice snort of coke when you called me," he laughs again.

"Shit… sorry…" Unsure if I should apologize for doing it in general or that he caught me.

"Don't worry, I get it. Just make sure you're being safe. Listen, I don't want to be *that* guy right now, but your mom called me last night asking how you were doing. You have to tell her you're not here anymore."

"No, I know. I am going to. I am going today."

"Today? You don't want a day to get it together?" He suggests.

"I think the haziness of my day will help me deal with her," I sigh and laugh concurrently.

"Alright. Well, you know she won't be too thrilled about missing your wedding. So prepare for it. I will let you go so you can rest up. Congratulations, I am happy for you, son. Send me your new address so I can send you and the new Mrs. a gift. Love you."

"Love you too," I hang the phone up and lie down on the porch, and close my eyes. I think about how I am going to handle this mom situation. Do I call her ahead of time so she knows I am coming, or just show up? I think back to how we left things before I left.

"Benjamin, you understand, right?" My mom asks me as I pack my suitcase.

"Is it okay if I leave the rest of my shit here, or does that need to be gone too?" I ask.

"No, leave it. You're going to come back," she responds.

I grab her lightly by the arm and pull her closer, "This is bullshit, you know that, right? You're picking this guy over your own son-" I let go of her, "you know what, I am just so disgusted by this. You can throw my shit out. I am never coming back here, got it?"

She starts crying and grabs my hand, but I pull it away from her, "I just want you to get better, and I don't know what else to do. You don't listen to me. I can't have you here if it isn't safe and you aren't being proactive,"

"So, throwing me out is going to help?" I zip the suitcase. "I am telling you right now, this is the last time you'll see me, unless I am fucking dead. And that is a promise," I grab the letter I wrote for Sean and put it in his room before I walk down the stairs.

Paul stands at the bottom of the stairs watching me come down as if to make sure I actually leave. I take the pill bottles from my pocket and throw it to him, "here are the drugs you say I so desperately need."

"We just want you to get better," Paul says as he fumbles to hold the bottles.

"Fuck you, I should've sho- no, I will leave it at that," I close the door behind me.

In the past few months after not seeing or talking to her, the anger for her and Paul lies at rest. At the end of the day, I understood where they were coming from. Nobody wants to feel unsafe in their home and my job is to make people safe. But the wound of her silence still cuts the deepest.

Willow and I hold hands the whole car ride to my mother's, my palms getting increasingly sweaty with each passing mile.

"So she doesn't know we're coming?" Willow asks, turning down the music.

"She doesn't know I am even back in town," more sweat forming at my fingertips.

She changes the topic, "So, how was trying coke for the first time?" She brings up and lets out a laugh.

I laugh even harder, "Oh, my girl. That isn't my first. Just first with you," I kiss her hand and smile.

We pull into the driveway and thankfully there are no guest cars in the driveway. Just Paul and my mom's sitting there peacefully. Willow and I interlock fingers right away again after we both get out of the car. I cling to her hand with my right hand and hold a bouquet in my other hand, the red roses sticking perfectly straight despite the humidity that crawls into our skin.

My stomach drops as I knock on the front door, and after what felt like an eternity, the door opens and Paul stands there with a glass of whiskey in his hand. "Oh.. oh! What… I didn't…" he stumbles to find words.

"Hi!" Willow breaks the tension as I stand there trying to find words myself.

"Well, come in," he says and moves back, gesturing for us to come in. I notice him looking us both up and down, probably praying there are no suitcases following behind us.

"Who is it?" I hear my mom yell from the kitchen to Paul. As soon as I hear her voice, my heart picks up speed. I look over at Willow, and she gives me a reassuring smile.

Paul walks ahead of us, and we trail behind him to the kitchen. I look around the house, noticing the grand entrance has new pictures on the entry table. My eyes scan across the faces of my mom, Paul, and Sean until I see an unfamiliar picture of a screenshot my mom must have taken on our video call from my first Christmas away. It was shortly after deployment, and I still have life in my eyes while I wear a Santa hat that she sent me in a care package.

"Who was it?" She asks again as Paul gets to the kitchen before us. She then looks over and sees me and Willow, dropping her wine glass from her hand into the sink. "Oh my God, oh my God," she starts crying and runs over to us and wraps her arms around me. Willow lets go of my hand so I can hug her back. I think of the picture that stands at the table and lift my arms to return the hug. But my mind flickers to the days I spent in my dark room, not leaving my bed for days, and my mother telling me I need to leave her house, and I put my arms back to my side.

I look over at Willow and see a frown form on her face as she notices what I did. My mom sensed it because she let go and looks at me, "When did you get back?" She asks, putting space between us now.

"A couple of days ago, I was just getting settled," I tell her.

"Where are you staying for now?" She asks, looking between me and Willow.

"I moved in with Willow."

"Oh," her voice sounding shocked. "Well, Paul is making burgers right now. Sean is at his friend's house for the night. Do you want to eat dinner here?" She asks.

Unsure if Sean not being here and us staying for dinner had a connection, but I answered sure. I hand her the flowers that I forgot I was holding, and she smiles, grabbing them and putting them into a vase immediately.

"Well, go sit outside. We have the table set. I will bring out drinks," she tells us.

"How relieved do you think he was when I said I was living with you?" I ask Willow quietly as we walk outside.

"I think he is trying to hide the confetti he's about to pop over it," we both giggle and I pull her in to give her a kiss on the head before we sit down.

We make small talk and I tell them about the shit weather that lives in Seattle and the funny stories of the kids and my dad. My mother in return shares comedic stories about her students this semester.

"So, I wanted to come here to tell you that I am back in town and living with Willow. But I also wanted to tell you something else," she stops pouring her glass of wine and puts down the bottle looking at me in the eyes. I grab Willow's hand and pull it up to reveal her ring.

"Ahh! Oh my God!" She exclaims, "you're engaged?"

"Well, no," I then pull up my hand and show my wedding band that sits snug around my finger.

Then her smile drops and she grabs my hand to look at the ring, "I don't understand."

"We got married," I tell her.

"You're lying," she drops my hand down, "when?"

"Last night."

"Where?" Her voice getting increasingly aggravated.

"The courthouse."

"The courthouse? Benjamin, you could have had a beautiful wedding here in the backyard where your family could have been there to see you get married."

"Well, I didn't want that. Can't you be happy your son just got married?" I say, now also getting aggravated. Despite knowing her reaction, the daggers of disapproval still ache.

"Benjamin, I didn't even get to see you get married. You come here, which I didn't even know you were home to begin with, and tell me you got married behind my back? It's just never-ending with you. Was this your idea?" She looks over at Willow.

"Me?" Willow questions.

"No, it was mine," I hastily reply to help Willow from being berated.

"With your erratic behavior, I can't say I am surprised at this point," she starts clearing the table in frustration. Paul then grabs the plate from her so she doesn't walk away from the conversation.

"Erratic behavior? What does that even mean? Listen to yourself, does it sound like I would want you there?"

"Benjamin, I am so disappointed in you for this. I truly am hurt by this. You are my son, of course, I would want to see you say your vows and promise yourself to someone," her voice trembling at the end as she fights off tears.

"You're hurt? I am your son?" I echo her, "That is rich coming from you," I stand up from the table, pushing the chair back with my legs. Willow grabs my hand and tries to pull me down to sit back down. "This was a bad idea."

"Getting married without your family, yeah, it was," she says.

"No, coming here was. I should've kept my promise I made before I left."

She knows exactly what that promise was and winces as I say it and grabs the half-empty bottle of wine and throws it on the ground, "fuck you, Benjamin. Go then, keep your promise. Keep it up with this bullshit from you."

"Nice, Mom. Real fucking nice," I respond. I grab Willow's hand and pull her from her chair, and lead her to the back door to start leaving. I turn around to look at my mom before I step inside, "So this is how we're leaving it?"

"Guess I will see you when you're dead, apparently," I nod my head and turn back around and head out. Before I close the door behind me, I hear my mother let out a screeching cry.

The car ride is silent except for the sounds of me flicking my lighter on after each cigarette. We get home, and I stay on the porch, continuing to smoke. Willow goes inside the house and comes back with a joint that she lights and sits next to me, resting her head on my shoulder.

"Do you want to talk about it?" She breaks the silence.

"If your mom told you that you should keep your promise of not seeing her unless you're dead, would you want to talk about it?" I tell her.

"Fair enough."

Willow

I sent all the good vibes to dinner tonight with my family, enlightening them about the marriage. Hoping that it doesn't end with people telling each other that they will see each other when they are dead. But since we believe in reincarnation, it isn't much of an insult as it is for Ben's family. Saying you'll see someone when they're dead is like comparing them to a sunrise on a summer morning in an empty field.

Ben and I took a shot of liquid courage before walking next door to my parents' house. We both figured, how much worse could it be? Thankfully, Rain was also here, and she will add enough drama to any situation that will extinguish any arguments that I cause.

We walk into the house, greeted with the smell of cooked spinach with garlic and a mixture of alcohol and weed. Coy hands me a joint within seconds of our entrance. "My lil love birds," he says and kisses our cheeks before flowing into the kitchen.

Rain looks up at us as we walk in and stands up from her chair, "Holy fuck. He is still around?" She says in shock and hugs me, then Ben. "You are a brave soul," she whispers in Ben's ear.

"No Hank?" I ask Rain as I sit down at the table across from her.

She breaks eye contact with me. "No, he stayed home with the kids," she says and then opens up her napkin, placing it on her lap. "So how are you doing?" I can tell she is trying to avoid the question, and I decide to play along with it and drop it.

"We are good," I look away from her and look at Ben, doing the same thing in return that she just did. Avoidance.

Coy comes into the dining room and places a plate full of salad on the table, "All I know is that I am still fucked up from the other night with you two," he says, looking at me and Ben.

My mom then follows behind him before he can say anything with a plate of penne pasta with freshly cooked tomatoes that make them look like fingers that have been in the bath for too long. My dad shortly follows behind her with a joint in one hand and a bottle of moonshine in the other. He pours a shot for all of us in our mismatched shot glasses that sat at our table setting.

"Huzzah!" He shouts while lifting his glass. We imitate him, Rain showing her strong dislike to the shot with a face of displeasure, wrinkled nose, and a tongue sticking out for air.

Once everyone has started eating, Coy is already on his second helping, and enough shots have been taken, and weed has been passed around, I decided it was time to tell them the news. "So, I am glad we're all here because there is something I wanted to tell you all," I start saying. Ben looks at me and grabs my right hand and squeezes it. Coy continues eating and everyone else drops their forks quietly on their plate and looks at us. I hold up my left hand to showcase the ring and then Ben does the same, "We got married!" I blurt out.

"Oh!" My mom exclaims, not sure if she was excited or just overall surprised.

"Hmm," My dad adds.

The sound of a cry is let out by Rain, "I am so happy for you!" She then says in between another cry. I look over at Ben as we both smile at Rain's response.

"That is surprising," my mom quickly says and our smiles fade because I can already tell by the sound of her voice it will not be the same excitement that is emanating from Rain. "I mean I just never took you as a person who would get married. Well, you're not married *married*. You just signed legal documents."

"That is marriage," Rain snaps back.

"Marriage is more than that. It is about love, sacrifice, trust, and loyalty. You should know that, Rain," my mom responds and Rain looks down at her place as if Mom just hit a nerve on her. "I am assuming this is a monogamous marriage?"

"Yes, of course," Ben suddenly says. His sudden voice jars me.

"Well I am just surprised. Willow, you have always been in a polyamorous relationship. Just two weeks ago you and River were having sex and now you're married."

Ben's hand loosen a bit from mine, "And if Willow feels like she needs to be with someone else, then that is between us. But we are married, and I will take care of Willow. I will love her and be loyal to her," Ben then adds in, comforting me despite the fact that his hand has now disappeared from mine.

"She is a strong, independent woman. She made it this far without you. She doesn't need to be taken care of," my dad says, his voice sounding more intimidating than usual.

"Did you know about this? I am surprised you're not adding your two cents to this," my mom says, looking at Coy.

"Who do you think gave them the drugs to celebrate the night of?" Coy continues eating his pasta, now taking a third helping.

"All of you are about good vibes and all that bullshit. So how about you wish your best for us and all that and be done with it?" Ben says, his voice remaining calm but still more intimidating than my dad could ever be. I look down at Ben's gold wedding band as it clutches onto his finger and smile internally, knowing that this is what we both want and what makes us happy.

After Ben goes to bed, or at least just lies there and looks up at the ceiling that is now full of plastic glow-in-the-dark stars to help illuminate some light in the room, Rain and I sit on the couch drinking wine.

She begins to tell me how happy she truly is for our marriage and that it is beautiful that we both found each other despite the hardships that she is only half aware of. She questions me about the River relationship that Mom brought up at dinner, and when I tell her the circumstances of what happened, minus the incident that led to Ben leaving, I sense a relief from her.

"So, the reason Hank isn't here is because he cheated on me. We are in the process of getting a divorce now," she shortly tells me after.

"I am so sorry, Rain. What happened?"

"He said he was getting bored with me, and he got into a relationship with a coworker. I saw the texts between them, but I never said anything to him because I figured if I never brought it up, then he would never leave, and we could pretend everything was okay. But after a while, he just stopped coming home at night, and then suddenly he came back one day and packed his stuff and gave me the papers," she takes a sip of wine, and I grab her hand and squeeze it.

"Mom and Dad know, I will probably be staying with them for a little while. I figured it's best if the kids are around family to keep them distracted from what is happening," she continues.

"You can always stay here," I offer.

"No, you're newlyweds! You need your space!"

"Hey, can you take a look at something for me?" I get up and go into the end table drawer and pull out a paper, looking at the words on the paper again before I hand it to Rain.

Rain takes a minute to read the paper before responding, "Well it looks like he took out life insurance." Her voice confused as to why I would be asking.

"Yeah, I got that. But why?"

"To just have probably. Every person with a job has life insurance. I mean, if he is in the army, he probably should have it," she adds.

"But he isn't active right now," I say, grabbing the paper and looking at it again.

"According to this, he is."

I throw it on the floor in frustration. The frustration with him not agreeing that he won't go back, something that I knew would eventually be inevitable. Frustration at the overhanging gloom that hangs over him because of a war that I don't even understand our place in.

The sound of the running shower wakes me up in the morning. I look over at the bedroom door from the couch that I fell asleep on, and notice it's open. Rain must have left because she is no longer curled up on the couch with me. I look down and notice the insurance paper glaring at me. It's bold letters "active duty" taunting me, laughing in my face at my naivety. I pick it up and make my way down the hallway, clearing my throat as I enter the bathroom to give Ben a heads up, I am coming in and not to startle him.

I pull back the shower curtain and hold up the paper to him, "What is this?"

"I don't know. I can't see it," he barely glances at it, but knows exactly what it is.

"Don't play smart with me, Ben. What is it?"

"What does it look like, Will?" He continues to shower, putting shampoo in his hand and brushing it through his hair as if it didn't really matter if I was standing there or not.

"It looks like life insurance," I snap back at him to keep up with the unplayful banter we have entered.

"Then there is your answer," still not looking at me.

"For what? Why does it say active duty? Can we skip this whole thing where you give a smart ass answer?"

"It isn't a smart ass answer. It is life insurance, if I die, you will be covered," he makes eye contact with me, and his face is stone. My stomach twists at his words. "I want you to have something if something were to happen to me. Willow, I told you when I moved in that I am going back. I don't know why you're acting like this is new information. You're smarter than that."

"Do you need to be married to be put on life insurance?" I ask.

"No, but it'll be an easier process. Less legal shit to deal with," I watch the shampoo slide off his head and down his body. He turns away from me and looks at the shower head. The sight of his scars on his back makes me look away.

"So did you marry me for that? For less legal shit to deal with? So I can collect some money if you die?"

"I married you because I love you and want to be with you. This is to take care of you. Why is that confusing?"

"Dying and giving me money isn't taking care of me. You being here does. I don't want your money," I look back at him as he turns back around and looks at me.

"Then donate it or something, I don't know what to tell you. But if you're mad about that you aren't going to like what I have to say next," he shows a slight smirk and I have never hated it more than I do now. I raise my eyebrow at him. He sighs, "Georgia... in two weeks. They want me back at base to help train some of the news guys," he pauses for a second, "we will get a house there. It won't be for long, about three or four months. Then you will come back here when I get deployed."

"Do I have a say in any of this?" I ask.

"You have a say in whether you come or not. You will come back when I leave though, here."

We both pause and look at each other, after a few blinks he continues to wash his body in the shower, turning back around. Then it hits me, the reason he keeps persistently saying that I will come back here. He doesn't want me at Fort Moore by myself. My hands start to get clammy and my heart beats faster and yet sinks at the same time. He turns back around and without me noticing, he has my hands in his hands and is kissing them. "Please, come with me. Please, trust me. In all of this."

"How long is your deployment?"

"I don't know yet. Willow, I *have* to go," his eyes soften as desperation sits in. Desperation for a life he will never live again but will always try to fight for. Desperation for something that no one, not even himself, will ever give him.

Georgia:
Fort Moore

Ben

The house was slightly larger compared to Willow's, but it lacks any type of land. Every inch of the community we moved into is full of houses for everyone on base. I know Willow hates it. Every time she looks at the sand-colored walls and continually asks me if she can just paint at least one wall to add life to it, she falls more and more miserable. I remind her that it is only three months, but she looks at it with disgust before turning around and waiting a few hours to ask again if something had suddenly changed.

She sits on the front porch on the porch chair we got with her cup of coffee every morning and reminds me how terrible it is that there is no fresh oxygen due to the lack of trees. She attempts to meditate in the spare bedroom, but since the window doesn't open, she can't get good air flow in the room, and there is no backyard for her to even try to do it there.

But Willow being Willow, she has already made new friends in the neighborhood to spend time with while I work. The girls are nowhere near her type of people, but they seem to idolize her in a way; her lack of giving a shit about anything is commendable to them. Each week, the group of girls delivers food to houses for the women who are left here while their husbands are deployed or the men who can't make a bowl of cereal for themselves.

It felt like a weight was lifted off my chest when I found out Cohens was getting transferred here in a few days, a person who I knew would have my back at the end of the day. There were a few guys here that I knew previously, and they were fine. Most of them had their wives or girlfriends here with them as well, so we all bonded together. Klein's wife was part of the group that Willow was in, and she was one of the people who admired Willow.

The first week of training was great. It consisted of physical labor, lifting, running, and climbing, and it was empowering to be the one to command the trainees instead of being the one who had to crawl in the mud. Then in the second week, we started target practice. Klein has been back in the States for the same amount of time as I, attempting to be a civilian again but failing. We both noticed each other wince during target practice. Ignoring the intrusive thoughts that circled our heads each time.

"Willow?" I call Willow as I sit on the sidewalk of a bar that is a few miles from base, chain-smoking cigarettes.

"What?" Her voice quiet and low, she must be lying down on the couch watching TV.

"I need you to come get me. The bartender took my keys," I tell her. Klein has been passed out on the barstool inside for half an hour.

"Are you that drunk?" She asks, her voice getting louder as she starts moving around to get up.

"No, actually. The bartender says I am, but I'm not," I tell her, truthfully.

"If you aren't, then why did he take your keys?" We are both silent for a second, and I look down at my red, bloody knuckles. "Babe?"

"Bartender is pissed because I got into a fight," if I had a tail, it would be directly between my legs right about now.

By the time she gets there, I have moved to my second pack of cigarettes; in my defense, the first was not full. She pulls up to the curb and looks down at me as I am sitting there.

"Gross," she says and kicks the empty pack that is next to me. She takes a second and looks me up and down, "You aren't that drunk. So why did you get into a fight?"

"Dude in there said some stupid shit," I say, avoiding eye contact with her.

"What did he say?" She asks.

"I don't know, something stupid," I respond and shrug.

"What did he say to cause you to punch him, Ben?" Her voice grows increasingly aggravated, rightfully so.

"I said I don't know, Willow," I snap back at her.

"Ah, oh," she nods her head in realization that I have no idea what I did. "I am going inside to get your keys and to ask."

I roll my eyes as she walks inside. After about 10 minutes she comes outside and stands above me and by the look on her face

I know it isn't good. "Well the guy you knocked out isn't pressing charges because he has a warrant out for his arrest so lucky you."

"That's good," I say hesitantly. "Is that all the bartender said?"

"He told me what happened," her voice lowered. It's her sad voice, no, her pity voice. "The guy didn't say anything to you."

"Well, that is a lie," I rebutted in my defense.

"Babe, I saw the video. He showed me. He was sitting a few chairs down and you got up out of nowhere and just," her voice trails off, "it was hard to watch." She heads back to the car and as she opens the front door I hear her mumble something under her breath. I ask her to repeat herself and she ignores me, grabbing a joint from her purse and lighting it waiting for me to get in the car.

"What did you say?" I ask again as I open the passenger side door but resist getting in. She takes a drag and still doesn't respond. "When have you been one to not talk? What did you just say?"

"I said take your fucking meds," her head snaps to look at me and her eyebrow is raised, showing she is ready for a fight.

"I will walk home," I respond.

"Go for it, maybe you can imagine a car driving you home instead," I let out an audible laugh and get in the passenger seat, not taking offense to her rather unkind joke. "Glad it's a good joke for you," she replies sarcastically to my laugh, and I grab her hand before she can put it into drive. She looks at me, and a sly smirk starts to form on her face. I grab her belt loops and pull me to initiate her to come on my lap, which she realizes and does. She takes a drag of her joint and blows it in my face as she straddles me. In return, I grab it and throw it out the window.

I grab my gun from my holster and put it on the dashboard, and take the pocket knife out of my pocket, flicking it open to reveal the blade. Willow looks down at it but doesn't ask and just pulls my pants down just below my ass. I unbutton her jeans, take the blade, sliding it down from the bottom of the zipper, and about five inches back so I can get in her. She gasps as soon as I enter and starts panting in my ear as she rides me. I grab the back of her hair and yank on it as the inside of her vagina pulsates and becomes wetter as she orgasms, causing me to come instantly.

The dull headache from drinking and the blinding light from the sun made it incredibly difficult to concentrate during training. Klein is struggling even more and has to take breaks to vomit every five minutes.

"We got fucking soft from being civilians," he turns to me and says. I shake my head in agreement, and he turns to throw up again.

"Serg, are you good, sir?" A kid stops and asks.

"What did you say?" Klein replies. The kid asks again. "Do you think I am a pussy like you? Do another lap running." The kid winces and looks down, and takes off. Klein looks down, and I can see he feels bad but is trying to now prove to himself that he hasn't gotten soft. But he isn't wrong; we are soft now. I am feeling like shit because of a small hangover and the sunlight. I have spent days dehydrated, in 115-degree heat, while in full gear, and didn't feel anything.

And now, in thought, I need to overcompensate for feeling soft. I go up to one of the guys who is in push-ups and put my boot on his back to stop him, "What kind of pussy shit is this?" He stops his push-up, "Did I say stop?" I push down harder on his back, and he struggles to do a push-up. "What is your name?" I ask.

"Marcus, Sir," he bellows out, trying to hide his struggling voice.

"Marcus, which one of your fellow brothers is the strongest one here?" I ask.

"Giovanny, Sir."

"Giovanny, get your fucking ass over here," I yell out. I look over at Klein, and he comes up next to me. "Klein, Marcus here says that Giovanny is the strongest one here. Let's put that to the test."

Giovanny comes up to us and stands erect, "Yes, Sir?"

"Marcus says you're the strongest one here, I want to see if Marcus is a liar or if Marcus is just a pussy and can't do a push up," both of them glance at each other now realizing that either way one of them is screwed. Giovanny gets down to start his push ups and Klein puts his boot down on his back, which doesn't slow him down and I can see Klein push down harder. I bend down and look at Giovanny, "so Marcus is a little fucking bitch who can't do a push up, huh?" He keeps doing push ups.

"Sergent Phillips asked you a fucking question," Klein says and puts all his weight down on his back.

Giovanny's arms start to shake with the pressure but keeps going steady, "No, Sir."

"If he isn't a little bitch then why can't he do a push up with my foot on his back?"

"I don't know, Sir."

"Then ask him," I demand.

"Marcus, why can't you do a push up?" He yells out.

Marcus doesn't respond and keeps doing his push ups without the weight on his back, "Marcus, tell him it's because you have no cock and balls. You want a man who can't do a push up with a little weight being on your side in the middle of the desert?"

"Marcus is a good man, Sir," Giovanny calls back.

"A good man is what gets you and your brothers killed," Klein barks back. "Now, Marcus, tell everyone you can't do a push-up because you have no cock and balls like you were instructed to do."

"I have no cock and balls," he yells out.

"Louder for everyone to hear it," Klein demands.

"I have no cock and balls," his voice getting louder.

"Serg, I don't think that is loud enough for me," Klein says to me.

"I agree, he even says it like pussy," I respond.

"I HAVE NO COCK AND BALLS," Marcus raises his voice fully.

I kick Marcus to his side, and he looks up at me on his back, bending down on one knee. I look at him, "Do fucking better. You should be able to carry more weight than that. If you want to get yourself killed, then that's one thing. But getting others killed because you are a weak, inadequate fuck is just stupidity and murder," I get up and walk back over to the sidelines, and Klein follows.

"Don't fuck anyone up too bad, I don't want to do shit today," a familiar voice says behind me. I turn around and see Cohens standing there with a smile on his face. He comes up to me and gives me a brotherly hug. The relationship I have built with Cohens is built on trust, loyalty, and unquestioningly having each other's backs. Cohens was a great EMT but shit at aiming his gun.

He eventually developed the nickname Parky, alluding to Parkinson's Disease. He was looked at as a liability because he would never be able to have your back in combat. It was after a while that he told me that he isn't bad at aiming, but as soon as he knows there is a person at the end of his gun, he can't do it. He said he is the one to help people with gunshot wounds, not be the cause of it.

I developed a sense of need to protect Cohens any time he came to the field with us because, at the end of the day, who better to be a close friend in combat than the EMT who will save you? This became an unspoken pact between us: I will have his back in combat without telling anyone what is going on, and he will fix me, no questions asked. This led to Cohens being the #1 witness of what was happening with Reynolds and being the one to initiate for me to pick up meds when I returned home.

After we discussed the basics of the typical catch-up, the "how are you", "how are you still alive", "how is the family", I invited him over for dinner to meet Willow. I saw her eyes glisten when I told her because she knows it is the one person who knows all the answers to her questions.

"Anything specific I should make for dinner?" She asks, while looking around in the cupboards for something.

"Anything you have?" I respond. I start to clear off the coffee table and notice a notebook full of Willow's handwriting.

*Subject one states that the hardest part of returning was adjusting to the idea that not everyone around him is a threat.

*Subject two (there seems to be no life to her eyes, I have seen this before, *Memorial day morning) she says it is hard to talk to people. Everyone feels like a "nuisance".

*Subject three told me "it is none of my god damn business" how he feels.

*Subject four says that even though people say welcome back and thank you for your service it feels as if everyone hates him, the protests, the social media posts, the look people give when they realize you have killed a person "I feel like I am living someone else's life."

*Subject five "everyone is a fucking idiot" "I am having a hard time finding a career that I enjoy now." "It feels like I need something that has a purpose, a desk job would never do. That is why I am back here. I need some type of meaning in my life."

*Subject six says that he loves his job and can't imagine anything better. (He says this as he lights a cigarette and drinks a beer, his legs up on a coffee table, this is an important picture to paint since he is showing his empowerment.) He says the idea of holding a gun makes him feel like "he knows what he is doing" (his gun is sitting on the table as we have this conversation)

*Subject seven said that he is worried about his wife and kids and how they will adjust if he dies, will she find someone else? Will his one-year-old ever call someone else daddy? "I love my wife; she is the greatest person. She is so loving, and I want someone else to feel her love when I die. It is not fair to her if she thinks I am the end-all all be-all just because she was mine. I just wonder if she will love again... I hope she does. God, I hope so. She deserves to be loved."

"What is this?" I ask Willow, holding it up. She looks across the kitchen into the living room at it and turns back around, waiting to respond.

"I am working on something," she finally says.

"What is it?"

"Another book, everyone is anonymous. It is just asking them how they feel about coming back and any adjustments they have struggled with. I think it will help others know they aren't alone."

"I don't think this is an appropriate thing to be doing, Will. It just doesn't look good," I glance over at the notes again, subject seven specifically catching my attention. Of course, I have thought about what will happen to Willow if I die, which is why I took out life insurance. But I never thought about what would happen in regards to her relationship life afterwards. I look over at her as she is sprinkling salt in a boiling pot of water, her hair swinging carelessly in a ponytail as she moves around the kitchen.

Willow

Cohens comes into the house with a giant smile on his face and a bottle of wine in one hand. His hair is on the longer side, long enough to push side to side, and it makes me miss Ben's grown-out hair.

"So you are the one who had to deal with Ben over the years, huh?" I say and hug Cohen.

"And you're the one dealing with him now!" He responds as he hugs me, squeezing tighter than a normal hug. I look over at Ben and look at his eyes as he watches me and Cohens hug, I can see his brain turning with thoughts. I poured us all a glass of wine as we sat at the table, Ben bragging about the homemade wine I make back home.

"So, Cohens, how long have you been back?" I ask.

"You can just call me Ian. But I have been back in the States for about two months now. I was back home in Maryland, my mom had passed away, so I was spending time with my family."

"I am sorry to hear about your mom," I say.

"Yeah, man. I am sorry to hear. She was wonderful. His mom would always send us both care packages."

"I bet she was great," I give Ian's hand a small squeeze before I get up from the table to start serving dinner. "Ian, I would love to hear some Ben stories. Got any good ones?" I ask.

"Oh man, do I have stories about this guy!" We begin eating, and Ben grabs a bottle of Patron to have with dinner and pours us each a shot. "This actually reminds me of the time we got drunk in this little city in Turkey one weekend. It was a big group of us, and Phillips and I stayed in the same room, and we were beyond shit faced. On our way to the room, this idiot somehow got us into the wrong room, and we walked in on this giant dude who hired a Turkish hooker, and we walked in and just saw his balls dangling."

Ben lets out a laugh and pours another shot for all of us, "I forgot about that. Yeah, that was rough."

We cheers in the center of the table before we throw back our shots and take our shots. I watch Ben as a different type of life and amusement fills his face. "Phillips and I have our fair share of sharing a room. I swear, I have slept next to this guy more than I have slept next to any girl. We were in the desert one night, and we had to curl up next to each other to keep each other warm."

"Yeah, cause no one else would ever sleep with us," I replied.

"And they still won't! I don't know how you convinced this one," Ian pointed at me.

I pull out a joint and light it up, I gesture to Ian if he wants a hit and he shakes his head no and takes another shot. Ben then pulls out his pack of cigarettes and lights it, "now that I will have," Ian says and Ben lights him one and hands it over.

"Then do you want to sleep with my wife?" Ben suddenly says, and Ian just responds with a laugh. I look at Ben, and there is no smile on his face to indicate that he is joking. No one responds, and Ben says, "Do you want to fuck my wife?"

"What the fuck?" I question.

Ian looks at him, puzzled, but when doesn't Ben say something absurd? "I am just thinking, if I were to die, I know Cohens would look out for you, wouldn't you?" He looks over at Ian.

"Yeah, of course. But I am not sure what you're getting at here," Ian says innocently.

"I just want to know what it would be like if I were to die. Your subject seven just got me thinking. And a way for me to understand how life would be without me is you fucking someone else," he replies it so coolly. I am more impressed with his composure and this thought-out plan than anything. He takes a drag of his cigarette and waits for either one of us to respond.

Ian's eyes scramble between both of us, waiting for one of us to burst into laughter and tell him this is some sort of prank. But the joke is on Ian because there is no punchline to this. While he knew War Ben, I know Schizophrenic, PTSD, Anxiety Ben, the one who pisses the bed at nightmares, the one who held a gun to his little brother's head because he was hallucinating. But Ian doesn't know that Ben and Ian doesn't know he is being serious right now.

"He isn't joking," I break the silence and smoke my joint.

"I can't say I don't understand where you're coming from. But…" Ian starts to say. He then looks over at me, "I mean, if you're okay with it."

"Monogamy isn't made for humans," I state, and I notice Ben breaking his cool for a split second in the corner of my eye. It took half a bottle of tequila and another joint before we moved from the table, all of us in fear that as soon as one of us moved, it meant it was time. But the fifth shot of tequila got to me and I started feeling risky and frisky. I get up from my chair and start to walk over to Ben. He must've felt my vibe because he puts his finger up and waves it as a way to say no. I then turn and go up to Ian and get on his lap to straddle him. He puts his hands up, unsure of where to put them.

"Just go for it," I whisper in his ear and grab his face to start kissing him. He starts getting erect under me as he puts his hand on my ass and pulls me closer in. My tongue goes in his mouth and circles around his, his hands fumble around when he takes off my shirt, exposing my tits in front of his face. He lets out a slight gasp when he realizes there wasn't another layer under my shirt. My hands fall to his belt to take it off effortlessly.

I grab his dick in my hands and start stroking it. I try to talk myself out of looking over at Ben because I know if I see him, I will want to go fuck him. Ian is extremely handsome; he reminds me of a mixture between Ben and River. He still has this boyish look about him, like River does, an innocence in a sense. But he has the look of toughness that Ben represents. He has black curly hair, his eyes are a deep blue, which makes it look like there is more joy in them than Ben's, but his arms aren't as filled out as Ben's. I still do not doubt that he could easily pick me up and throw me around.

My eyes make the mistake of looking over at Ben, and he just lights another cigarette and is in the process of taking another shot, so we don't make eye contact. I stand up from Ian's lap and grab his hand to pull him into the bedroom, not looking behind me to see if Ben is coming, but once we get halfway down the hallway, I hear his chair move. I wasn't sure what his plan was going to be, but Ian and I were staying on track with our mission. Ian's hands grab my waist as we walk into the bedroom, his hands feeling like they are somehow everywhere on my body, then pushing me back on the bed. I stumble slightly over my own two feet, the weed and alcohol hitting me all at once.

I start to pull off my pants, and Ian pushes my hands out of the way, "allow me," he says, and pulls off my shorts. I don't remember Ian getting undressed, but I gasp out loud as I suddenly feel him enter me. My eyes look to the door frame of the bedroom, and I see Ben standing there. This time, we do make eye contact. The feeling of anger rushes through my body, filling my veins, going into the marrow of my bones. I keep eye contact with him and wrap my legs around Ian, pulling him closer in.

"Fuck," Ian whispers in pleasure in my ear. I break eye contact with Ben and push Ian over to get on top of him.

"Your dick is so big," I say out loud. I bounce on top of him, my boobs following along.

"You're so wet," he replies and grabs the back of my hair, giving it a tug.

"Yes, Ian, yes! I am going to come all over your cock," I moan and lean down to reintroduce our tongues. I let out a loud moan, and Ian grabs onto my hips, pulling me further down on him as he comes. Our tongues linger in each other's mouths for a few more seconds, and then I roll off of him onto the bed, the bedroom door closing to break the silence.

"Do you think he's mad?" Ian suddenly asks, "I mean, he told us to so-" already defending his actions. "If I knew he would be mad, I wouldn't hav-"

"He is a bipolar schizophrenic who the fuck knows," I say and get up from the bed, putting on a loose pair of leggings.

"What?" Ian sounds surprised, which makes sense I suppose when they were catching up Ben didn't go into much detail about his current mental state.

"Just stay here," I say, closing the bedroom door behind me.

I see Ben standing in the hallway, he turns to look at me, "have fun?" he asks, his voice dismal but sincere at the same time.

"If I knew I would be having sex with your best friend I probably would've popped an E or something."

"I know you don't get it. But I just need to know what it'll be like when I am not here."

"You're right, I don't get it. I don't get any of it."

He comes closer to me, backing me up against the wall, putting his hands on the wall between my shoulders, "did you come?"

"Do you want the truth or for me to lie?" I ask.

"I already know the truth. Lie to me," his voice growing huskier, his eyes not breaking contact from mine and for some reason the anger in me dissipates and my heart starts racing.

"Yes, I did," I lie. There was nothing wrong with Ian's dick or the sex itself. But in the moment of riding him I realized I have learned there are three categories for sex. There is making love, which is what I do with River. Making love is when you feel safe, there is a spiritual connection, you take time to explore each other's bodies. Then there is sex, which is Ian's category. Sex is like an exchange of payment, you go there to get the job done, and it'll be fun, but there is nothing remarkable about it. Then there is fucking, Ben's category. There is no safety in fucking, fucking can take place anywhere, and there is passion and roughness to it.

Ben puts his hands down my pants and starts to finger me, the feeling of his fingers tapping inside of me already getting me wet. He is a pianist, and my vagina is the keys; he knows all the right melodies. My breathing gets heavier, and I wrap my arms around his neck to help keep myself up as my legs start shaking.

"Don't come for me, tell me you don't need me," he quietly demands as he continues.

"I don't need you," another lie.

"Don't come, don't you dare come for me," he knows I am getting close, but continues.

"That…is… a… little difficult," I say between breaths. And like that, I come.

"Did you come?" he asks, already knowing the answer.

"No," third lie. He smiles and yanks my pants down. I pull my ankles out of them as he pulls out his dick, picking me up, I wrap my legs around his waist as he starts to *fuck* me. I put my hands on his upper arm, feeling his muscles move as he thrusts and holds me up. He starts to carry me to the living room, but we don't make it there and end up on the dining room table instead, pushing the plates and cups to the side.

"His cock was so much bigger than yours," I tease as he continues to fuck me.

He puts his hand on my throat, "Did you like me watching you?"

"Did you like watching me make someone else come?"

"Yes. You are so fucking good at it," as he continues to hump me, we are interrupted by a knock on the front door. Ben doesn't acknowledge it until there are two more getting increasingly louder each time.

"Phillips," a deep voice behind the door yells. He rolls his eyes and sighs, pulling away from me.

He opens the door, remaining partially behind it to cover himself and the fact that his wife is naked on the dining room table ten feet away. "Yeah?" He says.

"Do you mind coming out?" the voice asks, the voice getting lower.

"Can you give me a minute? I am in the middle of fucking my wife. What is it?"

"Sir, your cadet Marcus Lowry has been in an accident."

"What kind of accident?" Ben's tone is getting irritated.

"Sir, he has killed himself."

Ben lets out a sigh, "Give me a minute, I will be right there." Ben closes the door and briefly looks at me before turning down the hallway towards the bedroom to get changed. I jump up to follow him, and I hear him already telling Ian what happened.

"Babe, what happened?" A silly question since I know the same information he knows. He doesn't respond. "So where are you going?" I look over at Ian who is already dressed and waiting for Ben to finish dressing.

"To deal with it, Willow," he snaps at me.

"So what happens now?" my questions coming out without thinking. He doesn't respond again. "What do you have to do? Why did he do it?" Once again asking questions that I already know he doesn't know hoping he magically has something to tell me.

"I don't know, Willow."

"How well did you know him? Was he someone you were in charge of?"

And that was the last straw for him, that was the question that pushed him to the edge, "Jesus Christ," he yells and slams his fist down on the dresser. "Please, I am begging you to shut the fuck up."

"So you knew him? How old was he?" He was a cadet so he must have been young, I imagine a mother of his hearing the news that her son didn't even get out of training before wanting to kill himself.

Ben puts his gun in his holster and takes a deep breath, "if you don't stop I swear to God, Willow I am going to be next."

"What kind of thing is that to say? Are you kidding me right now? That is what you say?" And suddenly the anger I had previously comes back, and now it is full rage.

"Yes, I knew the fucking kid, Willow. Eight hours ago, I told him he was inadequate and going to get his fucking team killed. So I am sorry, but I am feeling a little bothered right now. So if you don't mind, please shut the fuck up and let me deal with this. Cohen, you should come as well in case they need medical shit, I don't fucking know." Ben walks out of the room, and I just stand there.

"You okay?" Ian asks me before he follows behind Ben.

My heart drops at the guilt I know Ben is going to carry now, "Ian," I try to find words to say, a way to make him understand in a second Ben's state of mind, to ask him to watch him when I am not there, to warn him. "This is going to hit him hard."

Ian puts his hand on my shoulder, "I will talk to him."

Ben

There are two cracks on the wall left of the bed. They must be about an inch long. I take a breath about 12 times a minute, but when I become hyper aware of it, then it is either 8 or 16. Three birds live outside the window. One chirps every 19 seconds, the other one chirps every 43 seconds, and the other one does every 67 seconds. Typically, a car will pass about every 9-12 minutes. Willow peeks into the bedroom every 27 minutes and gets closer to the bed to check for movement every 54 minutes. Typically, when she comes into the bedroom, I am number 3 of my breath for that minute or 7. I see blood on my hands every 83 minutes, but it goes away after a minute and 2 seconds.

Nimaah asked me why everyone around me dies.

Nelson also asked me.

Marcus didn't say much; he had a lot on his mind.

I didn't have an answer for them, I just turned to see if there were any new cracks in the wall.

Willow comes in with a plate of food and sits next to me on the bed with it. "You should eat something," she sits there quietly before she starts talking again, "Don't you have to pee?"

I point to a cup that sits on the nightstand, "Oh," she says sullenly. "So is this what we are doing now?" I shrug and roll over so I don't see her anymore. Her embarrassment and shame don't even come close to matching mine. How do I tell her that this is my fault, that he is dead? And even if it wasn't my fault, the last thing I said to the kid was that he was an inadequate fuck.

I thought by rolling away from her, she would leave, but for some reason, she took that as an invitation to join me on the bed. "Ben, for once, can you just talk to me and not close up and leave this all on yourself?"

A part of me wants to tell her, but another part doesn't want me to let her know what a piece of shit her husband is when she isn't there. "If only it were that easy," I muster up to say to her.

"It is, you're just making it so much more difficult," she opens her nightstand and starts to light up a joint for herself, probably hoping that it would somehow calm me down as well. "Will you talk to Ian then?" she says after a minute.

I let the idea sit in my head for a minute, her and I both knowing that she will end up interrogating him for the answers after I confide in him anyway. But even knowing that, it still feels better for him to tell her than me. I let out a quiet okay, and she jumps up and runs to the living room.

The sound of the front door woke me up from the sleep I didn't intend to take. I hear Cohens' voice as it gets closer to the bedroom, and then he appears in the doorway. "You awake?" He asks as we make eye contact.

I don't respond, but he sits next to me on the bed. "Last night you were in bed with my wife, and now with me, you're really getting your way around," I tease him.

"Yeah, yeah. Fuck you," he lies next to me silently. His presence alone feels like enough for me.

"She is going to hound you for answers when you leave," I tell him.

"That is up to you if you want me to tell her. Or if you're even going to tell me," Cohens just always knew, knew what was wrong, and knew not to push. But I did. I did tell him. Not just some of it, but from the second it started going downhill while we were away. I told him about the assaults, the unjustified murders, the guilt. He didn't try to sympathize with me or make me feel better; he agreed it sucked and that he understood. He pushed taking medication for it, but I know that he is just scared of what could happen if I don't; he has seen it before.

I tell him what Willow already knows, and when she asks for answers from him, to give her a softer, sanitized version of it all. Enough for her to learn about what is going on so she can have an understanding and stop asking, but not enough for her to know the whole madness of it all.

After four days of lying in self-pity and hatred, I push myself to return to work. Returning to the same shit of yelling at young boys who can't do a proper push-up. I think about asking Giovanny how he is holding up with the death of his friend, and before I can fully form a thought on whether I want to or not, I am calling him over to speak to him.

He tells me he is okay and knows this is part of the job, friends dying. And while he isn't wrong, it's a shit lesson to need to learn. "His mom died, and he felt guilty for not being with her, so I think he just hit a breaking point," he tells me. Selfishly, I am glad it had nothing to do with him feeling inadequate, but still knowing that that's the last thing he heard from a person who is supposed to guide him, stings.

"Keep your head up," I tell him before he walks away, and I need to yell at him again for running too slowly.

"Full of inspirational quotes there, Phillips," it takes me a second to wonder if I am actually hearing this voice or if it's in my head. Even when I look at him, it still doesn't click if it's real or not. I stare at him blankly. "I am glad to see your girl didn't forget where I live," I turn back and watch the cadets struggle their way through the course, not wanting to show them that I could possibly be hallucinating while training them.

Klein makes his way over to me. "What do you say? Want to give them a 15-minute break?" He asks.

"Yeah, sure."

"Hey, Reynolds," he then says.

"It's a great surprise to have you back," Reynolds says and slaps my back. He and I both know the point of his slapping my back is to serve as a reminder. "Your girl looked good the other day. We caught up, and we had lots to discuss. When you see her later, tell her I said that yellow looks good on her."

"What the fuck are you talking about?" I finally snapped. Unsure if what he is saying is pissing me off more or the fact that he now knows it's bothering me.

"She stopped by my house the other day. But she can tell you all about that," he winks at me and walks away.

The memory of her being at his house months ago floods my brain. Visions of him taking her clothes off and feeling her bare skin bring bile to my mouth, my stomach churning after every second. I go to the bathroom before I actually vomit and leave a reminder of his being at my feet.

Looking in the mirror, I barely recognize the person looking back. My reflexes punch the mirror out of anger, frustration, and overall loss of feeling of knowing what is going on around me. The glass shatters into the sink, and with one swift motion, I grab a shard and jam it into my leg without thinking or without any type of reasoning.

Eyes glare at me as I walk out with blood pouring down my leg, creating a puddle with each step I take.

"Cohens?" I say as I walk into his medical tent while he shows trainees how to repair the damage on dummies. Right as the perfectly damaged dummy walks in for repair.

Trainees look at me with wide eyes, Cohens' eyes slowly looking up while in mid stitch, "fuck!" He drops what he's doing and clears a gurney for me.

As soon as I lie down, the loss of blood hits me as fast as it's coming out. "I don't know what happened," I managed to slur out.

"Did you do it to yourself?" Cohens asks.

"Before I know it, there is glass in my leg."

"Did he do it or did you?" He asks again as he and the trainees start working on my leg.

"I did," I respond.

"Alright, everyone, just as you were trained to do. Phillips, I will assume you don't give a shit if they work on you and you give consent to have them perform any medical tasks that are needed even though they are not fully trained, do we have your permission?" He asks. My eyes start to close. "Dude, just say yes so I can have verbal confirmation without any asshole suing me and I don't have to do this solo."

"Yes, yeah sure."

"Great. Everyone get to it. We need to cover-" I hear his voice slowly fade off as he is giving directions to everyone.

"Cohens, I think I am going to pass out," I whisper to him.

"I know you are, don't worry, I will take care of it."

Willow

There truly is no better smell than lavender filling the house. All feels right when it penetrates your nose and fills your lungs. I take another deep breath in to embrace the scent when the door swings open and Ian is helping Ben inside the house while he limps to the couch.

I look at them and see Ben's leg wrapped in gauze, "Do I dare to even ask?" Ian looks over at Ben, waiting for him to answer, but Ben just lies down on the couch.

"Training accident," Ian answers. I roll my eyes at the clear lie that he told me.

Ben doesn't look at me when I sit next to him on the floor. "What really happened?" I question.

"You heard him, training accident," his voice is cold.

"I know you too well to know that isn't the truth," I lean over and look at his leg, trying to investigate something about it.

"Did you go and see him?" He asks, not looking at me.

It takes me a couple of seconds to register the question and who he's referring to. I roll my eyes and go to stand up.

"Did you?" He grabs my wrist to prevent me from getting up, and then grabs my jaw, forcing me to make eye contact with him. Each time I try to yank my face out of his embrace, he grabs it tighter, waiting for an answer.

"No," I yank away again, and he lets go this time. "But I saw him. I was just making my rounds for my book, and he was there. Him being his cocky self just had to put some input to my interview. That is all. So are you going to tell me what happened to your leg or what?" I look over at Ian, and he sheepishly looks away as soon as we make eye contact.

"Why didn't you tell me when it happened?" I try to find the tone in his voice, sad, angry, hurt, but I come up blank.

"Are you going to stop ignoring my question? I am done answering yours until you answer mine."

"Why didn't you tell me? Now I look like a fucking idiot for not knowing where my wife is or what she is doing," he starts to stand up and Ian pushes him back down on the couch.

"I am not something you keep tabs on, Ben. You do know I am free to do as I please," I stand in front of him, showing him I am not going to back down from his tactics.

"Willow, if there is anything I know about you it is that I know you fucking do as you please," he rolls his eyes at me. "Pack your shit up, we are going back home for some time. I can't do anything with my leg, so I am on leave till I heal and then…"

"What? And then what?" There is suddenly a pit in my stomach.

"You know what, Willow. You knew the plan, baby," his voice is now soft as he attempts to look at me.

"I just thought…" The truth is, I don't know what I thought. I thought that after some time, he would give up on being deployed. Suddenly, things changed, and he wouldn't actually go.

"Ian is staying. He will be able to keep you up to date with everything, check in with you. Willow, you knew this was going to happen. I am sure you were hoping things were going to change, but I told you I have to do this," he stands up and limps over to me and takes my shoulders in his hands.

"You aren't going to come back, Ben. You might physically, but you won't be back," I look over at Ian behind Ben, "you know it too. You see how he is now. We aren't going to have a future if you go." Ian still doesn't look at me.

"We won't have a future if I stay here."

Home:
Yelton

Willow

Three older women linger in the romance section of the bookstore, fingering the pages of books while they whisper and look up at me in between sentences. I can't make out their entire conversation, but I hear key words to get a general idea. Words float around, such as "man", "gun", "boy", "army", "crazy", and "poor Sarah".

"Can I help you ladies find anything?" I start walking up to them with a big smile on my face.

"Oh, no, sweetie. We are good. You are the Phillips' boy's wife, aren't you?"

As if the devil himself heard his name, Ben walks right in. He is wearing a t-shirt that is soaked in salty sweat, gym shorts that cling to his legs from the humidity, and his army baseball cap. He looks at me with an infectious smile, sprawling across his lips, and most importantly, a coffee in his hand. He hands me the coffee and kisses my forehead while the women just stand there.

"Yes, he is my husband," I turn and say to them, to finally answer their question. They finish their conversation and leave empty-handed, clearly only coming in to gossip and gawk. "While I have you here. Can you grab that box of books and bring them down this way?" I head down Sci-Fi, and Ben follows behind with a box of books.

He drops the box in the middle of the aisle and pushes me up against a bookshelf, my head in between his arms as they rest behind me. He kisses my neck, and I get a catch of his cedarwood deodorant and the spearmint gum that he was chewing before he came in. I take a sharp breath when his hands go down my pants and tease me by playing with the lips of my vagina.

"We can't do this here!" I say in between breaths.

"Will the owner of the bookstore kick us out?" He says right before putting his fingers fully in me.

"What if someone comes in?"

"Someone will definitely be coming, and also nobody reads Sci-Fi," I let out a light giggle and shove my forehead into his neck as I enjoy his fingers dancing around inside me. "Fuck this," he suddenly says and then turns me around, pulling my pants down to my thighs and suddenly thrusting himself in me. I grab the shelves as he fucks me, knocking down books with each thrust he does. I can't help but moan louder and louder as he goes harder and harder.

"I couldn't stop thinking about you on my run," he whispers in my ear. His hand goes between my thighs and starts rubbing my clit. I can feel myself tighten around his dick, begging for some type of release.

"Ben," I moan. He starts to slow down the flicking of my clit to prolong my orgasm, "Please. I need to come," I beg.

"Baby, you know I will get you there. But what is the rush?" He moves his hand away, and I sigh in frustration as his thrusts also become slower. His hand goes up my shirt, and he starts to twist my nipple between his thumb and pointer finger. I might die if I don't have an orgasm. The wetness from my vagina starts to drip down my leg.

"Please, I can't take it," I softly beg. If someone came into the store right now, I am not sure I would even stop him.

"You need it that badly, love?" He whispers in my ear and grabs my throat lightly.

"I really do."

He knows all the spots to get me there quickly, and he reaches his hand between my ass and starts fingering it. The sensation of feeling him everywhere instantly gets me. I grab onto the shelves for support.

We both climax together, his knuckles turning white while holding the shelves as he comes. "God, I am going to miss you," he says while pulling his pants back up. And suddenly the excitement from the sex plummets as I think about him leaving in a week.

The entrance bell rings as he starts walking up front, and I fix my hair to make it look less like I just banged. Before I get up front, I hear Ben let out a loud HA, and the bell rings again. And then there is Sarah standing right there.

"He didn't stop and talk?" I ask her as she looks expressionless. She shakes her head no.

"Ben!" I yell down the street to him before he gets too far. "Are you going to talk to her?"

He turns around, cigarette already in his mouth, "Am I dead?" he keeps walking. His mom's face still looking expressionless when I come back inside.

"I heard he was back in town and I just wanted to see him and talk," she says to me as I walk behind the counter, putting the straw in my iced coffee, finally taking my first sip. "I am assuming he is still mad at me," she walks closer towards me.

"We don't talk about you, but I would assume the answer is yes," I continue to move around the shop, putting books away, organizing misplaced titles, smirking any time I pass the Sci-Fi section, all while Sarah follows closely behind me like a lost dog.

"Are you still mad at me?" She asks.

"There is enough anger in the world, I don't need to add to it."

"I just want to talk to him. Can I come over to your house so I can?"

"I can't really tell you what you can and can't do. So do whatever you want."

Ben goes from room to room fixing whatever needs to be fixed. First was checking the smoke alarm batteries, then the shower head that needed to be replaced due to rust, and the clogged bathroom sink from loose hair. After that was the living room window that didn't close and lock completely. Now it is the dining room chair that has a loose screw.

"You know all of this doesn't need to be fixed, right?" I say to him while I clean up the leftover homemade pizza.

"Well, the window was a must. But I am also leaving in a week and won't be back for 6 months. What if more screws fall out of the chair and you sit on it and fall and crack your head open?" He says while continuing to tighten them.

"Is this a bad thought you have, or did you like hallucinate this?" I tease.

"Yeah, yeah," he mocks a laugh, and suddenly there is a knock on the door.

Ben

My mother stands at the doorway just looking at me. I see tears start to form in her eyes, but she pushes through, and they're gone within seconds.

"Hi, I wanted to see you… Say hi…" She says, trying to find her voice.

I grab her hand, and I see a smile start to curve on her mouth. I put it on my chest and push down hard. "Do you feel that?" I ask her, pushing her hand down harder on me.

"Feel what? Your heart?" She looks at me, puzzled.

"Yes, do you feel it beating?" She looks at me, still confused, and nods yes. "Which means I am still alive," I let her hand go and shut the door in her face, turning around to look at Willow, who has her mouth agape.

"Ben…" She begins to say.

"Will, I don't want to hear it. I just want to spend this time with you, not stressed. So I am going back to fixing these damn chairs," I see her roll her eyes, but I decide to just ignore it.

I keep making notes in my head of things that need to be looked at before I leave. Tomorrow is the leaky kitchen faucet, cleaning out the fridge and pantry, and making sure I put a note on the dryer to empty the lint trap, just in case, even though I am sure she will be drying most of her clothes on the clothes line I installed last week. She keeps telling me all of this doesn't need to be done because she can survive without it being fixed, or if it gets bad enough, she can call someone. And I keep asking myself why I feel compelled to do it all, guilt? Earning my keep while I am gone? A reminder I am here?

I toss and turn in bed thinking about that last part. I can't help but think about River coming here like he did while I was in Seattle, granted that was different circumstances, so I can't hold it against her, especially since it wasn't like I was all that lonely either.

"Psst," I whisper to her in bed.

"Yes, dear?" She responds. Her voice is pretty awake as well. I know she hasn't been sleeping well lately, but we have silently agreed not to discuss it.

"Can we talk about something real quick?"

She turns on the lamp on her nightstand and sits up to look at me. She is wearing a white tank top, and I can see her nipples through it when she moves her hair behind her back. Anybody would be blessed to see her naked, and here I am just leaving her.

"While I am gone, this marriage is still just between us, right?" I finally ask after looking at her for a minute.

"What do you mean?"

"As in, no intimacy with anyone else."

"The only thing touching my vagina is my own fingers while thinking about you," she kisses my cheek and goes to turn off the light. I grab her before she can turn it off and pull her underneath me, yanking off her tank top at the same time. I just stare at her, and she smiles at me and pulls my shorts down. I finish the job and take them off while not leaving my eyes off her.

"Can you promise me something?" She pushes my chest back before I lean down and kiss her. I raise my eyebrow, inviting her to ask the question. "No hookers while you're gone."

I laugh, but she looks at me with a serious face, "hookers?" I ask while still laughing.

"I have just heard stories of guys getting lonely, and they go to like brothels or just find girls in the cities."

"The only thing touching my dick is my own hands while thinking about you," I lean back down as she lets go of my chest. Nuzzling myself into her neck, I kiss it and breathe in her scent with each kiss. My hand reaches down between her legs, and she opens them wider for me. My dick throbs for her as I enter her.

"God, I can't wait to have her to myself," Reynolds says, standing next to the bed.

"Me too, I miss how sweet she is," River adds right next to him.

"Don't worry, man. I will take care of her," Ian inputs and winks at me on the other side of the bed.

I push up off her and look down at her, "I'm not fucking kidding, Will."

She wraps her arms around my neck, and her legs wrap around my waist as she pulls me back down to her. "I know," she starts kissing my neck as I melt into her.

I look at the clock as it reads 3:23 am, and it feels like any time I check the clock, it is just a countdown till I leave. Rolling over, I stare at Willow. Her lips are red and swollen from kissing, and I can still taste her in my mouth. Suddenly, she starts moving her lips and whispers, "I can feel you staring at me. Go to bed."

"You wouldn't know that if you were sleeping too, though," I playfully respond.

"I enjoy watching you sleep; it is the only time you ever actually look relaxed and peaceful," she grabs my hand and plays with my ring that sits comfortably tight around my finger. "Naturally, I am scared you could die while you're gone," she begins to say.

"Well, you brought that in so gracefully."

"Not sure how else to bring it up, I guess. But what I was going to say is that I am also nervous you are going to come back even more... fucked up to say lightly. I have learned this version of you, and I am scared of it being worse. I wish I could have known you before," her voice trails off.

"You wouldn't have liked me then, though. Admit it, a part of you enjoys this idea of trying to fix me. You would have been so bored with old me. Even the sex would have bored you. You would get the same version of me every day, and Willow, my dear, you need excitement and fun, and no part of you runs on routine or ordinary. I love that about you because you keep me excited for the next minute, because God only knows what is going to come out of that beautiful mouth of yours."

Enough beers couldn't get me through the night with Chris and the guys, especially Jason. Jason pregamed before he got to the bar with us, and it visibly shows. There were at least five comments about "the wife letting me out" type jokes, and I told myself by the sixth, I will punch him.

"So how long will it be before I see you again?" Chris turns to me and asks while handing me another beer.

"Not long, I am only gone for six months this time."

"Aren't you going to get lonely?" Jason butts in, saying.

"I think I will be busy enough not to get lonely," I reply.

"What about the wife?" He says, his shot spills over in his glass onto the floor.

"Tread very fucking lightly," I warn him. He replies by just taking his shot.

And just when I think I am in the clear of his dumb comments, he opens his mouth, "Have you ever had sex with one of those girls? Ya know, the one with the towel on their heads? Oh man, I would love to just rip that off and see what they're hiding."

My fist turns into a clench, and Chris must notice because he starts to step in front of me to put more blockage between us than just the shitty high-top table. "Jason, how about we get you some water?" Chris says, trying to get him away from the table and, more importantly, me.

"What? Did one of the turban girls break his heart?" He says, pulling away from Chris's hands that are holding his arms. "Come on, just tell me. What was the sex like? Was it that mind-blowing?"

Before I could even realize what I was doing, I found myself shoving him against a wall, my arm in his neck and my fist in the air, "tough guy, huh?" he mumbled out the best he could. I know everyone behind me is telling me to stop, but I can't fully hear their words. My hand is about to meet his face when suddenly he manages to grab a beer bottle from the table next to us and smash it across my head. I stumble back, and he pushes me to the ground.

"Get one punch in because that is all you're going to get," I tell him. I allow it, I allow the one punch, and I flip him off me and straddle him and punch him. Once I start, I can't stop. I need to stop, though. I tell myself I need to stop, but I can't control myself.

Someone pulls me off of him, and I turn around and hit whoever it is without even seeing who it is.

"Don't fuck up your deployment," the voice says. I realize I can't fully see who it is because blood is pouring into my eye from the beer bottle that hit my head. The person yanks me out of the bar and pushes me onto the street.

"Fuck that guy," I mumble as I take out a cigarette and light it up.

"And to think, last time I saw you, Jason was pulling you off of me during a fight at a bar," the voice says.

I wipe the blood from my eye and try to figure out who it is, "Syed?"

"Full circle, huh," he sticks his hand out to indicate he also wants a cigarette.

"Why would you even bother breaking up the fight?" Passing the cigarette and lighter to him.

"Because you weren't wrong for fighting him."

We stand there in silence for a while, the humid air causing an even more uncomfortable stillness between us. It took me halfway through my cigarette to realize I didn't have my car with me, and there was no way I was going back in there to ask Chris to bring me home. When I mumble "shit" under my breath, Syed looks over at me.

"Have to figure out a way home," I tell him.

"Here, let me give you a ride. We can let bygones be bygones."

We force small talk on the way home to break the painful silence between us. He asks me about Willow, and I ask him about his relationships, in which he tells me his parents will start working on an arranged marriage if he doesn't find a girl within the next year. I guess none of us has any control over our futures.

"Sorry, by the way," I eventually say.

"For what?" He glances over at me with a smirk.

"All of it, but I also meant for hitting you just now," I wipe the blood that is still coming off my head and wipe it on my pants.

"All good, I have been in a fight with you before, so I can't say I didn't know what to expect. By the way, I have napkins in the glove compartment," I take them out and just push it against the cut, letting it absorb as much blood as it possibly can. "Uh, are you good, dude?" He then asks.

"Yeah, I am used to it. I could probably stitch it up myself," I apply pressure harder.

"Not what I was referring to. I know it happened a while ago but I heard about everything with your brother, and then you just kind of left, and now you're back, but you're also going back. So I just wanted to ask."

I never really thought about how many people probably found out about what happened with Sean, especially since he probably told his friends. I also have no idea how much they all know is the actual truth, even more so because I don't even know the whole story.

We pull into the driveway, and I realize I haven't even responded to his question, "Thanks for the ride and all."

"Be safe, man," the light in the car shines enough on his face for me to recognize the look in his eyes. It's the look someone gives you before you deploy when they think they won't see you again. They are looking at you and taking in this moment, thinking it will be the last.

Willow

The sound of the keys jiggling in the doorknob causes me to perk up from the couch. I wish I could say I am not surprised by seeing Ben in blood anymore, but it still shocks me to my core when I do.

I jump up and run to his side, and he pulls napkins off his head that are soaked in blood and looks at me. "What a night," he kisses my forehead and walks into the bathroom.

"Are we going to talk about this?" I ask while following behind him. I just see him looking at himself in the mirror as more blood comes from his cut. "Does it need stitches? Should we go to urgent care? Or do you think you could do it? At this rate, I should learn how to stitch you up."

He just keeps staring at himself in the mirror without saying anything or moving, and I see his chest starting to rise faster with each breath. He grabs the edges of the sink. His head turns, and he looks into my eyes. His eyes go dead as he says, "This is what I would look like if I got shot in the head."

My brows furrow, and I move closer to him as he turns away from me and looks in the mirror again, "Who the fuck says that to someone? Do you think that's what I want to think about before you leave?"

"Well, at least if it happens, your imagination doesn't need to run wild as to what it would be."

"If your deployment doesn't kill you, I fucking will at this point." I close the bathroom door and walk away. When I go outside to the porch to smoke a joint, I hear him mumbling and cursing under his breath as he tries to stitch himself up. It isn't until I am halfway through that he makes his way outside to me.

"Do you think I am not scared?" His voice stern and ready for an argument.

I roll my eyes at the fact that he is the one who decided to go, so I don't really care how he feels, which I tell him outright. He doesn't respond because there is nothing to say to that; it is the truth. He takes the joint from my hand and takes a hit before throwing it away. He pulls me up by my arm so I am standing in front of him, our eyes locking.

"Don't give me that look. I don't want that look from you. Anyone but you," he says quietly, pleading.

"What look?" But we both know what is going through my head right now, and we both know what he is referring to.

"I already got that look tonight from someone. I don't want it from you. I want you to look at me like you want me in you. I want you to look at me like you want to taste my cock. I want you to look at me like you need me in every way possible. I want you to look at me like you're craving my touch."

"Even though all of that is true, I can't help how I look at you right now, so you'll just have to hallucinate a different expression on my face."

He smirks at me, the corner of his mouth just raising a bit. His eyes narrow and darken, and he steps closer to me, "You'd better watch that mouth of yours." My back is then up against the house and his body is looming over me. I know it's only a matter of seconds before some part of his body is inside me. He bends down and starts to kiss my neck down to my collarbone. His mouth then makes its way to my breast, where he slowly kisses it through my shirt. The lack of direct touch makes me want it even more. My nipple hardens immediately, and he has no problem finding it and starts to tug at it with his mouth. He gets down on his knees and starts to kiss my stomach, his lips soft and tender with each kiss. My skin raises in goosebumps, and I just want to push his head a little lower.

He suddenly stops, and I look down at him, "That is the way you should be looking at me," he says. As he stands back up, he reaches under my arms to lift me. I immediately wrap my legs around his waist. My lips kiss every inch of his neck, and I allow my hands to dance around any part of his body I can reach, trying to take it all in. His head slightly falls back, allowing me to kiss more of his neck while his fingers get lost in my hair.

"I want to remember every moment of this," he whispers in my ear. He crashes into the bedroom and throws me on the bed without breaking contact with our bodies. He takes his time as he kisses all over my body, rubbing his finger over any freckle or birthmark he sees.

When he gets down to my thigh, his phone rings, but he doesn't hesitate and keeps going. Until another ring, then another, and on the fourth one, he lets out a frustrated sigh and picks it up.

"Yes?" he answers.

I sit up so I can hear the other person and hear his dad say, "You should really talk to your mother before you leave."

"I am spending the rest of the night fucking my wife, so it's not going to be now," he hits the end button and tosses his phone across the room, and goes to the same spot he left off. Remembering exactly where he left off to make sure he didn't forget anything.

Ben

"So, this is it," Willow says to me as we stand face to face, feet away from my airport gate.

"You have the email address written, I will call when I can, don't forget to drive my truck, remember the plumber is coming next Tuesday…" She wraps her arms around me. Her body starts shaking as she lets out tears. I rest my chin on her head and pull her as close as I can into me. "We have waited our entire lives to find and get each other; these next couple of months will be nothing," her arms wrap tighter around me. "Please wait for me," I whisper.

"I am with you. Just make sure you come home. Just *be* home."

Willow is then behind me as I walk towards everything I tried running from, everything I need to face head-on to be a better man for myself and my wife. The only difference now is that I know what to expect, and I am not sure if that makes it any less terrifying.

www.ingramcontent.com/pod-product-compliance
Lightning Source LLC
Chambersburg PA
CBHW020007120726
47903CB00004B/1177